Praise for ~~FAERIE~~

'A crossover title from which few ~~adults~~ ~~should~~ ~~hold~~ cross
back. Brennan writes with all the ~~conviction~~ ~~at~~ ~~the peak~~
of his form. Inventive as Harry P~~otter~~ ~~and~~ as
intelligently probing as Philip Pul~~lman~~ ~~...~~ ~~for the~~
dreariest of winter days.' ~~Nicholas Tucker,~~ *The Independent*

'*Faerie Wars* is an astounding blend of fantasy, mythology and science.
Herbie Brennan is a master of all three.' *Eoin Colfer*

'*Faerie Wars* (is) ambitiously, impressively and marvellously plotted ...
With its gutsy details, terrific descriptions and great storyline *Faerie Wars*
is a winner – an inspiration, never perspiration. And don't take my word
for it. Several 12-year-olds I know, boys and girls, have read it; their
verdict: brilliant!' *Irish Times*

'Brennan is a terrific writer, with a grasp of his intricate plot that ensures
that readers are swept along. His central characters are feisty and
vulnerable and utterly convincing. It's not necessarily easy reading, but it
certainly is compelling.' *Lindsey Fraser, Guardian Education*

'Excellent, fast-paced but touching ... one of the best fantasy works to hit
the shelves for a long time.' *Times Educational Supplement*

'Brennan's fairy world is a mixture of mythical beasts and hi-tech
wizardry that has engaged kids' imaginations.' *Evening Standard*

'This is a lengthy, exciting novel that glitters with a jigsaw of bizarre
characters and situations. It gallops along with wit and suspense and it
thrills with imaginative magic and invention.' *Books for Keeps*

'The interplay between the human and fairy (faerie) worlds is redolent of
Eoin Colfer's *Artemis Fowl* ... This is an imaginative tour de force that is
underpinned by encyclopaedic knowledge of science and science fantasy.'
Glasgow Herald

'For older readers, there is some really great stuff this year. From
Bloomsbury, by Herbie Brennan, for yer Eoin Colfer and JK Rowling
fans: *Faerie Wars*. And you thought a gripping thriller starring hard nut
fairies couldn't possibly exist.' *Families South East*

'Exciting, romantic and very clever, it has you gagging for the sequel.'
The Independent on Sunday

Faerie WARS

Herbie Brennan

BLOOMSBURY

First published in Great Britain in 2003 by Bloomsbury Publishing Plc
38 Soho Square, London, W1D 3HB

This paperback edition first published in 2004

A CIP catalogue record of this book is available from the British Library

ISBN 0 7475 6467 1

Printed in Great Britain by Clays Ltd, St Ives plc

1 3 5 7 9 10 8 6 4 2

All papers used by Bloomsbury Publishing are natural, recyclable products made
from wood grown in well-managed forests. The manufacturing processes
conform to the environmental regulations of the country of origin.

For Jacks
always

One

Henry got up early on the day that changed his life. He was making a cardboard sculpture and he'd left it the night before for the glue to dry out. All he had to do now was add a toothpick shaft and some decorations and the flying pig was finished. Three weeks' work, but today he'd turn the handle and the pig would take off, flapping cardboard wings. *Pigs might fly.* That's what it said on the base.

He was out of bed at seven, dressed by three minutes past and testing the set of the glue just one minute after that. It was solid. What else would it be when you left it overnight? That was the secret of cardboard models – never hurry. Take your time with the cutting out. Proceed stage by stage – which was what it said in the instructions: *proceed stage by stage.* Leave lots of time for the glue to set. Just do those three things and you ended up with cardboard sculptures that were as solid as the Taj Mahal. He had seven in his room already, including one that really *was* the Taj Mahal. But the flying pig was his best yet. It had a mechanism inside, made up from cardboard cogs and shafts. The mechanism raised the pig from its base and caused the wings to flap.

At least that's what it said in the instructions. Henry was about to find out.

Using a small nail, he bored a tight hole and inserted the toothpick. It was the last thing he had to do, if you didn't count the decorations. But it was tricky getting the toothpick seated just right. Trouble was, you couldn't tell until you tried it. And if you tried it and it *wasn't* right, it could wreck the mechanism. There was a red warning about that in the instructions. Get it wrong and you were back to square one. But get it right and you were *king*.

He thought he had it right.

Henry looked at his handiwork. The base was a black cube with nothing on it except the handle and the wording *Pigs might fly*. The pig itself crouched on the top, all pink and porky. Its wings were so cleverly folded you couldn't see them. The model was finished except for the last few stupid decorations. But he might even forget about those. The decorations didn't have anything to do with the mechanism. This was the real moment of truth.

Henry held his breath, reached out and turned the handle.

The pig took off smoothly on its pillar, onwards and upwards, unfolding cardboard wings. As it reached the end of the pillar, a hidden cog fell into place so that it stayed aloft, flapping. It would stay there until you turned the handle backwards. But Henry didn't turn the handle backwards. He kept the old pig up there, flapping, flapping.

Pigs might fly.

'Yes!' Henry exclaimed, punching the air.

His mum was in the kitchen, sitting at the table staring into a cup of coffee. She looked wretched.

'Morning, Mum,' Henry said cheerfully. He headed for the cornflakes cupboard. 'Got it working,' he said as he shook cornflakes into his yellow bowl. He carried it back to the table and reached for the milk jug.

His mother dragged her eyes out of the coffee cup and let them settle on him, large, liquid and entirely vacant. 'What?' she asked.

'Got it working,' Henry said again. 'Flying pig. Got it working. Never thought the machinery would hold up – cardboard machinery, give me a break – but it's cool. I'll show it to you later, if you like.'

'Oh, yes,' his mum said, but in that dreamy, distant tone that made him wonder if she *still* didn't know what he was talking about. She forced a smile and said, 'That would be nice.'

Martha Atherton was a good-looking woman. Even Henry could see it. Her hair was starting to go grey, but the FBI and the Spanish Inquisition would never get her to admit it. To the world she was brunette with auburn highlights. Her build was curvy – not exactly plump, but enough to stop her looking starved. Henry liked that, even when she looked like death. Who didn't look like death first thing in the morning?

Henry spooned cornflakes into his face. 'Where's Dad?' he asked. 'Did he come home last night?' Sometimes Dad stayed over when he was working late. He wasn't back last night when Henry crashed. But then Henry crashed early last night. He'd been so tired out by Mr Fogarty that he'd hardly managed to glue the last bit of the flying pig together.

For a second he thought he saw something in Mum's eyes. Then it was gone and so was the vacant look and she was saying casually, 'Oh yes. I expect he'll be down in a minute.'

Henry expected so as well. His father had his train to catch and hated to rush. 'What you got planned for today, Mum?' She was headmistress of the local girls' school, but it was closed for summer holidays.

'Nothing much,' his mother said.

Henry wondered if he'd turn into a zombie every morning when he was his parents' age. He finished his cornflakes and shook out some more, then reached for a banana from the fruit bowl. He had another busy day with Mr Fogarty. Slow-release carbohydrates were what he needed.

He heard his father's footsteps and looked up in time to see him on the landing headed for the bathroom. 'Hi, Dad!' Henry called and was rewarded with a grunt. As the bathroom door closed, he tilted his chair and reached into the drawer for a knife. He cut his banana into chunky slices – weird how the size made a difference to the taste – then cut in an apple as well. 'We got plenty of bananas?' he asked his mother.

'What?'

'Bananas, Mum. Have we got plenty?'

She stared at him for a moment, then said, 'Yes, I think so.'

'Mind if I have another one?' Henry asked, wondering what was wrong with her. This was way beyond her usual *Morning of the Living Dead*.

Her eyes drifted up to the landing. 'Have as many as you like,' she said in that offhand way he usually interpreted as disapproval. But why make a big deal about a lousy second banana? He felt the familiar flash of guilt, but took the banana anyway and cut it in as well.

Then he got up and headed for the fridge to see if there was any strawberry yoghurt.

He was doing justice to the mixture when his father came out of the bathroom, showered, shaved and dressed in his natty blue-grey business pinstripe. Something suddenly occurred to Henry. When the old man had been *heading* for the bathroom, he wasn't coming from his and Mum's bedroom – he'd been coming from the direction of the spare room.

Or had he? Henry frowned into his cornflakes, trying to remember. He *thought* Dad had been coming from the spare room, but he wasn't sure. Why would the old boy want to sleep in the spare room anyway? Unless he got back so late Mum had already gone to bed and he didn't want to wake her. Except he'd been home late lots of times and that had never worried him before. Maybe Henry just got it wrong. He'd only caught a glimpse after all.

'Hi, Dad,' he said as Timothy Atherton walked into the kitchen. 'I got my new model working.'

There was something wrong and Henry couldn't figure out what it was.

'Will you be late again tonight?' This came from Mum, without preliminaries and sort of sharp. Maybe she was freaked because Dad came home late last night.

'I'm not sure,' his father said. 'I may well be.'

'Tim, we need to – ' She stopped and Henry could have sworn it was because his father threw a warning glance in his direction.

'I'll phone you, Martha,' his father said tightly.

It wasn't what they were saying, since they weren't

actually saying very much. It was more the tone of voice. Not just Mum, but the two of them. Henry frowned. Maybe they'd had a fight last night, after Dad got home. Henry was fast asleep by then: they could have shouted the place down and he wouldn't have heard them. His mind went back to something he'd thought earlier. Maybe Dad really *had* slept in the spare room. Maybe Mum sent him there. Must have been bad – far as he knew, they'd never slept apart before.

Out of nowhere Henry wondered if his father had another woman. Lots of businessmen did: they slept with their secretaries. Maybe that's what the row was about. He felt a sudden chill. Other women were bad news. Couples got *divorced* because of other women.

Henry glanced surreptitiously at his father. He was looking thinner and older lately, with lines of strain across his forehead and around the eyes. If he really was sleeping with Anaïs, it wasn't making him any happier. But he couldn't be sleeping with Anaïs – not Dad. He just wasn't the type.

His mother said, 'Aren't you going over to see Charlie this evening?'

For a beat, Henry didn't realise she was talking to him. Then he woke up and said, 'Yes. Yes, I thought I would.'

'Mrs Severs will probably feed you – she usually does.'

'Yes, I thought – '

But his mother had already turned back to his father. 'I thought perhaps if you could get back a little early, we could have something to eat together, maybe go out somewhere. For a meal, I mean. Aisling won't be back from Pony Club until the weekend. Henry's going out. There'd just be the two of us.' She swung back to Henry. 'You wouldn't mind that, would you? If you're having supper with the Severs?'

'No,' Henry said. 'I could stay over if you like.' He often stayed over at the Severs's, but she ignored him, which presumably meant she didn't want him to. Hey-ho.

He saw his father glance at the clock. He had half an hour to make his train. 'I think that would be an excellent idea. I'll ring you later.' His voice was strained.

Tension had spread over the kitchen like a rug. Henry tried to defuse it. 'Wow, another nice morning!' he exclaimed brightly, looking at the sunshine through the window. 'Pity I have to go to Mr Fogarty today.'

'I thought we might talk,' Mum said. 'About ... things.'

Dad closed his eyes briefly, then said, 'I'd better go now.'

'You haven't had your breakfast,' Mum said at once.

'I've had coffee,' Dad said. Which was true, although only one cup.

'I'll make you something,' Mum said. Her chair scraped on the tiles as she stood. 'You've plenty of time.'

'I don't have plenty of time,' Dad said flatly. 'If I don't leave now I'll miss the train.' He stood up. For just the barest instant they faced each other, very close together. Then Dad looked away and muttered, 'Better go.'

'Can you drop me off at Mr Fogarty's, Dad?' Henry asked quickly. He purposely avoided looking at his mother – for some reason he had a guilty feeling he was taking sides.

'I thought you weren't going to Mr Fogarty's until this afternoon,' his mother said sharply.

'No, this morning, Mum,' Henry said, still without looking at her.

'You haven't had any breakfast either.'

'Yes, I have.' He gestured at the empty cornflakes bowl.

'That's not enough.'

'I put *bananas* in it, Mum,' Henry said. 'Anyway, I can have something with Mr Fogarty. He likes the company.'

'Mr – '

'You'll have to come now if you want a lift,' Dad cut in.

'Bye, Mum,' Henry said. He ignored the stricken look and kissed her on the cheek.

Dad left without kissing her at all.

'What was all that about, Dad?' Henry asked as he clicked his seatbelt.

His father said nothing, but pulled out of the drive far too fast and without really looking. Henry noticed Mum wasn't standing at the door to wave them off as she usually did.

Henry sat in the passenger seat feeling nervous. He hated it when his parents fought. You could cut the tension with a knife and now Dad was in a mood. They didn't do it very often which made this one all the more worrying. Henry told himself it was probably nothing, but that didn't stop the worry. He knew five kids at school whose folks were divorced.

His father said something, but Henry missed it. He dragged his attention back from his thoughts. 'Sorry, Dad?'

'This Mr Fogarty – what's he like?'

'Old guy. You know ... ' Henry shrugged. He didn't want to talk about Mr Fogarty. He wanted to find out what was wrong between his mum and dad.

'No, I don't know,' Dad said shortly. 'Why don't you tell me?'

He was uptight because of Mum. Henry said, 'Pensioner. Seventy, eighty – I don't know. Old guy. His house is a mess.'

'And you're cleaning it for him?'

If this had been Mum, the question would be followed by *So how is it you never clean your room?*, but with Dad what you saw was what you got. Or sort of. They'd been through all this before. But Dad was clearly hassled because of Mum. He was driving too fast, for one thing. 'Sort of,' Henry said. 'I clean up a bit, but some of the time he just wants to talk.' And some of the time he didn't. Mr Fogarty was weird, believed in ghosts and fairies, but he wasn't about to mention that. Weird or not, Mr Fogarty paid on the nail and Henry was saving for an MP3 player.

'About what?'

'What?'

'Talk about what? You said some of the time he just wants to talk. Talk about what?'

'This and that,' Henry said.

All his father's pent-up frustration suddenly exploded. 'Oh, for God's sake, Henry, has he made you sign the Official Secrets Act? I just want to know what sort of thing you chat about. You're my son. I take an interest.'

Henry said, 'You wouldn't slow down, would you, Dad? You've got the heir with you.'

His dad glared at him for a moment, then grinned for the first time that morning and the tension in the car suddenly lifted. 'Sorry, old son,' he said softly. 'I really shouldn't take it out on you.' He eased his foot back off the pedal.

Henry sat back in his seat and watched the trees and hedges whizzing by.

Mr Fogarty lived in a small two-up, two-down at the end of a cul-de-sac on the edge of town. Henry's father pulled in on the corner. 'There you go,' he said. 'Don't work too hard.'

'You too,' Henry said. He reached for the handle, then stopped.

Dad said, 'Might see you this evening, son. Before you go off to Charlie's.'

Henry said, 'Are you having an affair with Anaïs, Dad?'

The silence was so deep it seemed to overcome the ticking of the car's engine. Henry sat quite still, his hand still on the door handle, looking at his father. He thought his dad would be angry, but instead he just looked distant, as if he was in the hot seat on *Who Wants To Be a Millionaire?*

Are you having an affair with Anaïs?
A. Yes.
B. No.
C. Not any more.
D. We're just good friends.
One of those answers is worth £64,000, Mr Atherton. But the drop's a bit steep if you get it wrong.

After a while, Dad said, 'If you don't go now, I'll miss my train.'

'Come on, Dad,' Henry said. 'Don't you think I have a right to know?' He stopped himself adding, *You've plenty of time to make your train,* knowing it would sound too much like Mum. What he did add was, 'If you are, I won't tell Mum.' As he said it, he felt about six, promising not to tell the teacher.

Dad still didn't say anything. When the silence stretched further than he could bear, Henry opened the car door. 'OK,' he said.

His father said something as he climbed out. Henry was closing the car door at the time and didn't catch it. He opened the door again and bent down.

His father said quietly, 'I'm not having an affair with Anaïs. Your mother is.'

Two

The teashop was in a converted mews-house situated in a warren of side streets so narrow that Henry's father had to pull the car half on to the kerb to park.

'Have I left you enough room there?'

Henry opened the passenger door cautiously. 'Loads of room, Dad.' He managed to squeeze out, if only just. As his father was locking the car he said, 'Aren't you going to miss your train?'

'Stuff the train,' his father said.

Three steps took them down to a cosy, carpeted room with chintzy tables, only a few of which were occupied. The smell of frying bacon met them as they entered. His father led the way to a table tucked beside a door marked PRIVATE, well away from any of the others. Henry sat down underneath a window that looked out into a tiny, empty yard. There was a menu card propped up in a plastic holder in the centre of the table. 'Fancy bacon, egg and sausage?' his father asked without looking at it.

Henry felt his stomach tighten. 'I'm not hungry.'

His father sighed. 'I'm going to have the lot – I need it. You sure you don't want something? Scrambled egg? Toast? Cup of tea?'

'Cup of tea,' said Henry, smiling weakly, just to shut

him up. He wished he'd never asked about Anaïs. His father's sudden change was positively scary. Henry didn't want to know about Anaïs. He'd only asked so Dad could say, 'Anaïs? Of course not – don't be silly.' Which was what Dad *did* say, more or less. Except Henry didn't want to hear his mum was having an affair either. His mum having an affair was just as bad, maybe worse. And who was she having it *with*? Henry had never seen his mother look twice at any man except his dad. Maybe Dad was just plain wrong. Maybe it would all turn out to be a misunderstanding.

The swing door swung open and a young waitress hurried out carrying two plates of eggs. 'Hi, Tim,' she said as she walked past.

'Morning, Ellen,' Tim said shortly.

Henry blinked. Looked like his dad came here quite often. For some reason that felt just a little spooky. There seemed to be too much about his parents that Henry didn't know.

The waitress Ellen came back, tugging a notepad out of her apron. She was a pretty brunette, maybe eight years older than Henry, wearing a tight black skirt, a white blouse and sensible shoes. The shoes reminded him of Charlie, who kept saying she preferred comfort to looks and always would, even when she grew up.

'Usual, Tim?' she asked cheerfully. When he nodded she glanced at Henry and grinned. 'Who's the hunk?'

Henry blushed. Tim said, 'My son Henry. Henry, this is Ellen.'

'Hi, Henry, you want a heart attack as well?'

'Just tea,' Henry murmured. He was aware he was blushing and that made him blush more.

'Got some nice scones,' Ellen said. 'Fancy one?'

'Yes, OK,' Henry said to get rid of her.

It didn't work. 'Plain or raisin?'

'Plain,' Henry said impatiently.

'Butter or clotted cream?'

'Butter.'

'Strawberry jam or marmalade?'

'Strawberry.'

'Gotcha,' Ellen said. She closed her notebook and went off at last.

'Nice kid,' Tim remarked.

'You come to this place often, Dad?'

Tim shrugged. 'You know ...' he said vaguely.

Henry looked out through the window. 'You want to tell me about Mum, Dad?'

The bacon, eggs and sausages must have been waiting in a bain-marie because Ellen carried them right back through the swing door. She had a teapot in her other hand. She set the plate in front of Tim. 'Your scone's coming,' she told Henry.

They waited in silence as she bustled away and returned immediately with a scone that shared its plate with a pat of butter and a tiny plastic tub of strawberry jam. Henry stared at his father's breakfast, thanking heaven he hadn't ordered the same. The bacon was fat and the eggs were hard. With absolute revulsion he noticed there was a kidney lurking behind the fried tomato. This was his father's *usual*?

Ellen gave him his scone and laid out cups and saucers. 'Milk's on the table,' she told them as she left.

Tim glanced at his plate, then at Henry. 'You sure you don't want some of this?'

Henry shuddered and reached for a knife to cut his scone. The sooner it was started, the sooner it would be over. 'I want you to talk to me, Dad.'

'Yes,' his father said, 'I expect you do.'

Tim Atherton so didn't want to tell his son anything. But he talked. He poked at his breakfast and talked and once he started, he couldn't seem to stop.

'You know your mum and I have been having ... problems ... don't you, Henry?' Henry didn't. At least not before this morning. He opened his mouth to say so as his father said, 'Of course you do, you're not stupid. And you're not a child any more. You must have seen the signs – God knows they're obvious enough.'

They hadn't been obvious to Henry. To his profound embarrassment, a tear oozed out of his father's eye and rolled down his right cheek. The worst of it was Dad didn't even notice. Since he couldn't think of anything else to say, Henry waited. Eventually his father said, 'I don't know if you're too young for this, but our ... relationship started to go downhill a couple of months ago. Well, maybe a little more than a couple of months. She ... she just seemed to change. It got sort of obvious her heart wasn't in the marriage any more. You ... you can tell. It's not hard. That's when I started to get irritable with you and Aisling. I'm sorry about that, but I couldn't help it.'

Well, you asked for this, Henry thought. He hadn't noticed his dad getting irritable with him and Aisling, at least not any more than usual and only when they deserved it mostly. He kept his eyes on his plate.

'So,' his father said. 'You see.'

That was it? *So. You see.* Henry said quietly, 'You have to tell me about Mum's affair, Dad.'

His father sighed. He looked wrecked, but curiously

relieved. 'Hard to believe, isn't it? I still can't get my head round it.' He straightened up in his chair and pushed the plate away. Henry noticed he hadn't eaten one of the congealing eggs, or the hideous kidney.

Henry took a deep breath. 'Who's the man?' he asked.

His father looked at him blankly. 'What man?'

'The man Mum's having an affair with.'

The intensity of his father's stare was almost frightening. 'I told you, Henry. Didn't you hear me? It's not a man. Your mum's having an affair with my secretary Anaïs.'

The words lay there, stretched out across the air like a shroud.

His father offered to drop him off, but Henry said he'd walk. He took to the back streets and they were all so empty it was spooky. He walked and thought. He felt he was moving on an island a yard or two across and the world ended right outside it. On this island (that moved right along with him as he walked) he kept replaying the conversation with his dad.

Henry said, 'You're telling me Mum is having an affair with *another woman*?'

The distress on his father's face was pitiful. 'Yes. I know it ... it ... it's ...'

Henry said, 'But you and Mum – I mean, she's had *children*. Aisling and me. If she's ... you know ... that would make her a *lesbian*. Dad, that doesn't make any *sense*!'

His father shifted uncomfortably. He was obviously finding all this even more painful than Henry. 'It's not as simple as that, Henry. A lesbian isn't something you're born as. At least it can be, but not always. And it's not all or nothing either. People can go for years not realising they're attracted to their own sex.'

It didn't sound likely to Henry. 'Yes, but Mum's had *children*!' he said again.

His father managed a wan smile. 'Having children isn't all that difficult,' he said. The smile disappeared. 'I'm afraid there's no doubt. Martha and Anaïs ... Martha and Anaïs ...' He looked as if he might be about to cry again.

Henry pushed it. 'How can you be *sure*?'

His father told him.

In business you could set your watch by good old Tim Atherton. If he said he would be in at nine, he was in at nine. If he said he was going out for half an hour, you could be certain he'd be back in thirty minutes, not a minute more, not a minute less. Yesterday he'd said he would be back at five, but his appointment got cancelled due to some emergency. There was no reason for him to stay away from the office and he got back a few minutes before three.

The office itself was in one of those tall buildings developers put up all over Britain in the 1980s. Tim's company had all of the third floor. The doorman snapped a salute, a ground-floor receptionist gave him a nice smile. If you were a casual visitor, you had to be issued with a name tag that acted as a security pass, but Tim headed straight for the lifts.

It took a while for one to come down, but when it did, he had it to himself. The ride to the third floor took perhaps fifty seconds. He stepped out into the Newton-Sorsen company reception and said hello to Muriel who told him his wife had just called and was waiting for him in his office. He wasn't expecting Martha, but sometimes she popped in when she was shopping. Anaïs would tell her he was out until five of course – he hadn't bothered to phone in to say the meeting had been cancelled – but maybe he'd catch her before she left again.

He walked down the carpeted corridor to his office. Jim Handley came out of a door and collared him about the new presentation. By the time he'd finished with Jim and walked the rest of the way, it was seven minutes after three.

To reach his own office, he had to walk through the smaller office of Anaïs Ward, who guarded him the way most secretaries did their bosses. He was a little surprised to find Anaïs wasn't at her desk, but only a little – there was a coffee machine down the corridor or she might have slipped off to the loo. He was more surprised that Martha wasn't there either. He'd have thought he would have bumped into her if she'd left in the lift. But maybe she'd gone down the back stairs: she did that sometimes for the exercise.

He locked his office when he wasn't in it – some important documents in there – so he pulled his keys from his pocket as he walked across Anaïs's room. He had the key in the lock and the door open in maybe a second, two at the most. His wife and his secretary were both inside. They were startled, breaking apart at the sound of the door. They'd been kissing.

'Maybe it was just ... you know, a friendly thing,' Henry suggested, sick to his stomach. 'Women kiss each other all the time.'

'It wasn't just a friendly thing,' his father told him firmly.

After a while, Henry said, 'You only found out *yesterday*?'

They were bound to divorce. He couldn't see any way out of it after what his father had told him. The funny thing was Dad never said a word about divorce. Or leaving. Or separating or anything like that. But that could change tonight after he had his talk with Mum. Obviously he couldn't just ignore what had happened. Unless, of course, he was hoping Mum would get over it. Did you get over being a lesbian? Henry was so far out of his depth he felt he was drowning.

For once Mr Fogarty opened the door so fast you'd have thought he was standing behind it. 'You're late,' he said. 'And you look like shit.'

'Sorry,' Henry mumbled. 'I had to do something for my dad.'

'You want to talk or you want to get started?' Mr Fogarty had a wiry, old man's frame, no hair at all and on wet days his right hip hurt like hell. But his face looked as if it was cut from granite and his eyes were so sharp they were almost scary.

Henry'd had enough talk for one morning. 'I'd like to get started,' he said. 'Seeing as I'm late.'

'Suits me,' Fogarty said. 'I can't get into the garden shed any more. Bin the crap and tidy up the rest. But don't touch the mower.'

Mr Fogarty's garden was a stretch of dusty-looking lawn with a tired buddleia bush and little else, all surrounded by a high stone wall. The shed was a ramshackle wooden affair that had seen better days. The old boy had pushed three empty wheelie bins outside. It looked as if he was expecting Henry to throw out a lot of rubbish.

Henry straightened his back. It was going to be heavy, dirty work, but he wasn't sorry. Heavy dirty work would take his mind off things for a while. As he pressed the latch of the shed door, a small brown butterfly detached itself from the buddleia bush and fluttered briefly on to the ledge of the tiny window before dropping to the ground. Mr Fogarty's fat tomcat Hodge appeared out of nowhere to grab it.

'Oh, come on, Hodge!' Henry exclaimed. 'Don't eat butterflies!' He liked cats, even Hodge, but hated it when they killed birds and pretty insects. The trouble was, once they got hold of something like a butterfly, you couldn't take it from them without killing it yourself. 'Drop it, Hodge!' he shouted firmly, but without much hope.

Then he saw the thing struggling in Hodge's mouth wasn't a butterfly.

Three

What Pyrgus Malvae valued most in all the world was his Halek knife. Since the fight with his father, he'd had to work for every little thing and the crystal blade had cost him six months' pay on a bet.

The hideous expense was the fault of the Halek. They refused to make more than ten knives a year, and eight of those were replacements for old blades broken or beyond their use. The new blades were cut from cold spires of rock crystal in the Halek homeland, then polished to a blue, translucent sheen. Blood grooves were sanded down each side and the blade bonded to an inlaid handle. Then the knife was charged and dedicated by a Halek wizard.

The result was a weapon guaranteed to kill.

There was no such thing as a minor wound from a Halek blade. Once it entered a living body – and it would pierce any known skin, hide or armour – fierce energies coursed through the victim, stopping his heart. There was nothing it wouldn't kill, neither man nor beast. But there was a chance the blade would shatter. When that happened, the energies flowed backwards to kill the man who held it. Thus Halek blades were more often used in threat than anger, but they were always comforting to have when times got tough.

Pyrgus fingered the handle of his now. He had a feeling there was someone nasty watching him.

It was a weird place to get that sort of feeling. He was on Loman Bridge, the vast, creaking structure with its ancient shops and houses that spanned the river north of Highgrove. Day or night, the bridge was always thronged. It attracted bumpkins like a lodestone. They wandered slack-jawed past the shops and houses, waylaid by trulls, thieves, cutpurses, pickpockets, huggers, muggers, card sharps, thimble-riggers and assorted lowlife, not to mention the packs of greedy merchants who were the worst of the lot. Goods of every description were on sale, but you had to learn to haggle – and recognise rubbish. Each merchant was as expert at extracting gold from a purse as any thief.

''Ware!' someone shouted from above. Pyrgus stepped nimbly sideways to avoid the curdled contents of a chamber-pot slopped out from a high window. The move took him underneath the awning of an apothecary's cart and the feeling of being watched grew stronger. Pyrgus glanced cautiously around. He was surrounded by a thousand faces, most unwashed and none familiar.

'A little chaos horn?' the apothecary stallholder whispered.

Pyrgus glared at him so fiercely he took a step backwards. 'Sorree,' the stallholder said. 'Pardon me for breathing.' Greed caught hold again and his expression softened. 'Something else then? Gold attractors? A purple humunculus?'

Pyrgus ignored him and stepped back into the heaving throng. His instincts were screaming at him now and he trusted them. He quickened his pace, elbowing his way through the crowd. A burly man with a shaven head cursed and tried to grab his jerkin, but Pyrgus dodged aside. He pushed and shoved and shouldered, ignoring all the protests, until he reached the far side of the bridge and left the river. There were fewer people here, but he still felt he was being watched. He headed towards Cheapside, neck hairs crawling as he waited for the hand on his shoulder.

He knew what it was about, of course. Pyrgus had been caught leaving Lord Hairstreak's manor at an unsociable hour. Well, not caught exactly, but certainly spotted. The fact he was leaving by an upstairs window was probably what made the guards suspicious. Or it could have been that he was carrying Black Hairstreak's golden phoenix. Hairstreak wasn't the type to let anybody get away with that. He wasn't the type to go to court about it either. If his men caught up with Pyrgus now, he'd pay for the phoenix in broken bones and blood.

Pyrgus wasn't sure if he was safer among people or alone. The trouble with crowds was that you could never tell friend from foe. Not until it was too late. And Hairstreak's men could leave him pulped before anybody found the courage to intervene. Cheapside was crowded – it was a warren of stews and music dens that attracted the best and the worst of the city – and his instinct told him he'd be better somewhere he could see an attacker coming. He moved like a crab into Seething Lane, which was nearly always empty now on account of the smell. He hurried down the narrow street, then stepped quickly into the shelter of a door-way and waited.

He could see the head of the alley and the milling

crowds of Cheapside. Nobody had followed him and he was just starting to relax when a broad form silhouetted at the junction. The man looked huge, but the other three who joined him looked larger still. Together they began to saunter down the alley.

There was a chance they weren't looking for him, but Pyrgus wasn't about to bet his life on it. He began to wonder if Seething Lane was such a good idea. There was no way he could get past the four men and back to Cheapside. But if he made a break south, he was running towards a dead end. Not so long ago the lane led into Wildmoor Broads, but since Chalkhill and Brimstone built their new glue factory there was no way through.

A thought occurred to Pyrgus. In all the best adventure stories, heroes trapped in doorways pushed the door and found it open. Then they went inside, charmed the pretty young daughter of the household and persuaded her to hide them until the danger was over. Maybe he should try that now. He pushed the door and found it closed.

Shoulder to shoulder, the four men filled the entire width of Seething Lane. Their movements appeared casual, but they were carefully checking every doorway they passed. In minutes they would be checking his. Pyrgus knocked softly, silently praying the pretty young daughter of the household had good ears. After a moment, he knocked again more loudly. The four men were so close now he could hear their breathing, which meant they could hear his knocking. They quickened their pace. Pyrgus kicked the door violently. When it failed to splinter he turned and ran.

'That's him!' one of the big men shouted. All four broke into a lumbering run.

Pyrgus was fast, but that just meant he reached the dead end quicker. Since Chalkhill and Brimstone built their smelly factory, Seething Lane ended in high metal gates, lavishly decorated with fierce warning notices about guards and lethal force. Why they needed that sort of security in a grotty glue factory Pyrgus had no idea, but Chalkhill and Brimstone were both Faeries of the Night, a notoriously suspicious breed. Besides which, they made a great fuss about the secret process that produced their glue. He grabbed the gates and found them locked. Behind him the running footsteps drew closer.

There was a speakhorn fastened to the gate above the lock, but Pyrgus knew better than to get into conversation with some gluehouse guard. Without bothering to glance behind, he jumped on to the gate. The combat shirt and breeches he was wearing underneath his jerkin made him look like some great, green insect as he climbed.

Despite the fierce notices, the only thing on the other side of the gate was a spacious sweep of cobbled yard surrounded by the factory buildings. Although the place was new – opened no more than a month or two ago – it somehow managed to look old. Grime clung to every surface. Beyond the office buildings he could see the squat glue-oven chimneys belching foul black smoke. Chalkhill and Brimstone Miracle Glue would glue anything to anything.

It would be only a matter of time before his pursuers reached the gate. He didn't think they'd climb over, but they might bribe a guard to let them in. In any case, he couldn't afford to hang around. He was about to make a dash across the yard when a fat rat darted from one of the buildings. It had got no more than six feet when a cobblestone exploded.

Pyrgus froze as chips of stone and bits of rat rained down on him. Chalkhill and Brimstone had laid *mines* around their factory? He shivered. He'd been about to run across those cobbles.

What were Chalkhill and Brimstone trying to hide? A minefield was more than Faerie-of-the-Night suspicion, way more than anything you'd do to protect a formula for glue. What was going on in the factory?

A uniformed guard emerged from a doorway, fastening his trousers. Pyrgus was in plain sight and too terrified to move, but the man was looking towards the crater in the courtyard where the mine had exploded. All the same, it was only a matter of seconds before he'd look in Pyrgus's direction. Where to go? What to do? With Hairstreak's men in Seething Lane, he could hardly climb back over the gate. But if he tried to cross those cobbles he risked blowing himself to rat-sized bits.

The speakhorn blared suddenly.

'Coming,' the guard shouted sourly, but without turning round. He reached the crater and stared down into it as if he hoped to find some clue as to what had triggered the mine. He was moving without any great haste.

There was no way Pyrgus could stay standing where he was. Once the guard turned, he'd be spotted. He wasn't sure which would be worse: Chalkhill and Brimstone's fury at finding someone trespassing in their factory or Hairstreak's men exacting rough justice for the missing phoenix.

The speakhorn sounded again, louder this time. 'All right! All right!' the guard called out impatiently.

A scary thought occurred to Pyrgus. Not every cobble was a mine. The rat had run at least two yards before it got blown up. If he ran too, he might get lucky.

Or he might not.

Another scary thought occurred to Pyrgus. Suppose he didn't run. Suppose he jumped. Suppose he bounded like a kangaroo. That way he wouldn't touch so many cobbles and so cut down his chances of triggering a mine.

He glanced around and estimated he was about thirty feet from the nearest doorway. If he covered six feet with each leap, he'd touch down on just five cobbles altogether. How many cobbles were mined? There was no way he could know, but surely it wasn't likely Chalkhill and Brimstone had booby-trapped one cobble in five.

Or was it?

No, of course it wasn't. If he only touched five cobbles altogether, he had a chance – a very good chance, a very, *very* good chance – of reaching the doorway in one piece. The rat must have crossed at least ten cobbles before it got blown up. And even then it probably wasn't a very lucky rat. A lucky rat could have crossed fifteen, twenty, maybe even thirty cobbles safely. Pyrgus had to ask himself, was he a lucky rat? He also had to ask himself, would the door he was aiming for be locked?

The speakhorn blared and kept on blaring. It was

the perfect time to move – the noise would cover any sound he made. Pyrgus leaped.

The world went into slo-mo so he watched with terrified fascination as his leading foot approached a cobble, then gently touched the cobble, then slammed down hard on the cobble. He winced, but the cobble failed to explode.

Then he bounded off again and watched with horror as his foot landed full force on a second cobble ... which also somehow failed to explode. In the middle of his third leap he saw the cobblestone beneath him was a different colour from the others and closed his eyes as he approached it. He landed, stumbled, trod on three more cobbles – *three!* – but somehow bounded off again.

Then the slo-mo stopped, everything blurred and seconds later he was standing in the doorway. The guard was headed for the gate, amazingly not caring where he stepped on the cobbles, his muttered complaints suddenly audible as the speakhorn silenced.

Pyrgus pushed the door. It opened.

He was in an empty whitewashed corridor. There were doors along the right-hand side and, with the first one he tried, his luck changed massively. He found himself staring into a cupboard lined with uniform white coats, the sort issued to glue-factory workers. He noticed that the coats were tagged and suddenly realised why the guard could walk safely through the minefield. The tags had to stop the mines exploding. It was the only thing that made sense – there would have to be *something* so the ordinary factory workers wouldn't get killed. He grabbed one of the coats and shrugged into it.

Pyrgus closed the cupboard door and took time to have a little think. Tag or no tag, he wasn't going back the way he came. He'd have to find another way out.

He was still looking for it when he stumbled on the secret of Chalkhill and Brimstone's Miracle Glue.

With his white coat and tag, Pyrgus discovered he could go anywhere in the factory and nobody showed the slightest interest. All the same, he was careful to keep to himself, and do nothing that would arouse suspicion. Mostly he walked with a confident air as if he knew exactly what he was doing, where he was going. The trouble was he didn't really have a clue and, far from discovering an exit, he found himself wandering deeper and deeper into the maze of factory buildings.

Eventually he wandered into what must have been the production plant.

The heat was horrendous, the stench hideous: it was all he could do to stop throwing up on the floor. But he controlled himself and looked around.

The floor space was packed with evil-smelling vats of bubbling liquid and criss-crossed with encrusted pipes. Banks of heavy machinery drove pumps that strained to push the viscous fluids to a giant stoup set inside an enormous open oven at the south side of the chamber. Inside the stoup, a yellow-greenish mass of something ghastly roiled and boiled. The room was packed with workers, their uniform coats stained with residues and sweat. Some of them tended the machinery, others stirred the liquids in the bubbling vats. A hardy few hovered by the open oven, their faces ruddy from its glow.

Fighting back the urge to gag, Pyrgus moved

forward cautiously. There was an observation gallery about fifteen feet above the main floor. A few guards lounged on the railing, staring down with bored expressions, but most of those on the platform were inspectors using the high vantage point to check the fluids in the vats. One or two workers threaded among them, part of a constant stream parading up and down the metal stairway near the oven. With a surge of relief, Pyrgus noticed there was a door towards the end of the gallery prominently marked EXIT.

Pyrgus moved forward into the swarm of workers, confident the few bored guards would never notice him. With a purposeful expression, he made his way towards the metal stairway, stopping from time to time as he pretended to adjust machinery or inspect the contents of a vat. No one paid him any attention.

As he approached the stairway, the heat from the open oven reached such a peak that he began to pour with sweat. By the oven itself, some of the workers had taken off their coats and were working naked to the waist. He noticed a cage hanging close by. It was not a great deal larger than a birdcage, but inside was a small cat patiently nursing five sturdy little kittens.

Pyrgus stopped. He liked animals – Hairstreak's men were after him because he'd rescued Hairstreak's phoenix – and while it was nice to see Chalkhill and Brimstone had adopted company mascots, the kittens were far too close to the oven to be comfortable. He hesitated for a moment at the foot of the staircase, then walked over to one of the oven workmen.

'It's too hot here for those cats,' he said bluntly, nodding towards the cage. 'You should move them further from the oven.'

The man turned towards him with a sour expression on his face. He wiped sweat from his brow with the back of his arm and eyed Pyrgus's clean coat. 'You new here or what?' he asked.

'Yes,' said Pyrgus. 'What about it?'

'Then you won't know, will you?' said the workman.

'Won't know what?' Pyrgus demanded impatiently. It looked as if he'd picked the village idiot. The man had the dull, smug expression of a child pulling wings off flies.

'Won't know that it doesn't matter if they're a bit hot now, 'cause they'll be hotter in a minute, won't they? – at least one of the little ones will be.'

Something about his tone set off an unpleasant tingling near the base of Pyrgus's spine. 'What are you talking about?'

The man smiled slyly. 'That's the secret ingredient, ain't it? That's what puts the miracle into Miracle Glue.'

Frowning, Pyrgus said, 'What's the secret ingredient?'

The man's smile broadened. 'Kittens!' he told Pyrgus expansively. *'Kitten a day sends the glue on its way!* Didn't they tell you that one when you joined? Chuck in a live kitten and it makes a batch of glue stick better than anything else on the market. Nobody knows why. Mr Brimstone found it out by accident when he was drowning a litter and couldn't be fagged to go down to the river.' He leaned forward and tapped the side of his nose. ''Course that's a secret. Lot of people wouldn't use the glue if they found out it was made from kittens.'

There was a distant commotion behind him near the door where he'd come in, but Pyrgus ignored it.

'You … put kittens in the glue?'

'One a day,' the man said proudly. 'There's one due to go in about now, so you can see it if you like. Mother cat's quiet now, but she howls for hours afterwards. Keeps calling the dead kitten, stupid little toad. It's a great laugh.'

The commotion behind was nearer and louder. Pyrgus glanced over his shoulder and saw to his horror a team of guards pushing purposely towards him through the workers. He looked up the stairway. There was nobody between him and the exit door.

'Tell you what,' the workman said. 'You can throw the kitten in, seeing as you're new and all. Best fun you'll have here all day.'

Pyrgus hit him in the mouth. The man stumbled backwards, more surprised than hurt, but as he flailed to keep his balance, he set one hand firmly on the glowing surface of the oven. 'Yoooow!' he howled in sudden agony.

Pyrgus pushed past him and grabbed the hanging cage. For a moment he couldn't get it free, then it came away from the chain. The mother cat looked up at him warily but continued to feed her kittens. Pyrgus spun round and discovered a burly guard between him and the staircase.

'Oh no you don't!' the guard said, grinning. He spread himself to block Pyrgus's way.

The target was too good to miss. Pyrgus kicked him hard between the legs and leapfrogged over him when he bent double.

Then, still carrying the cage of cat and kittens, Pyrgus sprinted up the staircase towards the door marked EXIT.

four

Silas Brimstone locked the door. He had a grin on his wizened old face and a book in his wizened old hands. The book looked even more ancient than he did, a massive, dusty parchment tome bound between heavy boards. Brimstone's wizened old fingers stroked the faded gold leaf of the inlaid title: *The Book of Beleth*.

The Book of Beleth! He could hardly believe his luck. *The Book of Beleth!* Everything he'd always wanted was between those heavy boards. Everything.

He was in his attic room, a gloomy, poky, low-ceilinged chamber with few furnishings and more grime than the glue factory. But it had everything he needed. Oh yes, it had everything he needed. Brimstone giggled to himself and scratched a scab on his balding pate. Everything he needed to bring him everything he wanted.

Brimstone carried the book to the single, grubby window and opened it beneath the light. On the title page there was a heavy black sigil made up of curls and loops like the doodle of an idiot child. Below the sigil some long-dead scribe had written six stark words:

Beleth holds the keys to Hell.

'Yes,' chuckled Brimstone. 'Yes! Yes! Yes!' His rheumy old eyes glittered with delight.

Everything he'd always wanted and the book had cost him nothing. What a bonus that was. What an unexpected pleasure. What a strange, deep turn of fate. For years he'd searched for Beleth's book, fully expecting to pay out a small fortune when he found it. But when it came to him, it came so easily – and at no cost whatsoever! Well, no cost worth considering. A pittance to the bailiff who threw the widow from her home and seized her pitiful possessions in lieu of rent.

What fun that had been. Brimstone stayed for the eviction. He tried to attend all his evictions. He enjoyed the way the tenants begged and pleaded. The widow was no different from the rest, except a bit younger and better-looking, which added to the pleasure. Her husband was just three hours dead. Tripped and fell into a vat of glue, the clumsy cretin. Ruined the whole batch. But then he'd always been a trouble-maker – one of those bleeding-hearts who wouldn't boil the necessary kitten. Brimstone hurried round to tell the widow – he loved bringing bad news – then asked her about the rent while she was still in shock and crying. Just as he suspected, she couldn't pay now that her husband was dead. He had the bailiff round in twenty minutes.

It was an exceptionally entertaining eviction. The woman wailed and screamed and fought and howled. At one point she even threw herself at Brimstone's feet, begging and pleading and scrabbling at his trouser-leg. It was as much as he could do to stop himself giggling aloud. But he maintained his dignity, of course. Gave her his more-in-sorrow-than-in-anger lecture about fiscal rectitude and the responsibilities of the tenant. God, how he loved giving that tight little lecture. The bailiff knew the form and didn't drag her off his leg until he'd finished. Marvellous. If it hadn't been for her little dog, it would have been his best eviction ever. Her little dog peed on his shoe.

The bailiff's men brought her possessions round to his office. Not that she had very much, but he liked poking through his tenants' belongings and destroying anything that might have sentimental value. The young widow was much like the others – a few shreds of pitiful clothes, a handful of well-mended pots and pans, one or two cheap ornaments. But there was a wooden chest that looked far better quality than anything else she owned. It was bound with metal bands and padlocked.

'What's this?' Brimstone asked the bailiff's man suspiciously.

'Dunno,' the man said dully. 'She said we shouldn't take it because it wasn't hers. Keeping it for an uncle or some such. But we took it anyway.'

'Quite right,' Brimstone told him. He fingered the padlock with sudden interest.

That padlock gave him a lot of trouble when the bailiff's man left. It was too well-made to pick and the metal binding round the chest wasn't iron as he'd thought at first, but something far stronger. There was even a security charge running through the wood that made it impossible to smash open unless you wanted to risk considerable injury. Brimstone had to drain it off before he tackled the chest seriously. By then, of course, he knew it had to contain something valuable. Nobody took that much trouble just to store their washing.

When the chest resisted all other attempts to open it, he invested in a piece of firestone that turned the lock to molten slag while leaving the remainder of the chest intact. It was nearly half an hour before it had cooled down enough for him to touch and by then his heart was thumping with excitement. What was it the widow had been storing? Gold? Jewels? Family secrets? Artworks? Whatever it was, Brimstone wanted it. But before he threw back the lid, he had no idea how much he wanted it.

As he stared into the chest, he simply could not believe his eyes. The book lay on a bed of straw. It was bound shut with an amber ribbon, but he could still read the faded lettering: *The Book of Beleth*.

Brimstone's hands shook as he reached inside the chest. He took several calming breaths. It might be a forgery. Heaven knew there were enough of them about – he'd even bought two himself from dealers who turned out to be no better than thieves. But when he slid off the ribbon and opened the boards, he knew at once this was the real thing. The parchment was brown and foxed with age. The hand-drawn lettering was archaic in style, the ink authentic in its fading. But most important of all was the content. Brimstone knew enough about magic to recognise the ritual as genuine. He'd found it at last! He'd found *The Book of Beleth*!

For three days and three nights, Brimstone studied the book. He refused all food except for a little gruel and declined all strong drink. For once he allowed Chalkhill to run the business affairs without interference. The idiot wasn't likely to lose too much money in so short a time; and even if he did, Brimstone would soon make it up now he had *The Book of Beleth*. It was the portal to Hell, the key to riches. The man who had *The Book of Beleth* had all the gold in the world. What a fool that widow was. If she'd only known what was in her safekeeping, she could have paid the rent a thousand times over. She could have owned Chalkhill and Brimstone. She could have overthrown the Purple Emperor himself! But she hadn't known and her stupid dead husband hadn't known and now the book belonged to Silas Brimstone.

In the attic room, he prepared to put it to use.

Brimstone left the book by the window and shuffled over to the cupboard in the west wall. From it he took a bag of coffin nails, a hammer and the dead body of a young goat. It smelled a bit since it was more than four hot days since he'd sacrificed it, but nobody would notice once he started to burn incense. He set a bucket to one side to catch the remains, then drew his dagger and began to skin the goat.

It was sweaty work, but he was good at it. He'd been killing animals all his life and in his younger days he'd skinned most of them. When the pelt was removed, he threw the naked corpse into the bucket, then set about cutting the kidskin into narrow strips. Using the coffin nails, he fastened them to the wooden floor in the form of a circle. The noise of the hammer echoed through the attic room, but he'd given orders he wasn't to be disturbed and the servants knew it was more than their lives were worth to disobey. The circle had to be nine feet in diameter. He banged in the last nail and stepped back to admire his handiwork.

The ring of kidskin had a sinister look. In places it seemed almost as if some rough beast was oozing up out of the floor. Brimstone grinned and cackled. It was perfect. Perfect. Beleth would be pleased.

After he'd rested for a bit, he went back to the bucket where he cut open the stomach of the goat and carefully drew out its intestines. The book hadn't specified what guts he should use, but waste not, want not: it was cheaper than going out and killing something else. He used the last of the coffin nails to tack the intestines in the shape of an equilateral triangle just outside the circle of skin in the south-east corner. It was good. It was *very* good.

He went back to the cupboard and brought out the energy equipment he'd had made to the specifications in the book. It consisted of three metal lightning globes, each set on top of its own steel tower and linked by cables to a small control box. Everything was ridiculously heavy, but the cables were long so he managed to drag it a piece at a time. He set a tower at each point of the triangle, with the control box between the triangle and the circle. Fabrication of the gear had cost him more than five thousand gold pieces, a hideous expense and a huge nuisance since every penny had to be embezzled from the company and the ledgers cooked so his partner wouldn't find out. But everything would be worth it when he called up Beleth.

Brimstone was getting antsy now, anxious to begin his ritual, but he knew the preparations were important. One wrong step and Beleth might break free. Not good. There was nothing as much trouble as a demon prince on the rampage. They ate children, blighted crops, created hurricanes and droughts. Much more trouble than the skinny little big-eyed demons he was used to. Besides, a freed demon never granted wishes.

Carefully he checked the circle and the triangle. Both were equally important. The triangle was where Beleth would actually appear, but the circle was Brimstone's protection if the demon got out. It was growing dark in the attic – there was a storm brewing outside as often happened with a demon evocation – so he lit a candle to make the examination. There were no breaks in the circle. The intestines outlining the triangle glistened wetly in the candlelight, but there were no breaks there either.

Brimstone went back to the cupboard and collected the rest of the things he needed – charcoal, a metal brazier, a large bundle of asafoetida grass, a rough haematite stone, several wreaths of verbena, two candles in their holders, a small bottle of Rutanian brandy, camphor and, most important of all, his blasting wand.

It was a beauty – fully eighteen inches long and carved from premium bloodwood polished to a high sheen so that the tiny veins were clearly visible. A Northern Master – now long dead, curse his greedy, grasping, black little wizened heart – had graciously accepted an enormous fee to carve the microscopic runes that acted as channels for the energies. It had been attuned to Brimstone's personal harmonic by the Virgin of Ware. All very expensive, but worth it. Especially since the cost was hidden in the company ledgers.

The Book of Beleth was the last thing he carried into the circle.

Brimstone checked to make sure he had everything. Once he started the operation, there'd be no going back for something he'd forgotten. When you were calling demons, you stayed inside the circle until they were safely gone if you knew what was good for you. So you made sure you had everything to hand before you started.

When he was certain there was nothing missing, he took the haematite stone and used it to inscribe a second triangle, inside the circle this time, touching the circumference at all three points. Then he put two large black candles in their holders and set one to the left of the triangle, one to the right. He surrounded each with a verbena wreath before lighting the wick with a brief touch of his wand. Going nicely, going *very* nicely.

Thunder rumbled distantly as he inscribed the protective lettering. He used the haematite stone for that as well, leaning cautiously over the edge of the circle to write the word *Aay* on the floor in the east. Then he moved to the bottom of the internal triangle and wrote *JHS* along its base. As he finished the 'S', the lettering of both words began to glow slightly, a good sign.

Next he filled the brazier with charcoal soaked in the Rutanian brandy. It lit with a *whoosh* when he applied the blasting wand. Once the flames died down a little, he added the camphor and a heady smell began to fill the attic room. He took a deep breath. He was ready to go!

Brimstone took up *The Book of Beleth*, drew himself to his full height and closed his eyes. 'This incense of mine, Oh Great One, is the best I can obtain,' he intoned in a voice that sounded like the rustling of dead leaves. 'It is purified like this charcoal, made from the finest wood.' He waited for a moment, then went on: 'These are my offerings, Oh Great One, from my deepest heart and soul. Accept them, Oh Great One, accept them as my sacrifice.'

In his hands, *The Book of Beleth* began to glow softly.

Brimstone droned on about the Great One for some time, even though the Great One had never done much for him that he could remember. But *The Book of Beleth* insisted so he supposed he should pay lip service, just to be on the safe side. When he'd ploughed through all the prescribed prayers and added more camphor to the brazier, he got down to the real business.

'Prince Beleth,' he intoned, his eyes wide open now so he could read the conjuration directly from the book, 'master of the rebel spirits, I ask thee to leave thy abode, in whichever part of the world it may be, to come and speak with me. I command and order thee, in the name of the Great One, to come without making an evil smell, in fair form and pleasing face, to answer in a loud and intelligible voice, article by article, what I shall require of thee – ' How to get more gold, for a start, he thought. How to get more power. 'I command and oblige thee, Prince Beleth, and I vow that if thou fail to come at once, I shall smite thee with my frightful blasting wand so that thy teeth shall drop out, thy skin shall wrinkle, thou shalt have boils on thy bottom and be subject to night sweats, ringing in the ears, falling sickness, flaking dandruff, arthritis, lumbago, uncontrollable dribbling, deafness, runny nose, ingrowing toenails. Amen.'

So far it was all standard stuff. Not word for word, of course, but the sort of evocation he'd used to call up a dozen lesser demons at one time or another. What came next was different. Oh yes, very different.

Brimstone held his breath. After a moment, the first

spark crackled from the head of the furthest globe. Almost at once, trapped lightning arced from globe to globe, creating a triangle above to match the triangle below. A heady smell of ozone filled the air and the equipment crackled and roared.

'Come, Beleth!' Brimstone shrieked above the racket. 'Come, Beleth, come!' The book was glowing fiercely now and trembling in his hands. He'd read somewhere the tome was what made all demonic invocations work, whether you had it with you or not. So long as it existed somewhere, the road to Hell was always open to a man who knew the spells.

He stopped to listen. Behind the crackle and roar of the lightning, there was the faint sound of a distant orchestra, then a shimmering within the triangle. Brimstone swung his blasting wand to point it like a musket. 'Come, Beleth!' he repeated.

The music grew louder and the shimmering turned into a hooded form that gradually became more solid before Brimstone's eyes. The creature in the triangle was more than eight feet tall, broadly built with staring, bloodshot eyes. It threw back its hood. There were powerful ram's horns growing from its forehead.

'Enough!' Beleth roared.

Brimstone swallowed. There was something about Beleth that made him nervous. Well, actually *everything* about Beleth made him nervous. He'd called up demons before, but they'd all been small fry. This was the first time he'd managed a prince. He licked his lips. 'Oh mighty Beleth,' he began, 'I beseech – no, I *command* thee to remain within thy triangle of goat guts for such time as I – '

Beleth growled. 'Command? You dare to *command* me?' He had a surprisingly piercing voice for something that rumbled like the thunderstorm outside.

'C-c-command thee to remain within the triangle of g-guts for such time as I determine and – ' Most demons blustered. You had to be firm with them otherwise they'd try to walk all over you.

'Quiet!' Beleth thundered.

Brimstone shut up at once. He hoped the monster couldn't see he was trembling. It occurred to him that maybe this whole business hadn't been such a bright idea. You were always hearing horror stories about how difficult the larger demons were to control. Of course, much of it was Faerie of the Light propaganda, but there was obviously a grain of truth. To his horror, Beleth leaned forward so that the upper half of his body loomed over the boundaries of the triangle and even impinged across the edge of the circle. This wasn't supposed to happen. This wasn't supposed to happen at all. He swung the blasting wand to point at Beleth's head.

The demon stared at the weapon and smiled.

'Beware, Beleth,' Brimstone said tightly, his jaw clenched to stop his teeth chattering. 'For I shall so smite thee with my frightful blasting wand that thy teeth shall – '

Beleth's smile widened and a curious discordant ringing sound began to fill the attic room. It crawled into Brimstone's head to fuzz his thoughts and cause an eerie blood-red veil to rise behind his eyes. The wand in his trembling hand began to droop, then melt. Even in his terror, Brimstone set up a howl of protest. The money! Beleth watched as the wand dissolved completely, then raised his gaze to Brimstone's face. 'You don't have to threaten me.'

'I don't?' Brimstone said.

Beleth shrugged. 'A simple contract of sacrifice will bring you what you want.'

Relief flooded through Brimstone like a balm. Every demon asked for a sacrifice. 'Doves? Cats? Dogs? Nice little sheep?' he asked. 'You don't want a bull, do you?' Bulls were expensive. Not to mention tricky to kill. A sudden thought struck him. 'Wait a minute – it's a rare breed, isn't it? Something on the endangered list?'

'No, nothing like that. I just want you to sacrifice the second person you see after you leave the circle.'

Brimstone's eyes widened. 'You mean a *human* sacrifice?'

'Exactly!' Beleth rumbled.

Brimstone released an explosive sigh of pure relief. 'Piece of piss,' he said.

There was a knock on the attic door as Brimstone was intoning the ritual licence to depart. He had his contract now, properly signed in blood by both parties, but Beleth still hovered in the triangle.

'I told you I didn't want to be disturbed,' he shrieked. 'Go away! Go away!' He dropped his voice and went back to mumbling the licence: '...adjure and conjure you to leave this place, fully and without hesitation, returning whence you came, there to remain until – ' A part of his mind was wondering how he was going to turn off the lightning box now his blasting wand was destroyed.

'Something out here you should see, dear boy...' It was the voice of Jasper Chalkhill.

Brimstone abandoned the licence and tossed a handful of asafoetida on the fire. Beleth popped like a balloon as the smoke rolled over him. Asafoetida always did for demons, commoner or prince. The stench was so foul it made burning sulphur smell like perfume. 'Coming!' Brimstone called. He snuffed the candles hastily and stepped out of the circle fumbling for his key. Behind him the trapped lightning hissed and spat from globe to globe, but he'd find a way to switch it off later. He unlocked the door and opened it a crack. The first person he saw was Chalkhill, grinning broadly. He'd been doing something to his teeth so that they fizzed and sparkled in the light.

The grin died as Chalkhill sniffed. 'Have you been dismissing demons?'

Brimstone ignored him. 'What is it? What do you want me to see?'

Chalkhill gestured with his head and the grin returned. 'A handsome young man,' he said. 'We caught him skulking in the factory.'

Brimstone opened the door a little wider so he could see who Chalkhill had brought with him.

five

The commotion behind him swelled until it sounded like a riot, but Pyrgus Malvae was more concerned with what was going on in front. The guards on the observation platform were no longer looking bored. They were running from every direction to head him off. Two of them were already between him and the EXIT door.

Pyrgus dodged to one side. A guard lunged after him and Pyrgus tripped him up. The second guard was a lot more cautious. He drew a stun wand from his belt, placed himself squarely between Pyrgus and the door, and waited.

Pyrgus hesitated. There were running footsteps on the platform, footsteps on the stairway behind him. Time was not on his side. He feinted to the right, but the guard refused to move. His eyes were locked on Pyrgus and stayed there. He was not a particularly big man – only a little taller than Pyrgus himself – and Pyrgus might just have taken him in a straight fight. But this wasn't a straight fight. The guard had a stun wand and Pyrgus was hampered by the cat cage.

They stared at one another. The pursuit closed in on Pyrgus from all sides. His eyes flickered from the guard for just a second and he saw that the kittens had left their mother and were lined up with their noses pressed against the wire, watching him with great round trusting eyes. Pyrgus did the only thing he could do. He drew the Halek knife.

The guard's eyes widened when he saw the translucent blade. He spoke to Pyrgus for the first time. 'I got a stun wand,' he said.

'And you might stun me with it,' Pyrgus nodded. 'But you'd better do it first time, otherwise you're dead.'

The guard stared at him, his gaze wavering between Pyrgus's face and the knife in his hand. Charged energies writhed like serpents beneath the crystal surface. Pyrgus held out the blade and flicked it so sparks trailed from the tip. 'Just a touch,' he said. 'That's all it needs – just one little touch.' He thought he caught a flash of fear in the guard's eyes and made a snap decision. If he didn't get away within the next few seconds, the guards would be on him like an avalanche.

Pyrgus hurled himself forward. But he twisted his body so there was no chance that the knife might touch the guard. For just the barest moment the man held his position, then his nerve broke and he jumped to one side, the stun wand flailing wildly. Pyrgus was through the exit door before he recovered his balance.

He slammed the door behind him and raced up the corridor.

He knew he wasn't going to get away. The guards were already boiling into the corridor behind him, alarm sirens were sounding all over the place and any idiot could figure out the first thing they'd do was close the exits. So in a minute he'd be caught and the cat and her kittens would be taken back into the foul production plant. Pyrgus didn't care much what happened to him – he'd wriggled out of worse predicaments – but he couldn't let the kittens be killed. He raced round a bend in the corridor and lost sight of his pursuers for a moment. A sign hanging from the ceiling said TOILETS with an arrow pointing right.

He made the right-angle turn without hesitation. A quick glance told him the toilets were empty (and none too clean). He hesitated. It was possible the guards might run past without realising where he was, but he was not about to bet on it. He spun round to see if he could bolt the doors, but they were spring-loaded affairs without locks. Outside, he could hear the guards approaching in the corridor. There were loop handles on the doors and he looked around for a broom or something he could jam between them. There was no broom, nothing. The sounds were closer now. Would they run past?

'Check the toilets!' he heard someone call.

It was all over. Unless he could find something to jam the doors. A thought occurred to him, but he dismissed it. Then he looked at the kittens in the cage and thought it again.

Pyrgus set down the cage and pulled out his Halek knife. Six months' saving and even then he'd had to win it on a bet. He'd never own another one. Incredibly, he heard the kittens' mother purr. 'Oh, shut up!' Pyrgus muttered. All the same, he couldn't let her die. He shoved the Halek knife between the two looped handles.

It would shatter at the first onslaught, of course. But when it shattered, it would send a charge through the door. The wood would absorb most of it, but enough would get through to stun anybody within the first few feet. And that would give the rest very good reason to pause. It wouldn't stop them, but it would buy him time. He swooped down to grab the cage as the first wave of guards struck the doors. Pyrgus didn't even bother to look back, but he heard a howl as the Halek blade shattered, then screams and a scuffle outside. He hurled himself towards the little window at the far end of the toilets.

He had to stand on a washbasin to get near it. For a moment he didn't think he was going to get it open, but desperation gave him strength. The window looked out over a steep roof and was just big enough for him to climb through. He pushed the cage ahead and flicked the catch. The cage swung open, but the cat and her kittens only looked at him.

'Go on!' hissed Pyrgus. 'Get out of there! Get out of there *now*! For heaven's sake you're *cats*, aren't you? Cats are supposed to be at home on rooftops.'

There were crashing sounds behind him as the guards found their courage and piled in. The queen cat stood up, glanced at Pyrgus briefly, then stepped out on to the roof. Her kittens followed her sure-footedly. Pyrgus flung the empty cage away and started to wriggle through the window. Rough hands grabbed his ankles.

'Oh no you don't!' an angry voice growled.

Kicking and struggling, Pyrgus was dragged back down from the window. The last thing he saw was the cage arcing out over the edge of the roof to drop down towards the ground below.

Pyrgus relaxed. At least the kittens were safe now and the guards would hardly kill him for rescuing a cat. 'All right, all right!' he said. 'I'll come quietly.'

'Let's kill him,' muttered one of the guards. There were more than a dozen of them milling round. Two had Pyrgus by the arms. A burly man with a sergeant's insignia on his uniform stepped forward. 'Yus, let's kill him!' he muttered as he punched Pyrgus in the stomach. Pyrgus doubled up and fought to catch his breath.

'Great idea,' said one of the men holding him. 'We could beat him to death and say he was resisting arrest.' He grabbed a handful of Pyrgus's hair and jerked him upright. The burly sergeant hit him again.

Pyrgus groaned and the whole hideous scene faded briefly to black. He shook his head fiercely, more aware of a drumming noise than anything else. Then consciousness returned and he realised three guards were now raining punches on his chest and stomach. With his arms still pinned, there was nothing he could do to defend himself. He tried to kick his attackers, but his legs wouldn't work – he felt they were moving through treacle. His body slumped and the thought occurred that he might really be beaten to death. The guards had the goblin look of Faeries of the Night, like most of Chalkhill and Brimstone's people. You could never tell how far they'd go.

Pain was flaring through his body and a blood-mist crawled across his eyes before a dark-eyed man in a green captain's uniform pushed his way through. 'What's going on here?' he demanded angrily. 'What do you think you're doing to that child?'

The guards punching Pyrgus stepped back quickly and the two holding him snapped to attention, dragging him upright as they did so. 'Nothing, sir. Sorry, sir.'

'Who is he – one of our workers?'

'Trespasser and thief, sir – that's not his coat,' one guard said smartly. 'Broke into our factory and stole our cat.'

'And five glue kittens,' the second guard put in.

The captain frowned. 'And you were beating him for *that*?'

'No, sir. Not necessarily, sir. He threw them through the window. Poor little things are probably dead by now.'

Poor little things? Even through the haze of pain, it was almost funny. Pyrgus tried to speak, but all that came out was a groan.

'Shut it, you!' the guard hissed in his ear.

'Let go of him!' the captain ordered coldly.

'Sir?'

'You heard me. Let go of him at once!'

The guards released their grip on Pyrgus's arms and he felt himself slide gratefully down into velvet darkness.

He came to with the captain bending over him, a look of deep concern on his face. 'Are you all right? For a minute there I thought they'd killed you.'

Pyrgus moved cautiously. The whole of his body ached and burned, but nothing seemed to be broken. He expected he'd be a mass of bruises by the morning. 'I'm OK,' he croaked, his voice little more than a whisper.

'Take your time,' the captain said. 'Those idiots beat you badly.'

Pyrgus struggled to sit up. 'I'm OK,' he said again and his voice was stronger now. He seemed to be in some sort of poky office, probably the captain's. The furnishings consisted of a desk, a filing cabinet and a couple of chairs. The woodwork was encrusted with grime, like everywhere else in the factory.

The captain stepped back to give him room and Pyrgus climbed shakily to his feet. But he knew he wasn't going to stay there. He grabbed one of the chairs and sat down. A wave of nausea swept through him and he ignored the pain in his body to push his head between his legs. When he sat up again, the captain said gently, 'OK? Better now?'

Pyrgus nodded.

'I'm Captain Pratellus,' the captain told him. 'And the first thing I want to do is apologise for those imbeciles. What they did to you was inexcusable.'

Pyrgus stared at him wearily and said nothing. Captain Pratellus was nearly a head smaller than the guards who'd beaten him and would have been almost handsome if he hadn't had such really rotten skin.

The look of distress on Pratellus's face increased. 'The thing is, you *did* trespass, so I have to ask you some questions. You understand that, don't you?'

Pyrgus nodded.

'Are you OK for that now, or would you like me to wait a little while?'

Pyrgus swallowed. 'No, it's OK.' The sooner this was done with, the sooner he could get out of this lunatic asylum. And see how quickly you can close it down, a voice hissed fiercely in his mind. Now he knew what they did to cats, there was no way he was going to let the factory stand. He'd take his story to the Emperor himself if need be. Chalkhill and Brimstone might have one or two decent employees like the captain, but that still didn't justify what they were doing. He was astonished they'd been able to keep their treatment of the kittens secret, even if the factory had only been open for a short time. You'd have thought something like that was bound to leak out.

'Well, I suppose I'd better start with your name?'

'Pyrgus,' Pyrgus told him. 'Pyrgus Malvae.'

'A royal name!' Pratellus exclaimed. Pyrgus smiled weakly. 'Well, Pyrgus, I'll try not to detain you a minute longer than absolutely necessary. Would you like to tell me what you were doing in the factory?'

Pyrgus stared at him for a moment, then decided on the truth. 'Somebody was chasing me, so I climbed over the gate.'

The look of concern was back on Pratellus's face. 'Who was chasing you?'

'I'm not sure,' Pyrgus said. 'I think it might have been Black Hairstreak's men.'

Pratellus sucked breath through his teeth. 'That degenerate! Yes, well, I could see you'd be advised to keep out of *his* clutches. So you climbed over the gate?'

'Yes, sir.'

'Crambus, Pyrgus – call me Crambus. I've a feeling we might be friends when all this is over.' Pyrgus nodded. Crambus Pratellus said, 'You know that was a dangerous thing to do?'

Pyrgus nodded again. 'I do now.'

'I argued with Mr Brimstone about the extreme security precautions.' Pratellus threw his eyes briefly upwards. 'But would he listen? Some day somebody's going to get killed and then where will we be? But you didn't get killed?'

'No, sir – no, I didn't, Crambus.'

'And, of course, it might have been far more dangerous to let yourself get caught by Black Hairstreak.'

Pyrgus nodded. That was probably true. Especially

when you'd stolen his phoenix. He decided he wouldn't mention the phoenix to Captain Pratellus.

'So you weren't breaking into the factory *for* anything? It just happened to be your ... escape route.'

'Yes.'

'What about the kittens? The guards said you stole kittens.'

Pyrgus hesitated, then said, 'I didn't steal them – I rescued them.'

Pratellus sighed. 'You're an animal lover. So am I. I hate what they do to cats here.'

'Then why don't you stop it?' Pyrgus asked with sudden passion.

Pratellus spread his hands helplessly. 'It's not illegal,' he said. 'Believe me, I've looked into it and there's absolutely nothing I can do.'

'You could tell people!' Pyrgus said. 'Once people knew what was going on, they'd put a stop to it!'

Captain Pratellus smiled sadly. 'I'm afraid people just don't care. I know this is difficult to accept at your age, but it's true. Let's not quarrel – there may be something we can do about the kittens later. I have to make a report, you see. Just for now, would you like me to say you're a little soft-hearted about cats – lots of young people are – and that was all there was to it really? Boys will be boys sort of thing?'

It was probably the best way. Pyrgus nodded gratefully.

Suddenly Captain Pratellus was no longer smiling. 'You must imagine I'm a total cretin!' he hissed furiously.

Jasper Chalkhill's office smelled of perfume. Lush carpet covered the floor and heavy velvet curtains hung from every wall. There were two rare white tiger skins in front of the enormous desk and several works of oriental statuary on display in elaborate crystal cases. But the most exotic thing in the place was Chalkhill himself. He wore a feathered hat and peacock robe with cloth-of-gold slippers. Folds of fat hung from his face and arms.

'Why, Pratellus, dear Pratellus, what have you brought for me?' He tripped across the room with remarkable grace for so bulky a man and examined Pyrgus minutely. 'A boy! How thoughtful, Pratellus, how thoughtful.' Close up, Pyrgus could see he was wearing rouge.

'Caught breaking in, Mr Chalkhill,' Pratellus said ingratiatingly. 'Stole one of our cats and all her kittens. I suspect he was after – ' he dropped his voice and glanced behind him before completing the sentence ' – the formula.'

Chalkhill looked positively delighted. 'A thief! A dear little thief! Well, he must be punished, mustn't he? What shall we do, Pratellus? Shall we beat him? Shall we teach him a stern lesson? Oh, what fun we might have!' He leaned forward in a perfumed cloud and, for the first time in his life, Pyrgus realised here was a man he would cheerfully use a Halek knife on.

Pyrgus briefly wondered if he should spit in Chalkhill's eye, but satisfied himself with hissing fiercely, 'Keep away from me, you smelly tub of lard!'

'Ooooh,' said Chalkhill, smiling at Pratellus. 'What spirit! What ferocity!'

'He's bad-tempered all right, Mr Chalkhill. He was beating up my guards when I found him. Heaven knows what damage he might have done if I hadn't come along.'

Pyrgus gave the captain a filthy look, but said nothing. He was coming to realise the whole of Chalkhill and Brimstone was full of liars.

'Then you are to be commended, Captain Pratellus,' Chalkhill said. He smiled at Pyrgus and rainbow sparkles danced across his teeth. 'Well, now, my little terrier, what are we going to do with you?'

'You're going to let me go at once!' Pyrgus told him. 'Otherwise my father – '

'Ah, a father's boy, is it? I was always much more fond of my mother, but no accounting for taste. I'm afraid I'm not terribly impressed by your father, boy. Big, is he? Bulging muscles? Wooo, I'm *so* afraid.' He turned to Pratellus. 'Now, captain, I assume you questioned him?'

'Yes, sir, Mr Chalkhill. Sly one, sir – gave nothing away. That's why I brought him to you. I thought you might like to torture him.'

'Oh, yes,' Chalkhill said enthusiastically. 'I'd like to torture him, all right. But before we go to … extremes, perhaps I shall ask him some questions myself. I find quite a few people are prepared to chat with me when they refuse to talk to anybody else.' He turned back to Pyrgus. 'What makes a dear boy like yourself break into a respectable business premises?'

'Respectable?' gasped Pyrgus, sudden anger overcoming a determination to keep silent. 'What sort of factory drowns kittens in glue?'

Chalkhill's eyes widened sympathetically. 'Worried about little kittens, are we? But don't you realise, my poor child, there are far too many stray cats around the city? Most of them lead dreadfully unhappy lives. Illness ... starvation ... it's a kindness to kill off a few of them.'

'And profitable,' snarled Pyrgus.

'Nothing wrong with profit,' Chalkhill told him cheerfully. 'Young people don't appreciate these things, but I expect your saintly father would agree with me. Earns a crust, does he? Works for some *profitable* company?' He held up a hand. 'No, spare me the lectures, boy. The captain is quite right. If you won't tell us why you're here, we must *wring* it out of you.'

'I did tell him why I was here!' Pyrgus shouted. He wondered if he should make a break for the door. Chalkhill looked too fat to outrun a tortoise, but there was still Pratellus and two guards were stationed outside. 'I was being chased by some men Lord Hairstreak sent after me!'

'I can see why you didn't believe him,' Chalkhill said to Pratellus. He turned back to Pyrgus. 'Lord Hairstreak is a friend of mine – a *bosom* friend. He has much bettter things to do than send his men chasing after young boys. It was Paphia, wasn't it?'

Pyrgus blinked. 'Paphia?'

'Argynnis Paphia,' Chalkhill spat. 'He's had it in for us for years, poor Mr Brimstone and myself. Don't bother to deny it – I can see the truth in your eyes and I shall have it from your lips, mark my words.' He placed the back of one hand on his forehead. 'But I had a broken night. I am much too *enervated* to torture you myself. Captain Pratellus –'

'Yes, sir?' said Pratellus eagerly.

'We will take him to Mr Brimstone, captain. Mr Brimstone's *demons* will get it out of him.'

Six

The second person you see ...

Chalkhill was the first – a pity that, in some ways – but, as Brimstone swung the door back, an unfamiliar face came into view. It belonged to a boy with red hair wearing the sort of green battle fatigues that were the ridiculous fashion among young people these days. He wasn't handsome, whatever Chalkhill claimed, but his features were pleasant enough in a disorganised sort of way. Although Brimstone was useless at guessing ages, he couldn't imagine this lad was much more than fourteen years old.

An interesting sacrifice for Beleth.

That sycophantic idiot Pratellus was standing just behind the boy. Behind them both were two wooden-top guards. Everyone was po-faced except for Chalkhill, who liked showing off his fancy magic teeth.

'Ah, Silas, my dear fellow, we have need of your little friends.' Chalkhill bobbed his head, trying to see over Brimstone's shoulder. Inside the attic room, trapped lightning spat and crackled. 'Any of them in there? Or have you sent them all back home with your stinky grass?'

'What's happening here?' asked Brimstone. You had to be careful with Chalkhill.

'What's happening, Silas, is that Argynnis Paphia has sent this boy to disrupt our latest enterprise. Fortunately Pratellus caught him in the act.'

'What act?' Brimstone snapped.

Chalkhill looked taken aback and waved his hands feebly. 'In the act of ... of ... of disrupting our latest enterprise.'

'He told you that, did he?'

'Told me what?'

Brimstone sighed. 'Told you Argynnis sent him.'

'No, of course he didn't, Silas – what a *silly-billy* boy you are! He denied everything. Of course he denied everything. But that's where you come in, isn't it? You and your little friends.'

'You want me to get the truth from him?'

'Yes,' said Chalkhill.

'Very well,' Brimstone said. The turn of events suited him down to the ground. This child was the second person he'd seen since he stepped from the circle, so this child must be sacrificed to Beleth. Once Brimstone made the sacrifice, he could always claim the boy died during questioning. Chalkhill would accept that. He was always killing people himself. It was one of the reasons they'd gone into glue – the factory was perfect for disposing with bodies.

Chalkhill blinked. 'You'll do it?'

'Yes.'

'You'll turn him over to your little demons?'

Brimstone nodded. Not so little, but ... 'Yes.'

'You'll get them to torture him?'

'Yes.'

'They'll ...' he licked his lips '... they'll do *medical experiments*, won't they?'

Brimstone shrugged. 'Probably.' Demons usually did.

'When do we start? I want to help,' said Chalkhill.

Damn! He should have seen it coming. The fat fool wanted to get involved. He was always trying to interfere with Brimstone's demon work. Well, Brimstone couldn't have that, couldn't have that at all. 'Won't do,' Brimstone said shortly.

Chalkhill looked stricken. 'Won't do? Won't do? Why won't it do? I must help. Tell him I must help, Pratellus. You shan't have the boy unless I can help, Silas.'

'My dear Jasper,' Brimstone said, trying to put a little warmth into his voice. 'I wasn't trying to spoil your fun – surely you know me better than that? No, no, I merely wanted to say we couldn't begin *right away.* There are preparations to make. I have to be sure I call up the right demons. What I would suggest,' he went on easily, 'is that you leave the boy here with me – Captain Pratellus can stay to see he comes to no harm. You go and have a rest, perhaps have a little drink. Then, when everything's ready, I'll send Pratellus to fetch you so you can join the fun. How would that be?'

He held his breath, not altogether sure Chalkhill would go for it. The man might look like a beached whale with the IQ of a lettuce, but he had a certain animal cunning when it came to his pleasures.

Chalkhill was frowning. 'Pratellus can stay with him?' he asked suspiciously.

'Of course!' Brimstone exclaimed.

Chalkhill's teeth flared and dazzled. 'Capital!' he said. 'Capital! A rest, a drink. And you *will* send Pratellus to fetch me the *minute* it's all ready?'

'Of course,' said Brimstone kindly.

'Then I shall leave my little man in your capable hands!' Chalkhill exclaimed grandly and swept off down the stairs.

Brimstone dismissed Pratellus and both guards the minute they had the boy tied up securely and deposited inside the circle. None of the three made the slightest protest and Brimstone knew exactly why. Pratellus in particular realised which side his bread was buttered. He might suck up to Chalkhill for the little favours of his job, but Brimstone was the one with power, even if Chalkhill was the one with money. Brimstone was the one you kept sweet at all costs. He was the one who could fire you, throw you on the rubbish heap. He was the one who could send a demon hunting through your dreams if you irritated him too much.

He was the one with a sacrifice to make.

Brimstone stared at the boy, wondering why Beleth wanted him so much. He was certain in his own mind now that Beleth *had* somehow engineered this situation. It was all too neat and tidy for any other explanation. The boy's arrival the minute he stepped out of the circle – even *before* he stepped out of the circle, now he came to think of it. His position behind Chalkhill so he had to be the second person Brimstone would see. Even the way Chalkhill offered him and the ease with which he'd agreed to let Brimstone take him away. That wasn't like Jasper, not like him at all. It had to have something to do with Beleth. Once you called a demon, you gave it an opportunity to interfere with the world. Small demons just made mischief, but princes could be more subtle. And far reaching.

Yet why had Beleth chosen *this* child for the sacrifice and no other? Why had Beleth chosen a child at all? Why not someone of importance, someone rich and powerful? Chalkhill's boy seemed fearfully ordinary. Even his clothes weren't up to much. The breeches looked as if he'd mended them himself – and none too expertly.

Brimstone tore his mind away from the puzzle. It was really no business of his why Beleth wanted the boy. Just so long as the demon kept his end of the contract. Oh yes, that was all that mattered. He scuttled across the room for *The Book of Beleth* and turned to the chapter that described the sacrifice. It all looked simple enough. You called up Beleth in the usual way, then cut the victim's throat. Beleth absorbed the life essence, sealed the contract and took the boy's soul with him back to Hell. Easy-peasy. Once Beleth was gone, the only thing Brimstone had to do was dispose of the body, which would be simple with the glue vats in full production. He wouldn't even have to worry about Chalkhill any more. With Beleth's contract in Brimstone's pocket, Chalkhill was yesterday's news.

He went to the cupboard and found a sharp-edged knife. Then he came back and started to re-fortify the circle in preparation for the calling-up of Beleth. Two evocations in one day! That must be something of a record.

Pyrgus watched the old man skeetering about the attic room like a sun-dried cockroach and tried to figure out how much time he had left. He couldn't believe no one had searched him. The guards had been too busy beating him up. Captain Pratellus had been too busy playing Good Cop. Chalkhill had been too busy organising fun for himself. And this old boy – Brimstone – seemed to have other things on his mind as well. As a result, Pyrgus was now quietly sawing at his bonds with the little blade he'd fished from the button-down pocket on the leg of his breeches. It wasn't very sharp, but it would do the job. Providing he had time.

He wished he knew what Brimstone was really up to. Chalkhill wanted him to call up a few demons to torment Pyrgus and this place certainly looked as if it was ready for a conjuration – and Pyrgus himself was right inside the magic circle. But Pyrgus had never seen a triangle of trapped lightning before and he didn't like the look of that knife Brimstone had brought into the circle. The old man was about his own business, something even Chalkhill didn't know about. Pyrgus also guessed this was not good news. There were worse things than being tormented by a few minor demons and that knife looked like one of them.

If he could just cut through the ropes in time, he was certain he could get away. Brimstone looked like he'd been dead for years. He was lively enough for an old boy, but he was frail. Pyrgus reckoned he could outrun him easily, probably even take the knife away from him without much trouble. But only if his hands and feet were free. Until that happened, he was helpless.

He redoubled his efforts with the little blade.

Brimstone redrew symbols and lit candles. He glanced at Pyrgus. 'Nearly done,' he said cheerfully.

'What are you going to do to me?' Pyrgus asked him. He wasn't expecting an honest answer but, if he could keep Brimstone talking, it might give him extra time.

'Nothing you need worry about,' Brimstone told him promptly.

'What do I need to worry about?' It was horribly difficult to tell how far he'd got with the ropes. They certainly hadn't parted yet. But at least Brimstone was talking.

'Nothing,' Brimstone said. 'Nothing at all. You won't feel a thing. Well, hardly anything.' He turned away from Pyrgus and picked up a large book. 'Now please be quiet – I have work to do.'

So much for keeping Brimstone talking. Pyrgus watched with trepidation as he began an evocation.

Pyrgus couldn't believe what was materialising in the triangle. Like most boys, he'd seen pictures of demons and read about them in his schoolbooks. But they'd all been small creatures, just a few feet high. Bad tempered, admittedly; and dangerous. Put enough of them together and they could strip the flesh from your bones with those sharp little teeth. Some breeds even had magical powers – they could wither plants and cause all sorts of illnesses. And all of them could get into your mind if you were silly enough to look them in the eye. Even though you wouldn't want one as a pet, they weren't really all that scary.

But the thing in the triangle was something else.

It was huge. It was ugly. It was loud. It was smelly. It oozed malevolence and naked power. Worst of all, it was smiling.

'Aha,' it said. 'You found the boy.'

'You knew it would be him,' Brimstone said. 'You knew, didn't you? All that business about the second person I saw – you knew who it would be.'

'Of course I knew who it would be,' Beleth growled. 'You don't think I'd leave that sort of thing to chance?'

'Why him?' Brimstone asked. The creature seemed to make him nervous. He was dancing from foot to foot.

'Show me the clause in our contract that says I have to explain myself to you,' Beleth hissed.

Brimstone backed off at once. 'Just curious, just curious. None of my business, none at all. The deal's still on, isn't it?'

'Signed in blood,' said Beleth. 'And sealed once you complete your part of the bargain. Speaking of which …'

Brimstone took the hint. 'Yes, yes, I'll do it now. No sense in dragging these things out.' He raised the knife and bent down over Pyrgus. 'Hold still, boy,' he said.

Pyrgus snapped the ropes around his wrists.

His feet were still tied so he couldn't run, but he brought the little blade round and jabbed it into Brimstone's hand. Brimstone squealed and dropped the knife. 'You stabbed me!' he exclaimed in astonishment. He looked at his hand. 'I'm bleeding!'

Pyrgus rolled away from him and tried to grab the knife. He wasn't quite sure whether he was going to use it on Brimstone or the ropes that bound his legs. But he was never to find out because Brimstone moved with astonishing speed for someone of his age and snatched the weapon away just as Pyrgus's fingers closed on it. 'Oh no you don't!' Brimstone said. Pyrgus kicked out with both bound feet and caught him in the shin. For a moment Brimstone stood, arms flailing, then lost his balance and fell half in and half out of the circle.

'Aha,' said Beleth. 'Freedom!'

'No – ' Brimstone screamed. Pyrgus noticed he'd dropped the knife again.

Pyrgus made no mistake this time. With his feet still bound, he rolled once more and grabbed the weapon. From the corner of his eye he saw the massive form of the demon step out of its triangle. Since there was no way he could fight the two of them, he ignored Brimstone altogether, jack-knifed upright and slashed at the ropes round his legs. The knife must have had an ion edge because it cut through them like butter.

'Keep away from me!' Brimstone howled.

Pyrgus leaped to his feet and jumped right over Brimstone as he raced for the door. He couldn't remember if he'd seen Brimstone lock it, but it was the only chance he had.

'I'm on your side, fool!' the demon growled, apparently to Brimstone. It crossed the room in two huge strides.

Pyrgus was reaching for the door handle when the huge clawed hand fell on his shoulder.

The jolt of power that surged through his body felt like trapped lightning. Pyrgus jerked as every muscle went rigid. His momentum carried him forward, but his whole body felt as if it had been seized by rigor mortis so that he toppled forward to fall flat on his face on the floor. Blood gushed from his nose and a loud knocking filled his ears. Behind him he could hear Brimstone wailing like a child. The demon roared. Then everything went deathly quiet.

For an eternity Pyrgus lay there waiting for the demon to kill him. The knocking noise started up again and he realised it wasn't inside his head at all – it was coming from the door. Experimentally he tried to move his arm. His body ached from head to toe, but the muscles had started to work again. He rolled over, tasting blood in his mouth, and slowly sat up. The room was a shambles. Bits of trapped-lightning equipment were strewn across the floor and a whole segment of the circle had been torn up and destroyed. The brazier was just a piece of twisted metal. Brimstone lay against one wall, a dazed expression on his face. He looked as if he'd been thrown there like a rag doll. He was cradling his large book in both arms.

The knocking became a pounding and suddenly the attic door burst in, hinges shattered. Four large men marched through with military precision. Beleth vanished instantly. Brimstone scrambled to his feet. 'Get out!' he screamed. 'Get out! Get out! Who do you think you are?'

Pyrgus stared. He knew who these men thought they were. Each one wore the uniform insignia of His Supreme Majesty, the Purple Emperor.

'Where's my *boy*?' wailed Jasper Chalkhill.

'Shut up!' Brimstone muttered. He was staring at the wreckage of his attic room, still bewildered by the sheer speed of events. One minute he'd been about to bring his greatest plan to glorious fruition, the next his hopes were shattered. Beleth was gone. The boy was gone. All his expensive equipment was broken. It would take him weeks to replace it – weeks! No matter how much he paid, it would take him weeks! But he still had the book. That was something. And the contract. Although he didn't really like to think about the contract. The contract had a penalty clause.

'I insist you speak to me! I insist, Silas! I absolutely, positively insist!' Chalkhill stamped a slippered foot in the extremity of his frustration.

Brimstone sighed. 'They took him away.'

'Who took him away? Why didn't you stop them?'

'I didn't stop them because there were four of them and one of me. I didn't stop them because they were the Emperor's Guard. That's why I didn't stop them.'

Chalkhill blinked. 'The Emperor's Guard? The *Purple* Emperor's Guard?'

'What other Emperor is there?' Brimstone snapped. He wished the fat idiot would go away. He needed time to think, to plan. He needed to decide the best thing to do next.

'What's the Purple Emperor want with that boy?'

'How should I know? Maybe you should write a letter and ask him.'

'You're being horrid, Silas. Imagine what a disappointment this has been to me.'

Brimstone decided on diplomacy. 'To us both, Jasper, to us both. But what was I supposed to do – defy an order from the Purple Emperor?'

'They had an order? From the Emperor himself?'

'I don't know if it was from the Emperor himself. Maybe they print out those things by the dozen. All I know is they waved a bit of parchment underneath my nose, then marched him away.'

'Did you read it?' Chalkhill asked.

Brimstone stared at him as if he was insane. 'What am I – a lawyer? These were the *Emperor's* men!' Actually he was sorry now he *hadn't* read it. Might have given him some clue to what was so special about this boy. First Beleth wanted him, now the Purple Emperor.

Brimstone walked across the room and took Chalkhill by the arm. He made a massive effort to put sympathy and reassurance into his voice. 'Look, Jasper, give me time to clean things up in here, then I'll work out some way to get the boy back.'

'You will?'

'That boy broke into our premises. He stole several of our cats. Heaven alone knows what other damage he may have caused.' Brimstone nodded soberly. 'He *broke the law*, Jasper. That may give us prior claim. I don't know why the Emperor wants him, but we may have prior claim. Even His Supreme Majesty is not above the law. What I'd like you to do, Jasper, is give me half an hour to clean things up in here, then send Glanville and Grayling to my office – '

'Our lawyers?'

'Yes,' Brimstone nodded patiently, '*that* Glanville and Grayling. I'll have them prepare a petition – a *legal* petition.' He stared at Chalkhill for some clue he was following this. 'A petition to the Emperor, you understand. With a little luck, we could have the boy back here within a day.'

'You really think so, Silas?'

'I really do, Jasper,' Brimstone lied.

Brimstone's office was nothing like that of his partner. It was far smaller, more cluttered, gloomy and dusty. Every wall was lined with ancient tomes of sorcery and demonology, books that had taken a lifetime to collect. Brimstone's desk was a sea of parchment texts and the antique wooden floor an obstacle course of bulging folders and files. Brimstone himself was playing with a Hand of Glory when Glanville and Grayling marched in.

The lawyers might have been twins. They were both small, pot-bellied men with very little hair. They both wore three-piece suits and highly polished shoes. Both carried elephant-hide briefcases with ornate 'G' monograms embossed in gold leaf on the side. Both wore rimless spectacles and both were trying unsuccessfully to grow moustaches. They looked around vainly for somewhere to sit and sighed together when they didn't find it.

'Jasper Chalkhill claims you wish to see us,' Glanville said.

'Alleges you have work for us to do,' Grayling nodded.

'We understand – without prejudice – there is a boy,' said Glanville.

'Some miscreant,' said Grayling.

'Some tort-feasor,' Glanville added.

'Larcenous.'

'Trespassing.'

'And missing,' Brimstone said drily, to shut them up.

'Ah, yes,' said Glanville, 'missing! Taken by the Emperor's men, to the best of our information, knowledge and belief.'

'Abducted, one might say,' sniffed Grayling slyly.

Glanville smiled. 'And Mr Chalkhill would like him back.'

Grayling smiled. 'Mr Chalkhill would like him back,' he echoed.

'Never mind about that,' said Brimstone. 'I want you to run your eye over a contract.'

'Contract law!' Glanville exclaimed, not at all put out. 'Your speciality, I believe, Mr Grayling.'

'I want you *both* to look over it,' hissed Brimstone.

'I want the best legal advice you can give me.' He flicked nervously at the thumb of the Hand of Glory and small flames ignited at the fingertips. Brimstone blew them out hurriedly.

'You shall have it,' said Glanville.

'You shall have it,' said Grayling.

Brimstone pulled a single sheet of parchment from the drawer of his desk and handed it across. Glanville took it, read it, then passed it without comment to Grayling. Grayling took a little longer reading, but looked up eventually.

'Is it binding?' Brimstone asked.

'Yes,' said Grayling.

'Yes,' said Glanville.

'It's with a demon,' Brimstone pointed out.

'Makes no difference,' Grayling said. 'Demonic contracts still have force in law.'

Glanville reached out and took the parchment. 'I know everyone tries to get out of them and demons are notoriously slapdash when it comes to legal matters – '

'They prefer to kill you,' Grayling explained, smiling brightly.

' – but the fact remains,' Glanville continued, 'if this – ' he raised his spectacles and peered at the parchment closely ' – *Beleth* wished to institute proceedings on foot of this document, they would certainly be entertained in court. Unless, of course, your signature is forged or you could prove duress. That means the demon forced you into signing,' he added helpfully.

Brimstone shook his head. 'I signed it all right. Without duress.' The Hand of Glory was beginning to sweat a little so he set it down. 'There's a penalty clause …'

'I noticed that,' said Grayling soberly.

'I take it this contract has not yet been executed,' Glanville said.

Brimstone shook his head again. 'Not yet.' The Hand of Glory began to crawl away and he pinned it to the desktop with a paper-knife. All five fingers wiggled weakly. 'I want to know my chances of getting out of it.'

Grayling jiggled his spectacles. 'My dear Brimstone, this is signed in blood.'

'The form of words is clear,' said Glanville. 'You have agreed to make specific sacrifice to Beleth. He has agreed to grant you a specific wish.'

'The penalty clause is equally specific,' Grayling said. 'Should you fail to make the sacrifice within a month, this Beleth creature takes your soul.'

'No getting out of it,' said Glanville.

'No getting out of it at all,' Grayling confirmed.

Seven

Pyrgus could only see as far as the backside of the Imperial Guardsman walking three strides ahead of him. The man was so large he blocked much of the view in front. There were stone-faced guards on either side of him and one behind. If he tried to run, he would get maybe a stride and a half. These characters were experts.

But he had to try.

'I've a pebble in my shoe,' he announced loudly. If they stopped to let him get it out, there might be a chance of distracting them.

They ignored him.

'I could be crippled if you keep me walking on a rock. Your officers won't thank you for delivering an injured prisoner.'

Apparently their officers didn't give a hoot. The guards continued to ignore him.

They reached the bridge where the four men around him were joined by six more of their colleagues. They wore helmet masks and uniform riot gear with stun wands in every holster. This was beginning to look like a serious bust.

As the new men fell in, Pyrgus started to wonder what it was all about. When the four first took him into custody, he'd been so relieved to get away from Brimstone and the demon that he'd never thought to ask himself why the Emperor's Guard had been sent after him. 'Where are you taking me?' he demanded. 'I've a right to know where you are taking me!' He waited vainly for an answer, then added sourly, 'Or not.' It didn't matter anyway, because by now he had a fair idea where they must be going.

They crossed the bridge in fine style. The crowds melted before the marching phalanx of Imperial Guard but reconvened to watch the prisoner. At the far side, they followed the course of the river until they reached the official ford. When they stopped to await the Imperial barge, Pyrgus knew he'd been right. They were going to the palace. These men had been sent to bring him to the Emperor.

Pyrgus sighed. What on earth did his father want with him now?

The Imperial palace was set on an island in the widest part of the river. There were nearly two square miles of formal gardens surrounded by a miniature forest where the Emperor sometimes went off hunting boar. The palace itself had been built more than four hundred years ago using purple stone. The stone had weathered over centuries until now it was almost black; although it did take on a faintly purple sheen at sunrise and sunset. The colouring combined with the archaic architectural style to give the building a sinister, cyclopean look. Most visitors found it intimidating. For Pyrgus it was simply home.

He walked in step with the guards through the main entrance, then halted as Gatekeeper Tithonus slithered out to meet them. The old man was wearing his official green robes and looked more like a lizard than ever.

'I'll take him from here,' he said.

'Our orders is to bring him to the Emperor direct.'

'Your orders have been changed,' Tithonus said, unsmiling. He held the guard's eye and Pyrgus could almost feel the soldier's willpower crumble.

Eventually the guard mumbled, 'Yes, sir.' He motioned to his colleagues and they wheeled off in perfect step.

'I see you haven't lost it, Tithe,' Pyrgus grinned.

'And I see your dress sense has got worse,' Tithonus told him drily. 'Do you want to change before you meet your father?'

'I think I'll stick with what I'm wearing – let him see what he's reduced me to.' Pyrgus's grin faded. 'What's happening, Tithonus? Why did my father send the heavy squad?'

'It's Blue,' Tithonus said. 'Walk with me. We'll take the long way round – there's a great deal I must tell you.'

'What's the matter with Blue?' Pyrgus asked quickly. Holly Blue was his sister. She was the thing about palace life he missed most. 'Is she ill?'

'Far from it,' Tithonus said. 'But she *is* up to her old tricks.'

Pyrgus groaned. 'What's she told Father this time?'

'That you've fallen foul of Lord Hairstreak. Is it true?'

'Sort of,' Pyrgus said. How on earth had she found out? She was a year younger than he was, yet she'd somehow set up a network of spies that was the envy of the Imperial Espionage Service.

'What does "sort of" mean in this context?' Tithonus asked.

'He caught me stealing his golden phoenix.'

Tithonus closed his eyes briefly. 'Good grief!' He opened them again. 'I was half hoping it wasn't true. Have you any idea of the implications?'

'He was mistreating it!' Pyrgus protested.

'Of course he was mistreating it. This is Black Hairstreak we're talking about. He mistreats his own mother. I don't suppose you stole her as well?'

Pyrgus smiled despite himself and shook his head.

'What did you do with the bird?' Tithonus asked.

'Released it in the wild. I fed it first.'

Tithonus stared at him, then shook his head slowly. 'You fed it first. Pyrgus, do you even know what it costs to trap a golden phoenix?'

'No.'

'I thought not. But you do know Hairstreak is a powerful man?'

'That doesn't mean he's entitled to mistreat – '

'Spare me the lecture,' Tithonus cut in with a sigh. 'I happen to agree with you, but that's hardly the point. The point is that Hairstreak is a member of a Noble House – '

'He's a Faerie of the Night!'

'He's a *noble* Faerie of the Night. He has considerable political connections and even greater political ambitions. He's already the major spokesperson for that whole unruly breed.'

'How is Comma, by the way?' Pyrgus asked. He grinned. 'Speaking of unruly.'

'Please don't try to divert me,' Tithonus said coldly. 'And especially not so crudely. Comma is Comma.

Your stepbrother has no terminal illness so far as I am aware and beyond that I care very little. We were discussing Hairstreak. You should not have taken his bird. He is in the process of making mischief for you.'

'I can handle myself,' Pyrgus said confidently.

'Doubtless you will tell that to his Imperial Majesty.' Tithonus sighed. 'Pyrgus, I think the time may have come for you to realise who you are. You are not a young soldier of fortune. You are not some merchant's son or artisan, however much you like to disguise yourself. You are His Highness the Crown Prince. That carries certain responsibilities even if you no longer live at the palace.'

'It's serious, isn't it?'

Tithonus nodded. 'This business between you and Lord Hairstreak has disrupted some very delicate political negotiations. Most people may not recognise the Crown Prince without his finery, but Hairstreak's men had no problem at all. He had a full report inside the hour. He may not treat his phoenix very well, but he knows its value. He is making demands that will be hard to meet. Meanwhile, he has men searching for you. In the circumstances he is quite entitled to seize you if he finds you – seize and hold you. Can you imagine the scandal that would cause? The Crown Prince in the custody of a Faerie of the Night? It doesn't bear thinking about. Your father is very, very angry.'

Pyrgus felt his heart sink as it often did when his father was the subject of discussion. 'What's he going to do with me?' he asked.

'I prefer he tell you that himself,' Tithonus said. 'Indeed, I have explicit instructions to that effect. But I can give you one piece of advice. Don't lose your temper with your father. Whatever happens.'

Pyrgus lost his temper with his father. 'I didn't flounce out of my home!' he shouted furiously. 'I didn't walk away from my responsibilities! I didn't abandon my sister, not that she needs me to look after her. You *forced* me to leave! I can't believe you still hunt animals. I can't believe you keep a zoo. I can't believe you still cling to medieval – '

'You seem to care far more about animals than you do about people,' his father said coldly. 'But this isn't about animals, Pyrgus, however much you'd like to think it is. This is about the future of the Empire.'

'Oh, don't be so melodramatic,' Pyrgus sniffed in just the tone of voice he knew would infuriate his father most.

They were together in the conservatory behind the throne room, breathing in the heady scent of orchids. The Purple Emperor was not a tall man, but he was broad: Pyrgus seemed to be taking after him in that respect. His head was shaved in the papal tonsure – as Emperor he also led the worldwide Church of Light – and he was wearing an open shirt that showed off his official butterfly tattoos. They seemed almost to flutter as he fought to control his temper.

For once he succeeded rather better than Pyrgus. His voice was almost calm as he said, 'This is no melodrama, Pyrgus. This is real life – your life as well as mine. I expect Tithonus reminded you of who you are.'

'I expect you told him to.'

'Yes, I did. I'm aware you're far more likely to listen to him than you are to me. I had hoped he might get you in a reasonable mood before we talked, but I can see now that was far too much to hope for. Pyrgus – '

'Did you know there's a factory in Seething Lane that makes glue from live kittens?' Pyrgus asked him furiously. 'Did you know there are Faeries of the Night who call up major demons? Did you know one of them almost killed me? Did you know Black Hairstreak goes into his phoenix cages three times a week and – '

'We all know Faeries of the Night leave a lot to be desired when it comes to their behaviour, but – '

'A lot to be desired?' echoed Pyrgus. 'A lot to be desired? Father, you're *negotiating* with these people! You're treating them as *equals*!'

'I'm treating them as subjects of the Empire, which they are. Whether you like it or not. They're difficult, it's true – '

'Difficult?' Pyrgus exploded. 'They're trying to overthrow everything we stand for!'

'Yes, they are,' his father agreed. 'Indeed they are. And that is exactly why they need careful handling. I have been in negotiation with Night leaders – including Lord Hairstreak – for several months. Those negotiations have reached a critical stage. The last thing I need is my idiot son blundering in where he isn't wanted and handing them new leverage on a plate!'

'My mother would never have agreed with what you're doing!' Pyrgus hissed.

His father swung round furiously. 'You leave your mother out of this! You've no idea what she would or wouldn't have agreed with. You don't even know what's going on! I've tried to make you take an interest in politics, but all you ever think of is your damned animals and yourself! Oh, you're so sensitive, Pyrgus, so sensitive to birds and little creatures. But if we don't reach an accommodation, it won't just be birds and little creatures they'll be killing – it will be people!'

'The Nighters are killing people anyway,' Pyrgus said, deliberately using the insulting term.

His father looked briefly apoplectic, then managed at last to get his temper under control. 'Enough,' he said. 'I've had enough of this. I didn't get you here to discuss politics or explain my decisions. I am Emperor and that must be enough. When *you* take the throne, you can set up sanctuaries for every stray cat and dog in the kingdom, but until – '

'I don't want to – '

'Be quiet!' his father thundered. 'Just *listen* for once! This is *your* future I'm about to talk about – yours! Now, will you do me the courtesy of *listening*?'

Pyrgus glowered at him sullenly, but said nothing.

His father stared down at his hands which had somehow shredded a precious orchid. He dropped the remnants on the floor and looked up again at Pyrgus. 'You are in peril,' he said softly.

'Blue doesn't know what – '

'You're supposed to be listening,' his father said quietly.

'Sorry,' Pyrgus said.

'This isn't Blue's information. Oh, she told me about your escapade with Hairstreak, but this comes straight from the Espionage Service. Double-checked and copper-fastened. Apparently you've been a target ever since you left the palace.' He held up a hand to stop Pyrgus interrupting. 'I know you've been keeping your identity a secret. I know you've been living like ...' he gave Pyrgus's clothes a look of sheer disgust '... some sort of ballad singer. I appreciate your face isn't particularly well known. But we're not the only ones with spies. It would be naïve to imagine our friends on the Nightside didn't know all about our ... differences. Even more so to imagine they didn't know you'd left. Our information is they've been systematically hunting for you. The plan was – the plan *is* – to kidnap you and hold you to ransom. Not for money, of course, but to make sure I agree to their political demands. Your little raid on Hairstreak's phoenix – '

'Father – ' Pyrgus began, distraught for the first time in their conversation.

His father's voice remained soft. 'I'm not really blaming you,' he sighed. 'The man is a reptile. He treats everyone abominably, servants, animals, followers – it doesn't matter. I expect at your age I'd have done exactly what you did. But the fact is, you've rather handed them your head on a plate. They don't have to kidnap you now – Hairstreak can hold you legally. And if you think he treated his golden phoenix badly...' The Emperor paused briefly, then continued, 'He knows I know this. He will use it to try to wring concessions.'

'But they must know you couldn't put me before the welfare of the Empire,' Pyrgus protested.

'Of course I could,' his father said. 'I love you.'

They walked together along the broad corridor that was the spine of the Imperial palace. For the first time in his life, Pyrgus noticed the maroon carpet underfoot was a little threadbare in places. 'What –?' He hesitated. He'd been about to ask, *What are you going to do to me?*, but decided to phrase it differently. 'What do you want me to do?'

Servants bowed as they passed, like waves on a beach. 'I want you to go away for a little while,' his father said.

'I understand,' Pyrgus said.

They turned off into the private quarters. A permanent spell of silence meant they could talk freely without risk of being overheard. 'There's nowhere really safe for you within the kingdom,' Pyrgus's father said.

Pyrgus said nothing.

'I've made arrangements for you to translate,' his father said.

'The Analogue World?' Pyrgus had suspected as much.

The Emperor nodded. 'Of course you won't be going alone. Tithonus is too old, but Lulworth and Ringlet will be with you as servants and bodyguards. Blue wanted to go as well, but I told her it was out of the question: I expect you're quite relieved. We're targeting a remote Pacific island with no other inhabitants. Good climate, quite a few exotic fruits, although we've laid in our own stores, of course.' He smiled wanly. 'Lots of wildlife – you'll feel right at home. Once the negotiations are over, you can come back. Should be no more than a month at most. You can look on it as a little holiday.'

After a moment, Pyrgus said, 'When do I go?'

His father put a hand upon his shoulder. 'Lulworth and Ringlet have already translated. They're waiting for you on the island. The portal's been established in the chapel. I'd like you to go at once.'

'For a month?'

His father nodded.

Pyrgus took a deep breath. 'Don't get angry, but

there's something I really have to do ...' His father waited, watching him. Pyrgus swallowed. 'There's a factory – '

The Emperor nodded again. 'Chalkhill and Brimstone. I wondered how long it would take you to discover it.'

Pyrgus felt his anger rising again, but for once it wasn't directed at his father. 'They're killing animals! They're killing – '

His father held up a hand. 'We know about it. We're trying to do something about it. The trouble is, what they're doing isn't strictly against the law. Glue has been made from slaughtered animals for generations.'

'But – '

'I know, I know. This goes beyond humane slaughter. Our problem is proving it.'

'I can prove it!' Pyrgus said. 'I saw it! I saw what goes on!'

'Your word against theirs, I'm afraid. But don't worry, we *will* do something about it. I have lawyers working hard to find a way to close the factory down. That's the only real solution. I know how you feel, Pyrgus, but you're going to have to leave this one to me. Will you trust me to do the job?'

'Yes, of course,' said Pyrgus quietly. He felt a great deal older than he had that morning.

His sister Blue and stepbrother Comma were already in the chapel. She ran across to fling herself into his arms. 'I thought that dreadful Hairstreak must have killed you! It was nearly *three days* before I could get any word of you at all!'

Pyrgus disentangled himself gently. 'Hairstreak never

got near me. It was someone else who nearly killed me.' He regretted the words the moment they were out of his mouth.

His father fortunately hadn't heard – he was engaged in conversation with the technician priest who worked the portal. But Blue picked it up at once. 'Who nearly killed you?' she asked fiercely. 'If you don't want to tell Father, I can do something about it, you know.'

He didn't doubt she could. Not for the first time he wondered what his little sister would be like when she grew up. Already she was one of the most formidable people he knew. Even Tithonus treated her with respect. He shook his head. 'It's nothing, Blue. Just a joke.'

She stared at him suspiciously and he knew as soon as he was on his way she would be putting out feelers about where he'd been and what he'd done before his father's guards caught up with him. But Comma broke the moment. 'Our brother likes his little jokes, Blue – don't you, Brother?' he said with his sly twisted smile. 'But now perhaps we should let him get on with his trip. The sooner he goes, the sooner he'll be safe …' His eyes sparkled like Jasper Chalkhill's teeth.

The portal had already been established between the pillars by the altar, for all the world like a raging blue fire. If Pyrgus hadn't known better, he'd never have believed anyone could step into that fire and live. But despite appearances, the flames were not really there. If they existed at all – and philosophers were far from sure about that – they had their being *between* the worlds. As such, they were nothing more than a visible separator, a demarcation line that indicated the transition between one dimension and the next. The real power of the portal lay in its enhancements by the hideously expensive machines that distorted space and time in this one spot. Everyone in the Faerie Empire knew this technology existed – it had been the stuff of legend for centuries – but only the Imperial Family could afford it. Thus the Analogue World, where the portal led, was the ultimate escape route for threatened royals. No one could find them there.

The Emperor joined them in time to catch the last remark. 'Comma's right,' he said. 'The sooner you go, the sooner I'll know you're safe. Have you had your vaccines?'

One of the medical priests bustled over with a hypodermic needle. 'We're ready for that now, Majesty.' Pyrgus pushed back one sleeve and looked away as the needle slid underneath his skin. It stung slightly, then subsided.

'Ready to go?' his father asked.

'I think so,' Pyrgus said.

'There's nothing you need to take,' his father reassured him. 'We've equipped the island with everything you're likely to want and Lulworth and Ringlet will have it all set up and ready waiting for you.'

'Thank you, Father.'

Blue threw her arms around him and kissed him soundly on the cheek. 'I shall *so* miss you!' she whispered. 'Be safe.'

Pyrgus grinned weakly and gave her a brief peck in return.

'Aren't you going to kiss your little brother too?' Comma said. 'It could be *such* a long time before we see each other again.'

Pyrgus ignored him and stepped into the portal.

Eight

For a moment Henry Atherton just stood there, mouth open, eyes blinking furiously, as he tried to decide what he was looking at. Hodge had caught a butterfly, of course, but it wasn't a butterfly Henry was seeing. He was seeing a tiny winged figure. The wings were like butterfly wings, but the figure ...

Henry shook his head. He was looking at a *fairy*!

The trouble was he didn't believe in fairies. He didn't even *know* anybody who believed in fairies. Except, a voice said in his head, Mr Fogarty. Mr Fogarty believes in fairies! For some reason it brought him up short. Mr Fogarty believed in fairies. Along with ghosts and flying saucers. Mr Fogarty believed the world was run by a secret conspiracy of bankers based in Zurich, Switzerland. Just because Mr Fogarty believed in something didn't make it real.

But Henry was looking at a fairy. In a lunatic moment he wondered if Mr Fogarty had somehow *created* it. Then his paralysis broke.

'Hodge, you idiot!' he screamed. He threw himself on the tomcat and grabbed him by the scruff of the neck, the way mother cats do with kittens. Hodge howled in protest and dropped the ... dropped the ... Hodge dropped whatever it was he'd had in his mouth.

Then Henry dropped *him*. He glared at Henry accusingly and stalked off no more than a yard or two before stopping to sit down. Henry snatched the fairy between cupped hands, taking care not to crush the wings.

As Hodge washed himself to regain his dignity, Henry cautiously opened his hands to take another peek. The creature looked dazed. Its head was twisted to one side, possibly as a result of being chewed by Hodge. There might have been blood on one shoulder, but it was difficult to tell.

Henry forced himself to consider what he was holding, even though he knew it was more or less impossible. It was a little winged man of sorts. Well, actually a little boy. Or not a *little* boy exactly – he looked somewhere around Henry's own age – more of a young man, but tiny. He was wearing clothes: a jacket and breeches that might be dark green – the actual colour was difficult to tell. The wings were dun, marked like a grizzled skipper butterfly.

Henry swallowed. 'Who are you?'

The fairy – it *had* to be a fairy – clapped his hands to his ears and tried to launch himself out of Henry's grasp. Henry slid his thumbs across quickly to block the exit. He opened them again a slit and asked again more softly, 'Who are you?'

It occurred to him suddenly that he was assuming an awful lot. In all the storybooks, fairies could talk. But what happened in real life? What was a fairy anyway? It looked like a little person, but since it clearly wasn't human, maybe it was some sort of *animal*. It was weird thinking of fairies as animals – or insects, an errant thought intruded: they had wings like insects – but maybe that's what they were. Just poor dumb creatures. Very *rare* poor dumb creatures ...

And if they weren't, who said they spoke English?

It was kind of dark inside his cupped hands, but he thought he saw the fairy's mouth move. No sound came out. Henry decided to assume it understood English and said very softly this time, 'I'm not going to hurt you. I rescued you from the cat.' He had a sudden inspiration and added, 'Nod your head if you understand me.'

The fairy's head poked out between Henry's hands and nodded.

'Will you promise me you won't try to fly away if I open my hands?'

The fairy's head nodded again enthusiastically. Henry started to open his hands and the fairy tried to launch himself out again. Henry snapped them shut. 'Oh no you don't!' He carried the fairy into the shed and looked around until he found an empty jamjar. Carefully he dropped the creature inside and covered the mouth with one hand while he manoeuvred the lid. He screwed it tight and held the jar up for inspection. The fairy was gripping his throat and writhing in a pantomime of suffocation. 'Oh, all right,' Henry said. 'You keep well clear.' There was no way he was going to loosen the lid, but he did punch a few air-holes in it with his penknife. The fairy watched and kept well clear. Obviously he was no dumb animal.

What now? What did you do when you caught a fairy?

A thought occurred to him. He pushed it away, but it came right back. After a moment, feeling really stupid, he asked softly, 'Do you grant three wishes?'

The fairy cupped his hand around his ear.

Henry licked his lips. 'Do you grant three wishes?' he asked again, more loudly this time.

The fairy nodded vigorously, then pantomimed unscrewing a lid.

'Oh, no,' Henry said firmly. He had the feeling he was being got at. Only little kids believed in three wishes. But then only little kids believed in fairies. He scratched his head. What was he going to do?

Maybe Mr Fogarty would know. Mr Fogarty had one big advantage over Henry: he actually thought fairies existed. That probably meant he'd studied them. Maybe he'd never *seen* any, but if you read enough books, one of them usually told you what to do. The more Henry thought about it, the more it seemed sensible to show the fairy to Mr Fogarty. Before he could talk himself out of it, he grabbed the jamjar and dropped it into the pocket of his jacket.

He found Mr Fogarty in the kitchen, making a mug of instant coffee. 'You finished?'

Henry shook his head. 'Haven't really started yet.'

'You want coffee?'

'No. I – '

'Good,' Fogarty said, 'because this is the last. Goes on the supermarket list tomorrow. Instant Crap with Toxic Additives, one jar, large. Food stores? Should close those places down.'

Henry didn't want to get into that. He said, 'Can I show you something, Mr Fogarty?'

For some reason Fogarty became instantly alert. 'Did you find it in the shed?'

'No, not in the shed exactly. Outside actually.' The jar caught in his pocket as he tried to drag it out, but he freed it eventually.

Fogarty bent over, frowning, to look through the speckled glass. 'Some sort of kid's toy?' The fairy moved. 'Good God!' Fogarty exclaimed and jumped. Then he grinned. 'That's good. That really got me going for a minute. What is it – radio control?'

'It's a fairy,' Henry said.

They sat facing each other, the jarred fairy on the kitchen table between them.

'You think it can talk?'

'The lips move, but I can't hear anything,' Henry told him.

'Could be pitch,' Fogarty said. 'That thing's vocal cords must be really short. Any sound he makes has to be in the high register, like a bat. Can you still hear bats?'

'Squeaking?' Henry asked. 'Yes, I can.'

'You lose it when you get older. Something happens to your ears. I haven't been able to hear a bat in fifty years.' He looked back at the fairy. 'Or it could be volume, of course. Not much lung capacity there either.'

'He can hear me,' Henry volunteered. 'And understand.'

'Oh, he'll understand all right. They're intelligent little scrotes, by all accounts. Dangerous too.'

Henry frowned. 'How can something that size be dangerous?'

Fogarty looked at him soberly. 'Animal cunning,' he said. 'They lure you into Fairyland and then they have you.'

He couldn't mean what Henry thought he meant. 'Like ... magic or something?'

'Weight of numbers,' Fogarty snorted. 'Some of them have poisoned stings, like African bees.'

'You really think there's such a place as Fairyland?' Henry asked. 'A sort of … magic place?'

'Why do you keep going on about magic?' Fogarty asked him sourly. 'I'm talking about another reality. Don't they teach you physics at school?'

'Actually – '

But Fogarty wasn't listening. 'Einstein – you know who Einstein was?' Henry nodded. 'Einstein figured there were about a billion universes next door to this one. Quantum boys say the same thing, some of them. You never hear Hoyle's Different Spouse Theory? Every morning you wake up beside a different spouse because you've moved into a whole new universe, only you don't know it because now you've got a whole new set of memories.' He caught Henry's expression and added, 'Never mind that. I'd say that thing's from a parallel universe. Any sign of UFOs?'

Bewildered, Henry shook his head.

The fairy was sitting cross-legged in the jamjar, staring out at them. If he could hear their conversation, he gave no sign.

Fogarty said, 'Take the top off.'

'What? What happens if he flies away?'

'Where's he going to go? The windows are shut and the back door's closed. Besides, if he tries that I'll get my fly swatter.' Fogarty grinned suddenly. 'Heard that, didn't he? Sneaky little scrote's listening to every word. Look at his expression. Fly swatter for you, my lad, if you try anything stupid. Got that? Comprendez?'

Inside the jar, the fairy nodded.

'Told you,' Fogarty said to Henry. 'Take the top off.'

Henry reluctantly unscrewed the lid and set it on the table beside the jamjar. After a moment, the fairy reached up to the rim of the jar and pulled himself out. Henry noticed he didn't use his wings much. He dropped down on to the table, watching Fogarty warily.

'Now, listen,' Fogarty said. 'I think you and me need a little talk, boyo. Trouble is, you can hear me but I can't hear you. But I can fix that. If it's pitch or volume I can rig something. Won't be pretty, but it'll do the job. Now you can do this the hard way or the easy way. You can try running off or flying off or whatever it is you do, but you aren't going to get far. I won't use a fly swatter. That was just a joke – you're far too valuable. But I can catch you, easy as pie, in a butterfly net and when I do, you're going back into that jar. So what's it to be? You going to be good?'

The fairy nodded.

'OK,' Fogarty said. 'This shouldn't take long.'

The fairy sat down with his back against the jamjar and watched while Fogarty took down an old shoebox from a top shelf. It was full of tangled wiring and dusty electrical components. Fogarty scrabbled through them, laying out bits and pieces on the kitchen table. Henry noticed they included a tiny speaker from an old transistor radio. He found a half-used tube of instant solder and unscrewed the top to inspect it. 'Nobody uses this stuff any more,' he remarked. 'All bloody microchips and circuit boards.'

Henry watched, fascinated, as Fogarty began to assemble something with the speaker at one end. His old hands were flecked with liver spots but amazingly deft, as if he was well used to intricate machinery.

Halfway through, the fairy got up and walked across to hand things to Fogarty as he needed them. The little creature appeared to have an instinctive grasp of how the contraption was going to work.

When the last piece was in place, Fogarty said to Henry, 'See if there's a battery in the drawer under the sink. Nine volt. Little square thing.'

The drawer seemed to hold nothing but string, but Henry eventually found a battery in the bottom. 'This do?'

Fogarty was making some finishing touches and barely glanced across. 'Yes, that's the ticket.' He took the battery from Henry and wrapped wires round the terminals. 'Talk into that,' he told the fairy, pointing to a button mike larger than its head.

The fairy crouched down at the mike, looked at Fogarty, then at Henry. Lips moved and a tinny voice crackled from the speaker. 'You were very rough on that cat.'

Henry blinked. 'That cat was trying to eat you!' he protested. 'That cat thought you were a butterfly.' All the same he grinned a little. He rather liked cats himself, even great podging cats like Hodge.

'I could have handled it,' the tinny voice told him.

'Never mind the cat,' Fogarty cut in. 'We've got more important things to talk about. You can understand what I'm saying to you?'

'Certainly.'

'So you speak English?'

'If that's what you're speaking.'

'Of course it's what I'm speaking. Where did you learn it?'

'Didn't have to,' the fairy said.

Fogarty frowned. 'So it's your native language?'

'Wouldn't think so,' said the fairy.

'You trying to be clever with me?' Fogarty asked.

The fairy gave him a look that would have done justice to a sphinx. 'I don't know why you're going on about the language. You can understand me, I can understand you. I need you to help me.'

'We're not talking spying here, are we, because – '

Henry interrupted, 'Help you how?' Maybe the fairy would do something in return. He kept thinking about his parents. He kept thinking of the three wishes business. But he couldn't ask about three wishes in front of Mr Fogarty. Or talk about his parents.

'Get back to where I came from.'

Henry hesitated. 'Like … Fairyland?'

'If that's what you call it.'

'What do *you* call it?' Fogarty asked aggressively.

They both saw the fairy shrug. 'I don't call it anything much. The realm, I suppose. Or the world.'

'But it's not *this* world?'

'It's some sort of parallel dimension, right?'

'Yes.'

Fogarty looked at Henry. 'Told you. We're dealing with an alien.'

Henry said, 'What's your name?'

'Pyrgus,' said the fairy. 'Pyrgus Malvae.'

Mr Fogarty went back to the language business, which he seemed determined to worry like a bone. Pyrgus the fairy sighed audibly through the little speaker. 'Look,' he said, 'I don't understand the physics of it very well, but Tithonus once told me – '

'Who's Tithonus? Your leader?'

'He used to be my tutor when I was a child. He told me this world is an analogue of mine. Or mine is an analogue of this one. Or they're analogues of each other – it all amounts to much the same thing.'

'What's that mean?' Henry asked. 'Analogues of each other?'

'Connected,' Pyrgus said. 'Tithonus says it's like dreaming, except you don't leave your body behind. Dream worlds can be pretty weird, but you always know the language, don't you?'

It made no sense at all to Henry, but Mr Fogarty seemed satisfied. 'So you travelled here from this other world?'

'It's not exactly travelling,' Pyrgus said. 'We call it *translating*. You don't actually go anywhere. You just move into another state of being. But it feels as if you've gone somewhere,' he added helpfully.

'You people have been translating here for centuries, haven't you?' Fogarty asked casually.

'Some of us,' Pyrgus said. Even through the speaker his voice sounded guarded.

'You mean like not everybody can afford it?' Henry put in.

'Something like that.' Pyrgus moved position, but the mike continued to pick up his voice perfectly. 'Look, I don't know who you two are – '

'I'm Henry Atherton,' Henry told him promptly. He'd decided he liked Pyrgus. The little fellow was feisty.

Pyrgus ignored him. ' – but I don't think I'm going to answer any more questions until you promise to help me get back.'

'You can't get back to your own world?' Fogarty asked, frowning.

Pyrgus said nothing.

'How can we help you if you won't answer questions?'

Pyrgus folded his arms and studied the ceiling.

Fogarty gave in. 'All right, all right, we'll help you. But you're getting nothing for nothing.'

'What do you want – three wishes?'

'We'll work that out later,' Fogarty scowled. 'Just so you know there's no such thing as a free lunch.'

'How do I know I can trust you?' Pyrgus asked suspiciously.

'See anybody else round here who's going to help you?'

Pyrgus glared at him.

'Take my point?'

Pyrgus continued to glare for a long moment, then muttered something that sounded like, 'Can't be any worse than Brimstone.' More loudly he said, 'All right, we'll make a deal. You help me and I'll send you gold when I get back.'

'Hah!'

'Well, what do you want?' asked Pyrgus crossly. 'How much gold do you think I can carry when I'm this size?'

Something about the way he said it made Henry ask, 'Weren't you always this size?'

Pyrgus shook his head. 'Didn't have these stupid wings either.'

'I think you'd better tell us what's going on,' said Fogarty.

Once Pyrgus got started, it seemed as if he couldn't stop. There were details that didn't make much sense and gaps he glossed over. But the story was fascinating.

The Faeries of the Light first discovered the Analogue World nearly five thousand years ago when three families of seed merchants were shipwrecked on a remote volcanic island in the Land of Faerie. The place was barren and they might have starved to death if one of the children hadn't stumbled on something very odd – two basalt pillars that burned fiercely without giving off the slightest heat. The child – her name was Arana – walked between the pillars. Where she found herself wasn't barren like the rest of the island, but lush, well watered and packed with a jungle of enormous plants and flowers. Even more exciting, she'd been turned into a creature with wings who could fly from one giant flower to another.

Arana played for a time in this amazing world, then started to miss her family and plucked up enough courage to go through the fiery pillars again. She found herself back on the barren island. Her wings had disappeared.

When she told her family, they didn't believe it, but she talked her older brother, Landsman, into coming with her to see the fiery pillars. Before Landsman could stop her, Arana ran into the flames. Landsman lunged forward to try to save her and they both found themselves winged creatures in the green land. Landsman was old enough to realise he wasn't surrounded by giant flowers and plants, but had himself shrunk. When he led his sister back through the pillars, they lost their wings and returned to normal size.

The discovery of the portal saved the shipwrecked families, for while the barren island couldn't feed them, the world beyond the pillars certainly could. Since they were seedspeople, they already knew a lot about plants and even introduced a few new species from the Realm of Faerie, using seeds they'd managed to save from the shipwreck.

'Which ones?' Fogarty asked.

'Bluebells … foxgloves … most of the flowers with bells came from my realm.'

In the early months, Landsman made regular trips through the pillars in the hope of spotting a passing ship that would rescue them, but, as time went by, he did this less and less. Eventually he left a written record of their experience somewhere on the island where it would be safe from weather and painted a large notice on a rock near the pillars explaining where this record could be found. He hoped if anybody ever landed on the island, they'd find the diary and follow his family into the Analogue World to bring them home.

Nobody ever did. Landsman updated the record every six months at first, but this dropped to once a year, then every few years. Eventually he stopped updating altogether. By now he was middle aged and little Arana a full-grown woman. The younger members of the families were intermarrying and producing winged children of their own on the far side of the pillars. The new generations had never experienced the Realm of Faerie (beyond that tiny patch of barren island) and had little interest in it. Their home was among the plants and flowers of the Analogue World.

It was nearly four hundred years before anyone else landed on that remote little island. But it was eventually visited by a wizard named Arion, who was experiencing some problems with the engine of his fishing boat.

'You have wizards in the Realm of Faerie?' Henry asked eagerly.

Pyrgus blinked at him. 'They're just people who can make things work. Like Mr Fogarty here.'

'Get on with it,' growled Mr Fogarty.

Arion found the notice on the rock, faded but still readable. He followed the directions and rescued Landsman's record, which had survived rather well. But search as he might, he couldn't find the basalt pillars with the fire between them or any sign of the original shipwreck. He decided the record was a hoax, but since it was a centuries-old hoax it had curiosity value, and he donated the documents to the library of the Wizards' Guild.

'You have a Wizards' Guild?' Henry interrupted again, but Mr Fogarty shushed him.

Landsman's record lay unnoticed for a further sixty years before it was taken up by an adventurous nobleman named Urticae. Pyrgus called Urticae a Faerie of the Night without explaining what that meant.

'You have *nobles*?'

'Shut it, Henry!' Fogarty growled.

With nothing better to do, Urticae managed to find the original island. He couldn't locate the basalt pillars either, but he did discover evidence of an ancient earthquake that might have toppled them. Before long he'd convinced himself that the portal had really existed and sensed that an entrance to another realm could have important political and military possibilities. He also decided that the portal must have had something to do with natural conditions on the island. To the amusement of his family and friends, he spent the next three years visiting active volcanic sites in the hope of finding another one. The day after his thirty-third birthday he did.

The new portal, only the second ever discovered in the Realm of Faerie, was on property owned – but never visited – by another noble, a Faerie of the Light named Iris. Urticae tried to buy the site, but Iris became suspicious and wouldn't sell. Urticae's House launched an attack on House Iris, thus beginning a conflict between Faeries of the Night and Faeries of the Light that was to cause trouble right to the present day.

House Iris won the war and it was only after Urticae's forces were defeated that Iris himself found out what the fuss was all about. He searched the disputed property and eventually stumbled on the natural portal. Although he didn't recognise it for what it was, investigation soon enlightened him. His discovery was to lay the foundations of the vast power and wealth that eventually accrued to his family.

Fogarty leaned forward. 'You mean there's just one portal between our two worlds now?'

Pyrgus shook his head. 'No, eighteen have been discovered altogether. But they don't stay open. Some of them get buried, like they think happened to the first one. Some of them just stop working, nobody really knows why. New ones are found from time to time. There are about five known now, including the Purp – ' Pyrgus stopped himself, then went on, ' – including the one Urticae lost to Iris.'

Fogarty's hard old features were expressionless, but there was a curious glint in his eyes. 'How come that one lasted so long?' he asked. 'Way you tell it, it must be thousands of years old.'

Pyrgus hesitated, then said, 'That one was... modified.'

Fogarty waited for him to go on and, when he didn't, asked, 'Modified how?'

'The Imp – the, ah, some wizards made a study. I mean, this was before I was born. The portal was just an ordinary portal for, you know, centuries, but House Iris eventually built machines to stabilise it and change the way it worked. The other portals just lead to one place each and two of them aren't even useful. One opens underwater near the bed of some ocean and one opens inside an active volcano. That's the only place they go. They're sort of *just there* in both worlds. But you can aim the House Iris portal so it opens up anywhere you want it to.'

'That's the one you came through, isn't it?'

Pyrgus nodded. 'How did you know?'

'I think I'd have noticed a portal that was always *just there* at the bottom of my garden,' Fogarty said drily. 'It had to be one that opened up specially for the occasion. Why did you want to come here?'

Pyrgus hesitated. 'I didn't. I wasn't supposed to come here at all. Or shrink to this size. Or grow wings. There's a filter on the House Iris portal that stops you shrinking when you translate, but it didn't work for some reason.'

Fogarty sniffed. 'Sounds to me like you were sabotaged,' he said.

Nine

'How much of that did you believe?' asked Mr Fogarty.

Henry blinked. He'd believed it all. 'Don't you think he's telling the truth?'

'Not much,' Fogarty said. 'All that business about shrinking and growing wings…?'

'But he's small and he does have wings!' Henry protested.

'I know,' Fogarty said. 'But that doesn't mean he's shrunk or just grown them. He may have always been that way.'

They were together in Mr Fogarty's cluttered living room, having left the fairy Pyrgus Malvae in the kitchen eating a potato crisp that was nearly as big as he was.

'Why would he say he did if he didn't?'

'To keep us off our guard,' Fogarty told him soberly. 'What could be more innocent than a sweet little fairy with butterfly wings … in trouble?'

'Keep us off guard about *what*?' Henry asked.

Fogarty pursed his lips, leaned forward and dropped his voice. 'The alien invasion.'

'Alien *invasion*?' Henry echoed. '*Alien* invasion?'

'Well, you can drop that attitude for a start,' Fogarty said crossly. 'You know how many Americans got abducted by aliens last year? Six million!'

'Mr Fog – '

'And that's just America. You think what it's like world-wide. Believe me, there's something going on and this may be a part of it. He's already admitted he comes from a parallel universe. What do you think that makes him – a teddy bear? How far do you think you'd trust him if he was green with tentacles? Or that thing that came out of John Hurt's chest in *Alien*?'

Henry hadn't seen *Alien*, but he imagined what came out of John Hurt's chest must have been pretty awful. He opened his mouth to say something, but Fogarty was in full flight.

'You wouldn't, would you? You'd be on your guard. Think about it. If you looked like hell and dripped slime, wouldn't it make sense to come on like something a lot more harmless? So you use advanced alien technology to change your shape – molecular adjuster, I'd say. But what do you change it to? Fairy, that's what! A *fairy*!'

'Why?' asked Henry. He'd seen Mr Fogarty like this before and the only way to stop it was to meet it head on.

'Why? Why what? Why a fairy? Because a fairy is familiar ...' he narrowed his eyes ' ... yet strangely unfamiliar. Every kid on the planet's seen fairies in a picture book, but how many've seen the real thing? Everybody loves a fairy – tiptoes through the bluebells, butter wouldn't melt – but at the same time, fairy says *Don't mess with me otherwise you don't get the gold at the end of the rainbow.* You heard that thing talking about gold, didn't you?'

'That's leprechauns,' Henry said.

It stopped him. 'What's leprechauns?'

'Gold at the end of the rainbow. Irish leprechauns. They promise you gold, but don't give it to you. Fairies just help plants grow.' Then, before Mr Fogarty could get his breath back, he went on, 'Anyway, if he *was* part of the alien invasion, why would he tell us he'd shrunk?'

'What?'

'Why would he *tell* us? Why wouldn't he just pretend he was a normal fairy?'

'To get our *sympathy* – '

'If we thought he was a real fairy, he wouldn't *need* our sympathy,' Henry said patiently. 'He'd have it already. Everybody loves fairies – you just said so yourself.' He waited while Mr Fogarty considered it. The old boy might be batty, but he wasn't stupid.

Eventually Fogarty said, 'You think I should trust him?'

'Yes!' Henry said emphatically.

'You think we should help him?'

'Yes,' Henry said, but less emphatically this time. It was the 'we' that got to him. He wanted to help Pyrgus the fairy. In fact he wanted to help quite badly. But a little voice in his head muttered that maybe he wouldn't be able to do all that much. Henry had other problems in his life.

Fogarty shrugged. 'OK,' he said. 'Let's go back in.'

'We've had a discussion,' Fogarty said briskly, 'and we've decided – '

'What was that thing?' Pyrgus asked, interrupting.

'What thing?'

'That thing you gave me to eat.'

'Potato crisp,' Fogarty told him. 'It wasn't poisoned, if that's what you think.'

Pyrgus looked at him in surprise. 'Didn't think it was – I just thought it tasted nice.'

'Potato crisp,' Fogarty said again. 'Cheese and onion.'

'Haven't you ever eaten one before?' Henry asked.

Pyrgus shook his head. 'We don't have them in my realm.'

'Don't you?' Henry was fascinated. He couldn't really imagine a world where you couldn't buy yourself a packet of crisps. 'What do you do for snacks?'

'Brindles,' Pyrgus said. 'They'd be the most popular. Bubble smoke, I suppose. And nants, if you've got a sweet tooth. Slice of ordle. Then there's chaos horn, but that's a sex thing. In Cheapside they sell retinduculus from stalls.'

'This chaos horn – ' Henry began.

'Can you talk about all that some other time?' Fogarty cut in. He glared at Henry, then at Pyrgus. 'As I was saying, we've had a discussion, young Henry and me, and we've decided to give you the benefit of the doubt – '

'What doubt?' asked Pyrgus.

'What doubt?' asked Henry.

Fogarty ignored them. 'We've decided you might just be who you say you are, although you haven't really said yet, have you? But we need to ask you a few more questions.' He waited, then when Pyrgus said nothing, went on: 'This shape you're in, this fairy business – little, wings, skinny – you say that's not natural? That's just what happens to you when you come through a portal?'

'Unless it's got a filter,' Pyrgus said. He scowled. 'Or the filter doesn't work.'

'It's important how you answer this,' Fogarty said, 'so think carefully. Every country in the world – our world – has got folklore about fairies. Little stick-insect people like you with big wings. Every country.'

'What's your question?' Pyrgus asked.

Fogarty's eyes darkened. 'No smoke,' he said. 'No smoke – that's what they say, don't they? Mean to tell me all those stories about fairy folk are just coincidence? Don't have anything to do with your people?'

Bewildered, Pyrgus said, 'No, I'm not trying to tell you that.'

'So an awful lot of your people – your *alien* not-human-at-all people – must be swarming through the portals. Without filters.'

'Mr Fogarty – ' Henry began. He'd thought they'd cleared up the alien stuff.

But Pyrgus cut him off. 'I'm not trying to tell you that either. We don't have very many people using gates to your world. Why would we? It rains a lot here. And who wants to shrink and grow wings? You think it's fun getting eaten by cats and put in a jamjar? There's only one filtered gate and it's expensive to operate. My fa – the people who have it are always complaining about the cost, so it's only used when you really, really have to. I told you there's only one other gate that gets you anywhere useful just now. Believe me, nobody's *swarming* through it.'

Fogarty had the look Hodge got when he was about to pounce on a mouse. 'So where do all our fairies come from?' he asked triumphantly.

'They're descendants of Landsman and the shipwrecked seeds people,' Pyrgus said.

Fogarty's jaw dropped. 'Oh.' But he recovered quickly. 'All right. Answer me this then. What do you look like when you don't look like a fairy?'

'Handsome,' Pyrgus said and grinned.

It went on like that for a while. Pyrgus answered Mr Fogarty's questions and gave reasonable explanations. By lunchtime, enough trust had been generated for Mr Fogarty to let Pyrgus out of the kitchen while they all ate lunch in the cluttered living room. Henry made them beans on toast, as he often did for Mr Fogarty and himself. He cut up a baked bean for Pyrgus, who ate each piece in his hands like watermelon. When he'd finished, he wiped his mouth on his sleeve and gave Henry a thumbs up. They tramped back into the kitchen with Pyrgus sitting on Henry's shoulder. He fluttered down to his microphone as Henry pulled up a chair.

'That was even better than your potato crisps. What was it?'

'Baked beans,' Henry said.

'You're a super cook, Henry,' Pyrgus told him. 'How did you make that brilliant sauce?'

'Comes in a tin,' Henry muttered, embarrassed.

Fogarty said, 'See if there's a small box in the drawer, Henry. We need to make the speaker portable.' He pushed himself to his feet. 'Never mind, I'll get it – I want to look for a different mike.' He rummaged in the drawer and came up with a rusting tin box that had contained tobacco sometime around 1918. 'This'll do. Ah – ' From the jumble of wiring and components, he picked out a throat mike even smaller than the button mike currently linked to the speaker. 'Should make things easier.'

While Henry and Pyrgus watched curiously, he packed the various bits of the speaker into the tin box and replaced the button mike with the smaller throat mike, extending the wire as he did so. 'There,' he said when he'd finished. 'Portable. More or less.' He went back to the drawer and returned with two rubber bands, which he attached to the throat mike. 'OK, young Pyrgus, think you can carry something this size on your back?'

Pyrgus examined the throat mike. 'Think so,' he said cautiously. He folded his wings and slipped his arms through the rubber bands, pulling on the microphone like a knapsack. When he spread his wings again experimentally, it sat comfortably between them.

'Say something,' Fogarty instructed.

After a moment, Pyrgus said, 'What do you want me to say?' His voice emerged from the tin box, slightly muffled but still perfectly audible.

'Right,' Fogarty said briskly, 'you carry Pyrgus and the box, Henry. We've got some investigating to do!'

Henry held out his hand so Pyrgus could climb up his arm on to his shoulder. 'Where are we going, Mr Fogarty?'

'Just down to the end of the garden,' Fogarty said. 'If we're to find a way to send this little fella back, I want to see the spot where he arrived.'

Henry smiled to himself. It sounded as though Mr Fogarty had decided Pyrgus wasn't an alien invasion after all.

They walked together from the house. Pyrgus was seated on Henry's shoulder, casually holding on to his ear. The wire from his backpack microphone trailed down to the tin box which Henry had strapped to his wrist. 'Hope that cat's not still there,' came Pyrgus's tinny voice.

'Kick in the backside'll soon sort him out,' said Mr Fogarty, who liked to pretend he didn't share Henry's soft spot for animals.

As they reached the shed, Fogarty said, 'Somewhere round here, was it?'

'Over by the buddleia, I think,' Henry said.

'Actually it was a bit beyond it,' Pyrgus told them. 'I'm not exactly sure because I was confused. I mean, I didn't expect to end up here and I didn't expect to be a titch with wings, so I staggered around a bit. Then I got drawn towards the bush – '

'The buddleia bush?' Fogarty asked.

'If that's what you call it. That one.' He pointed.

'What do you mean, *drawn towards* it?'

'It's just … I don't know … I sort of liked the feel of it. Or the smell or something. Felt as if I'd be safe there.'

Fogarty shook his head. 'Weird, that. Buddleias attract butterflies.'

As they moved towards the buddleia, Henry saw there were several butterflies on the bush and examined them carefully in case another one turned out to be a fairy. Pyrgus must have noticed what he was doing because he said quietly, 'I came through on my own.'

Henry nodded, but checked the rest of the butterflies anyway. He was beginning to realise just how weird this whole business was. Yesterday he hadn't believed in fairies. Today he actually *knew* one. And he knew there were others, generations descended from Landsman and his people who'd probably forgotten where they came from in the first place. A thought struck him and he asked Pyrgus, 'Landsman and Arana and those ... where did they come out in our world when they went through the portal on the island?'

'Don't know,' Pyrgus said.

'It's just that they spread all over the world,' Henry said. 'So it would have to be somewhere they could spread *from*. I mean, it couldn't have been another little island, for example – they'd never have got off it.'

'Don't know,' Pyrgus repeated. 'I got taught this stuff when I was a kid, but I forget half of it. Anyway, nobody's sure where the first ones came through. Don't forget, it was hundreds of years before anybody else used a portal and hundreds of years after that before anybody made contact with the descendants of the originals. By then they'd nothing much in common with the people in my world and the stuff about the portal had turned into myths. Maybe it was England.'

'This is England!' Henry said excitedly.

'I know,' Pyrgus grinned. 'Mr Fogarty told me.'

'Just kidding me?' Henry said. He didn't mind. He liked Pyrgus.

'Sort of,' Pyrgus told him. 'But I'd actually heard of England. I mean before I came here. So it must have been mentioned in my lessons, although I can't remember why.'

They moved beyond the buddleia bush into a corner that was all shrub and weeds. Mr Fogarty had abandoned a couple of decaying oil drums and several rusting machine parts, including a car engine sump. They poked up out of the long grass like tombstones.

'It was here,' Pyrgus said at once.

'You sure?'

'Yes,' Pyrgus said. 'I thought I'd gone mad when I saw the junk.' He looked round at Henry apologetically. 'You have to remember I wasn't expecting to shrink. Took me a couple of minutes to figure out what had happened.'

'Remember exactly where?' asked Fogarty. He looked around as if expecting to be attacked.

'Not sure,' Pyrgus said. 'I think it might have been over there.'

They walked in the direction he was pointing. Even before they reached the spot, Henry could see a ring of discoloured, flattened grass. 'Is that a fairy ring?' he asked Mr Fogarty.

Fogarty was frowning. 'More like a crop circle. Small one. You also get marks like that in UFO landings.'

'Is it big enough for a UFO?' Henry asked. He found he was frowning now too.

'Naw, too small. Unless aliens drive compacts. But look at the colour of the grass. That's some sort of radiation.' To Pyrgus he said, 'How does this portal of yours work?'

'I'm not sure,' Pyrgus said.

'You're not sure?' Fogarty rounded on him. 'You use the thing to get you from one dimension to another and you don't even know how it *works*?'

To make peace, Henry said, 'Maybe it's like television, Mr Fogarty. I mean, I know how to switch it on and that, but I don't know how it works, not really.'

'I do,' Fogarty said. 'I know exactly. Could build one if I had the parts.'

'Yes, but you know stuff like that,' Henry said. Not for the first time he wondered what sort of engineer Mr

Fogarty had been before he retired. He seemed to be able to build anything.

On Henry's shoulder, Pyrgus said, 'It's an energy thing. The portal is some sort of energy that goes with volcanic action – ' He hesitated. 'Actually, I'm not sure of that. All the natural portals appear near volcanoes or at least places where there's volcanic activity – hot springs, that sort of thing. But there hasn't been a volcano near the one I came through for five hundred years or more. The old one went extinct and they, I don't know, flattened it or something.'

'Maybe you just need the volcano to start it off,' Henry suggested helpfully. 'Maybe once it starts, it stays on of its own accord.'

They both ignored him. Pyrgus said, 'The filter works through trapped lightning.'

'Trapped lightning?' Fogarty frowned. 'You mean electricity?'

'I don't know.'

'Same stuff that drives your speaker.'

'I don't know,' Pyrgus said again.

'It has to be electric,' Fogarty muttered. 'And the portal must be some sort of field. The flames you see aren't hot at all, not even warm?'

'No.'

'Henry, poke around a bit. See if you notice anything odd. Pyrgus, try to remember anything, anything at all that might be useful.' He crouched down to examine the circle of discoloured grass more closely.

Henry made his way cautiously into the undergrowth, casting his eyes around for anything that might look unusual. It was tough going. The corner was full of stones as well as the junk Mr Fogarty had abandoned. On his shoulder, Pyrgus said, 'You've no idea how peculiar it is to be this size, Henry. Nothing looks right and you get lost every five yards. I think I came through where there's that circle on the grass, but I'm not sure.'

'Don't worry,' Henry said. 'We'll find some way to get you back.' He wished he felt as certain as he tried to sound.

They circled back to Mr Fogarty, who was still staring at the grass. Henry opened his mouth to say something when a loud ringing sound made him jump.

'Careful!' hissed Pyrgus.

Fogarty dragged a tiny mobile phone from his pocket, switched it on clumsily and placed it to his ear as if it were a bomb. 'What do you want?' After a moment he muttered, 'Right', and pushed the phone back into his pocket. 'Brain cancer if you use it too long.' He looked over at Henry. 'Your mother,' he said shortly. 'She wants you to get home. At once.'

Henry's heart sank to his boots. In all the excitement, he'd nearly managed to forget what was going on at home.

Ten

Her Serene Highness Princess Holly Blue thought something was amiss when she stepped from her bed-chamber to find a priest running down the palace corridor outside. Priests never ran anywhere, even technician priests. They *processed* in a dignified fashion at a stately pace and, if you wanted one in a hurry, you damn well had to wait. But this one was running, the skirts of his ceremonial robes flying up to show his hairy shanks. He made a screeching turn around the corner and seconds later she heard his footfalls on the main staircase.

Blue stepped back into her chamber and walked over to the window. The running priest emerged from a doorway below, scattering a group of servants, and careered across the courtyard to disappear through an archway on the other side. He might be heading for the chapel or the kitchens or even the main entrance to the palace. But why was he running?

Blue chewed her lower lip. There was far too much going on she didn't know about just now. It had taken her days to find Pyrgus and heaven only knew what might have happened if someone else had found him first. Not that she entirely blamed herself – Pyrgus was unbelievably stupid sometimes and this bee in his bonnet about living as a commoner was about as thick as it got. A *commoner*. She shuddered. It took lifetimes of self-sacrifice to get born a prince and Pyrgus was prepared to throw it all away. Besides, he wasn't just a prince. He was Crown Prince. He should be learning how to *rule* instead of mixing with hoi polloi. Luckily he'd have her to advise him when he became Emperor, but even so ...

Except it wasn't just Pyrgus. There was something going on between her father and the Faeries of the Night. Not just the recent discussions. There was something else. She could smell it. Too many comings and goings. Too many little chats in shadows. Too many strange faces at the palace. The other thing was that her father had stopped talking to her. Well, not stopped exactly. But if she tried to discuss politics, he changed the subject. If she so much as *mentioned* Faeries of the Night, he almost ran for cover. Even when she told him Black Hairstreak had it in for Pyrgus, he'd seemed more embarrassed than grateful. But at least he'd taken action, which was something.

Blue walked slowly back from the window and sat down at her dressing table. She stared at the ornate jewel case for a long moment. She'd never done this to her father before. But then she'd never had to. She reached out and fingered the clasp. Perhaps it was going a bit far. But then again, wasn't it going a bit far that her father had stopped confiding in her? What was a girl supposed to do? She flicked the clasp, but didn't open the lid.

Where was the harm? It wasn't as if she couldn't be trusted. It wasn't as if she was some sort of spy for the Nighters. She had Father's best interests at heart.

Everybody knew that. Even *he* knew that, if he cared to admit it. Besides, she was a Princess of House Iris. Third in line for the throne. Didn't that count for anything? Didn't that mean she should never be kept in the dark?

Blue stood up abruptly, walked across the room and locked her door. Princess of House Iris or not, what she was about to do was illegal and she would be in truly gigantic trouble if her father ever found out. Fortunately that wasn't very likely.

She walked back to the dressing table and opened the casket. After a moment, the psychotronic spider crawled out, its great eyes blinking in the light. The creature had a rainbow back, like a skim of oil reflecting sunlight. It crawled aimlessly around the dressing table for a moment, examining her brush and comb, lurking near her perfume bottles. Then it moved purposefully towards her, halted at the edge of the table and waited.

Blue reached for her little wicker sewing box. She hated this bit, but it had to be done. She took out a silver needle, licked her lips nervously, then pricked the tip of her finger. She wiped the needle clean and dropped it back into the sewing box. The spider seemed to quiver in anticipation.

Ignoring the pain, Blue squeezed the finger until a single drop of bright red blood welled up and dropped beside the insect on the table top. The spider turned towards it at once and began to feed. In a moment, the table top was clean again. Blue sat back and waited, willing her slim body to relax. Impatient minutes passed before – at last! – she felt the familiar scratching on the edges of her mind. The blood was the link, of course. Her blood, her mind. It was a small enough sacrifice, she supposed, but without it the spider was no more useful than an ordinary bug.

Blue closed her eyes and opened her mind. She felt the alien presence of the psychotronic spider at once, alert, cautious and strangely familiar. She reached out a mental tendril and stroked it gently. The spider wriggled and trilled like a kitten. It was ready to accept her. In her mind, she touched it, held it, felt it blend with her.

It was as if a shutter opened and light flooded through. Her perceptions suddenly expanded. She caught her breath and fought down the sudden excitement as she became aware of not just her room, but the whole upper storey of the palace, then the palace itself, then the island, then –

Rein back! she told herself. This was the most dangerous time. If her perceptions continued to expand, she would be insane within minutes. Yet even knowing that, she *wanted* the expansion to continue. The feeling that went with it was like nothing else she'd ever experienced, an exhilaration that bordered on ecstasy. This was precisely why the use of psychotronic spiders was outlawed, even in the Imperial Espionage Service. Too many good operatives had ended up as cabbages, happily crooning to themselves as their minds examined distant reaches of the universe.

Rein back! She had a talent for it. Her curiosity, her *need to know*, had always been far stronger than the pull of pleasure. Now she imposed a focus that drew her attention away from the all and everything, back to the palace, back to her room. With a curious flicker, she saw the room through the eyes of the spider itself, all distorted planes and angles filled with giant furniture and sweeps of patterned textures. She released her mental grip a little and expanded again, but not too much. Now it felt only that she had escaped from her body and was rushing through a windswept tunnel to her goal.

An instant later she was standing in the private quarters of her father, Apatura Iris, the Purple Emperor.

There were two men in the book-lined chamber, her father himself and Gatekeeper Tithonus. Both were informally dressed and held brandy balloons, but the expressions on their faces showed this was no casual meeting.

' – did lose his temper. Both of us did,' her father was saying. 'But at least he listened. I think I may have you to thank for that.'

Tithonus shrugged. 'He's safe now. It's all that matters.'

'Indeed,' the Emperor nodded. 'But unfortunately that doesn't solve our problems.'

'No, sire, but it does simplify them a little,' Tithonus said smoothly. He set down his glass and turned to look directly at Blue.

The illusion was so real she felt she should duck behind a screen and hide. But she knew she didn't need to. However much it felt like she was here, her physical body was still in her bedroom. Only her consciousness was visiting and that was quite invisible.

'Any further intelligence on the troop movements?' her father asked.

Blue was instantly alert. Troop movements? She hadn't heard anything about troop movements. Who was moving troops? Her father? She'd have known. She was sure she'd have known. Besides, he wouldn't have used the word intelligence if he was talking about his own soldiers. Intelligence meant information collected by the Imperial Espionage Service. Information on somebody else's troop movements.

Even without her body, she felt a chill. There was something going on between her father and Black Hairstreak, negotiations that were supposed to heal the ancient rift between Faeries of the Light and Faeries of the Night. They'd been under way for months so far as she could gather. Until now she'd assumed it was the usual horse-trading, each side jostling for the best position possible, after which things would settle down for a few years. But troop movements meant something far more serious. Troop movements meant war. Or at least the threat of war. No wonder her father looked worried.

Tithonus said, 'Lord Hairstreak continues to insist it's just manoeuvres, nothing to do with the current negotiations. But the build-up's very large for a routine exercise and reinforcements are still coming in.'

'Sabre-rattling?' the Emperor asked. 'His way of wringing a few more concessions out of the negotiations?'

'Possibly,' Tithonus said. 'I have, however, taken the precaution of placing our own forces on alert.'

'You really think he would risk an all-out attack?'

Tithonus frowned. 'I find it hard to believe. But whatever he has in mind may be part of some larger scheme. Don't forget he was planning to murder Pyrgus.'

Murder? Blue blinked phantom eyes. She hadn't

known that! Why would he want to kill her brother? It would gain him a lot less than simply taking Pyrgus prisoner. That way he could use him to bargain.

'I still don't understand what it would have gained him,' her father said, echoing her own thought.

'Neither do I,' said Tithonus, 'but there's no doubt it's what he was planning.'

'Perhaps – ' The Emperor stopped, interrupted by a sharp knocking on his door. He glanced at Tithonus.

Tithonus said nothing, but opened the door a crack, then murmured something to someone outside. Blue moved to eavesdrop on the exchange, but before she reached the door, Tithonus stepped back and a chapel priest entered. He moved forward nervously and knelt before the Emperor. 'Majesty, grave news.' Blue wasn't absolutely certain, but she thought this was the same priest she'd seen running in the corridor.

Her father waited, face impassive.

'Majesty, I –'

'Come on, man,' said the Emperor mildly. 'Spit it out!'

The priest could not meet his eye. He swallowed loudly, hesitated, then said all of a rush, 'Majesty, Crown Prince Pyrgus has not reached his destination.'

For a moment, the only expression on the Emperor's face was puzzlement. 'What are you talking about?'

'Sire, the translation appeared to be routine. As you saw. We had no reason to – No reason to – ' He looked up at the Emperor imploringly. 'Sire, we have made routine contact with Lulworth and Ringlet. Prince Pyrgus has not joined them.'

'What?' the Emperor exploded.

Tithonus said sharply, 'I saw him enter the portal myself.'

The priest glanced at him miserably. 'We all did, Gatekeeper.'

'Then where has he gone?'

'I don't know.'

'Where *could* he have gone?' Tithonus asked insistently.

The priest dropped his eyes again. 'Anywhere,' he murmured.

Blue withdrew her consciousness so violently her body went into spasm in the bedroom. She gasped, then stretched to unlock her muscles. Her heart was racing. *Pyrgus had vanished!* She grabbed the psychotronic spider and dropped it back into the jewel box. Then she ran from her room.

The chapel was in chaos. Dozens of technician priests seemed to be running here and there to no purpose whatsoever. Blue's eyes went at once to the portal. The space between the twin pillars was devoid of the familiar flames. In their place hung a dirty grey fog, all that was left of the natural portal owned by House Iris. To one side, part buried in the chapel floor, were the great machines that maintained it now and gave it life. But their metallic covers had been stripped away and component parts were strewn about.

She stepped forward to find her way barred by a near-hysterical priest. 'No admittance!' he screamed wildly. 'Nobody is permitted – ' He recognised her belatedly and stepped aside. 'I'm sorry, Your Highness. Forgive me.'

Blue swept past him without a word. She was fighting to control her emotions. Pyrgus would be fine. Pyrgus *was* fine. This was just a glitch, just some silly mistake or misunderstanding. Whatever had gone wrong could be corrected. Pyrgus was still safe. She looked around until she spotted Peacock, the Chief Portal Engineer, and marched directly up to him. He was a man she'd spoken to before and liked. Although technically a priest, he cared very little for the ceremonial aspect of his profession. It was the mechanics of portal transportation that fascinated him. He was just the man she needed at this moment. 'What's happened?' Blue asked.

Peacock looked worried and distracted. 'Your brother is missing. He never reached the portal destination.'

'I know that,' Blue told him. 'I want to know what happened.'

'That's what we're trying to find out.' He nodded towards the scattered components.

'Was there a fault in the equipment?'

Peacock hesitated, bit his lip, then said, 'Could be, but my money's on sabotage.'

She fought down a growing panic and managed to hold her voice steady. 'What makes you think so?'

'Well, we know the portal's not working properly since it didn't send him where he was supposed to go. But the filter's not working properly either. I've just stripped it down myself. It *looks* OK on the outside, even *tests* OK so long as you only run a routine check. But it's not doing its job. The filter and the portal mechanism are different things – they work quite independently of each other. Chances against two major faults like that developing at the same time are far too high for my liking. I think somebody's been up to something.'

Blue said, 'Isn't the filter working at all?'

'Only up to a point, Your Highness.'

'What's that mean?'

'When he went through, he'd have translated into the small winged analogue, just like going through a natural portal,' Peacock told her soberly. He caught her expression and added quickly, 'But it wouldn't last. There was enough of a charge in the filter to pull him back to his natural size and shape sooner or later.'

Blue stared at him. 'How long?'

'Difficult to say.'

'Then *guess*!' Blue snapped.

'Few days ... week or two. Month at most. Hard to say.'

'Days? Weeks? A month?' Blue echoed. 'He could be killed by anything. A mouse could kill him. A *dragon-fly* could kill him!'

'Yes, but they probably won't.'

It was an empty reassurance and she ignored it. 'Do you know – ' She stopped because her father had entered the chapel, trailed by Tithonus. They spotted the Chief Portal Engineer and headed towards him. Around them, the scurrying priests froze in place, apprehension showing on their faces.

'Holly Blue,' her father said, 'I'd like you to go to your room. I need to speak to the Chief Portal Engineer on a – '

'I know what's happened, Father,' Blue told him. 'And I'd like to stay.'

He hesitated for less than a second, then turned to Peacock. 'Do we know if he's alive?'

'No, sire.'

'Assuming he is, do we know where he's gone?'

'Not yet, sire. But we're working to find out.'

'How long will it take?'

'About a week, sire.'

'A week!' the Emperor flared. 'I can't wait a week to find out if my son is alive or dead!'

'Sire, we have to strip down and analyse every component in the machinery. After that, we have to run tests. We might be lucky and get an answer sooner, but ...' His face said clearly that he wouldn't bank on it.

'Someone's tampered with the filter,' Blue said.

'Tampered?' The Emperor rounded on the Chief Portal Engineer. 'You mean this wasn't just an accident?'

'It *may* not have been an accident,' Peacock said carefully.

'I'm afraid it's certainly no accident,' a new voice put in. They turned to find the Senior Medical Priest had joined them. He was a smoothly handsome grey-haired man, but his eyes were bloodshot now and his face showed strain. 'Your Majesty, may I speak to you in private?'

Blue moved to follow her father as the two stepped away, but he waved her back. She watched their huddled conversation with increasing frustration. She could read nothing from their faces. After a moment they broke apart and her father returned, his features like a mask. 'Holly Blue, please come with me. Tithonus, I'd like you to find Comma, then bring him to join us in my apartments.'

'Yes, sire,' said Tithonus, and left without another word.

Blue knew better than to push her father at a time like this, but in the event she didn't have very long to wait.

Tithonus entered after a discreet knock and announced formally, 'Prince Comma, Your Majesty.' Comma came in looking distinctly shifty, as if he expected to be accused of something; but since he had a nose for trouble, this was much his usual attitude around his father.

'I'd like you to stay, Tithonus,' the Emperor said. 'Please sit.' He looked gravely from one to the other. 'Comma, I asked you here because you are next in line to the throne after the Crown Prince. Holly Blue, you are a blood member of House Iris, so what I have to say concerns you too.' He drew a deep breath and sighed. 'Tithonus, you are my Gatekeeper and in the present circumstances I shall need your counsel more than ever before – there is a possibility we may be facing a covert act of war.'

Blue's jaw dropped and she looked at Comma, but he was staring sullenly at his shoes. Tithonus seemed impassive as ever.

The Emperor went on, 'Blue, I know how close you are to Pyrgus and if I knew any way to break this gently I would. I'm afraid your brother, the Crown Prince, may soon – ' he stopped, then corrected himself ' – *will* soon be dead.'

'I know about the filter,' Blue cut in quickly. 'The portal may have shrunk him, but he's clever. I know some people get killed, but Pyrgus can look after himself, no matter what size he is. And it won't last for ever – the Chief Portal Engineer told me himself he'd come back to his normal size and he can always hide until – '

Her father gestured her to silence. 'It's not the filter, although clearly that was part of a broadly based assassination attempt. But the critical factor was never the portal. I believe that was tampered with as back-up to make sure Pyrgus could get no help when he discovered he'd been poisoned.'

'Poisoned?' Blue exclaimed, eyes wide. Comma looked up from his shoe inspection and even Tithonus seemed stunned.

The Emperor said tightly, 'The Senior Medical Priest has just informed me that the vaccine ampule used on Pyrgus was tampered with. There are traces of triptium on the syringe.'

'What's triptium?' asked Comma, speaking for the first time.

The distress was evident on the Emperor's face. Tithonus put in softly, 'It is a drug sometimes used by Darkside assassins.'

The Emperor said, 'Thank you, Tithonus, but they deserve to hear the whole truth.' He turned back towards Blue and Comma. 'Your brother has been injected with a slow-acting toxin. The substance reacts with natural agents in the bloodstream and spreads almost like a bacterium. There are no symptoms at first, but after a period of time – it can vary from a few days to about two weeks – the triptium collects in the brain and begins to ferment. As the pressure builds, the person experiences nausea and increasingly severe headaches. Eventually – ' He swallowed. ' – eventually – ' He stopped, unable to go on.

'What?' Blue demanded, terrified. 'You must tell us what!'

The Emperor closed his eyes. 'Eventually his head explodes,' he said.

Eleven

Pyrgus watched Henry leave with a feeling close to nausea. He'd moved on to Mr Fogarty's shoulder now and the old boy smelled a bit, but that wasn't the problem. The problem was ... the problem was ... well, there wasn't just one problem. There were so many problems he hardly knew where to start thinking about them.

He didn't like being small and powerless, for one thing. All his life he'd been able to do things for himself, even as a kid. Now he couldn't even talk without the magical pack strapped to his back. And it wasn't magic he understood. This was his first trip to the Analogue World and its magic was completely different from the magic of his own.

But that was just the immediate thing. He kept thinking of the Chalkhill and Brimstone glue factory and the kittens that would drown for every day he stayed here. He kept thinking of his father and the negotiations that were going on with the Faeries of the Night. Most of all, he kept thinking about the comment Mr Fogarty had made when Pyrgus told him how the filter on the portal had failed. *Sounds to me like you were sabotaged*. It sounded to Pyrgus like he was sabotaged as well, and the more he thought about it, the more he believed it. The question was, who had sabotaged him?

It had to be somebody who wanted him dead. Pyrgus had no doubt at all about that. Sending you to a strange location without preparation or guards was asking for trouble. He hadn't mentioned it to Mr Fogarty or Henry, but all the history books told how hundreds, even thousands, of early visitors to the Analogue World had lost their lives within an hour of arrival. In time, of course, the Faeries learned to take precautions – and the greatest precaution of all was the filter – but until then, the Analogue World had been a death trap. It had come very close to killing him inside the first hour as well. If Henry hadn't happened along, the cat would have crunched him like a mouse.

But his biggest problem was how would he get back? That thought came crashing down on him like storm waves on a rocky shore. Natural portals existed in both worlds at once. You went through, you turned round, you went back. About as easy as it got, assuming the portal didn't open at the bottom of the sea. But the modified portal in his father's palace worked differently. Because you could aim it to open anywhere in the Analogue World, it had no permanent existence in the Analogue World at all. It appeared where you aimed it once you switched on the power and closed again once the power went off.

Pyrgus tried to collect his thoughts. If he'd been sent to the South Sea island as his father planned, the gate would have stayed open long enough for his guards to report everything was shipshape, then closed again. After that, the palace technicians would probably have reopened it at an agreed time every day to make sure no problems had arisen.

'What's the matter?' Fogarty asked.

Pyrgus realised he'd started at the thought. 'They may reopen the portal,' he said.

'Who?'

'The people who sent me.' He'd decided to keep unnecessary details from Mr Fogarty until he knew him better.

'When?'

'I don't know. I'm not sure they will. I was just thinking what would have happened if I'd gone where I was supposed to go. Once I'd got there safely, they'd have opened the portal maybe once a day to check up on me.'

'How would they know you'd got here safely?' Fogarty asked.

Pyrgus glanced at him admiringly. Fogarty might be old, but he certainly wasn't stupid. His father must know something had gone wrong by now. The priests and wizards would be trying to find out exactly what. They'd be trying to locate him and get him back. That should have been reassuring, but somehow it wasn't. He'd no idea how you traced somebody who'd been translated to the wrong place – or even if you could.

'In this case they wouldn't,' Pyrgus said, answering Mr Fogarty's question. 'I mean they wouldn't know I'd got here safely. But they *would* know I *hadn't* got to the Pacific island safely.'

It sounded confusing even to him, but Fogarty seemed to get the hang of it because he said, 'Your people will know something's gone wrong and they'll start looking for you?'

'Yes. Almost certainly.'

'So they'll reopen the gate if we hang around here long enough?'

'I'm not sure. I suppose so. It depends if they can figure out where I went. I'm not supposed to be here.'

'So you said,' Fogarty said shortly. 'Listen, if they did open the portal again – suppose they figured out where you'd gone and opened the portal again – would it open at the same place you came through?'

Pyrgus thought about it. They'd try to trace the coordinates – that would be the only thing they could do. He nodded. 'Yes.'

'We'd better keep an eye on that circle,' Fogarty muttered. He turned and strode towards the house with Pyrgus on his shoulder.

'I thought we were already keeping an eye on it,' Pyrgus protested.

'Can't watch it twenty-four hours a day,' Fogarty said. 'I'm going to rig up something that will trigger an alarm if your portal reopens.'

Henry caught a bus at the end of Mr Fogarty's road and sat near the front staring into a bleak future. He felt ... peculiar. Now he was away from Pyrgus and Mr Fogarty, everything suddenly seemed unreal. There were no such things as fairies. Even though he'd just had one sitting on his shoulder ... and talking to him through a microphone strapped on with rubber bands. Ha-ha, single to the Funny Farm, please!

Whatever he looked at seemed to have black edges. The business with Pyrgus had distracted him, but now everything was crashing in. He felt the bus seat was suspended in space. There were flurries of darkness beyond the window. He could hear his own breathing. Every time he moved his head he seemed to be floating. Above all, he felt sweaty and afraid.

He still didn't believe it. Mum had two children, for heaven's sake!

Henry found himself standing up and walking down the aisle of the bus. He hovered by the door, holding on, until it reached his stop. If it was his stop. He was feeling so confused he hardly knew any more. Not that it mattered. Nothing could make him feel much worse than he did already.

Stupidly he left the bus before it had quite finished moving, tripped on the kerb and ran to keep his balance. Before he could stop himself, he'd crashed into a woman climbing from a taxi.

'Sorry,' Henry said. 'So sorry. Are you – are you all right?' He felt his face flush with embarrassment, but at least he hadn't knocked her down.

'Henry?' said the woman hesitantly. She stared at him as if she couldn't believe what she was seeing.

Neither could Henry. The woman was Anaïs Ward.

Everything snapped into sharp focus, but Henry, without knowing why, suddenly felt very much afraid. He stood there looking at her and all he could think was that Anaïs Ward just couldn't be a lesbian. She was far too feminine, too pretty.

'It's Henry, isn't it?' she said.

Henry nodded dumbly. He was still trying to figure out what he was going to say. He looked at Anaïs. She was younger than his mum. In fact she wasn't really *that* much older than Henry himself.

So what was he going to say to her? What could he possibly say to her? *Keep your hands off my mother?* He caught the first hint of his face flushing again and offered a silent plea to God not to let him blush. To cover his embarrassment, he came up with something really stupid. He took a deep, rattling breath and said, 'How are you?'

Anaïs glanced around nervously, at Henry, at the street, at the taxi driver waiting for his fare. Then she got caught up in it and said, 'Fine, Henry.' She looked almost stricken. 'How are *you*?'

'OK,' Henry said. He blinked.

She looked terribly, terribly pretty. She was wearing a tailored suit with sheer black tights and high-heeled shoes. She had big brown eyes and long brown hair. She wore make-up, but nice make-up, not tarty or anything. She smelled good, some sort of perfume. He liked the shape of her nose. He liked the shape of her mouth. He wondered how she would look with butterfly wings.

If he was older, he could imagine falling for a girl like Anaïs, asking her to come to a movie or something. He could imagine his dad falling for her, although his dad was older than his mum which meant his dad was *plenty* older than Anaïs. But then older men often fancied younger women and younger women sometimes fancied older men. Except it hadn't happened that way.

'Are you having an affair with Anaïs, Dad?'

'I'm not having an affair with Anaïs,' his father had said. *'Your mother is.'*

Pyrgus Malvae had to be around Henry's own age. It was hard to think of him like that, an ordinary boy like

Henry doing whatever things they did in his world, but that had to be the way it was. Except he'd come through a portal and now he wasn't an ordinary boy any more. He was a grizzled skipper butterfly with a tiny human body. A cat could kill him and he didn't know how to get home. How did you help somebody like that? How did you help somebody whose wife was in love with somebody else? How did you help somebody whose mum fancied women?

Henry's eyes filled up and he began to weep.

Twelve

'There's good news,' said Grayling.

'And bad news,' put in Glanville.

Brimstone watched them, scowling. He wanted to nail them to the floor and saw their feet off, but he knew from bitter experience that nothing would divert them once they started talking. It was what made them so devastating in court. Innocent men confessed to murder when subjected to their relentless double-act. But at least they were on his side.

'The good news is, we have a case,' said Grayling, smiling.

'No doubt about it,' Glanville said.

'The boy may be our Crown Prince,' Grayling went on, 'but in the eyes of the law, he is a common felon.'

'Trespasser.'

'Cat burglar.'

'In that he burgled a cat.'

'Or, more precisely, burgled you and stole a cat.'

'The law dislikes that,' Glanville said. 'Indeed, the law will not tolerate it. We have seen the judge – '

'Indeed we have.'

'And she has ruled the boy may be seized and held awaiting trial.'

'By us or our officers, acting as your agents in your

capacity as director of Chalkhill and Brimstone, the injured body corporate.'

'She has issued a warrant. I have it here.' Glanville extracted a piece of parchment from his briefcase and waved it in the air.

'How long can we hold him?' Brimstone asked.

'Oh, a very long time,' Grayling told him. 'Six months without court intervention. Then, when we bring him to trial, we may request a further six-month continuance to prepare our case. A year in all. It seemed sufficient.'

'Ample!' Brimstone exclaimed. He rubbed his hands and grinned. This was turning out to be one of his better days.

'The bad news,' said Glanville, 'is that all this good news has become quite academic.'

'Useless information. Unsupportable judgment.'

'What are you talking about?' Brimstone asked them irritably. His grin had turned to a frown.

'The warrant cannot be executed,' Glanville said. 'As matters stand it is a worthless piece of paper.'

'Worthless,' Grayling echoed.

Brimstone leaned forward. 'Why?' he growled.

Glanville put the parchment back in his briefcase and closed it with a snap. 'The boy – or defendant as we must now call him – is no longer in the jurisdiction. He has left this world.'

'He's dead?' Brimstone asked in sudden panic. It wasn't enough that Pyrgus died. He had to be sacrificed to Beleth. And by Brimstone. Nothing less would satisfy the terms of the demonic contract.

'Not to my knowledge. The Royal Household – on whom we sought to serve the warrant, you appreciate – claims he has been translated.'

'To the Analogue World,' Grayling put in helpfully.

'The Courts of Faerie have no jurisdiction in the Analogue World. While he remains there, he is beyond legal redress.'

'Are you sure that's really where he is?' Brimstone asked suspiciously.

Glanville looked shocked. 'We have a formal statement to that effect bearing the Emperor's official seal. These are Faeries of the Light. They would never put a lie in writing. I think we may safely assume that if they say he's in the Analogue World, then that is where he is.'

Brimstone glared. 'We have to get him back.'

'Ah,' said Glanville.

'Ah,' said Grayling.

'What?' Brimstone demanded. 'What? It's simple, isn't it? We send some bully-boys into the Analogue World and drag him back by the scruff of the neck. Not even illegal, from what you tell me – our laws don't extend there.'

'An admirable strategy,' said Glanville. 'But flawed.'

'*Fatally* flawed,' said Grayling. 'We have no way of knowing where to find him – in the Analogue World that is.'

'Unlike other portals, the portal of House Iris is multi-directional. They could have sent him anywhere they wished.'

'Can't we force them to reveal his destination?' Brimstone asked.

Glanville looked at Grayling. Grayling looked at Glanville. They turned together and looked at Brimstone. 'Possibly,' Grayling said. 'But if they resist, it could take some time. And time, we know, is of the essence.'

'House Iris has excellent lawyers,' Glanville said. He glanced down at the floor. 'They elected not to contest our warrant since they knew we could not execute it.'

'I've got spies in the palace,' Brimstone said. 'So has Chalkhill. Between us we should be able to find out his translation coordinates.'

'Possibly,' said Grayling. 'But even if we do find out, we cannot follow. House Iris owns the only multi-directional portal in existence.'

'Perhaps not *quite* the only one,' said Brimstone thoughtfully.

Even with Chalkhill's help, it took him days to get an appointment and then it was only with a lackey. Lord Hairstreak's representative was a big, unsmiling man named Harold Dingy. He wore a silver-grey suit and was accompanied by a bloodshot endolg. For some reason he'd insisted they meet at the zoo.

'It's nice to see you,' Brimstone said untruthfully, holding out his hand.

'The pleasure's all yours,' Dingy said, ignoring it.

His endolg rolled several times around Brimstone's legs before remarking, 'He's clean, boss. No weapons and just the routine spells and charms.' It spread itself out like a mangy rug and watched them both.

'Did Mr Chalkhill tell you what it was I wanted?' Brimstone asked, shouting above the noise of the parrots.

Chalkhill had long claimed to be Lord Hairstreak's friend, but if Dingy was impressed by the mention of his name he didn't show it. 'No.' He looked as if he didn't care.

This was the tricky part and Brimstone didn't really feel like shouting it out at the top of his voice. 'Can we get away from these damn parrots?' he asked.

'I like parrots,' Dingy said.

'He *likes* parrots,' said a parrot clinging to the wire mesh of its cage.

'So do I,' lied Brimstone, 'but what I have to say is confidential.'

'Doesn't want us to repeat it,' said the parrot smugly.

'All right,' Dingy said. 'We'll talk in the Reptile House.'

The Reptile House was hot and dry and played hell with Brimstone's sinuses. But at least it was quiet and lizards didn't play back what you'd said. The endolg climbed up one of the glass-fronted cages and embarked on a staring match with a cobra. Dingy glared at Brimstone.

Brimstone glanced around to make sure they weren't being overheard, then lowered his voice. 'I wanted to talk to you about—'

'Can't hear you,' Dingy interrupted.

'This is *confidential*!' Brimstone hissed. He gestured Dingy closer and, when the man took a reluctant step forward, stretched to whisper in his ear. 'I wanted to talk to you about Black Hairstreak's portal.'

'What about Lord Hairstreak's portal?' Dingy asked suspiciously.

Brimstone looked around him again. 'I understand Lord Hairstreak may have a *multi-directional* portal,' he whispered.

'Who told you that?' Dingy sniffed.

Brimstone laid a finger along the side of his nose and tried to look knowing. 'I have my sources,' he said. His source was actually his partner Chalkhill, who'd once let the information slip while drunk. The trouble was Chalkhill let a lot of things slip when drunk that simply weren't true. Brimstone was praying this wasn't one of them.

'Somebody's been tickling your ferret,' Dingy said.

'You mean he doesn't?' Brimstone asked, then added slyly, 'It's just that if he *did* have a multi-directional portal, I should be prepared to pay a great deal of money for its use. A *great deal* of money.'

'Pity he doesn't have one then,' said Dingy. The endolg began to detach itself from the glass. It looked as if the interview was over.

'Just a minute,' said Brimstone hurriedly. 'When I said a great deal of money, I meant a million gold pieces.' He'd have to mortgage the business to raise that sort of cash, but if he didn't find Pyrgus he was dead and if he did, he'd have all the money in the realm.

Dingy stared down at him impassively. The endolg was tugging at his trouser-leg as if anxious to be going.

'For Lord Hairstreak,' Brimstone said. 'And a quarter of a million more for you.'

'You must need a multi-portal very, very bad,' Dingy said. 'Mind telling me why?'

Brimstone weighed up the pros and cons. He'd expected the question, but assumed he'd be talking to Black Hairstreak himself, not one of his stooges. All the same, this clown was probably more shrewd than he looked – Hairstreak would hardly employ him otherwise – so he might spot a lie. Besides, he had the endolg with him. They were supposed to be able to sniff out anything fishy from a hundred yards. Which was, of course, the reason Hairstreak used them. Not much trust left in the realm these days.

As against that, it was well enough known Lord Hairstreak had little love for the Purple Emperor, so he might actually welcome the death of his son. Brimstone decided to tell the truth. It was such an odd feeling he thought he'd make that *part* of the truth. Enough to squeeze past the endolg. 'I need to find Crown Prince Pyrgus,' he said.

'Why?' asked Dingy innocently. 'Is he lost?'

'He's in the Analogue World. I need a multi-portal to reach him.'

'Why would you want to reach him?'

'I have business with him,' Brimstone said with dignity.

'What sort of business would that be then?'

Oh, bog it, Brimstone thought. 'I want to kill him.'

The endolg trilled excitedly. 'What about that, boss?' it said. 'He wants to slaughter the Crown Prince.'

Harold Dingy leaned forward soberly and suddenly he seemed very menacing indeed. 'I'm going to do you a favour, Mr Brimstone. I'm going to tell you something that will save you a great deal of money. Are you listening, Mr Brimstone?'

Brimstone took a step backwards. 'Yes.'

'I'm going to tell you there's no need for you to kill Prince Pyrgus. Want to know why, Mr Brimstone?'

'Yes,' Brimstone repeated in a small voice.

To his astonishment, Dingy smiled abruptly. 'Because Prince Pyrgus is already dead!'

'As a coffin nail,' confirmed the endolg. 'Or at least as good as.'

Brimstone felt as if the sky had fallen in. He thought

he might have gone pale, but fought to keep his voice steady. He swallowed. 'Are you sure?'

Dingy was positively beaming. 'You just heard it from the endolg.'

Even with a floater spell, the gold was heavy. Brimstone tried to lift the case and felt his back creak. It was no good. He'd have to get somebody to help him. Kill him afterwards, of course – a little something in his soup or, better yet, a knife across the throat. Only way to make sure he kept quiet. Only way to make sure no one knew where Silas Brimstone went.

The trick was to go quickly. Now, in fact. Beleth was back in his own dimension now and wouldn't start to look for him before the contract expired. By then he'd be long gone. That was definitely the way to do it. Cut his losses and go. But what losses. The factory, the other businesses, his home, most of his books. It wasn't weight with the books, it was bulk. He could take a few – the more important ones. Enough so he could start again. And he'd have his gold, which was something.

Unless Beleth somehow caught up with him. Unless Beleth somehow *tracked him down*!

How had it all gone so horribly wrong? One minute he was getting ready to cut the brat's throat, the next he was running for his life. For his *life and soul*. Beleth wouldn't play around. Demon princes never did. The minute he caught up with Brimstone, Brimstone was dead meat. And his soul, what was left of it, would be used to drive a golem, or guard some stupid tomb, or have slivers sliced from it perpetually to nourish demon children. It was dreadful. Ghastly. Beyond thinking about.

He opened the door of his office and roared, 'Porter!'

He couldn't carry all his gold, of course, not even with a porter helping. He'd have to leave so much behind. Tens of thousands of pieces. Hundreds of thousands of pieces. The pain he felt was almost physical. He'd have to start again. Somewhere where no one knew him. Have to start without contacts or friends. Well, actually, he'd never had many friends, but it was the principle of the thing. And starting without contacts was a nightmare. He'd have to live in some dingy little back street in some dingy little set of lodgings in some god-forsaken dungheap of a farming village where nobody would ever think of looking for him. And even when he started up another business, he'd have to make sure it never became *too* successful. Once he disappeared, he must never, never, ever draw attention to himself.

There was a man standing in the doorway.

'What the hell do you want?' Brimstone asked.

'Porter, sir. You called for one.'

'So I did,' said Brimstone. 'Can you lift that?' He pointed to the chest of gold coins on the floor beside his desk.

The porter walked across and hefted it on to his shoulder as if it were a feather. 'You've got a floater spell on this,' he said in some surprise.

'Take it downstairs and load it into my hansom – it's the black one parked outside,' Brimstone ordered. 'When you've done that, come back here – ' he cracked a smile ' – for your tip.'

When the man had left, Brimstone opened his desk drawer and examined the selection of knives inside.

They were all long-bladed and razor sharp. He picked one with a curved edge and an ion blade that was capable of decapitating the porter, let alone slitting his throat. Then he hid behind the door and waited.

He usually disliked cutting throats. The amount of blood that pumped from the jugular was appalling, took ages to clean up. But since he was unlikely ever to come back to his office, that would be somebody else's problem. Pity, though – he'd always liked this office. Such a shame never to be seeing it again.

He heard the porter's footfalls outside and steeled himself to strike the moment the man entered. One quick stroke, step over the corpse, then out of the building before anybody noticed he was gone. The horses were fresh, the hansom unmarked. He could be –

The porter turned the handle of the door. Brimstone raised the knife and had a sudden thought. He didn't need to run away at all! He didn't need to hide! How had he missed it? All he had to do was burn *The Book of Beleth*! He froze in place. So simple. It was the book that had called him into Brimstone's world in the first place. Destroy the book and Beleth had no way to reach him. It solved the problem absolutely. With Beleth out of the picture, Brimstone could ignore the contract. He could forget about sacrificing the boy – who'd turned out to be trouble anyway – and forget about Beleth grabbing his soul. He could keep his gold, keep his businesses, keep his books. He could carry on exactly as before and, when things settled down a little, he could work on other plans to get richer and more powerful. Suddenly life was wonderful again!

Brimstone dropped the knife as the porter stepped

into his office. The man started a little at finding Brimstone lurking behind the door, but recovered enough to say, 'The chest is in your carriage, sir. You mentioned something about a tip, Mr Brimstone ... ?'

Brimstone grinned at him. 'You can whistle for it!' he said gaily. 'I'm not going! I'm not going!' He danced past the man and ran downstairs to the passage that led from the factory to his lodgings and the attic room. The place was still in a mess after the last disastrous evocation, but he ignored the debris and headed straight for the cupboard, chanting the code that removed his protection spell. The cupboard door sprang open as he reached it.

The Book of Beleth was no longer there.

Nor, when he went back to the factory a little later, was his chest of gold. Brimstone only just stopped himself from screaming. That damn porter had taken his own tip!

Thirteen

It had clouded over and begun to rain by the time Henry reached his road. He plodded miserably towards his house. Mr Fogarty's voice sounded like a refrain in his head. *Your mother. She wants you to get home. At once. Home at once. Home at once. At once, At once.* He'd a pretty good idea why his mother wanted him home at once.

Despite the cool touch of the rain, Henry's face was burning. He simply couldn't believe what he'd done. Stood in the street in front of Anaïs and cried like a baby. Huge, racking, incoherent sobs with blubbering attempts to apologise without knowing what he was apologising for.

She came over to him. That was the worst bit. She came over and put her arm around his shoulders and cuddled him as if she was his mum or something. 'Oh, Henry, what is it? What's wrong?' He'd let her hold him. She smelled nice and she was soft and warm. But now he felt guilty, as if he'd betrayed his dad. 'Do you want to talk about it?'

He didn't want to talk about it. How could he talk about it behind his father's back? Besides, he couldn't speak for sobbing. He just stood there, his head pressed to her breast, and cried. Then, to finish him completely, a stream of snot poured from his nose all down her crisp, white blouse. It went on and on and he couldn't stop it. The awful thing was she didn't make a fuss. She didn't even move, just kept holding him and stroking his hair and asking what was wrong, as if she didn't know already.

His house came into view and he noticed at once his dad's car was in the driveway.

His mother must have seen him through the window because she met him at the front door. She managed to look anxious, furious and guilty all at once. 'Where on earth have you *been*, Henry? Didn't Mr Fogarty tell you to come straight home?'

Been blubbing at your girlfriend, Mum. But instead of answering, Henry pushed past her, head down, dripping water on the Welcome mat. He wouldn't bet on getting much of a welcome today. His dad emerged from the kitchen and grinned at him weakly. 'Your mother's a bit upset,' he said.

Henry shrugged out of his coat and hung it to drip from the hallstand. 'You're soaked,' his mother said. 'Go up and change your clothes before you catch your death.'

'I think I'll take a bath,' he said, just to be bolshie. He knew they wanted a family conference.

He stood there dumbly, watching the conflicting emotions cross his mother's face, and felt a tiny twinge of guilt, a tiny twinge of satisfaction. Eventually she said, 'Yes, all right, but don't be long.'

The bath was a bad idea. He lay in the warm, soapy water, looking up at the light fitting and feeling afraid. Whatever happened next wouldn't be good and he wished now he hadn't put it off. They might get divorced. They might ask him and Aisling to go into a home. He couldn't see how to work out anything that wasn't a disaster. AOS. All Options Stink. He closed his eyes and wished there was somewhere he could go to hide.

He put on clean jeans, but the only shirt he could find was that stupid lumberjack thing Aunt Millie had bought him for his birthday. He stared at it blankly, then pulled it on. What the hell, he wasn't making a fashion statement.

They must have been listening out for him because they both shot out of the kitchen while he was on the stairs. 'We're in here, Henry,' his dad said. 'Can you come in a minute?' He hesitated, then added briskly, 'Things to discuss.'

Henry tramped into the kitchen without a word.

His dad tried to take charge. 'This would be better if your sister was here, but we thought it best to have a talk as soon as possible. We can fill in Aisling when she gets back at the weekend.'

Welcome home, Aisling. Your mother's run off with my secretary and I've booked my passage to Australia. They really should change the wording on the mat.

'Do you want to sit down, Henry? Will I get you tea or something?'

His mother cut in tiredly, 'Don't waffle, Tim.' To Henry she said, 'I understand you've been talking to your father?'

Henry nodded and walked over to the fridge. There was half an apple inside, neatly sliced on a small plate. He bit into it and it tasted like sawdust. He went to the table and sat down, staring at them both with large eyes. At least he didn't think he'd blubber now. He was all cried out.

'I suppose the first thing I want to say is this has got nothing to do with you or Aisling, Henry,' his mother said. 'I mean, it obviously concerns you, but I want you to know you're not ...' She gave a stiff little shake of her head. '... you know, to *blame* or anything like that.' She actually tried to smile.

She'd been reading her psychology books. Parents divorce, children get it in their head they're somehow to blame. Years later they're spilling it all out to some shrink. Henry said, 'I don't think anybody's to blame.' And surprised himself. It sounded far more grown-up than he felt.

His mother blinked. 'Well, no. No, of course not. I just wanted to make sure you ...' She let it trail.

Poor old Dad stuck his oar in again. He wasn't really a match for Mum, but he was a fairly big deal executive after all, so he wasn't exactly a wimp. He said, 'The thing is, Henry, something like this changes things. That's inevitable, whatever people want – '

Henry's mother said quietly, 'You agreed to let me handle this.'

With just a flash of anger, Henry's dad said, 'I was only trying to reassure him – ' But he let it go.

Henry's mother said, 'Your father told me about his conversation with you this morning and we've been discussing the situation. Trying to decide what to do, really. He's been – ' She looked embarrassed and a little green. 'He's been very understanding.' She dropped her eyes. 'Probably more than I deserve.' After a moment she looked up at Henry and said in an explosive breath, 'We've been talking most of the day and we realise we're not the only ones involved in this. There's Aisling. And there's you. I mentioned Aisling first because she's younger and less likely to understand. You're older, so ... Anyway, the point is that neither your father nor I can just think of ourselves and what we want. We, ah, have to consider what's best for Aisling and you. And ourselves too, of course.'

Henry's mind wouldn't function. He could usually second-guess his parents by a mile. Now he'd no idea whether his mother was trying to prepare him for the divorce court or the firing squad.

'What I want to tell you,' his mother said. 'What I want to tell you is that we've talked this through from every viewpoint and I suppose the first thing to say is that we're not going to get a divorce. We don't think that would be fair on either of you.' She licked her lips. 'But we *are* going to separate.' She stared at Henry, obviously trying to gauge his reaction. After a moment she said, 'You needn't worry – nothing's going to happen right away. It'll take several weeks, maybe a month or so, to get everything organised. And we won't be separating *completely*. We'll get together from time to time, like family, so it'll seem more like, you know, long holidays, trips abroad, that sort of thing.' She wound to a halt, still staring at him.

'Who gets the house?' Henry asked dully.

Henry's mother glanced across at his father, who said nothing. His mother said, 'We thought it would be easier if your father moved out.' She waited for Henry to react and when he didn't she said almost eagerly, 'It's logical really. He can find somewhere nearer his work.' She forced a smile. 'You know how often he has to sleep at the office – it'll really be much easier for him.'

Henry stared at her. She actually believed it.

His mother said, 'This house is nearer the school.' She meant her school, where she taught.

'Who gets the kids?' Henry asked.

'Don't put it like that!' his mother pleaded. 'It's not like we're splitting up the family.'

'How else should I put it?' He felt numb inside, as if he didn't really care any more. He just wanted to know what was going to happen.

His mother sighed. 'We thought it would be less of a disruption if you and Aisling stayed here. With me. You wouldn't have to relocate, or make new friends or change schools or anything. Everything would just ... you know, go on as before. Your father would visit – visit often.' She forced the smile again. 'You might even see him more often than you do now, with everything that's been going on at the office.'

Bad choice of phrase, Mum, Henry thought. Aloud he said, 'Will Anaïs be coming here?'

His mother hesitated and looked at his father again. She licked her lips nervously. 'Eventually ... and obviously only if it's all right with you and Aisling ... I would, ah, hope Anaïs might ... visit, maybe even stay over sometimes. Just to see how we all get along.' Since she couldn't look him in the eye, she looked out through the window and added, 'Long term, who knows.'

'So long term Anaïs might move in?' Henry said.

'It's possible,' his mother admitted. 'But only if you and Aisling were happy about it.' She was watching him again, still hoping for a reaction. After a moment she said, 'Might be fun, Henry. Sort of like having two mothers.' She blinked. 'You like Anaïs.'

Sure he liked Anaïs. What wasn't there to like? But

two mums? No thank you. He was having enough problems with one. To his father he said, 'All this OK with you, Dad?'

'I don't like it,' his father said, 'but it seems the fairest way.'

Fairest? His mum has the affair so she takes the house and the kids and kicks Dad out to find another place. Then she moves her lover in. If she'd convinced Dad that was fair, she should be selling used cars.

'How do you feel about it, darling?' his mother asked.

Henry shrugged. She didn't care what he was feeling. Why should he get into it? 'It's what you and Dad have agreed.' He stood up.

'Where are you going?' his mother asked at once.

Henry stared at her numbly. 'To see Charlie,' he said. 'Mrs Severs is expecting me for tea.'

His parents looked at one another as he headed for the door. 'You won't discuss any of this with Charlie, will you?' his mother called after him.

'She's *what*?' asked Charlie when he discussed it with her.

'Dad has this secretary called Anaïs. Mum's having an affair with her.'

'Your mum's, like, *gay*?'

Henry nodded.

'Wow!' said Charlie. 'Cool!'

The rain had proved to be a passing shower, so they were together in the Severs's garden. Mrs Severs, who had the idea children never grew up, served them a tea of sausages, crisps, popcorn, jelly and a garishly pink cake, then left them to their own devices. The remnants were scattered across the garden table, along with two empty lemonade bottles. Henry had been surprised by the extent of his appetite. He hated what was happening, but now he knew the worst, he had the weirdest feeling of relief.

'You think it's cool my mum's a lesbian?'

'Sure. Don't you?'

'Never really thought about it like that.'

'I have,' Charlie said. 'The gay thing, I mean – not your mum. The girls talk about it a lot at school.'

'Do they?' Henry asked, surprised.

'Yes, of course.' She cast an overtly innocent glance towards the sky. 'Some have even ... dabbled.'

'The girls at your school?'

'Yes.'

'With each other?'

'Of course with each other – that's the whole point! It's supposed to be a phase you go through.'

'Have *you*?' She couldn't have. But then this morning he'd believed his mum couldn't have either.

Charlie laughed. 'Not my thing.' She tossed her hair. 'You're not upset, are you?'

'About Mum? Yes, I am.'

'That's terribly old fashioned, Henry.'

'I don't care,' Henry said. 'It hurts my dad.'

Charlie looked thoughtful. 'I suppose it does.' She was a short girl with fair hair and blue eyes. Outside school he'd never seen her wear anything but jeans and a boy's shirt. Sometimes he thought she was nuts, but the thing about Charlie was you could talk to her. About anything. The other thing about Charlie was she never told. She said, 'What are you going to do?'

'Me? What can I do?'

'Dunno,' Charlie admitted. 'They going to divorce?'

'They say they're not,' Henry said, 'but it's bound to come.'

'What are they doing now? Staying together *for the sake of the children*?' She rolled her eyes.

Henry nodded. 'Something like that.'

Charlie put her hand on his arm. 'I'm sorry, Henry, this is really upsetting you, isn't it?'

Henry bit his lip and nodded again. 'Yes. Yes, it is.'

Charlie said, 'My mum and dad divorced.'

Henry frowned. 'What – they got back together again?' Mr and Mrs Severs had always struck him as an easy-going couple without a care in the world.

Charlie gave a little smile. 'Peter's not my real dad, Henry.'

'He isn't?'

Charlie shook her head. 'Mum divorced my real dad when I was three. Or four. He used to come home drunk and beat her up. She stayed with him *for the sake of the kids* – well, this kid really. One night he broke her arm and knocked me out of bed on to the floor. I got bruised and cried a lot. Mum decided enough was enough. Walked out with me under her good arm and hired a solicitor. She met Peter eighteen months later and it was a lot better second time around.'

Henry was staring at her open-mouthed. 'I didn't know any of this.'

'No,' Charlie said, 'nobody does. When Mum remarried, Peter formally adopted me so I got his name as well as Mum. Peter's all right.'

'But what about your real dad?'

'What about him?'

'You ever see him?'

Charlie shook her head. 'Nope.'

'Not ever?'

'Nope.'

'Where's he living now?'

'Don't know.'

'Don't you want to see him?' Henry asked.

Charlie shook her head again. 'I don't even know what he looks like,' she said as if it were some sort of a triumph. 'I can't remember and Mum burned all his pictures. She says he's a turd.'

'Sounds right,' said Henry seriously.

Charlie suddenly grinned brightly. 'Anyway, the whole point is you're not the only one with a delinquent parent. Just that mine disappeared a long time ago. Thing is, Henry, it worked out well. Peter's as good a dad as anybody. Better than my real dad. They're happy together, more or less. You never know, this thing between your parents might be good in the long run.'

'Doesn't feel like a good thing now,' Henry said. To his horror he felt his eyes begin to fill again. He tried to turn away, but Charlie spotted it.

She did exactly what Anaïs had done. She came across to his plastic garden chair and put her arm around his shoulders and cradled his head to her chest. She was only really starting to grow breasts, so it didn't feel the same and somehow he managed to stop himself from crying.

Still holding him, Charlie said, 'Must have been a heck of a day.'

A butterfly fluttered past on an erratic course towards the hedge. Henry started, then relaxed. You don't know the half of it, he thought.

fourteen

Aisling came home Friday night full of news about a pony called Chester and some stupid instructor named Damien Middlefield. She looked astonished when her parents wouldn't listen and spirited her away into the living room to explain that life, for once, was not a bowl of cherries. Henry waited patiently in the kitchen, ate some yoghurt, then two fudge brownies, but eventually it got so late he went to bed. The following morning he found Aisling heavily into denial.

'He's so *big*,' she told him enthusiastically, 'but so *gentle*. And he'll try anything, real have-a-go no matter how high they set the fences. I just wanted to pack him up in my case and bring him home with me.' She was talking about Chester, the wonder-horse. 'Do you think Mum and Dad would let me have a pony? I mean, there's room. Well, there would be if we got rid of the pergola. Chester might actually be *for sale*. And if Dad bought the field from Dr Henderson, we'd have more than enough grazing and I could – '

'What did they tell you?' Henry asked. They were alone in the house. Mum had gone shopping and Dad, despite the fact it was Saturday, had taken himself off to the office. Both had stressed they would not be back until the afternoon. Henry suspected it was a deliberate give-the-children-time-to-talk-things-over sort of thing.

'Well, I didn't actually ask them about Chester,' Aisling said. 'I mean I *hinted* but – '

'Oh, come on, Aisling!' Henry said tiredly. 'We're going to have to talk about it some time.'

'Talk about what?' Aisling asked.

'What's happening between Mum and Dad.'

'What's happening between Mum and Dad?' Aisling asked brightly.

Henry felt like strangling her. 'Did they tell you Mum's been having an affair with Dad's secretary?' he asked brutally.

'Oh, that,' Aisling said. 'It doesn't mean anything. Mum's not gay.'

'Mum's not gay?' Henry echoed.

'No,' said Aisling sniffily. 'How could she be? Besides, she told me last night.'

'Mum told you she isn't gay, but she's having an affair with Anaïs Ward? Didn't you see the tiniest little contradiction between those two statements?'

'No,' Aisling said. She glanced around vaguely, like somebody looking for an escape route. 'Don't you have to go work for that old poop Fogarty or something?'

Henry ignored it. 'They told you they were splitting up? Dad's going off somewhere and we're supposed to stay here with Mum?'

'Won't last long,' Aisling told him confidently.

'What won't?'

'The thing about Mum and Dad living apart. Mum's not serious – it's just an early menopause or something. It's not like it's another *man*. She's just at an age when women like to experiment. You're a boy – you wouldn't understand. It'll blow over and then Dad will come back. They mightn't even get as far as separating. They both said that would take ages because Dad has to find a flat. Mum could have stopped with Anaïs before then.'

He'd never thought of his sister as Brain of Britain, but this was dim even for her. 'And you think Dad will just … forgive her?'

'What's he got to forgive? It's not another man.'

Henry gave in. Aisling seldom made much sense and today she wasn't making any at all. But then everybody coped with these things their own way. Aisling obviously wanted to believe everything was going to be all right, nothing was going to change. Or if it did, it wouldn't change for long. Then she could get back to the important things in life, like persuading Dad to buy her a pony. 'OK,' he said.

'OK what?' Aisling asked suspiciously.

'OK, it's not happening.' He got up and started to shrug on his jacket.

'Where are you going?'

'To work for that old poop Fogarty,' Henry said.

For some reason it made her angry. 'Maybe if you stayed home a bit more, this whole thing might never have happened!'

He stared at her, speechless for a minute. She was just back from a week at her damn Pony Club, she treated the house like a hotel and she was telling *him* he should stay home more? Before he could think of a suitable riposte, something bitter and hurtful, she said, 'What do you do for that dreadful Fogarty person anyway? I mean, old man living alone, no wife. What's somebody like that want with a young boy coming round two or three times a week? You sure it's *Mum* who's the gay one in this family, Henry?'

'You shut up!' Henry snapped. He took her by the arms and shook her, so her head bobbed like a rag doll. 'You … just … shut … up about … about everything!' But some half-buried part of him knew she wasn't talking to him at all, wasn't talking *about* him. She was just shouting aloud to drown her own fear, trying to hold someone else to blame for what was happening to their parents.

'All right,' she challenged. 'What do you do?'

The thought that popped into his head – *We rescue fairies* – was so ridiculous he almost smiled. With a huge effort he managed to make his voice sound calm and reasonable. 'I clean his house, sometimes his shed. He lets things slide a bit. I think he's over eighty.'

But Aisling was in no mood for calm and reasonable. 'That all you do?' she asked, in his face. 'Just cleaning?'

'No, as a matter of fact. Not just cleaning.'

Absolute triumph took command of her features. She stood looking at him, waiting.

What the hell, Henry thought, she's not going to believe me anyway. And there was some sort of poetic justice about telling her the truth. He tipped his head to one side and this time actually did smile. 'As a matter of fact, we rescued a fairy. Little fellow with wings, name of Pyrgus.' Then, before she could recover, he headed for the door.

As he closed it behind him, he heard her sudden explosive shriek. 'You're the fairy, Henry! *You're* the bloody, bloody, bloody fairy!'

There was a few feet of tired lawn in front of Mr

Fogarty's house to match the few feet of tired lawn at the back. The grass looked grey, as if it were slightly blackened by soot. It seldom needed cutting – the soil was poor and badly drained – which suited Mr Fogarty fine since he didn't like working at the front where anybody could see him. Henry once offered to cut it for him, but Mr Fogarty had the idea he was too young to handle a lawnmower. Weird thing was, the old boy owned an incredibly powerful lawnmower, far too big for the amount of grass he had. It was greased and oiled and wrapped in plastic towards the back of the shed.

Henry thumbed the front doorbell, then rattled the knocker. Sometimes it took Mr Fogarty as much as five minutes to answer his door, sometimes he wouldn't answer it at all, so Henry had to go round the back and hammer on the kitchen window. But today his reaction was immediate.

'Go away!' called Mr Fogarty's voice from inside. 'Go on – push off!'

Henry bent down and pushed open the letterbox. 'It's me, Mr Fogarty,' he said patiently. He straightened up and waited.

After a moment the door opened a crack. Fogarty's rheumy old eye peered out. 'That you, Henry?'

'Yes, Mr Fogarty.'

Fogarty opened the door a little further and stuck his head out. He peered both ways along the street, then reached out to grab Henry and pull him inside. 'Where the hell have you been?' he hissed as he slammed the door. Quite unexpectedly he gave one of his rare feral smiles. 'Got somebody I want you to meet. Come on, come on.'

Henry followed him to the living room. Like much of the rest of the house, it was full of cardboard boxes and stacks of books. You had to step carefully to get from one end to the other. Mr Fogarty had taken to sticking brown paper over the lower windowpanes to stop his neighbours looking in, so the room was always gloomy. For a moment Henry didn't realise there was anybody in it except for Fogarty and himself. Then there was a movement to his left and a red-haired boy about his own age pushed himself out of a tattered armchair. 'Hello, Henry,' he said.

'Hello ...' Henry said uncertainly. 'Do I know you?' The boy had cheerful, open features and a peculiar way of dressing Henry hadn't seen before. His clothes were dark and loose, a bit like the military gear some kids liked, but the wrong cut and colour.

The boy stuck out his hand and grinned. 'Pyrgus,' he said. 'I'm Pyrgus Malvae.'

Henry frowned, wondering who Pyrgus Malvae was. Then it hit him like a thunderbolt. 'Pyrgus! It's you! But ... but ...' He looked round at Mr Fogarty who was grinning broadly as well. He looked back at Pyrgus. 'No wings?'

Pyrgus shook his head. 'Not any more.'

'And you're ... big!'

'You noticed?'

Henry took the proffered hand and shook it. The skin felt surprisingly hard and rough. He glanced over his shoulder at Mr Fogarty. 'How did you do it?'

'Didn't do anything,' Fogarty said. 'It just wore off.'

'Sometime in the night,' Pyrgus said. 'I went to sleep that little thing with wings and woke up normal.'

'Wow!' said Henry. He couldn't believe the solid boy

before him was the same delicate little creature that had been sitting on his shoulder a couple of days before.

Fogarty's eyes glinted. 'Other thing is, you have to call him Highness. That's *Prince* Pyrgus you're shaking hands with.'

'Don't listen to him,' Pyrgus said.

Henry grinned now. 'You're not a prince?' Pyrgus didn't look like a prince.

Pyrgus sucked air through his teeth uncomfortably. 'Actually, I am. My father's the Purple Emperor. But nobody calls me anything but Pyrgus.'

'Lot of things happened since you skived off home,' Fogarty said sourly. 'Pyrgus says Faeries of the Night must be behind the UFO abductions.'

Henry blinked. 'Wait a minute – how did we get to UFO abductions?' *And what are Faeries of the Night?*

Pyrgus said, 'Mr Fogarty has been telling me about how your people are getting kidnapped by small beings with large eyes and thin limbs. Faeries of the Night use creatures like that – in my world we call them demons.'

Demons, Henry thought. Pyrgus was as big a nutter as Mr Fogarty. Carefully he said, 'And Faeries of the Night are what?'

'Bit hard to explain,' Pyrgus said. 'They're sort of different from Faeries of the Light.'

Henry started to feel like he was drowning. 'What are Faeries of the Light?'

'My lot,' Pyrgus told him cheerfully.

'So you see why it's important you're here,' Fogarty said to Henry.

'No,' Henry said.

'So we can send Pyrgus *back*,' Fogarty told him

patiently. 'We were going to help him for his own sake, of course, but now there's another reason, isn't there? He gets back to his own world, he can get his old man to close down the portals the demons use. Stop the whole abduction business.'

'I see,' Henry said. Portals. Fairies. UFO abductions. Demons. He glanced at the brown paper stuck to the windows. He supposed it wasn't all that much more of a lunatic asylum than the one he'd just left. 'It's important I'm here so we can send Pyrgus back.'

'Good,' said Fogarty impatiently. 'Now let me show you how we're going to do that.'

As they followed Fogarty towards the kitchen, Henry whispered to Pyrgus, 'There's no such thing as flying saucers.'

Still frowning, Pyrgus said, 'But Mr Fogarty told me six million Americans were abducted last year. Americans are people – right?'

'Yes. Yes they are. But it didn't happen. Mr Fogarty just *thinks* it happened.'

'Why does he think that?' Pyrgus asked, bewildered.

Because he's barking mad, thought Henry.

'What are you two whispering about?' Fogarty asked suspiciously. He hated people whispering.

'Nothing, Mr Fogarty,' Henry said.

There was an enormous blueprint on the kitchen table. It showed a piece of machinery like nothing Henry had ever seen before. Two symbols were marked 'tesla coils' and seemed to be electrical, something borne out by what looked like a drawing of a power pack. But there was conventional machinery as well, the sort of cogs, levers and wheels you might see in a

Victorian flour mill. Strangest of all was a circuit diagram labelled 'Hieronymous Machine'. A spiral antenna emerged from one end, emitting – or absorbing – a little lightning flash with 'eloptic radiation' written beside it in Mr Fogarty's neat block capitals. Henry checked twice to be sure, but no part of the Hieronymous Machine was connected to the power pack. He looked up at Mr Fogarty. 'What is it?'

'That's a design for the first completely artificial portal between the Analogue Worlds,' Fogarty told him proudly.

Henry looked at Pyrgus, then back at the blueprint. Apart from the cogs and wheels, which he could follow well enough, none of it made any sense to him. 'How does it work?' he asked.

'While you were podging at *home*,' Fogarty said sourly, 'Pyrgus and I were working on this. Pyrgus told me every detail he could remember about his portal and eventually I figured out the basic principle had to be the same as a Hieronymous Machine.'

'What's a Hieronymous Machine?' Henry asked.

Fogarty gave him a withering glance. 'Don't they teach you anything at school? First one was patented by Galen Hieronymous in 1949. Little thing he lashed up to detect the metal content of alloys. Somebody sold you a gold brick, you could use the thing to tell if there really was any gold in it.'

'Never heard of – what? Hieronymous, was it? – never heard of it,' Henry said a little sulkily.

'That's because it didn't catch on,' Fogarty told him. 'Trouble was, about one in five people couldn't get it to work.'

'Too complicated?' Henry asked.

Fogarty shook his head. 'Naw, you switched it on, put a sample near the pick-up coil, then read off the results with your fingertips on a detection plate. Easy-peasy.'

'So what was the problem?'

'Nobody knew,' Fogarty said. 'But a character called Campbell found out. He set up experiments with people who could get the machine to work. One of them was a kid not much older than you. He switched on the machine, tuned it in and tested a whole heap of samples. Worked fine. Then Campbell noticed he'd forgotten to plug it in.'

'That's impossible,' Henry said. He didn't know a lot about electronic gadgets, but he knew enough to know they didn't work without power. An idea struck him. 'Maybe it was picking up static electricity or something.'

'Campbell tested for that,' Fogarty told him. 'Wasn't static. Run a phase test and you'd find there was no electricity in there at all. Looked like an electronic machine, worked like an electronic machine – valve blows, they used valves in those days, and it stopped – but it wasn't an electronic machine. Had to work some other way. Only thing that made sense. They finally figured what made it work was faith.'

After a second, Henry said, 'You're kidding me, aren't you?'

Fogarty, who had no sense of humour, looked at him soberly. 'Henry,' he said, 'everybody knows electronic machines work – we're used to them, see. They always work. So make something that looks like an electronic machine – but make it properly with all the parts in place – and it works anyway. Something happens

170

between your mind and the machine. Except for one clown in five who doesn't have the faith.'

Henry glanced at Pyrgus. 'Is this making sense to you?'

'Oh yes,' said Pyrgus seriously. 'Wizards use that principle in my world all the time.'

Fogarty said, 'Doesn't matter if it makes sense – the theory's sound. This thing will work. All we have to do is build it.'

Henry looked at the blueprint again. 'Where are you going to get the parts?'

'I've got a lot of bits and pieces here,' Fogarty said, 'and I know where I can buy the tesla coils. But there are one or two components for the Hieronymous circuits that could be a bit tricky if we want them in a hurry. Which we do.'

'So where do we get them?' Henry asked innocently.

Fogarty said, 'You'll have to steal them from your school.'

Fifteen

Henry walked into another heap of trouble when he got home. Aisling, who didn't believe their mum and dad would split up and didn't believe anything was ever going to interfere with her perfect world, had suddenly decided to believe that Henry thought he'd rescued a fairy. Or maybe she was just stirring it.

'We're worried about this fairy business,' his father said abruptly after supper.

Henry looked at his parents. 'What fairy business?'

'With Mr Fogarty,' his mother said sternly.

Aisling had told them! The little cow had *told* them! He hadn't thought she'd take him seriously, not the way he'd put it. She probably didn't believe it for a minute, but she'd told them anyway. 'Not much to say,' Henry shrugged.

'Well I don't suppose there is,' his father said. He smiled. 'I mean, I can't see a sensible boy like you suddenly starting to believe in fairies.' The smile faded. 'But I've made enquiries and I know a few things about your Mr Fogarty now. Frankly, he leaves a lot to be desired. He believes in fairies, doesn't he? And invasions of little green men? And a secret Jewish plot to run the world?'

'He never said Jewish – ' Henry tried to put in.

But his father wasn't really listening. 'There's a word for that,' he said. 'I'm not sure if you know it, Henry. Paranoia. It's a sort of madness.'

Henry knew the word *paranoia* all right. He even knew Mr Fogarty had it big time. It was one of the most interesting things about him. But that didn't make Mr Fogarty some sort of, like, Hannibal Lecter who'd cut you up and eat you. He sounded off a lot about stuff and he was a tough old fart, but Henry liked him. 'Dad, I – '

'The thing is, old man,' his father said soberly, 'just because Mr Fogarty believes in flying saucers doesn't mean you have to. And just because he's anti-Semitic – '

'Dad, he's not anti-Semitic.' He just didn't like the Swiss very much, as far as Henry could tell. The Swiss weren't Jews, were they? Henry thought most of them were Protestants.

' – doesn't mean you should hate Jews. And just because he believes in fairies doesn't mean you should waste your time chasing after moonbeams.'

'Dad, I said that about the fairy to annoy Aisling.'

'I thought it was something like that,' his mother said. 'All the same, that's hardly the point, is it? Mr Fogarty can't possibly be considered a suitable ...' She hesitated. '... friend for you, can he, Henry?'

'Mum, I just clean up the house for him,' Henry said, trying to retrieve the situation.

'Your sister seems to think it may be more than that,' his mother said.

'Mum, Aisling doesn't know anything *about* Mr Fogarty. And even if she did, she's not exactly – '

'But you have to admit she has a point,' his mother cut across him.

'A point about what?' Henry asked.

Martha Atherton sniffed. 'Middle-aged man ... young impressionable boy. You're not a child, Henry.'

'First off, Mr Fogarty isn't middle aged. He's *old*. Really old, like seventy-five or eighty or something. He's not interested in sex any more.'

'Who mentioned sex?' his mother asked. 'I didn't mention sex.'

It was one of her tricks, but Henry wasn't going to let her get away with it. 'It's what you meant, isn't it, Mum? You're worried in case Mr Fogarty and I are ... are –' He couldn't even say it.

'You have to admit it's a possibility. You have to – '

This time it was Henry who cut in. 'It's *not* a possibility, Mum. I'm not *interested* in old men – I'm interested in girls!'

Henry's mother said coldly to her son, 'Did you know your precious Mr Fogarty has a *police record*?'

Up in his room, long after the hassle, Henry stared at his sculpture of the flying pig and wondered what had gone wrong with his life. He turned the handle and the pig took off smoothly, flapping cardboard wings. He felt as if he'd made it in some other lifetime. Some other lifetime when he was just a kid. He didn't feel like a kid any more. At that exact moment, he felt older than Mr Fogarty who he'd been forbidden to see ever again.

A police record? His mother refused to say anything more, not even where she'd heard it, but his dad looked sheepish so Henry suspected this little titbit of information was part of the *few enquiries* he'd made. Not that Henry believed it for a minute. His dad could get things wrong just as easily as his mum. There was no way Mr Fogarty could have a police record. He was nearly eighty, for God's sake, maybe more than eighty. What sort of police record could anybody have when they were over eighty? Swatting somebody with their pension book?

His parents wouldn't listen. Neither of them. Not even when Henry tried the old ploy of playing them off against each other. Where it came to Fogarty, they stood shoulder to shoulder, all differences forgotten. Henry was not to see him again.

He lay down on the bed, not bothering to take off his trainers, and ran a replay of the last conversation he'd had with Mr Fogarty.

'So where do we get them?' Henry said, asking about the components of the Hieronymous Machine.

And Fogarty told him, 'You'll have to steal them from your school.'

Henry blinked and said something really dim. 'It's closed for the summer holidays.'

'Make it easier to nick them, won't it?' Fogarty sniffed.

'I'm not going to steal stuff from my school!' Henry protested. 'No way!'

'Well, I can't do it,' Fogarty said. 'Can hardly walk to the end of the road, let alone climb a wall. You'll *have* to do it, Henry. Pyrgus will help you. Won't you, Pyrgus?'

'Yes,' said Pyrgus promptly.

'Are you mad?' Henry asked them. 'What happens if I get caught?'

Fogarty gave him a withering look. 'Know how many larcenies ever get solved in this district? Ten per cent. Ten per *cent*. One in ten – know what I'm saying? Even then, half of them walk for lack of evidence or some legal crap. And it's only the stupid ones get caught in the first place. Little bit of planning, little bit of common sense and you'll be through that place like a dose of salts. It's an empty school! Not like I'm asking you to nick the Crown Jewels.'

'I'm not doing it,' Henry said.

'You want Pyrgus to get back, don't you?'

'Yes,' said Henry angrily. 'I want Pyrgus to get back. But I don't want to steal things from my school. Or anywhere else.'

'Tell you what,' Fogarty said, 'we'll put them back afterwards. So it won't be stealing – just borrowing. Short-term-loan sort of thing, if you're going to be prissy.'

Henry bristled at the *prissy* crack, but forced himself not to respond. 'What do you mean, *we'll* put them back? Pyrgus will be gone and you can't walk to the end of the road. You mean *I'll* put them back. So I'm supposed to break into the school twice. I'm not doing it.'

'Suppose I got somebody else to put them back, would you do it then?'

'Who?' asked Henry. 'Who would you get to put them back?'

'I got contacts,' Fogarty said.

'Then get your contacts to steal them!' Henry told him crossly.

'No time,' Fogarty said. 'Pyrgus has things of his own to do.' He sniffed. 'Anyway, I see you don't have any objection to taking the things just so long as *you* don't have to do it.'

'Of course I have an objection to stealing – breaking and entering and stealing. Of course I do. I'm not going to do it.'

Pyrgus said, 'Look, Henry, would you at least be prepared to show me where your school is? I'll go in and get the things we need.'

Henry glared at him. 'You can't just go around *stealing* things!'

'Yes, I can,' Pyrgus said. 'I don't like it, but somebody tried to kill me and I think my father may be in trouble and there's a factory drowning kittens in glue, and if it means stealing a few things to put a stop to all that, I'll do it. Especially if Mr Fogarty can arrange to put them back.'

Henry's mouth opened and shut a few times, but nothing came out. Fogarty said, 'Won't work, Pyrgus.'

'Why not?'

'You don't know what you're looking for.'

Pyrgus frowned. 'You can give me a list.'

'Sure I can,' Fogarty said. 'But it won't mean anything to you. Do you even know what a transistor looks like?'

After a moment Pyrgus said, 'You could draw it for me.'

'I'm not that good at drawing. Besides, we need a lot of parts. I can give *Henry* a list. Henry goes to the school. Henry gets taught in the lab. Henry knows where everything is and what it looks like. It has to be Henry.'

Pyrgus looked pleadingly at Henry. 'Would you at least come along with me and point things out, Henry? I'll do the actual stealing. And if we get caught, I'll say I forced you to help.'

Henry sighed. 'All right – I'll do it. I'll get you what you need. Make out a list.'

'That's the ticket!' Fogarty said enthusiastically.

'You don't have to come, Pyrgus,' Henry said. 'No sense in both of us getting caught.'

'I'm coming,' Pyrgus told him firmly.

Henry turned to Mr Fogarty. 'When do you want me to do this?'

'Tomorrow morning,' Mr Fogarty said promptly. 'Tomorrow's Sunday – there won't be anybody about.'

Tomorrow was still Sunday, but as Henry lay on his bed in a haze of frustration, he couldn't see how he was going to do it. The plan had been to meet up with Mr Fogarty early in the morning to pick up Pyrgus and the list. Then he and Pyrgus were to head for the school, break in if the coast was clear, and bring the necessary components back to Fogarty like two characters out of *Oliver Twist*. The three of them would spend the rest of Sunday constructing Fogarty's weird machine. The cover story was simple: Mr Fogarty wanted Henry to work an extra day.

Except now the cover story wouldn't work. Henry was forbidden to see Mr Fogarty.

Worse still, there was a family picnic planned for tomorrow. His mum was having an affair. His dad was going out of his mind with worry. His sister was in love with a horse. So the thing to do was have a family picnic, pretend everything was normal, thank you very much. Henry closed his eyes. With the picnic thing, he couldn't just sneak away to Mr Fogarty and hope his parents never found out. He was expected to fight flies off his food with the rest of them. He'd more than half decided the picnic was just a way of keeping an eye on him.

But what to do about it?

After a while, he got up and took off his trainers, then walked to the door of his room and listened. The house was quiet. He'd heard his parents go to their separate rooms more than an hour ago, so with a bit of luck they might be asleep. But even if not, they weren't likely to come down again. He'd heard Aisling come home earlier – she was a door slammer – and assumed she'd be in bed by now as well.

Henry opened the door. The landing was dark except for the glow of a little low-wattage light plugged into a wall socket so people could go to the bathroom in the night without falling downstairs. In his stockinged feet, he crept across the landing and looked over the balustrade. The lights were off downstairs too, but he could still see well enough thanks to the moonlight streaming through the curtains. He glanced around. There was a sliver of light under the door of the spare room. His father was probably reading, but once he went to bed, he never got up again before morning. The lights seemed to be out in his mother's room and Aisling's room. Henry tiptoed down the stairs.

There was a phone in the living room and an extension in the kitchen. He picked the living room because it was that much further away from the stairs. He had two numbers for Mr Fogarty – his house phone and his mobile. You never rang the house phone during the day because Mr Fogarty refused to answer it, but Henry didn't think he'd leave his mobile switched on late at night so he dialled the house phone anyway. On the fifth ring, he heard Fogarty's rough voice.

'Mr Fogarty – ' Henry said quietly, then realised he was listening to an answerphone.

'... in South America,' said the answerphone message. 'Don't leave a message because I won't be back this year.' There was a click and Henry was listening to empty space.

He hung up, then dialled Mr Fogarty's mobile, praying he hadn't switched it off. There was a pause, then a ringing tone. Henry waited nervously. If Fogarty didn't answer, the call would be re-routed to his answering service, but he wouldn't check that before tomorrow, which would be too late.

'This better be good,' Fogarty's voice growled. 'I'm in bed.'

Henry glanced over his shoulder. There were still no sounds in the house. 'It's me, Mr Fogarty,' he whispered. 'I'm sorry to get you out of bed, but – '

'Who the hell is that? I can't hear you.'

'It's Henry,' Henry said, raising his voice only a fraction, but trying to enunciate very clearly.

'Well, which is it – CIA or FBI? Don't you know what time it is over here?'

'It's Henry,' Henry said again in something closer to his conversational voice.

'Henry? That you, Henry?' Fogarty asked. 'What's the problem?'

'My mum and dad won't let me work for you any more. That means I – '

'I can't hear you, Henry. You're whispering. Can't stand people who whisper. Most of them are sly.'

Hell with it, Henry thought. 'My mum and dad won't let me work for you any more, Mr Fogarty,' he said loudly enough to be sure Fogarty would hear him.

'Been expecting that,' Fogarty grunted.

Henry wondered why, but only said, 'You know the job tomorrow? The one Pyrgus and I have to do together?'

'Yes,' Fogarty said quickly.

'I thought if we went early – very early in the morning, yes? If we did that, I might get back here before anybody wakes up. So they wouldn't know. You and Pyrgus will have to work on the machine without me.'

'Yes, that's OK.'

'Thing is,' Henry said, 'I'd need to be back here by eight. Get to you and then on to the sc – to where we'll be working, I'd need to leave here half four or so; before five anyway. To be on the safe side.' He took a deep breath. 'Buses don't run that early.' He couldn't see how it was going to happen, but at least he was showing willing.

To his surprise, Mr Fogarty said, 'Get to the top of your road by quarter to five. You'll be picked up.'

'Picked up?' Henry echoed.

'In a car,' Fogarty said.

'You don't have a car,' Henry said.

'I'm not picking you up,' said Fogarty.

Sixteen

It was already light when Henry left the house, but a little misty and quite chill. He reached the top of the road with five minutes to spare, but even so there was an old blue Ford parked with two wheels on the verge. The windows had been tinted black so he couldn't see in, but one of them was wound down as he approached.

'You Henry Alison?'

'Atherton,' Henry said.

'Yes. Right.' The man behind the wheel was much the same age as Mr Fogarty, but far smaller and bird-like. He either dyed his hair or was wearing a wig because it was a stark Asiatic black that didn't match the network of fine wrinkles on his face. He was dressed in a crumpled grey suit. 'Alan sent me,' he said.

'Alan?'

'Alan Fogarty. Your name's Henry, right?'

'Yes, sir,' Henry confirmed.

'Bernie,' said the man by way of introduction. 'Hop in.'

The car smelled of dust and mice droppings. Bernie drove it well below the speed limit and checked his rear-view mirror constantly. 'Thing about Fords,' he said, 'is reliability. Reliability and parts. Never did trust your foreign cars. They're like foreign women – good looking but anything goes wrong you could wait a month or more for parts. Now, your good old British Ford, made in Dagenham, that's different. Your good old British Ford, you can get parts anywhere, Land's End to John o' Groat's. And you don't need to go to some fancy garage to get the job done. Trained chimp could fix a Ford, probably on the side of the road. Alan always used Fords in the old days. Swore by them, he did. Wouldn't have anything else. You wouldn't even have to ask old Alan. You always knew he'd say Ford. Habit stuck with me. Always drove a Ford even after we retired. Now, this one guzzles, have to admit that. Any petrol station, she just heaves in of her own accord. Practically an antique, but she goes. Any weather, day or night. Just keeps going. Can't ask better than that, can you? Now, your average continental car …'

At first Henry tried to keep up his end of the conversation, but quickly realised it wasn't necessary. He sat back and let his eyes close as Bernie's words flowed over him like smoke. He felt nervous, but not nearly as nervous as he'd thought he would. Maybe it was something to do with the early-morning light and empty roads. Nothing seemed quite real.

'There you go,' Bernie said as the car pulled in discreetly outside Mr Fogarty's house. He sat staring straight ahead, hands gripping the wheel, as Henry climbed out.

This time Mr Fogarty answered the door at once. He was dressed in a blue serge suit that had seen better days, but still somehow had the feel of Sunday best. Henry found himself wondering if he was planning to go to church. Pyrgus was standing behind him, a look of keen anticipation on his face.

'You need a pee or anything?' Fogarty asked.

'No,' Henry said.

'OK, boys, off you go. Keep your eyes peeled and your wits about you. Get straight back here afterwards. And good luck.'

'How are we getting to the school?' Henry asked.

Fogarty looked at him in surprise. 'Bernie's driving you. That's what he does.'

Henry glanced at Pyrgus, then back at Mr Fogarty. 'He, ah ... I mean, he doesn't know what we're, you know ... I mean, how are we going to explain the stuff ... the stuff we bring back afterwards?'

'Of course he knows,' Fogarty said impatiently. 'What's the point of having a driver if he doesn't know the score?'

'But ... but ...' Henry protested. He looked at Pyrgus for support and got none. 'Won't he ... like ... you know, disapprove – ?'

Fogarty actually cracked a smile. 'What you talking about, Henry? *Bernie?*' The smile disappeared. 'Bernie and me *worked* together.'

'Yes, but that was *engineering*!' Henry said. 'This is something different.'

Fogarty looked at him in bewilderment. 'I wasn't an engineer,' he said.

Henry just stared back at him. Mr Fogarty could make anything. It was about the first thing Henry'd learned about him. Mechanical stuff, electrical stuff – even as an old man he had magic hands. Henry had always assumed he'd been an engineer of some sort when he was younger. 'What were you?' he asked.

'Bank robber,' Fogarty told him without a second's hesitation.

'Bank ... robber?' Henry echoed.

'Armed robber,' Fogarty said. 'Thought you knew.'

'No,' Henry said wonderingly. 'No ...'

'Did time in fifty-eight, but apart from that it was a good life. Decent money and didn't do much harm to anybody.'

'Armed robbery?' Henry stuttered. 'Didn't do much harm – ?'

'This was *banks*, Henry,' Fogarty told him. 'Put your savings in a bank and I nick them tomorrow, you still get your money back. Walk in day after and draw out every penny. So who's hurt?'

'The bank,' Henry said.

'Banks have more money than they know what to do with. Never missed the few quid I took from them. And I never hurt anybody,' Fogarty said soberly. He hesitated, then added, 'Except that guard, and he deserved it, cocky scrat. But he didn't *die* or anything. Couple of weeks in hospital and he was back on the job boasting to his mates.' He gave a little half-smile. 'Those were good days, Henry. Bernie was my driver. When he wasn't inside.'

'You mean Bernie drove your getaway car?' It was unbelievable.

'Great wheelman,' Fogarty said. 'You know what makes a great wheelman, Henry?'

'No,' Henry said. Although in the circumstances he thought he'd better find out.

'Anonymity,' Fogarty told him. 'Somebody doesn't draw attention to himself. Bernie gets himself an old, nondescript car – Ford usually, because of the reliability – never exceeds the speed limit, always signals when he's turning right, never gives the finger to another driver, quiet spoken, soul of tact. Coppers wouldn't pull him over in a fit. Mind you, he could put on a turn of speed when he had to. Used to have us bouncing like *Streets of San Francisco* sometimes. Used to jibe him about it afterwards, me and the boys.'

'What boys?' Henry asked quickly.

'Ran a gang,' said Mr Fogarty. He caught Henry's expression and added, ''Course I've been retired for years. So's Bernie, come to that, though he's younger than me. But he's still the best man for this sort of job. Wouldn't trust you and Pyrgus to anybody else.'

It was creepy driving round town so early on a Sunday. Every shop was shut, every street was empty. Bernie's monologue, which had now moved on from cars to the way Americans ruined tea, made it all seem even more unreal.

Pyrgus looked a little edgy, as if he had a headache, but that may have been because he'd never ridden in a car before. ('Where are the horses?' he asked as he climbed in.) Henry was feeling zombie calm. The news of Mr Fogarty's former career had produced a sort of overload in his brain so that he sank back into a torpor bordering on peaceful.

They reached Henry's school a little later than they'd planned, but not much. The school itself was set back from the road behind a high wall. The main gates were shut.

'Drive round the corner,' Henry instructed. 'There's a pull-in where you can park.'

Bernie, who hadn't monologued for at least three minutes, did as he was told. When the car was parked, Henry said in a take-charge voice, 'We'll go over the back wall. It's quite low and there's trees – the kids do it all the time. I don't know how long it'll take to get into the school.'

'Doesn't matter,' Bernie said. 'I'll wait. Got Alan's list?'

Henry patted his pocket. 'Yes.' It wasn't all that long and the components were mercifully small, so he and Pyrgus should be able to carry them without much difficulty. Now the moment had arrived, it was as if somebody had thrown a switch in his stomach and the butterflies had gone. He hoped they'd stay away, at least until the job was done. Pyrgus looked relaxed as well, but then Henry suspected he was more used to this sort of thing. He seemed to have led a very exciting life in his own world.

'Don't rush,' Bernie advised. 'Rush things and you make mistakes. Good luck.' He turned and stared through the windscreen, his hands on the wheel, exactly as he'd done outside Mr Fogarty's house. But this time Henry noticed he left the engine running.

Henry and Pyrgus went over the wall easily. A solitary car drove past as they were dropping down the far side, but Henry was fairly sure the driver couldn't have seen them. They were now among the trees that verged the cricket pitch. Beyond it were two tennis courts and beyond those the back of the school itself, a rambling grey Victorian building with a jumble of roofs and chimneys that hadn't been used since central heating was installed sometime in the 1960s.

'Come on,' Henry said.

The physics lab was housed in an incongruous,

low-slung, single-storey, wooden annexe to the west of the main buildings. It had been built in 1999, funded by a massive cash donation from a past pupil who'd made good in sausages. It was a self-contained unit, separate from the rest of the buildings, with its own entrance and a bank of windows set little more than shoulder height. For the first time it occurred to Henry that, from a burglar's viewpoint, it was a bit of a gift.

But not a complete gift. The stupidly optimistic bit of him had half hoped a window might have been left open, or even a door, but everything was locked tighter than a drum.

'These are strange windows,' Pyrgus said, standing on tiptoe. 'I understand the windows in Mr Fogarty's house – they go up and down like the windows in my world. But – ' He stopped suddenly.

'What's the matter?' Henry asked.

Pyrgus shook his head. 'Just a stupid pain behind my eyes – it's nothing. Anyway, these windows seem to open outwards and they have large metal fastenings.'

'They're supposed to be burglar-proof,' Henry said.

'I don't think so,' Pyrgus said. He looked around until he found a brick half hidden in the grass behind them and used it to smash a hole in the nearest windowpane.

'You can't do that!' Henry exclaimed.

'Just did,' Pyrgus told him.

'But somebody may have heard!'

'We need to move fast then,' Pyrgus said. He put his hand through the hole and, despite his unfamiliarity with the fittings, had the window open in a moment. A moment more and the two of them were standing in an empty classroom.

Somehow Henry'd had the idea burglary would be very difficult – it was such a big deal in the movies and the bad guys were usually caught in the act. But this one proved a doddle. He found every component on Mr Fogarty's list and even discovered two Harrods bags in a desk drawer to carry them. They were outside and heading back towards Bernie's car faster than he could ever have imagined possible.

There was a grassy bank on the inside of the wall, which made it even easier to climb. Henry reached the top of the bank first, pulled himself up on the wall, then dropped back down again at once, dragging Pyrgus with him.

'What's the matter?' Pyrgus asked.

'There's a copper talking to Bernie.' Henry pulled himself up and peered cautiously over the top of the wall again. A patrol car was parked behind Bernie's famous Ford and a policeman was engaged in conversation with him at the driver's window. From this distance, Henry couldn't hear what was being said, but, as he watched, the policeman stepped back, Bernie gave him a cheery wave and drove away. The policeman climbed back into the police car, which pulled away as well.

'What's happening?' Pyrgus asked.

'Bernie's gone,' said Henry.

'How do we get back to Mr Fogarty with the stuff?'

Henry thought about it for a moment. Then he said, 'We walk.'

Seventeen

The Situation Room was a modified cavern deep in bedrock underneath the palace. It was safe from attack – even magical attack – because the surrounding granite was unusually high in quartz, but the trip down took nearly twenty minutes, even using the suspensor shafts. Apatura Iris hid his impatience. It was important for the Purple Emperor to maintain the appearance of calm at all times, whether he felt it or not.

In fact, he felt anything but calm. There was still no word about Pyrgus, nothing to show whether he was alive or dead. The House Iris portal had yet to give up its secrets. Machine parts still lay strewn about the chapel. Technician priests still worked round the clock to try to find out where Pyrgus might be. So far with no result. Apatura had abused them all roundly this morning, but he was aware it was no more than a token show. The men were all as anxious to find out what had happened as he was. They had never lost anyone in a portal before. They took the disappearance of their Crown Prince as a personal affront. If anyone could get him back, it was these men.

The only question was whether they could get him back in time.

The Purple Emperor had spent hours with the Senior

Medical Priest learning everything there was to know about triptium. The action of the substance could be stopped, but only if caught in time. The treatment was a painful injection and full recovery might take days, but it was preferable to having your head explode.

How long did Pyrgus have before that happened? How long? How long? It was the only thing Apatura could think about at a time when he should certainly have been thinking about a dozen other things. The realm was edging steadily towards the most dangerous crisis in its history and its Emperor had to force himself to pay attention.

Which was probably what Hairstreak had planned. Apatura had no doubt at all Lord Hairstreak was behind this whole affair, although as yet he had no way of proving it. Nor was he sure – yet – of Hairstreak's motivation, but what had happened had his stamp all over it. There was no doubt at all now that the House Iris portal had been sabotaged, no doubt the only reason it had been sabotaged was to make sure Pyrgus died. How exactly that would benefit Hairstreak Apatura had still to discover, but the convoluted planning by someone who could reach into the palace itself meant this was no amateur operation. It required the sort of resources only Hairstreak could muster.

It also required traitors in the palace.

Without traitors, no one could have done what had been done to the House Iris multi-portal. The Chief Portal Engineer now knew exactly what had happened, even if he was still not in a position to say where Pyrgus might have gone. The sabotage required subtlety and a deft hand. So someone who knew what needed to be done had to be smuggled into the palace and protected from discovery while he carrried out the job. Then all signs of his work had to be hidden.

But that was only half the operation. The other half, the more important half, was ensuring Pyrgus was poisoned. And poisoned at exactly the right time he could be spirited away beyond help. This meant access to stores, knowledge of vaccination procedures and, again, split-second timing, since the medical priest who administered the injection might have selected any one of a dozen ampules. In fact the whole thing was carried out with such sophistication that Apatura was far from certain any outsiders were involved at all, except in the planning. Surely it would make more sense to suspect the whole thing was an inside job?

That was certainly the way Palace Security were thinking. Apatura knew they were working on the theory no outside agent was involved. Apatura himself wasn't quite so sure, although he was certainly leaning in the same direction. What worried him was the level of treachery. Whoever was involved would have had to move freely throughout the palace, including the most secure areas. That meant someone at a high level. Apatura didn't want to think the palace harboured a high-level traitor.

The filter had been repaired. That proved to be a simple job. The Chief Portal Engineer had also assured him the portal itself could be made safely operative within a matter of hours. But that was only *after* they discovered where Pyrgus had gone. Until then, the machinery had to stay dismantled for the ongoing analysis. It was a hideous frustration and one Apatura could ill afford when he needed a clear head to deal with all the other problems.

Two uniformed guards snapped to attention as he stepped from the shaft and shrugged off his harness. They fell in step beside him as he moved off along the starkly lit passageway. At other times he would have waved them back – he had never much liked the formalities of his office – but now even that small effort seemed beyond him. Besides, he might even need their protection. If his own son could be poisoned underneath his nose, who knew what else might happen in the palace?

Two more guards opened the door of the Situation Room at his approach and Apatura stepped inside, already dreading what he might be about to see.

The Situation Room, like so much of the palace these days, was a buzz of activity. The banks of crystal globes had been linked directly to the spy cameras of the Imperial Espionage Service so that all pictures were updated on a second-by-second basis. In the centre of the room was the huge operations table, with the entire landscape of the realm available, in three dimensions, when the proper chant was voiced. Just now, only a segment of the land was visible, recognisable by the indigo marking flags of Night Faerie. Young women moved briskly between the globes and the table, constantly rearranging the display. Three of Apatura's top military commanders were already in the room. So was Gatekeeper Tithonus.

The military men came to attention as he entered and Tithonus hurried across to greet him. 'What news?' Apatura asked.

Tithonus frowned. 'I fear the situation looks increasingly grave.'

'Is an attack imminent?'

'Possibly.' Tithonus dropped his voice. 'Any news of Pyrgus, Majesty?'

The Emperor shook his head. He walked over to the crystal globes. They were all displaying different viewpoints on what appeared to be a mass rally of Night Faerie troops. Apatura selected a low-level aerial view and forced his body to relax. In a moment he felt the familiar sensation as the globe drew him in.

He was looking down on a vast stadium packed with a cheering throng. Black-uniformed troops marched in tight formation to create a torchlit serpent winding its way into the stadium to the insistent beat of drums. The lead contingents bore the insignia of House Hairstreak, but others following wore uniforms of various other Night Houses. Most were members of the old Nightside Alliance, but, in a worrying development, some additional Houses appeared to have joined them. Lord Hairstreak, it seemed, was growing in popularity.

The update from the Imperial Espionage Service gave the scene a jerky, unreal quality, but, even so, Apatura watched with growing unease. The marching soldiers looked like grim-faced robots and their discipline was impressive, as doubtless it was meant to be. They split into several streams and wizards marching with each one changed the colour of their torches so that they became a rainbow throng. The colours spun and danced as the men marched, then, with breathtaking speed, became a living insignia of House Hairstreak. The drumbeats reached a crescendo as spotlights picked out a single figure on the rostrum.

The soldiers halted, the drumming ceased, the vast crowd fell completely silent. After a moment the figure spoke, his words carried by amplification spells throughout the stadium. 'Behold,' he said, 'the might of Night Faerie. May our enemies beware!'

Apatura thought briefly it must be Black Hairstreak himself, but now he realised it was Hamearis, the Duke of Burgundy, Hairstreak's closest ally. He looked more impressive in public than Hairstreak and was an infinitely better speaker, which was probably why he was addressing the crowd now. But there was another possibility. Hamearis had been to the forefront of the negotiations lately. His appearance on the rostrum may have been designed to send a signal: *take me seriously or else!*

Apatura had not the slightest doubt this rally was meant to be seen by himself and as many of his people as cared to watch. There had been no public announcement, but nor had there been the slightest attempt at secrecy. A few relatively simple spells would have discovered most of the Espionage Service cameras, a few more put them out of action. Yet not one had been touched. The conclusion was obvious.

Apatura withdrew. 'Very impressive,' he said drily. 'Now, where is the real action?'

Tithonus gestured to one of the technicians and at once the rally disappeared from the globes, to be replaced by a less spectacular but far more sinister scene. Only one of the realm's twin moons had risen, so the light level was low – far lower than the torchlit rally – and it took a moment for Apatura's eyes to adjust.

This time there was no easy aerial view. Rather he felt he was standing on a hilltop, looking out across a grassy plain. This was one of the new Seventh System espionage units, virtually impossible to detect, whatever the expenditure on spells, but with some problems in its colour resolution. As a result, the scene took on a bleached appearance and fine detail was lacking. But all the same, he knew what he was seeing. A vast military camp stretched across the plain. Rows of black tents were laid out with geometric precision, silhouetted against a scattering of camp fires. There were soldiers here too, thousands of them, perhaps tens of thousands, but unlike the black dress uniforms of the rally, these men were in combat fatigues. They moved quietly, with a purposeful air. No drums were beating. No crowds were cheering. Indeed no sounds at all reached Apatura's Seventh System vantage point, as if the whole scene below was covered by a deadly pall.

Apatura closed his eyes. He knew the area. This was the Plain of Yammeth Cretch. The espionage unit itself was placed somewhere near the head of the Teetion Valley. He was looking into the Night Faerie heartland, that huge sweep of the realm which was virtually a state within a state, almost entirely populated by Faeries of the Night and absolutely under their control, whatever lip-service was paid to their allegiance to the Purple Emperor.

Apatura allowed his consciousness to withdraw from the globe again and opened his eyes. The Teetion Valley marked the unofficial border between the Night Realm and the rolling farmlands of Lilk tended by the Faeries of the Light. He looked at Tithonus. 'It's almost like a threatened invasion by a foreign country,' he said.

'In many ways a foreign invasion would be easier to handle,' Tithonus told him. 'Civil wars are notoriously difficult. And bloodthirsty.'

'You think it will come to that? Civil war?'

'I pray not, Majesty,' Tithonus said. But his tone of voice suggested he had little confidence his prayers would be answered.

The crystal globes switched back to the rally and the powerful voice of Hamearis Lucina filled the chamber: ' – would say to the Purple Emperor that the old ways no longer serve us, that no longer will the Faeries of the Night be treated as second-grade citizens within the Realm, that no longer – '

Tithonus waved the sound down, but something caught Apatura's attention and he waved it up again. ' – shall not wait beyond two weeks,' Hamearis was saying, 'and less than that if our Emperor does not see fit to right the wrongs set forth in – ' His final words were drowned out by thunderous applause and cheering from the crowd.

'Did that sound to you as it sounded to me?' asked Apatura as he silenced the globes completely.

'An ultimatum?' Tithonus frowned.

'Yes,' Apatura murmured. 'Please arrange to have a full draft of Lucina's speech delivered to my chambers as soon as possible. This is something I shall want to study.' He walked to the operations table and hummed the note rather than waiting for a specialist to do it for him. At once the landscape flowed into a representation of Yammeth Cretch and the surrounding Light Faerie territories. Apatura turned to his nearest general. 'Put up our forces, if you will, Creerful.'

'Yes, Majesty,' Creerful nodded. He stretched to touch a button on the side of the table and patches of bronze appeared on the map surrounding Yammeth

Cretch. Some fine adjustments changed their texture and tone to represent familiar strengths.

Apatura stared at the display for a long time. He was trying to remember something, but could not say exactly what. Then, suddenly, it came to him.

'There's something missing,' he said aloud.

'I'm sorry, Majesty?'

Apatura ignored Tithonus and signalled the three generals to move closer. 'Look at those patterns,' he said, gesturing towards the table display. 'What do they tell you?'

General Vanelke, always the first with an opinion, leaned forward frowning. 'That our defences are well placed,' he said. 'We have them contained.' He glanced at his colleagues as if daring them to contradict him.

'I see nothing missing, Majesty,' Creerful added. On his right, General Ovard nodded.

'Stop thinking of our forces,' Apatura said. 'Put yourself in the place of the – ' he almost said 'enemy' but caught the diplomatic gaffe in time ' – of our Nightside citizens. Assume for a moment that really *was* an ultimatum we just heard from Hamearis Lucina. An ultimatum is useless – even counterproductive – unless you are prepared to back it up. So far, all the indications have been that House Hairstreak plans to back it up by force of arms. Now ask yourself, gentlemen, if you were commanding Hairstreak's forces and not those of your Emperor … would you be happy with the disposition of your troops in Yammeth Cretch?'

There was a long moment's silence, then General Ovard said, 'By God, Majesty – no I would not!'

'You would not, Ovard,' the Emperor echoed. 'Nor would you, Creerful: nor would you, Vanelke. The numbers are wrong. I thought as much when I was using the vision-globe, but I had no immediate comparison then. They have deployed too many men for defence, *but not quite enough for attack*! Make the calculations for yourself, gentlemen. The posture is not defensive – we are all agreed on that. Their front lines seem to be in place for an attack and they could certainly mount a few successful sorties – hit and run tactics, modified guerrilla warfare, that sort of thing. But they could never back up the sort of ultimatum I believe Hairstreak has just delivered through his monkey Hamearis Lucina.'

'You think they are bluffing, Majesty?' Tithonus asked quietly.

'I think there is a missing element,' Apatura said. 'Can they have concealed troops we have not yet discovered?'

'Impossible!' Vanelke exclaimed.

Ovard said, 'Our intelligence is excellent, Your Majesty. Besides, as you saw, they are making little effort to hide anything.'

'Indeed,' said Apatura, 'they *appear* to be making very little effort at concealment. Which is, of course, part of their political strategy. What I want to know is whether or not it is possible they have *actually* concealed quantities of troops and munitions of which we are completely unaware.'

Before the military men could speak, Tithonus put in, 'It is possible, but extremely unlikely. Bear in mind, Majesty, that we have been watching them long before the current crisis.'

'Can they count on military aid from any source beyond the Nightside?'

'Difficult to imagine where,' Tithonus said.

Which was precisely Apatura's problem. Hairstreak's military deployment simply did not match his political strategy. There was a missing component of his attack force. If he had not hidden it – and like his generals and his Gatekeeper the Emperor doubted that – it was difficult to imagine where he might get it from. Yet Hairstreak was no fool and his military advisers were at least the match of the Emperor's own. So what was Hairstreak up to? Where was the missing component?

The Emperor was still trying to puzzle it out when the message arrived from his Chief Portal Engineer.

Apatura and Tithonus arrived in the chapel at a less than dignified run. The first thing Apatura noticed was that the portal was in place again. Beside it, the Chief Portal Engineer was making some final adjustments with a flexible spine-wrench. His hands and face were black with oil, but it did nothing to hide his smug expression.

'You've done it?' Apatura asked, grinning despite himself.

'Yes, Your Majesty.'

'You know where this damn thing sent my son?'

'Yes, Your Majesty. He reached the Analogue World all right, but not the island we targeted.'

'And the portal's working properly again?'

'Yes, Your Majesty.'

Apatura's grin faded to a sober expression. 'Right, Tithonus, let's put a party together to find out what has happened to Pyrgus.' He turned to look at the portal, already beginning to glow slightly as it entered its initial warm-up cycle. 'We leave in fifteen minutes!'

Eighteen

'Where have you *been*?' Henry's mother asked crossly. She was buttering bread for sandwiches on the kitchen table. Their old picnic basket was open on the worktop behind her, already well packed with fruit, soft drinks and what looked suspiciously like her ghastly vegetarian Scotch eggs.

'We were getting worried,' said his father, a lot more mildly. He'd abandoned his usual business suit for his weekend uniform of slacks and sports shirt, rounded off with pristine golf shoes. He was also wearing one of his more familiar expressions, the one that told Henry he was feeling miserable, but putting on a cheerful front. Henry suspected his father was looking forward to the family picnic about as much as he was.

'I went for a walk,' Henry said. It was a lie, but it was equally the truth, which made him feel a bit better. It was also simple, which meant you were far less likely to be found out. At least he'd got Pyrgus and the stuff safely back to Mr Fogarty.

'You *knew* we were going for a picnic,' his mother said. 'It's so late now it's hardly worth the trouble.'

'You aren't even ready yet,' Henry said, perhaps unwisely.

'That's because we didn't know where you *were*!' his

mother told him. 'Honestly, Henry, you've been behaving so strangely lately we hardly know what to think.'

He'd been behaving strangely? Henry looked at his parents, but decided not to get drawn down that particular road. 'I was just walking,' he said. Then, in the wicked hope of making his mother feel guilty, he added, 'I needed time to think.'

'He wasn't just walking.' Aisling's voice came from behind him. 'He went to see Mr Fogarty, even though you told him not to. I heard him making the arrangements on the phone last night.'

Henry spun round. Aisling was smiling smugly all over her stupid face. She'd known since last night, but she'd waited until now to tell their parents so he'd get into maximum trouble.

'Is this true?' his mother asked. The tone of her voice said she'd take a lot of convincing that it wasn't.

As he fought down a surge of guilt, a hideous thought slid into Henry's mind. Had he mentioned breaking into his school last night on the phone? He didn't think so, but he couldn't remember for sure. Was Aisling waiting to drop that little bombshell as well? He took a deep breath. There was only one way to find out.

Henry lowered his eyes. 'Yes,' he said, 'it's true.' He looked up again and added more forcefully, 'There was a job I had to do for him. I couldn't let him down.' His gaze flickered towards Aisling. If she did know what he'd been up to this morning, now was the time she'd tell. He could hear her triumphant voice: *And do you know what that job was, Mum? Breaking and entering and stealing!*

If Aisling knew about it, she kept quiet.

'Let him down?' his mother echoed. 'We told you – your father and I *both* told you – that you weren't to work for him again. As of now. Not some time next month or next week. Henry, this is for your own good. That man is wholly unsuitable company for a boy your age. But that isn't the point any more, is it? The point is, we can't even trust you—'

To his surprise, his father murmured, 'He may have had obligations, Martha.'

'All right,' his mother said. 'All right, we'll find out about his *obligations*, shall we?' She turned to Henry. 'Did you finish this job you had to do for your friend Mr Fogarty?'

Henry looked at her for a moment, then nodded. 'Yes.' Henry the Truthsayer.

'So you have no more *obligations* to Mr Fogarty?'

Henry shook his head. 'No.' Which was true as well. He'd told Mr Fogarty he couldn't help him build the portal, but that didn't matter because he'd only have been handing him components anyway. Mr Fogarty, armed robber or not, was still the one who made things. And if he needed help, Pyrgus was there to give it.

'In that case,' his mother said, 'you can no longer have *any* objection to the request your father and I made that you shouldn't see Mr Fogarty again. Can you?'

'No, I can't,' he told his mother.

'So you agree you will not see Mr Fogarty again?'

Henry nodded. 'Yes.'

'I want you to promise. Promise on your word of honour.'

'I promise on my word of honour,' Henry told her miserably.

'Good,' his mother said briskly. 'Now the only thing to be decided is your punishment.'

His punishment turned out to be two weeks' grounding. (His mother wanted to make it a month, but his father intervened.) He couldn't leave the house unless accompanied by one of his parents or – ultimate humiliation and Mum knew it – his sister Aisling.

But he made no protest, probably because he was feeling so guilty. He consoled himself with the thought that he'd played his part in helping Pyrgus get back to his own world.

He lasted three days before he tried to ring Mr Fogarty. His mum had forbidden him even that form of contact, but it wasn't what he'd promised. What he'd promised was that he wouldn't *see* Mr Fogarty again. But that had its own problems since Mr Fogarty didn't answer his home phone (as usual) and, when Henry tried his mobile, it was switched off.

He tried again the following day. By now, his parents had stopped watching him so closely. His dad was at work, of course, and his mum soon discovered that grounding somebody was one thing, but acting as his jailer was a real pain. Even Aisling stopped her little game of trailing around after him like some smug guard dog. Henry walked into the kitchen, helped himself to a doughnut, and dialled Mr Fogarty's mobile. It was still switched off.

It was switched off on Friday as well, and on Saturday morning. By now, Henry was taking more and more chances, calling the number just as often as he could. Fogarty's mobile seemed to be permanently switched off. Henry tried to tell himself it was just out of order, but he didn't believe it. Every time he phoned without result, the feeling grew that something was wrong. He didn't know what, but his imagination supplied some weird possibilities.

By Saturday afternoon he found it all so worrying he'd come to a horrible decision. He was going to break a promise made on his word of honour. He was going to go and see Mr Fogarty.

Nineteen

Alan Fogarty woke with a start. His bedroom was filled with a stark blue light and there was a high-pitched humming noise in his ears. They were coming to get him!

He rolled over and reached underneath his bed for the shotgun, then remembered, dammit, the thing was in pieces on the kitchen table, cleaned, oiled but not reassembled because he was an old man now and he'd got tired and gone to bed thinking he'd put it together in the morning, thinking it wouldn't matter if he went to sleep just one night without an equaliser handy. But he forgot Murphy's Law: if it can go wrong, it will go wrong. The one night he left himself without a firearm was the night they picked to come and get him.

He pushed himself upright. They weren't in the room yet, so he still had a chance. But he had to hurry, even though hurrying wasn't what he did well these days. Growing old was deadly. Thirty years ago he'd probably have fought them. Twenty years ago, he'd have been legging it down the road by now. But once you pass eighty, everything slows.

He swung his feet out of the bed and placed them firmly on the wooden floorboards. He had to hurry, but if he did this too fast he was in trouble. Any time he stood up suddenly he passed out. After a moment he risked pushing himself to his feet. Not so much as a hint of dizziness – great! He walked to the bedroom cupboard and took out a cricket bat.

They could pass through walls. It made no sense, but it was in all the books. Trick was not to let yourself get impressed. And to make your move before they did. He fondled the cricket bat and walked to the window.

There were figures moving on his lawn!

He let the curtain fall and scuttled from the bedroom. There was a good chance they weren't inside yet, which was to his advantage. A bit of him was wondering if he could get the gun assembled before they came in. There was a full box of cartridges in the table drawer.

He reached the kitchen in short order. There was a humanoid shape at the back door, its outline distorted by the frosted glass. It knocked sharply. Fogarty walked over and unfastened the five bolts that secured it. Then he took the key from its hook, unlocked the deadlock and opened the door.

As the figure entered, Fogarty hit it with the cricket bat.

The character in the cloak and purple jerkin wasn't what you'd call tall and Fogarty had seen a lot more imposing men, but the second he walked through the door you knew he was in charge.

'What's happened here?' he asked.

Fogarty said nothing, partly because the arm around his throat was cutting off his air supply, partly because he was feeling a bit embarrassed. These clowns certainly weren't aliens. They didn't look like Men in

Black or FBI either. Their clothes were all too colour-ful, too flashy in the cut. Besides, there was something about the man in purple that looked familiar.

'Doubtless a misunderstanding, Majesty,' said the man Fogarty had hit with the cricket bat. The man's arm was encased in a tight, white rigid sleeve cast that had been sprayed on by one of his colleagues.

'Why are you trying to strangle that man?' This was aimed at the soldier with his arm around Fogarty's throat. Fogarty knew he was a soldier from the cropped hair and the ramrod up his ass. They all looked the same wherever they came from and God alone knew where this one was from. If that was a uni-form he was wearing, Fogarty had never seen the like of it before.

'Danger to society, sire!' the soldier said, trying to snap to attention. The sudden movement came close to shutting off Fogarty's windpipe completely.

'You or him?' the man in purple asked. 'I think per-haps you had better release him.'

'Yes, Majesty!' the soldier said. He let Fogarty go, took a step backwards, stamped his feet and came to attention again, all in a single movement.

Fogarty massaged his neck. That was the second time they'd called the purple character *Majesty*. Was he some sort of king? And why did he look so familiar? Fogarty blinked. 'My God,' he said, 'you're Pyrgus's father!'

You'd have thought he'd dropped a nuke. Everybody froze in place. Eyes widened. Jaws dropped. The char-acter in the purple jerkin recovered first. 'I am Apatura Iris, the Purple Emperor,' he said. 'What do you know of my son?'

So they'd come for him. Pyrgus always said they would – or at least that they'd try. Not that it had stopped him sorting out his own problems: sort of son you wanted, that. Fogarty said, 'You're too late – he's gone back.'

The Purple Emperor exchanged glances with the thin man Fogarty had assaulted. 'Gone back?'

Fogarty nodded. 'Yes.' He looked from one to the other. There were five men in his kitchen and he was fairly sure there were more outside. 'What?' he asked the Purple Emperor. 'What's wrong?'

Apatura glanced at the disassembled shotgun on the table. 'Is that a weapon?' he asked.

Fogarty nodded. 'Yes.'

'*Your* weapon?'

'Yes.'

'Can you put it together again?'

Fogarty looked at him cautiously. 'I can.' He moved to the table and sat down without taking his eyes off the Purple Emperor. His hands reached out for the parts and began to reassemble them.

'This is Gatekeeper Tithonus,' the Emperor said, nodding towards the slim man.

'I'm sorry about that,' Fogarty muttered, glancing at the arm.

'It's just a fracture,' Tithonus told him drily.

Fogarty said, 'I'm Alan Fogarty.'

'I fear we have somewhat forced ourselves on your hospitality, Mr Fogarty,' Apatura said. His voice was polite, but his face was like a rock. 'However, I should be grateful if we could speak about my son. Please tell me how you know of him and what has happened.'

Fogarty had met the type once or twice before. You

didn't mess with them unless you absolutely had to. Pyrgus would be the same in a year or two and you could see where he got it from – even now he was a tough kid. Fortunately Fogarty had no quarrel with the Emperor. Quite the reverse: he liked Pyrgus and it was clear from everything Pyrgus had said that Pyrgus liked his dad. There were problems between them, of course, but that was just the age thing. Wasn't a kid anywhere didn't have problems with his father at that age. Something wrong if he didn't.

Fogarty said, 'Not my business, but if I were you I'd tighten up my security. I think somebody tried to do your boy a mischief.'

Apatura looked at him impassively. 'I came to much the same conclusion, Mr Fogarty. From the beginning, please.'

Fogarty took a deep breath and told him everything.

They were all watching him intently when he came to the part about sending Pyrgus back.

'How did you propose to do so?' asked the Purple Emperor.

Fogarty, who disliked being interrupted, said, 'Portal.'

One of the Emperor's party, a man named Peacock with an ornate crown of the Purple Emperor embroidered on his jacket, said just as shortly, 'Portal was down.'

'Not your portal,' Fogarty said. 'Mine.'

He could sense the sudden excitement. The Purple Emperor leaned forward. 'You have a natural portal somewhere near here, Mr Fogarty?'

Fogarty shook his head. 'I made one.'

There was absolute, stunned silence. Fogarty looked from face to face. 'You got a problem with that?' he asked.

The one called Tithonus, who'd generally kept quiet, probably because his arm was hurting, said, 'Do I understand that you made a portal from scratch, rather than modifying an existing one?'

'Yes,' said Fogarty, irritated by something in his tone, 'that's what you understand.'

'How can – ' The Emperor intercepted a warning glance from Tithonus and changed tack. 'You must be a man of exceptional talents, Mr Fogarty.'

A little mollified, but only a little, Fogarty muttered, 'Used to make things in my job.' Detonators, lock picks, alarm system jammers, but they didn't need to know that.

'Even so,' Tithonus said smoothly, 'I was not aware this world was familiar with portal technology.'

'Pyrgus told me the basics.'

'So you worked it out from first principles?' asked Tithonus.

'No big deal,' Fogarty said. 'Half the battle's knowing it can be done – saves you looking in the wrong direction.'

'I'm sure it does,' Tithonus said.

The man Peacock was leaning forward and, if Fogarty was reading him right, it was as much as he could do to stop himself shaking with excitement. 'Can I see it?' he asked.

'Mr Peacock is our Chief Portal Engineer,' Tithonus said. 'He is interested in the technical aspect.'

There was a directness about Peacock Fogarty liked. He opened the table drawer and took out a small brushed-aluminium cube.

'What's this?' Peacock asked when he handed it across.

'Portal,' Fogarty said.

Peacock stared at the cube, turning it over in his hand. Eventually he looked up at Fogarty. 'This isn't a portal.'

Fogarty grinned. 'Sure it is. Press the red button. Only take it outside – can break things if you use it inside.'

Peacock looked at his Emperor, who nodded briefly. In a moment they were all outside in the back garden. Fogarty noted he'd been right – there had to be maybe another dozen men lurking in the shadows, most of them with a military look about them. The Emperor was clearly prepared for trouble. Fogarty liked that in a man.

'Where …?' Peacock asked.

Fogarty shrugged. 'Anywhere here. Just so long as it's out of the house.'

Peacock pressed the red button. There was a ripping sound as reality tore apart. Through the gap they could see a carpeted corridor lit by crystal chandeliers. After a moment of stunned silence, Apatura whispered, 'That's the palace!'

'Thought it might be,' Fogarty remarked proudly. 'I was trying to home in on your own portal – that's in some sort of chapel, Pyrgus told me. Thought the palace might be close enough for jazz.'

'This isn't like our portals at all,' Peacock said, with something like awe in his voice.

Fogarty fought to keep his stern expression. 'Might have made a few improvements,' he said casually.

'What happens if I press the green button?' Peacock asked.

'Closes the thing down.'

Peacock pressed the green button. The portal disappeared without a sound. 'Where's the power source? You can't have packed it in this cube.'

Fogarty found himself grinning and didn't care. Peacock was a fellow engineer. 'Cube's just a control. Actual portal draws power from the planet.'

'Volcanic?' Peacock asked.

'Not round here.'

'Ours are volcanic.' Peacock ignored – or didn't even notice – warning glances from Tithonus and his Emperor. 'Ours are all volcanic.'

'Planetary resonance,' Fogarty told him. 'We had a man called Tesla worked it once. Dead now. Pumped electricity – Pyrgus says you call it trapped lightning. I used a psychotronic trigger.'

'Psychotronic trigger – wow!' Peacock exclaimed. 'We tinkered with the idea of planetary resonance, but I'd never have thought of using a psychotronic trigger.'

'Won't work without it, no matter how much electricity is pumped.'

'I know,' Peacock said. He looked delighted and amazed, both at the same time.

'Perhaps you could continue this conversation at another time,' Apatura suggested drily. He waved aside Peacock's hasty apologies and said to Fogarty, 'You tell me you used this portal to send Pyrgus home?'

'Ah,' said Fogarty uncomfortably. 'Not exactly …'

'Not … *exactly*?' Tithonus asked.

'Impatient lad, your son,' Fogarty told the Purple Emperor, who nodded sourly. 'He used the portal himself the night I finished it. Took off while I was asleep the night before last. Left me a note. I was a bit worried when I found he'd gone. I hadn't made the final adjustments or tested it or anything. But when I tried the thing myself, it was working fine.'

'You tried it yourself?'

'Oh, yes. Wouldn't rest easy until I was sure Pyrgus was OK.'

'And what happened when you tried it yourself?' the Emperor asked cautiously.

'What you saw,' Fogarty said. 'I stepped through into your palace. I recognised it from what Pyrgus told me.'

'There were no reports of your visit,' Tithonus said.

'Wasn't exactly a *visit*. Stepped through, looked around, then stepped back again. Got things to do here. I was just glad your boy got home.'

'That's the problem, Mr Fogarty,' the Purple Emperor told him soberly. 'My boy didn't get home.'

twenty

The mirror showed a slim boy with close-cropped hair and open features. His clothes were homespun and entirely drab: a muddy green jacket inexpertly repaired and itchy brown breeches tucked into cracking, down-at-heel, leather boots. He might have been a factory worker or a badly paid apprentice. Holly Blue examined her reflection with some satisfaction. Real disguise was always better than some erratic illusion spell that could be probed by counter-magic or fail completely when you least expected.

She was worried about her skin. Many boys her age were spotty, and apprentices spottier than most, but there wasn't a lot she could do about that. Besides, she'd used the disguise before and nobody seemed to notice. Although those missions hadn't been as dangerous as this one. She thought about it, then compromised by rubbing in a light stain to give a weather-beaten look. It helped a little.

Blue checked her armaments. They were pitifully scant. The trouble was everything had to be in character. No factory worker or apprentice could afford magical weapons, or even a simple sword. Most of them just carried a defensive cosh, if they carried anything at all. She settled for a small dagger and a screamer built into a copper coin. The dagger was just about acceptable – it looked a lot cheaper than it was – and if the screamer was discovered, she could always say she stole it. As an afterthought, she dropped a pickspell in her pocket. It looked much like a banana if you didn't examine it too closely.

She took a last glance in the mirror, then walked to her bookshelves and tapped a slim volume of Crudman's *Essays*. A section of the shelving slid back on silent runners. As Blue stepped into the hidden passageway beyond, glowglobes illuminated gently and the shelving slid back into place. In less than half an hour, she was mingling with the teeming crowds of Northgate.

The first playhouse had opened in Northgate five hundred years earlier and the district had been an entertainment centre ever since. Except now the entertainment offered was a bit more varied than theatre trips. Sparkle-spell signs advertised whirl booths, saturation dens, chaos-horn cafés, simbala music parlours, reality suites and – new to Blue – something called the Organic Fizz Experience. The pavements were crowded, as they always were at this time of night, and street entertainers worked hard to extract a few coins from the throng. Blue passed jugglers and acrobats, a tiny troupe of strolling players and an odd-looking individual who appeared to be eating his way through a live dragon. It was an illusion, of course, but a good one.

An elderly trull emerged from a doorway. 'Like to try a little chaos horn with me, young sir?'

Blue waved her away, grinning. At least her disguise was passing muster.

On a routine trip, she might have taken her time in

the main thoroughfare, enjoying the excitement and the sights. But this was no routine trip. Her father might think he could find Pyrgus in the Analogue World, but she wasn't so sure. For days now, a snatch of conversation had been replaying in her mind:

> *'I thought that dreadful Hairstreak must have killed you! It was nearly three days before I could get any word of you at all!'*
> *And Pyrgus said, 'Hairstreak never got near me. It was someone else who nearly killed me.'*

They'd been in the chapel, just before Pyrgus stepped through the portal and disappeared. *It was someone else who nearly killed me.* He'd tried to pass it off as a joke, but she knew her brother very well. That wasn't a joke – it was a slip of the tongue. There was something Pyrgus didn't want her to know about ... or anybody else for that matter. He always dreaded making a fuss. But there was somebody who'd nearly killed him. Not Hairstreak either, someone else. And minutes later someone tried to kill him again, someone injected poison into his veins and sabotaged the House Iris portal. Was that a coincidence? Holly Blue thought not.

She pushed past a chorus line of synchronised sword swallowers and entered Garrick Lane. This had been the site of the very first playhouse. The building was long gone now, but the lane itself was still the beating heart of Northgate's theatre district. She passed the garish façades of the Moon and the Globe and the Garrick itself before she reached the narrow, unassuming stairway next door to the old sorcery supply shop. A guardian illusion stopped her on the first landing.

'Who dares seek audience with the Painted Lady?' it asked portentously.

Blue smiled to herself. A typical guardian illusion was set to say something like *Please state your name and business*, but that would never do for Madame Cardui. She believed in creating an impression before you even met her. The illusion itself was custom made. Where most people were content to buy a standard doorman, this thing was an eight-foot-tall djinn complete with black beard, baggy pants and turban. Its eyes glowed like burning coals.

'Little Boy Blue,' said Blue quietly and the creature dissolved in a cloud of theatrical green smoke. She walked up another flight and knocked politely on a partly curtained door.

'Come in, my deeah, come in!' commanded a shrill voice.

Madame Cardui's salon was extraordinary by any standard. Lush, rich washes of colour writhed over every wall, occasionally dissolving into brief, mind-numbing vistas full of manticores and unicorns. The furnishings seemed to consist almost entirely of lavish silk and velvet cushions, interspersed with the occasional low table offering water-pipes of purple opium and shallow crystal bowls of Turkish delight. A heady smell of incense hung thickly in the air, its scent continually changing yet somehow retaining a constant undertone of jasmine. Sensual simbala music wailed and purred on the outer edge of audibility but managed, as simbala music always did, to insinuate itself inside your body and your brain.

But most extraordinary of all was Madame Cardui herself. The Painted Lady reclined in a black lace peignoir on a pile of cushions, attended by her orange dwarf and translucent Persian cat. Miniature mechanicals chattered busily on the table beside her, manufacturing exotic bonbons and sachets of strange powders. She was slim as a reed, except for her bust which retained the vast enhancements of her theatre days. The skin beneath the heavy make-up was veined and networked with fine wrinkles, but her eyes were dark and bright and liquid as they'd ever been.

She smiled to show her scarlet teeth. 'Boy Blue,' she greeted Blue warmly, 'what a delight to see you again so soon.' She patted a place beside her. 'Here. You must sit here, by me.' Her dwarf scuttled to arrange the cushions as Blue sat.

'Are we alone, madame?' asked Blue casually.

The Painted Lady drew a deep breath through her nose, as if sampling the heavy incense smell. 'Alone, but perhaps not yet entirely private,' she said grandly. She waved a languid hand. 'See to it, Kitterick.'

The orange dwarf grinned broadly as he hurried to a table near the door. He took a small brown cone from a cedar casket and held it to a nearby glowglobe until the tip began to smoulder, then set it down on a shallow metal incense dish. As he scurried back to his mistress, the cone erupted like a firework, scattering an ornate silence spell across the room.

'There!' the Painted Lady said, and sighed. She pushed herself into a sitting position and stretched. 'Well, Highness,' she said briskly, 'this will be about the Crown Prince, I suspect.'

Blue nodded. 'Yes, Madame Cynthia.'

'I thought he was back safely.'

'He was,' Blue said. 'My father decided to translate

him to the Analogue World.'

Madame Cardui pursed her lips. 'Probably the safest place until things settle.'

'Unfortunately,' said Blue, 'someone sabotaged the portal.'

'Ah,' said Madame Cardui. She looked at Blue thoughtfully. 'An attempt on his life, do we suspect, or simply someone making mischief?'

'An attempt on his life,' Blue told her. She decided not to mention the poison. She trusted the Painted Lady as much as, if not more than, any of her informants, but experience had taught her information was best dispensed on a need-to-know basis. 'The thing is, I think someone also tried to kill him before he returned to the palace.'

'We're not talking of Hairstreak?'

'No, someone else.'

'And you believe it may have been the same person who arranged to sabotage the portal?'

'I think it's possible,' Blue said.

'Do we know who it was tried to kill him while he was on his little adventure in the outside world?'

'I don't,' Blue said soberly. 'I was hoping you might.'

'I see,' said the Painted Lady.

The translucent cat climbed on to Blue's knee, curled up and went to sleep. She stroked it absently. Underneath the fur, she could just make out its swiftly beating heart, the shadow of its twined intestines and the outline of a half-digested mouse. 'You managed to track him down for me,' Blue said. 'At that time I wasn't interested in where he'd been. Now I am. Do you know?'

Madame Cardui pushed herself painfully to her feet.

'Have you realised even you must grow old one day?' Before Blue could reply, she waved a hand grandly and went on, 'No, of course not, my deeah. Why should you dwell on such things? You are scarcely a woman yet, for all your birthright and intelligence. Why think of winter when you have only just begun to enjoy the spring?' She sighed. 'Shall I tell you the worst thing about growing old – worse even than the pains and aches and loss of looks? Your memory wizens. Oh, the unimportant parts remain. You can still remember vividly some stupid boy you kissed when you were five. But you forget what you did last week. Such a bore. I believe I may be able to help you, but I shall have to check.'

The orange dwarf took her elbow solicitously as she walked to a section of the wall that transformed itself into a chaotic hypnopattern at her approach. 'Be still,' she murmured and the wall settled down at the sound of her voice. She placed the flat of one palm on the surface and a deep cavity appeared. From it she extracted a deck of playing cards. 'My marvellous deck,' she said. 'Did I ever tell you I was once a conjurer's assistant? The Great Mephisto. Such a handsome man and so skilled with his hands. But he never had a pack like this.' She riffled through it until she found the Jack of Hearts. 'Hold still, Kitterick,' she said and pushed the card into Kitterick's head.

Kitterick froze and his face took on a vacant look. 'Crown Prince Pyrgus Malvae,' he said woodenly. 'Son of Apatura Iris the Purple Emperor, heir to the Peacock Throne, colour of hair red, colour of eyes brown, height five feet and – '

She cut him off with a wave of her hand. 'Scroll to

Search Node Seven. Query all antagonistic encounters within a six-week – ' She hesitated and looked at Blue. 'Is six weeks enough?'

'Perhaps two months,' Blue said. 'To be on the safe side.'

'Within an *eight*-week period,' Madame Cardui told her dwarf.

'Lord Hairstreak,' Kitterick said promptly. 'Crown Prince Pyrgus broke into his manor and stole his golden phoenix after which Hairstreak ordered his immediate detention. Huntsmen – '

'It wasn't Hairstreak,' Blue said. 'Pyrgus told me that himself.' *Hairstreak never got near me. It was someone else who nearly killed me.* 'But I think it may have been after he took the phoenix,' she added.

'Scroll forward,' Madame Cardui ordered.

'Groumu,' Kitterick intoned.

'What?' Blue frowned.

'I think it may be a name,' Madame Cardui suggested. 'Is it a name, Kitterick?'

'Yes.'

'Who is this Groumu?' Blue asked.

'Continue listed enquiries, Kitterick,' Madame Cardui ordered.

'Groumu, Security Guard Sergeant, black hair, brown eyes, height six feet one inch, age forty years and four months, assaulted Crown Prince Pyrgus on the first day of the second moon. Jocurm, Security Guard, hair brown, eyes blue, height five feet ten and a half inches, age twenty-nine years and one month, assaulted Crown Prince Pyrgus on the first day of the second moon. Praneworf, Security Guard, hair brown, eyes blue-grey, height five feet eleven, age thirty-three years and seven months, assaulted Crown Prince Pyrgus on the first day of the second moon – '

'Busy day,' the Painted Lady murmured.

'Datches, Security Guard – '

'What did these guards do?' Blue asked quickly.

'Assault with grievous bodily harm,' said Kitterick. 'Attempted murder, level eight.'

Attempted murder! Blue felt her stomach tighten. Was this what Pyrgus meant? An attack by somebody's security guards? *It was someone else who nearly killed me.* That didn't sound like a bunch of guards. It sounded more like a single person. Unless Pyrgus meant whoever it was set the guards on him. But even then, it was only a level-eight assault, which was technically attempted murder, but actually only meant they'd beaten him unconscious. A serious assassination attempt would have to be at least a –

'Level nine,' Madame Cardui commanded Kitterick. 'Examine level-nine encounters.'

Kitterick clicked audibly and jerked his head. 'Pratellus,' he said. 'Crambus, Security Guard Captain, hair black streaked grey, eyes brown, age forty-four – '

Blue cut him short. 'What did he do to Pyrgus?'

Kitterick's face became immobile except for his eyes which began to circle in a clockwise direction. An odd sound emerged from his mouth, rather like a stuck ratchet.

'Probably this Pratellus did nothing himself,' Madame Cardui explained. 'A level-nine encounter carries the *potential* of serious harm, even death, but the person encountered may not be the one who does the deed.'

Blue frowned. 'I don't understand.'

'Well, for example, Pratellus might have held your brother's arms while someone else stabbed him. Or he might have handed someone a scimitar to decapitate him. Or he might have led him to the gallows or some other place of execution. Or – oh, please don't distress yourself, my deeah: I am speaking *hypothetically*. All we can say is that the brave captain was *involved* in an attempt on your brother's life, not that he was directly responsible.'

'How do we find out who *was* directly responsible?' Blue asked a little crossly. It was sometimes difficult dealing with people of Madame Cardui's age. They had a set way of doing things that wasn't always fast enough.

'Kitterick, move to level ten!' Madame Cardui said imperiously.

Kitterick clicked again. 'Chalkhill, Jasper,' he said loudly. 'Hair dyed, eyes baby blue, height five feet seven inches, age deleted from official records following substantial bribes. Brimstone, Silas, hair gone, eyes bloodshot blue, height five feet and ten inches, age ninety-eight years and ten months.'

'Chalkhill and Brimstone!' Madame Cardui breathed. 'It seems we have found who tried to kill your brother.'

'Who are Chalkhill and Brimstone, Madame Cynthia?' asked Holly Blue. The names rang a bell from somewhere, but they certainly weren't members of any of the Noble Houses and if they were in politics they didn't hold important offices.

'They are in *trade*,' said Madame Cardui, somehow

managing to make it sound like a disease. 'Faeries of the Night, of course.'

'In trade?'

Madame Cardui allowed her eyes to flicker upwards. 'My deeah, they sell pots of glue.'

That was where she'd heard the name. Chalkhill and Brimstone Miracle Glue – she'd seen it in the servants' quarters. 'They manufacture it as well, don't they?'

'I suppose so,' Madame Cardui said dismissively. 'Chalkhill's background is moderately interesting. He had something of a reputation as a hairdresser. Then he became an interior decorator. Distinctive style, but a little too flamboyant for my taste. He was brought up by an aunt. Quite a decent woman, by all accounts, but one understands Jasper poisoned her for her money.'

Blue was alert at once. 'Poisoned? He didn't use triptium, by any chance?'

'I've no idea. It was merely a rumour – nothing was ever proven. But he did inherit her entire estate which he sold off for a substantial sum. He was in the process of squandering it when he met Brimstone.'

'What's Brimstone's background?' Blue asked.

'Sorcery,' said Madame Cardui promptly. 'Necromancy and demonology of the very lowest kind. He even makes his fellow Nighters nervous.' She removed the card from Kitterick's head and he escorted her back to her cushions where she lay down again. 'No doubt about it, Your Highness – either or both of those two are quite capable of an attempt on your brother's life.'

Blue looked at her. 'Better tell me where to find them,' she said grimly.

twenty-one

'Did it hurt?' Blue asked curiously. 'The card-in-the-head thing?'

'Not exactly,' Kitterick said. Madame Cardui had insisted he come along with Blue as protection. 'But it makes you feel peculiar.'

'How does she do it? Some sort of spell?'

'Oh no, Serene Highness – I've got a slot.' He parted his hair and bent over so Blue could see. There was a metal-lined slot let into his skull. 'The information is coded on the cards – they're made to look like an ordinary deck so no one will suspect. All I do is read it off them. It requires a little training, but that's mainly so you don't fall over when you have a card in your head.'

'Good grief,' Blue said.

They were walking together in Cheapside, an area of the city Blue hadn't visited before and wasn't sure she wanted to visit again. They made an odd-looking couple. She was still disguised as a boy and Kitterick, with his bright-orange skin and clothing, scarcely came up to her shoulder. Although he was stocky, he seemed far too small to be much of a bodyguard, but Madame Cardui had assured her he was extremely toxic. One bite from Kitterick was usually enough to fell a carthorse, although it might take a little time.

It was very late now, yet Cheapside was just as thronged as Northgate, although Blue suspected the people here were in search of far less innocent pleasures than a trip to the theatre, or even a chaos-horn café. The whole area had the rough look of a mugger's paradise. She was pleased she was not on her own, even though Kitterick attracted too much attention for comfort.

'Nearly there,' he said. He pointed. 'That's it.'

He was talking about Seething Lane where Madame Cardui had said Chalkhill and Brimstone had their glue factory. It would be shut at this hour, of course, but the Painted Lady had given her the private addresses of both Jasper Chalkhill and Silas Brimstone. Chalkhill had an estate in Wildmoor Broads somewhere beyond the factory. Brimstone lived even closer. He had rooms in Seething Lane. Blue looked where Kitterick was pointing and saw a narrow, gloomy entrance flanked on one side by a tattoo parlour and on the other by a barber shop, both shut. It looked like the last place in the realm anybody would ever want to go. How on earth had Pyrgus got himself mixed up with these people?

Close up, Seething Lane was even less appealing. It oozed a smell that made her stomach turn. The thoroughfare was narrow and partly cobbled, so poorly served by street lights that substantial stretches were positively dark. Anybody could lurk in the shadows down there, waiting to pounce on the unwary.

As if reading her thoughts, Kitterick produced a flaming torch from his pocket and held it aloft. 'I think it best if I go first, Serenity,' he said quietly. Blue agreed. Even so, she fingered her concealed dagger nervously as she followed him.

The lane was empty of people and, once away from the main Cheapside road, their footsteps echoed eerily on the cobbles. The smell was even stronger here, but she fought down the urge to throw up. After a moment Kitterick said, 'This is it.' He held up the torch so that its light danced on the number branded into the narrow doorway. 'Eighty-seven. Mr Brimstone's apartments.'

The lane itself was flanked by ancient terraces, some of them with overhanging balconies. Brimstone's place was part of this, but wasn't a complete house. It was difficult to judge in the gloom, but it seemed to be squeezed between two other buildings, as if slipped in as an afterthought to take up unused space. It rose above them for three narrow storeys, none of them showing a single light.

'Looks like no one's at home,' Blue murmured.

'Shall I ascertain if that is indeed the case, Serenity?'

Blue thought for a moment, then nodded. She was in no hurry to meet either Chalkhill or Brimstone. Her plan, insofar as she had one, was to search for evidence of their attempt on her brother's life. Once she had that, she could act. She was prepared to talk to either of these men if she had to, but if Brimstone was not at home, it could be the perfect opportunity to do a little poking around. She wondered if he used security spells.

'Perhaps, Serenity, it would be a good idea if you were to stay out of sight for the moment. The place certainly seems empty, but one can never be certain and we may not wish Mr Brimstone to realise there is royal interest in him just yet.'

She very much doubted Brimstone would see through her disguise, but Kitterick was right. At this stage of the game it might be better not to take the chance. She nodded again and slipped back into the shadows. At once Kitterick set up a thunderous knocking on the door.

After a moment somebody flung open an upstairs window in one of the neighbouring houses and an angry head poked out. 'Stop that racket, you ugly little orange git, or I'll come down there and do you something grievous!'

'I have a delivery for Mr Brimstone,' said Kitterick, not at all put out.

'At this hour? What sort of cretin are you?'

'Special delivery. Something for his glue.'

'Then deliver it to the factory, you cross-eyed imbecile! Don't come round here disturbing people's sleep.'

'I fear, sir, the factory is shut. I thought it best to see Mr Brimstone.'

'Well, Mr Brimstone ain't at home, you bilge-rat. Take yourself on. Go on, piss off!'

'Will Mr Brimstone be home later?' Kitterick asked.

'Later? Later? How should I know if he'll be home later? Do I look like his nanny?'

'No, sir. Thank you, sir. I shall be on my way now. Sorry to disturb you, sir.' Kitterick made a great play of walking up the lane, but returned as soon as the head disappeared. 'Empty house, Serenity. I take it we shall be breaking in?'

'Oh yes,' Blue said. 'We shall indeed.'

Brimstone was security conscious all right. His front door looked as if a baby should be able to blow it down, but it resisted Blue's pickspell and, fifteen minutes into an assault by Kitterick's nimble fingers, it still wasn't open.

'I've never seen locks quite like this before,' Kitterick muttered. 'They're interlinked. Somehow when you open one it makes another close. Very simple idea, but I can't seem to get round it.' He straightened up and turned to Holly Blue. 'I wonder, Serenity, how you would react to a more muscular approach?'

'What are you thinking of?' Blue asked cautiously.

'I was thinking of a stick of dynamite,' Kitterick said. 'I happen to have one about my person.'

Blue frowned. 'Won't the noise attract attention?'

'Not if we use it in conjunction with a silence spell. If there is a drawback it's that we'll leave a gaping hole where the door used to be; and probably part of the wall as well. In other words, if Mr Brimstone does return, he will know at once there's been a break-in.' He hesitated. 'I don't think it will bring the whole house down.' He blinked. 'No, I'm sure it won't – these old places were sturdily built.'

'Do it,' Blue told him.

Kitterick produced a terrifyingly fat dynamite stick from a trouser pocket and lit the trailing wick. With the fuse burning down at a furious rate, he tucked it in against the door, then stood patting his pockets. 'Where did I put that silence spell …?'

Blue watched the sparkling flame race closer to the dynamite. She licked her lips nervously. 'Mr Kitterick – '

'Ah, here it – no, that's not it.'

'Mr Kitterick, don't you think – ?'

'Why is it things are never where you put them when you want them, Serenity? It may be we shall have to do without – No, I tell a lie: I've found it!' He drew a small cone from an inside pocket. 'What a relief that is.' He bent down and lit the cone off the fuse, which was now just inches from the dynamite. 'Hopefully our spell will detonate before the explosive.' He turned to Blue and smiled. 'Now, I would suggest we put a little distance between us and the door. If you'll permit me, Serenity – ?' He took her arm and together they ran pell-mell down Seething Lane.

They had scarcely gone fifty yards when an immense fireball erupted out of the doorway behind them and an invisible hand slammed into Blue's back as a wave of sudden heat swept over her. She almost tripped, but held her balance, and turned in time to watch a shower of debris. But the silence spell had beaten the dynamite. Not so much as a tinkle reached her ears.

Kitterick grinned. 'Let's see what his fancy locks made of that!' he said.

They walked back to find Brimstone's door had completely disappeared, as had much of the street directly in front of it and parts of the houses on each side. In the gloom behind, they could see a narrow stairway leading upwards.

'I think it best if you stay here, Mr Kitterick,' Blue said. 'That way you can warn me if Brimstone does turn up.'

She hoped he wouldn't argue. If there was any incriminating evidence inside, she preferred to sort through it alone – heaven only knew what Pyrgus might have been up to. But in the event he only said, 'Excellent idea, Serenity. The explosion will have absorbed the spell, so I shall whistle if there's any trouble. I can produce a very piercing whistle when I put my mind to it.'

Blue believed him. She'd formed a high opinion of Kitterick. She climbed over the heap of rubble to find the lower stairs were broken, but she managed to pull herself up without much difficulty and the rest of the staircase seemed sound. It took her to a landing with two doors leading off. The first one she tried opened into a smelly loo, the second into what seemed to be a living room.

She hesitated for a moment, wondering what to do about lights, then decided to risk it. As Kitterick said, if Brimstone came back he'd know there was an intruder anyway – a few lights on upstairs wouldn't make much difference. All the same, she stumbled across the room and pulled the curtains before triggering the glowglobes.

The room was packed untidily with furniture so old that some of it was falling to bits. There was no carpet on the floor and, while a few rugs had been scattered on the wooden boards, they were faded, worn and threadbare. She could see where Brimstone sat when he was in this room. There was an ancient easy chair to one side of the empty fireplace, a couple of dirty cushions fighting the protruding springs. Beside it was a small table with an empty cocoa mug. On the other side of the fireplace was a scuttle with a few pathetic nuggets of coal. To the right was a small wicker basket of kindling. She could imagine the old man on winter nights huddled before a pitiable fire, warming mittened hands on a meagre cup of –

Wait a minute. This wasn't adding up. Blue looked around. From the fly-blown glowglobes that didn't seem to give off nearly enough light, to the rubbish furnishings, the whole place reeked of poverty and decay. Yet Brimstone wasn't a poor man. He couldn't be – he owned a glue factory and had interests in several other businesses if Madame Cardui was to be believed. So why would a man of means decide to live like a pauper? Was Brimstone simply a miser? For some reason, Blue didn't think so. This had to be an illusion, maybe something set by Brimstone to protect against thieves. Anybody breaking in here would think at once there was nothing worth stealing. Very cunning.

She assumed the spell had been triggered by her opening the door, although there might have been a pressure pad on the landing outside. In any case the important thing was to find how to switch it off. Blue began, step by step, to examine everything in the room.

If she was right about this being an illusion, it was certainly a good one. Even close up, there was nothing that gave the slightest hint it might not be real. She reached what she thought of as Brimstone's chair and could smell it and touch it as well as see it. When she poked one of the filthy cushions, it gave off a little cloud of dust that made her cough. She was just beginning to wonder if she was wrong, if Brimstone really was a miser, when she reached a little portrait in a standing frame on top of a battered chest. The painting was of a thin old man, possibly Brimstone himself, staring out with a smug expression on his face. As Blue bent forward to examine it, the old man in the picture winked.

She was so startled she jerked back, but when nothing else happened, she bent forward again. The old man gave another wink. She shifted her head back and forward and discovered that, in a certain position, the portrait always seemed to wink. But why? You might attach a wink spell to a child's toy, but it was hardly the sort of novelty that would make anybody money in an adult portrait. So why had a wink spell been attached to this one? A growing suspicion almost made her smile.

Blue moved her head until the portrait winked at her, then winked back. At once there was the distinctive scent of an illusion breaking and the gloomy, fly-specked glowglobes flared into full, bright light. She straightened up and looked around. The room was transformed. The clutter of ancient furniture had disappeared to be replaced by a tasteful selection of stylish – and costly – antiques. The bare floorboards had given way to thick imported carpeting wall to wall. Brimstone's chair had turned into a modern recliner with an extendable tray for cocktails and cushions sculptured to the exact shape of his skinny bottom. But her attention was drawn at once to one of the antiques, a beautifully preserved roll-top desk.

She expected it to be locked, but Brimstone must have relied on his illusion spell for security since she opened it up easily. There were cubbyholes packed with papers, and more papers in the drawers. Blue ransacked them systematically, looking for anything that might provide a clue to what had happened to Pyrgus. Her hopes quickly faded. All the papers referred to Brimstone's business interests, most of them concerned with the Chalkhill and Brimstone company. To her surprise, the papers themselves seemed to be completely in order. There was not the slightest hint of under-hand activities or shady deals. There wasn't even a suggestion of anything unethical, let alone illegal.

Blue made a cursory search of the rest of the room, then returned to the stairs. There were two doors on the second-floor landing as well. One led into a neat little kitchen. Since she was determined not to be caught twice by an illusion spell, she inspected it carefully, but after five minutes decided it was exactly what it seemed. She came out again, crossed the landing and opened the second door.

The demons were waiting for her on the other side.

She heard them before she saw them, a distinctive insect-like chittering underlaid with a *click-clack* of lobster claws. Then the glowglobes flared.

She had the impression of a library, but the place was infested. She saw at least five demons. They were the familiar greys – small and thin with large heads and enormous jet-black eyes. Four were male, one female. All dressed alike in one-piece silver jump-suits and thick-soled silver boots. Blue knew at once what they were – a grouping technically known as a Goblin Guard. You conjured them, then contracted them to guard whatever it was you wanted guarding. It cost you the occasional sacrifice, but they did their job. Goblin Guards were lethal.

Blue jerked her head round – everybody knew you mustn't look a demon in the eye – and slammed the door. It was a reflex action. She knew perfectly well it wouldn't do any good, yet it made her feel safer. But not for long. Within seconds, a beam of blue light penetrated from the inside of the door and the first of the demons slid out along it. Blue ran for the stairs.

She was back on the first landing before she realised

the demons weren't following. She stopped, heart pounding, and looked back up the stairs. Nothing there. She caught her breath and chanced climbing a few steps. Still nothing. This was very odd. Once Goblin Guards had their sights on you, they nearly always kept coming until they killed you or something stopped them. But there was nothing to stop them here. The whole Guard should have been tumbling down those stairs like an avalanche. She climbed another step.

By the time she was in sight of the second landing, she knew for sure the demons were no longer there. Where had they gone? This was not usual demon behaviour. Had something frightened them off? After a moment she decided she didn't need to know. If they'd gone, it was all to her advantage – she could search the library room now. She pushed the door open cautiously and discovered to her horror they were all back inside.

This time she didn't even bother to slam the door, simply took off down the stairs as fast as her legs would carry her. She knew she wasn't going to get lucky a second time. She also knew that before demons killed you, they had a very gross habit of carrying out some particularly painful medical experiments on –

They weren't following now either! She stopped halfway down the stairs and there was absolutely no doubt about it. The Goblin Guard, which had begun to pour out of the room when she opened the door, had disappeared again.

It hit her like a thunderbolt. It was another illusion! Illusions seemed to be one of Brimstone's magical specialities. It was cheaper than conjuring up a real Goblin Guard and a lot easier on maintenance. You didn't have to sacrifice to an illusion or make sure it wasn't sleeping on the job. You just set it up, switched it on and allowed it to do its work.

She went back very cautiously until she was just a step from the landing, then stopped. She had to be extremely careful here. The library door was still open and, if the Goblin Guard caught sight of her, it would be on to the landing in seconds. An illusion demon could kill you just as dead as a real one. For as long as the illusion lasted, the creature was real enough – it just couldn't step outside the boundaries of the illusion spell. It looked as if Brimstone had set this one to guard the library room and the landing outside, but possibly not the staircase.

With the door open, she daren't step on to the landing. Once the demons saw her they would come after her again. But demons were tricky at the best of times and illusion demons trickiest of all. There was no way of making them intelligent. You set your illusion so they'd attack anything that opened the door but you couldn't set it so they would recognise you and leave you alone – illusion magic just wasn't that good. Which meant there had to be an easy way to switch the illusion off. Brimstone had to be able to get rid of the Goblin Guard before he used his library.

Where was the switch? *What* was the switch? In the room below, the trigger was the winking picture. That gave some clue to the way Brimstone's mind worked. Not that she thought it was another picture, but she did think he might disguise the switch to make it look like something else.

There were no portraits beside the stairs, no pictures of anything else. The walls were smooth, no ornamentation, no panelling, nothing that looked at all – not looked: sounded! One of the stairs squeaked. She'd noticed it vaguely on the way up and it had squeaked again when she ran down. She'd paid no attention, of course. Lots of stairs and floorboards squeaked, especially in a house this age. But suppose it wasn't a natural squeak? Suppose it was a specially built-in signal?

Blue retraced her steps down the stairs. She was still within sight of the landing when she reached the tread that squeaked. She trod on it a few times and the squeak never failed. It wasn't so loud you'd pay much attention, but loud enough so an old man would hear. Was this the illusion trigger? Did it switch the demons on when you climbed up? Or were the demons always there and the squeak just a way of marking the place to switch them off?

Frowning, Blue tried to work it out logically. If this really was the switch, then it couldn't just be a question of pressure on the tread. She'd made it squeak coming up, which might well have switched on the demons, but she'd made it squeak again running down, which certainly hadn't switched them off. Or had it? Maybe she'd switched them off running down, then switched them on again when she climbed back up?

It didn't seem right somehow. Mainly because it didn't do the job well enough. Brimstone wanted his house secure. He'd want to be sure that his illusions were all working. If this one was just a question of a pressure switch, anybody climbing the stairs two at a time would never trip it at all. She frowned. Couldn't be a simple pressure switch.

She thought of the winking picture. The illusion disappeared when you winked back. Maybe … maybe … maybe the Goblin Guard disappeared when you *squeaked* back. Blue trod on the step to make it squeak, then imitated the squeak as an answer. She waited, then, when nothing happened, climbed the stairs again. The door on the second landing was still open, but from this angle she couldn't see if there was anything inside. She'd have to take a chance and go right on to the landing.

She did it fast before she lost her courage. The library was empty.

Blue breathed a sigh of relief. Although he was someone she'd never met, she had a very strong picture of Brimstone in her head now. He was a dangerous and crafty old man, somebody who didn't care much what he did to people. Pyrgus was lucky to get away from him with a whole skin.

But she still didn't know what had happened between them. The library was packed with books on sorcery, wizardry, witchcraft, necromancy and magic – some of them rare tomes – but though she searched it thoroughly, there was nothing at all to show how Brimstone might have tried to kill her brother.

She left the library and climbed the stairs to the third floor. This time she listened carefully for squeaks and examined every inch of the way for another illusion trigger. She spotted none, but even so she was caution itself when she reached the final landing. It was laid out exactly like the others and it proved a complete anticlimax. One door led to a bathroom, the other a bedroom. There were no more Goblin Guards, no more illusions of any sort as far as she could discover. It seemed as if Brimstone was happy no intruder was likely to get past the second floor.

But she still hadn't discovered anything about Pyrgus.

Twenty-two

Pyrgus stepped into choking darkness. For an instant he thought he'd somehow wandered into one of the portals that opened at the bottom of the sea. Then he realised he was breathing air, not water, although it was air mixed with something sulphureous that caught violently in the back of his throat. He stumbled forward, arms outstretched, until his hands touched rough rock, then fumbled his way along, coughing furiously, in a desperate attempt to find fresher air.

It seemed an eternity, but eventually he reached a place where the worst of the choking fumes were behind him and a dim light appeared far ahead. He slowed down and made his way cautiously towards it. He'd already bruised a knee and grazed his ankle and it was still so dark in here (wherever *here* was) that he could easily fall to his death down some subterranean pit. So he edged forward, one hand still on the rock wall, testing each step before he took it. This was always the problem when you used a portal for the first time: you could never be really sure where it would come out. Mr Fogarty had reckoned he should emerge in the palace chapel – something to do with locking on to ion trails – but even he'd admitted there was a margin of error. Besides which, Pyrgus knew he'd been just the tiniest bit impatient. He'd used the control before Mr Fogarty had adjusted it completely.

The light ahead grew brighter and eventually resolved itself into an opening. As Pyrgus approached it, he was able to confirm what he already knew. He was in some sort of underground passageway. It seemed to be a natural formation, possibly part of a cave system. As the light level increased, he could see rock walls and floor. At one point where the passage widened, there was a single stalactite.

Now he could see the source of the light, he realised it was an opening to daylight high up in a rock wall. It wasn't very large, but he thought he should be able to squeeze through. The problem was reaching it.

Pyrgus examined the rockface. It was sheer, but rough, which meant there might be enough handholds for a climb but also meant that if he fell he would be dead. For the first time, he missed his wings. He stared up at the opening for a long moment, then wiped his palms on his breeches to dry off any excess sweat and tackled the wall.

It wasn't as hard as it looked, but he climbed slowly all the same, taking great care to establish firm footholds before reaching for the next handhold. By the time he reached the narrow ledge in front of the opening, his muscles were aching and he was breathing heavily. He sat on the ledge for a moment, allowing himself to recover, then turned to tackle the opening. It looked like a fissure in the rock and up close there was no doubt it was wide enough for him to squeeze through. He could see sky beyond, but nothing else, so he had no idea whether he was going to come out at ground level or high up on some cliff face. But no sense worrying until he found out. He wiggled through the crack.

Pyrgus tumbled out on to a rocky hillside and knew at once something was wrong. He wasn't near the palace portal, of course, or near the palace at all for that matter. In fact, he didn't even seem to be near the city. But it wasn't that. The air tasted foul. It still had a hint of the metallic sulphur that had nearly choked him underground. And the sky, now he was outside, looked the wrong colour. It had the dirty yellowish tint you sometimes got before a storm, except no storm was approaching – there was not a cloud in sight.

Pyrgus frowned. He still felt nauseous and wondered if there might be sulphur fumes venting from some volcanic source nearby. But now he was in the open air, fumes were no longer the first of his worries. He needed to find out exactly where he was; and then take the fastest route back to the palace. Although he'd been gone only a short time he was afraid of what might have happened. He'd never taken much interest in politics, but he wasn't a fool. Somebody had tried to kill him and for all he knew his father might be next. This latest attempt on his life was a political act and his father needed to know about it as soon as possible.

He climbed to his feet and looked around. The landscape was hilly, rocky and generally barren except for a few clumps of pod-like plants he didn't recognise. He was beginning to wonder if he was even within walking distance of the city – he knew the surrounding area well and none of this looked familiar.

The sun was low in the sky and the sulphur fumes, or whatever they were, had given it an angry, fiery hue. If he was to reach anywhere familiar before nightfall, he needed to get started. He made a brief check of his possessions, glad he'd taken up Mr Fogarty on his offer of a knife. The old man kept going on about how you never knew when you might need a weapon, and while Pyrgus hadn't expected to end up in the middle of nowhere, he knew from past experience his own world could be a dangerous place. The knife was no Halek blade – Mr Fogarty had found it in his kitchen – but it was better than nothing.

He also had a knapsack – Mr Fogarty called it a 'kit-bag' – with food. He hadn't thought he'd need that at all, but he liked the stuff you got to eat in the Analogue World and had packed the bag with crisps, Mars bars and a tin of baked beans. Things could be a lot worse. If he had a few miles to walk, it was no further than he'd walked before. Even if he was forced to sleep in the open for a night or two, it hardly mattered. He'd done that before as well.

He slung the knapsack over his shoulder and started down the hill.

He reckoned he'd walked for an hour before deciding something else was wrong. The landscape hadn't varied and the angry sun still hadn't set. By his calculation, it should be growing dusk by now, yet the sun hardly seemed to have moved from its original place in the sky. In fact, the more he thought about it, the more he was convinced it hadn't moved at all. That wasn't possible, so he had to be mistaken about how long he'd been walking.

Pyrgus stopped. His surroundings still looked much the same as they'd done when he'd reached the surface. Were they actually the same surroundings? Was he wandering around in circles? He pushed the thought aside. It couldn't be that simple. The sun hadn't moved. Which meant no time had passed. He felt a little tired, as you might expect after walking for an hour. He *remembered* walking for about an hour. But if the sun hadn't moved, he *couldn't* have been walking for about an hour. He wondered if the fumes had affected his mind. It was a scary thought, but could he be hallucinating?

He started to move again, very much aware of placing one foot in front of the other. He was walking. Of course he was walking! He slipped his knapsack off his back and dropped it on the ground, then watched it as he took half a dozen backward paces. The knapsack stayed put and he moved away from it, exactly as he should. He walked back and retrieved the knapsack. He was walking. Of course he was walking! He'd been walking for an hour or more. So why hadn't the sun moved?

He walked on, westwards, in the direction he'd been walking before. What else was there to do? But the mystery disturbed him. It was like the smell of sulphur – he *still* had that in his nostrils – and the yellow sky. Something was *wrong*, yet he couldn't figure out exactly what.

He topped a rise and found himself looking down on a ruined city.

The ancient buildings rose up out of the barren plain like rotten teeth. Collapsed walls left heaps of rubble, but enough remained standing to show this had once been a busy metropolis. He could see the remnants of a pylon gate and the foundations of stone towers. There was a central plaza, its paving split and cracked. Old roadways and streets were half hidden by patches of the same strange vegetation he'd seen earlier. Even in ruins, the city was impressive. The wall stones were enormous. Several must have weighed tons.

Pyrgus felt a sudden chill. He'd never heard of a city like this anywhere in the Realm of Faerie and certainly not anywhere near his palace. That meant it had to be undiscovered, probably in some distant country on another continent, which would explain the unfamiliar vegetation. How far was he away from home? It might take him weeks, even months, to reach his father and warn him about what had been going on.

If he could get back at all ...

Pyrgus had an optimistic nature, but, all the same, he knew he needed to be realistic. He'd been walking across countryside so barren it was almost a desert, confused by fumes and with absolutely no idea of where he was. He had food – of a sort – in his knapsack. With care, it might last him two or three days, but after that he'd have to hunt and so far he hadn't seen so much as a gruntrat in this desolate terrain, let alone anything edible.

More to the point, he hadn't seen water either and he had no water at all with him. He wouldn't last much more than a week without water. It was cool enough now with the sun near the horizon, but tomorrow at noon it could be leaching moisture from his body at a frightening rate.

He glanced towards the sun. It hung in the same place in the sky as if time itself had stopped.

Water had to be his first priority. He needed water to survive. Without it, he would never reach his father, never warn him, never find out who was behind the murder attempt, never – He cut off the train of thought and forced his mind on to the immediate problem. He might be able to squeeze some moisture from the curious plants, but that had to be a last resort since he'd no idea if they were poisonous. What he really needed was a stream or a pool or...

Or a well!

The ruined city must have had its water sources! The city planners might have built cisterns to collect rainwater, but there would be wells too – they were the only certain source of supply. Some, maybe even most, would probably have dried up by now. But there was a chance one or two might still hold water. All he had to do was find them.

He started down the slope towards the ruins. The thought occurred that he might be lucky enough to stumble on an inscription that would give him some clue to his whereabouts. Once he had water and knew where he was, he'd no doubt he could find his way home, however far away it was. Somehow.

Close up, the city was more impressive than it was at a distance. On several of the structures, the massive stones had been cut and slotted together like a jigsaw. There didn't seem to be any mortar between them, yet they were a perfect fit. He'd never seen anything like it before, although there were several enormous buildings in his father's realm, including the palace itself. He wondered how old these ruins really were – a thousand years? ten thousand years?

He wanted to search systematically, so he began at the surviving pylon gate and began slowly to follow the main thoroughfare that led to the central plaza. There were two possible types of well. One would be enormous borings to ensure a water supply for the city as a whole. These would probably be located somewhere near the centre. But there would be another type as well. Some families, particularly the wealthy ones, would want their own water supply and would have sunk shafts near their homes, possibly even inside them. It was these shafts that were more likely to hold some water now, rather than the over-used municipal borings.

He walked slowly, alert for residential buildings. They weren't as easy to find as he'd thought. Thousands of people must have lived here once, but their homes would have been the smaller, less-well-constructed buildings – the first to fall to rubble. What was left now were segments of the massive city walls, portions of temples, ancient factories, observatories and the like. And in their ruined state, it was tricky enough to tell one type of building from another, especially when all you had to go on were a few flagstones or sections of enclosure walls.

But one area looked promising. The buildings there had all but disappeared, leaving no more than tumbled stones and traces of foundations. It was those foundation outlines that attracted Pyrgus, for they seemed to show small houses clumped together. There were one or two dark crevices that could repay exploration. Even more exciting, there were two cracked slabs that might – just might – be covering shafts.

He was clambering across some rubble to investigate when the demons seized him.

Pyrgus fought like a demon himself. He had no chance to reach the knife Mr Fogarty had given him, but he punched and kicked furiously. There was something about the creatures that sent him into a frenzy of revulsion. They were nearly naked so he could see their repulsive, chalk-white, hairless bodies and their spindly limbs. When they touched him, his skin crawled.

Individually, they were smaller than he was, but there were dozens of them and more swarming across the rubble to help. He had never seen so many in one place, never *heard* of so many appearing at one time. Even the most skilled Wizard of the Night could call up no more than three at once, not dozens. They chittered like insects and darted excitedly towards him, snatching at his clothing, then jumping back to avoid his flailing fists.

He knew enough not to look at their faces. Instead, he concentrated on kicking at their legs, which were brittle and fairly easily broken. The trouble was, the demons knew that just as well as he did and took care to keep well clear of his boots.

Something grabbed his head from behind and held it like a vice. Despite their size, demons were strong. He jerked and twisted, trying to break free, but the creature clung to him. Then more demon hands seized his head and in a moment he could no longer move it at all.

'Nooo!' Pyrgus wailed.

He stopped fighting to concentrate on what he knew was coming. He closed his eyes tight shut and tried to hit backwards at the demons holding his head. Then his arms were caught as well and he knew he was done for. Probing fingers crawled across his face to prise open his screwed eyes. He looked down at once, but the creatures anticipated the reaction and pulled back his head. He found himself looking into a demon face.

The huge, black eyes stared into his own.

'Be still,' a voice said in his mind.

The sensation was hideous, like slime-mould oozing through his brain. He felt the paralysis beginning in his limbs.

'Be still,' the demon voice repeated.

'Rented a tent,' Pyrgus murmured. 'Rented a tent. Rented a, rented a, rented a tent.' It was something Tithonus had taught him. Sometimes rhythmic gibberish could lock your mind enough to break free of a demon's spell. 'Rented a tent. Rented a tent. Rented a, rented a – '

'Your name?' the demon voice demanded in his mind.

Don't think the name! Whatever you do, don't think – Once a demon knew your name, its power over you increased. He'd never heard of anyone escaping demons once they knew his name. *Don't think P – P – No, don't think it! Rented a tent. Rented a tent. Rented a – Don't think* – He felt the name hovering on the edges of his mind, waiting to rush in, to float in, to creep in. *– tent, a tent, a tent, a pent, a py – Don't think P-P-P-P … Don't think PYRGUS! Dammit, dammit, dammit! Well at least don't think Pyrgus Malvae. Oh, double dammit!*

'Come with me, Pyrgus Malvae,' said the slime-mould in his mind.

The demon hands released his arms and head. The demon horde fell back so that the way was clear. The demon speaking in his mind drew thin lips over tiny, pointed teeth. It took Pyrgus a moment to realise it was smiling. The creature turned and walked away across the rubble.

Pyrgus followed like a lamb.

Twenty-three

Arthritic hands or not, Fogarty had the pump-action shotgun all together now. He sighted down the empty weapon and worked the pump a few times to make sure it was functioning properly. It gave a satisfying, well-oiled ratchet sound.

'Your boy isn't here,' he said.

The Purple Emperor leaned forward to look him directly in the eyes. 'I believe you, Mr Fogarty. I believe everything you have told me. I believe you were a friend to my son, as was the boy Henry you mentioned. But Pyrgus has not come home and I hope you will be a friend to me as well.' He held Fogarty's gaze for a long moment before adding, 'You will not find me ungrateful. Or ungenerous.'

'What do you want?' Fogarty asked.

'I want you to help me find him,' Apatura said.

'What do I call you?' Fogarty asked. 'Highness? Majesty? Something like that?'

'You may call me anything you wish, Mr Fogarty. You are not one of my subjects. My given name is Apatura Iris.'

'All right, Mr Iris. I liked your boy. I liked him a lot. Tough little squirt – reminded me of myself when I was a kid. If I can help you find him, I will. But I don't see how.'

The Emperor looked relieved. 'I think there are three possibilities,' he said. 'One is that your portal malfunctioned – '

'My portal didn't malfunction,' Fogarty said promptly.

The Emperor smiled slightly. 'Just possibilities, Mr Fogarty. One, however unlikely, is that your portal malfunctioned and my son was sent some distance from the palace. Another, much more likely, is that Pyrgus set it wrongly, with the same result. You said he worked the thing himself before you even had time to test it.'

'Yes, that's true,' Fogarty agreed.

'The third is that he came back safely, more or less where he should, but felt he had to do something before he made his presence known.' He turned to Tithonus. 'Have I missed anything, Gatekeeper?'

Tithonus shook his head. 'Not that I am aware, Majesty.'

The Emperor turned back to Fogarty. 'If Pyrgus was accidentally sent a distance away, he is probably trying to make his way back to the palace. It would be useful if we could discover where the portal really did leave him. I thought you might co-operate with Chief Portal Engineer Peacock and his technical people to try to calculate exactly where he may have gone. At the same time, it's possible you might remember something he said that would give us a clue to where he went if he decided there was something he needed to do.'

'You want me to come back with you? To your world?'

'That would make sense. You and that boy Henry – Pyrgus may have said something to him too.'

Fogarty opened the drawer in the kitchen table and took out a box of shotgun shells. 'I'm going to load this thing – that OK with you?'

Tithonus glanced up sharply, but the Emperor said mildly, 'Please go ahead. Believe me, Mr Fogarty, if I did not trust you completely you would be restrained or dead by now.'

Fogarty grinned and began to feed shells into the chamber. 'Henry hasn't been here for a while, but I expect he'll tip up soon. I'll leave him a portal control. He can follow us through and you can talk to him then.'

Apatura hesitated. 'There was an attempt on my son's life. I'm not sure it's wise to have open access between our two worlds.'

Fogarty's grin turned into his feral smile. 'Don't worry,' he said, 'I'll make sure nobody but Henry will be able to get through.'

'Does that mean you will come with us, Mr Fogarty?' the Emperor asked.

Fogarty worked the slide on the shotgun to rack a round into the chamber. 'Lock and load!' he said.

Kitterick read Holly Blue's face. 'I take it we have not been successful, Serenity?'

Blue shook her head. 'Nothing. Not a thing.'

The dwarf pursed his lips. 'What now, Serenity? Shall we investigate Mr Chalkhill, or would you prefer it if I escorted you back to the palace?'

Blue didn't like either possibility. It was late now, very late. She was getting tired and needed to sleep if she was to have a clear head for the rest of her investigation. At the same time, it irked her she'd found nothing in Brimstone's rooms – and wasted most of the night into the bargain. The weird thing was she'd found nothing suspicious at all, not just about Pyrgus, but about *anything*. Every drawer she'd opened, every paper she'd read showed Brimstone was a model citizen. Yet from everything Madame Cardui told her, Brimstone *wasn't* a model citizen. Far from it. He was a liar and a cheat who consorted with demons. And he'd taken a lot of trouble over his security. The special locks on his door. The lethal illusions in his –

She froze. How had she missed it? How on earth had she missed it?

'Serenity, where are you going?' Kitterick called.

But Blue was already over the rubble and back on the stairs. 'Keep a look-out!' she shouted. 'I shouldn't be long!'

On the first floor she crashed into the living room. It was exactly as she had left it: the illusion spell removed, the comfortable furnishings, the roll-top desk packed with all its innocent papers, the winking picture on the chest. She ran to the picture and bent down until she found the angle where it winked at her. Blue winked back and knew at once she had been right. The scent of a broken illusion was unmistakable.

She spun round. At first glance, the room hadn't changed. Same carpeting, same furnishing. But she knew it *must* have changed. Brimstone was so clever. He'd set up an illusion within an illusion. Anyone who discovered the first one was supposed to think that was all there was – and she'd fallen for it completely. It never occurred to her there might be a second illusion spell cast over this comfortable room. But there was; and she'd switched it off now. All she needed to do was find out what the second illusion hid.

Her eyes fell on the roll-top desk.

She had it! She had it! These were Brimstone's *real* papers! As she sorted through them with excited hands, she found instance after instance of dirty business dealings. Fraud. Bribery. Embezzlement. Tax evasion. Illegal evictions. Dodgy contracts. It went on and on. Nothing about Pyrgus yet, but she was certain she would find it now. In one drawer she found records of Brimstone's work with demons. It was gross. He'd supplied them with animals – and even a few humans – for their rotten experiments. Blue wasn't as big a softie about animals as her brother, but even she found the details sickening. If Pyrgus had fallen foul of this smelly old nightmare, it was no wonder he'd got himself in trouble.

Blue forced herself to go through the papers systematically. It stretched her patience to the limit, but paid dividends. It was only a scrawled note just five words long, a reminder by Brimstone to himself:

Lock Beleth book in attic

There was an attic! It had never occurred to her there was an attic so she hadn't searched for one. And while she'd no idea what the Beleth book was, the note meant Brimstone hid stuff up there. Probably magical stuff – Beleth sounded like a demon name. Maybe Pyrgus had got mixed up in Brimstone's magic somehow. But whatever: there was another place for her to search.

She raced back up to the third floor, pausing only to squeak back at the stair tread so the Goblin Guard illusion wouldn't try to kill her. She thought there might be a trapdoor in the bedroom ceiling, but even when she stood on the bed there was no sign of one. She went next door to the bathroom and examined the ceiling there, again without result. Was there an illusion spell on this floor too? She spent another fifteen minutes searching for triggers and found nothing. If there really *was* another illusion spell it was well hidden.

Blue sat down on the bed to think. She knew she'd been here far too long. She knew every extra minute she spent increased the chances of Brimstone coming back and finding her. But there was an attic. There was another place where Brimstone hid things. She couldn't give up now – she had to find it!

She made one more search of the room, paying particular attention to possible illusion switches. There was a walk-in wardrobe full of Brimstone's clothes. The enclosed space had a nasty, old-man smell so she'd only taken a quick look before. Now she held her breath and actually stepped inside to tap the wood-panelled walls.

There was a false back to the wardrobe! She'd no doubt at all. The wall sounded hollow. She pushed and prodded, pulled, rapped, even kicked it, but the wall remained firm. She fiddled with the wardrobe rails, searched for secret catches and illusion triggers. Nothing. Nothing. Nothing. 'Oh, open up, you stupid thing!' she screamed in frustration. The back panel of the wardrobe slid back silently. Low-level glowglobes lit beyond.

There was another staircase. Blue hesitated. It led upwards, clearly a secret entrance to the attic. But it also led downwards into gloomy depths. Where to?

This was stupid, Blue thought. She *knew* Brimstone had hidden something in the attic. She *knew* she shouldn't really waste time investigating anywhere else. She knew that if she went down into those dark depths, she might run into more illusion spells ... or worse. She knew all this, but she also knew she couldn't resist – she simply *had* to find out where those stairs led if she went downwards.

Blue moved forward, then stopped. This was too easy. If she'd learned anything in the last hour, it was that Brimstone was one of the trickiest characters she'd ever come across. The whole house was full of magical illusions and traps, yet the panel in the back of the wardrobe – the panel that had to lead to Brimstone's secret attic room – was a mechanical device with the simplest possible *sesame* lock. Anybody could open it with a standard spoken *Open up*. And if she was honest, the panel itself hadn't been that difficult to find. She'd have found it far sooner if she hadn't been put off by the smell of Brimstone's clothes.

Blue took a cloth cap from a peg behind her and threw it on to the staircase, then watched with horror as it passed right through the tread and tumbled down into the depths below. The stairs did not really exist at all. They were another illusion.

If she'd stepped on to them, she'd have fallen to her death.

Twenty-four

Tithonus coughed discreetly.

'Yes, Gatekeeper?' the Emperor asked.

'Sire, there is the question of which portal we should use.' When the Emperor looked at him without speaking, Tithonus went on, 'We may use the House Iris portal, which I assume is what you had in mind – '

The Emperor nodded. 'Yes.'

'But we also have the option of using Mr Fogarty's portal – with Mr Fogarty's consent and co-operation, of course – which might give us some indication of where Crown Prince Pyrgus ended up when he used it.'

For the first time in an hour, the Emperor's face lightened. 'Sound thinking, Tithonus! So obvious now you've mentioned it, but that had not occurred to me.' He turned to Fogarty, who was standing by the door now with his shotgun presented to point up at the ceiling. 'Mr Fogarty, will you permit us to use the portal you constructed?'

Fogarty shrugged. 'Don't see why not,' he said.

Blue thought she had it figured out, but she wasn't sure. If she was right, the trigger she'd applied would make the staircase solid again. If she wasn't, it would remain an illusion. She found another of Brimstone's caps and tossed it on the stairs. This time it stayed. It looked as if she'd stabilised the illusion, but there was really only one way to find out. She took a deep breath, closed her eyes and stepped on to the staircase.

She released the breath explosively. She hadn't fallen. The stairs were real and solid now.

Blue opened her eyes and started downwards without a second's hesitation. Brimstone's house was far too dangerous for a return visit. If she was ever going to find out where this staircase went, it had to be now.

The stairs went down the full three storeys but didn't stop at ground level. If her calculation was correct, they continued for at least another twenty feet. When she reached the bottom, she found herself in a long, straight corridor where glowglobes were already lighting automatically at her presence. She had a good sense of direction and, so far as she could judge, the corridor ran underneath Seething Lane in the direction of Brimstone's glue factory. Which was probably exactly where it led. Heaven only knew what was brought from the factory to Brimstone's rooms and vice versa. Pyrgus himself might have been marched along this corridor for all she knew.

Should she follow the passage? She didn't think so. If Brimstone had information about Pyrgus in the factory, that would have to be another day's work. She still had to find the attic room and search there. Blue headed back up the stairs. In minutes she was standing outside what she knew must be the door to Brimstone's secret attic.

She pushed it open.

A long, carpeted corridor stretched directly ahead,

illuminated by elaborate crystal chandeliers.

'Not the chapel,' murmured the Purple Emperor, 'but clearly still the palace.'

'I believe this is the east wing, somewhere near the quarters of your daughter, sire,' Tithonus put in, looking around.

'Yes, I think you may be right. So if we're here, Pyrgus must have made it home safely.'

'Assuming this man Fogarty has been telling us the truth,' Tithonus said, his voice scarcely more than a whisper.

'My instinct is to trust him,' the Emperor whispered back. 'For now.' He raised his voice. 'Are we all safely through?'

'All accounted for, Your Majesty,' said Chief Portal Engineer Peacock briskly.

'Mr Fogarty, is this the same place you saw when you came through before?'

Fogarty sniffed. 'Looks like it,' he said.

'It seems my son may have taken himself off somewhere. But at least he is back in his own world.' The Purple Emperor gathered his cloak around him. He felt reassured by events, but there was still the possibility Pyrgus had set the portal wrongly and translated several miles away. The boy had a genius for getting into trouble. 'Mr Fogarty, I should like you to go with Chief Portal Engineer Peacock. He will arrange to have you comfortably quartered. I appreciate it's late and you must be tired, but first thing in the morning I hope you will be able to assist our engineers.'

'Do my best,' Fogarty said drily. He took a control from his pocket and switched off the portal.

'Gatekeeper Tithonus, come with me,' the Emperor

said and strode off briskly in the direction of the stairs. They were approaching his private quarters when a harassed servant caught up with the news that his daughter had now disappeared as well.

The attic smelled of blood. Strips of animal pelt had been nailed to the floor to make a crude and nasty circle. There were weird bits of equipment at the far side of the room. She'd never seen anything like them before, but they had the look of machinery for trapping lightning. Some of them were lying on their sides and possibly broken. There was an ornate metal incense burner filled with ash. Several bowls were strewn around and somebody had inscribed a triangle on the floor at the far side of the circle. There was a bunch of asafoetida grass in one corner. The walls were decorated with banners displaying mystic sigils. The whole place reeked of magic of the most debased sort.

Was it a trap?

Nervous and impatient though she was, Blue took time to think. After careful consideration she decided traps were unlikely. This was Brimstone's demonic workspace. It was well protected from intruders and she could imagine the grotty old sorcerer wouldn't want protection or illusion spells interfering with his magic. If you had too many spells going in the same place, they set up peculiar resonances that could sometimes shake a whole building apart. Chances were the attic was the one room in the house that Brimstone would keep absolutely free of magic until he started calling up his demons. That's if she was right. The only way to find out for certain was to walk in.

Blue walked in.

Her heart was pounding, but nothing happened. She couldn't absolutely rule out an illusion, of course, but somehow she didn't think there was one in this room. The whole place was just too chaotic, as if some ghastly ritual of Brimstone's had gone badly wrong. She started to search.

There was only one cupboard and it was locked with a simple protection charm, but she opened it easily with her pickspell – another sign that Brimstone considered his attic safe from intruders. The cupboard was packed with magical equipment – fire wands, blood chalices, pentacle discs, talismans, mandragores, air daggers and the like. A miniature humunculus began to crawl towards her, its sightless eyes turned towards the light, but what caught her attention were the books. There were two of them, pushed in towards the back of the cupboard and one looked suspiciously like a journal.

She pushed the humunculus to one side and grabbed them. The smaller of the two had a blank cover, but when she flicked it open, the pages inside were filled with Brimstone's familiar ornate script. His magical diary! She'd found the sorcerer's magical diary! It would have details of every demon he had ever conjured, every act of necromancy he had ever undertaken. She turned a page and the name seemed to leap out at her:

Pyrgus

This was it! This was it! Her heart was pounding as she looked around for somewhere she could sit and read under better light. Then a piercing sound struck her ears so forcibly it was almost painful. For an instant she thought she'd been wrong about the attic and had somehow triggered one of Brimstone's protection spells. But then she realised the sound was coming from somewhere far below and suddenly her mind clicked into gear. It was Kitterick's warning whistle. Somebody was coming.

Holly Blue tucked both books underneath her arm and fled.

Twenty-five

Henry went straight round the back. Even if Mr Fogarty was alive and well he wasn't likely to open the front door. The grass hadn't been cut and the flower beds hadn't been tended, so no change there. He glanced towards the buddleia bush for a portal – he knew that's where Mr Fogarty would try to open one – but there was nothing.

He peered through the kitchen window, then the glass pane in the back door. There didn't seem to be anybody inside. He knocked loudly on the door and then the window. The noise echoed, but no one came. Somehow it sounded like an empty house.

Henry fished in his pocket and pulled out a key on a long piece of string. *Didn't know about that, did you, Mum?* He opened the back door and slipped inside. 'It's me, Mr Fogarty!' he called reassuringly. 'It's Henry.' He waited. Once when he'd used the key and startled Mr Fogarty, the old boy'd come at him with a kitchen chopper.

Nobody appeared, not Mr Fogarty, not Pyrgus. 'Hello …' Henry called. 'Hello …' He moved cautiously from the kitchen into the cluttered living room. 'Mr Fogarty? It's Henry, Mr Fogarty.' The room smelled musty and there was nobody in it.

Ten minutes later, he'd been through every room in the house. The only living thing he found was mould on a half-eaten hamburger beside Mr Fogarty's rumpled bed.

He came back to the kitchen and noticed something he'd missed earlier, a brown envelope held down by an empty salt cellar on the kitchen table. There was one word written on the outside in black Biro:

Henry

Henry grabbed the envelope and found a single sheet of paper inside, torn from a ruled notebook. On it were just four words in Mr Fogarty's neat handwriting:

Npx uif gspou mbxo
6851

Henry stared at them. You could always read Mr Fogarty's handwriting, so there was no doubt about the spelling, but the words themselves didn't make sense. He didn't think they were in a foreign language – they certainly weren't French, which he learned at school – although they might be something weird and East European like Serbo-Croat. Except that Mr Fogarty didn't speak Serbo-Croat, or anything but English as far as Henry knew. Anyway, didn't languages like Serbo-Croat have a different alphabet?

It was code! All of a sudden, Henry knew it was code. It had to be! Mr Fogarty had never left him a note in his life, but if he'd left one now, it would have to be in code. Especially if it was something important, maybe something to do with Pyrgus and the portal. Fogarty would never leave stuff lying around for others to read – he was far too suspicious. Suddenly Henry was excited.

Then the excitement died abruptly. How was he going to crack the code?

All sorts of stupid thoughts poured into his mind. Maybe Mr Fogarty kept a codebook … maybe this sort of thing dated back to his bank-robber days … maybe there were clues hidden about the house … maybe the numbers were the clue … maybe … maybe …

Maybe he should stop flapping around like a headless chicken and see what he'd got here. It couldn't be too difficult. Mr Fogarty knew he wasn't Brain of Britain, so it would have to be fairly easy. Maybe a little like charades. Ignore the numbers for the moment and concentrate on the words. First word NPX. OK, first word, three consonants. But you didn't get words that were all consonants. So one of those consonants had to stand for a vowel. And it was a short word, just three letters, maybe 'the'. If the first word was 'the' that made 'X' stand for 'E'. Were there any more 'Xs' in the message? Yes, there was one in the fourth word. This was looking good.

If 'X' stood for 'E' then 'N' had to be 'T' and 'P' must be 'H'. Any repeats there? No more 'Ns' but there was another 'P' in the third word. So the whole sentence read:

THE / - - - / - - H - - / - - E - -

Henry stared at it for a while, then ran out of steam. Four words, first word 'The', second word unknown, third something with an 'H', fourth something with an 'E'. The something something something …

Suddenly, out of nowhere, Henry saw it. The first word *wasn't* 'the'. What you did was displace a letter of the alphabet. The simplest way was to displace by one: A became B, B became C, C became D and so on.

Mr Fogarty's code was a straightforward, one-place displacement. So to decode, you just displaced one back again. N became M, P became O, X became W. He found a leaky ballpoint in his jacket pocket and jotted down the transpositions underneath the original message:

NPX UIF GSPOU MBXO
6851
MOW THE FRONT LAWN
6851

He stared at the message stupidly. He'd cracked the code. He knew he'd cracked the code because everything fell neatly into place. But the message didn't make any sense. *Mow the front lawn?* Why would Mr Fogarty leave him an instruction like that *in code?*

The lawnmower! Mr Fogarty had always told him not to touch the lawnmower! Now he was telling him to mow the lawn. It had to be something to do with the lawnmower in the shed.

Henry crumpled the paper and stuffed it in his pocket, then raced down the back path to the shed. Inside was the usual mess. (He'd never got round to cleaning it for Mr Fogarty that day Hodge caught Pyrgus in his fairy form.) There were cobwebs and dust coating the largest collection of junk, machine parts, garden tools and flower pots he'd ever seen. On his left was an ancient grow-bag for tomatoes, with the wizened brown remains of last year's plants emerging from it like a spider. The lawnmower was at the far end of the shed.

Henry picked his way across. As he reached the mower, his heart began to pound. Mr Fogarty was up to something, definitely trying to send him some sort of message. He cautiously unwrapped the plastic covering the mower, looking for another envelope. There was none. He detached the grass box and looked inside that, but couldn't see because of the gloom of the shed. He stuck his hand in and fumbled around, then gave up and carried the box outside. When he tipped it to the light, there was nothing inside there either.

He started to drag the mower from the shed so he could see a little better. There was a cavity underneath it in the concrete floor.

The cavity had been covered by a thin sheet of plywood, but as Henry dragged the mower a loose fitting caught and moved it slightly. Even then he might not have noticed the cavity if he hadn't been so hyper. But he was watching out for clues and spotted the dark crack at once. He pushed the mower clear and lifted the plywood.

The cavity was no accidental flaw. It was a three feet by two feet rectangle, three feet deep with neat, clean edges, obviously built in when the concrete was first laid. Inside was a metal strongbox with a combination lock.

Mow the front lawn
6851

Henry's heart was thumping so loudly now it was making his whole body shake. That's what the numbers were for – the combination lock! His fingers were trembling as he dialled the combination and jerked the lid.

The lid didn't move.

Henry tried again, taking great care to do it right this time. 6 ... 8 ... 5 ... 1 ... But while he was certain he'd dialled exactly, the strongbox remained locked.

What was going on here? The numbers had to be the combination – nothing else made sense. He frowned. The message wasn't *Mow the front lawn 6851*. The message was *Npx uif gspou mbxo 6851*. To get it right you had to shift the letters. Maybe you had to shift the numbers as well!

Henry tried the new combination. 5 ... 7 ... 4 ... How did you shift *one* backwards? Zero, he supposed. He dialled in the final 0 and the strongbox opened easily. Inside was a brushed aluminium cube with two inlaid concave plastic buttons on the top. Lying beside it was another scrap of paper. He picked up the paper. There were eight words, but no code nonsense this time. Mr Fogarty's second message said simply, GONE ON AHEAD. FOLLOW SOON AS YOU CAN.

Gingerly Henry picked up the cube.

Twenty-six

Pyrgus had the impression of an open trapdoor with stone steps leading downwards, but his mind was no longer working. He felt as if it had been pushed into a tight, dark corner of his skull and locked there like a small, furry animal in a cage. He could still see through his eyes, still hear through his ears, but everything was at a distance, as if he was looking through the wrong end of a telescope. Nothing was important any more, not where he was going, not getting back to the palace, not his father, not his sister, not his new friend Henry. His thoughts crawled through treacle and were blurred around the edges, slipping and sliding away from him every time he tried to use them. His memory had collapsed and his head ached. He was no longer sure where he was before he got here or even who he was exactly. If he concentrated really hard he could recall his name, but not much else.

The demons led Pyrgus along a stone-flagged passageway that seemed to be illuminated only by a greenish fungus clinging to the walls. The light level was so low he stumbled constantly, although the demons themselves didn't seem to have much trouble. He could hear them oozing and chittering along the edges of his mind. The slime-mould had withdrawn a little, but he knew it was still there with the others, ready to pounce at the first hint of him trying to break free. Pyrgus couldn't fathom that. Why would he try to break free?

The passageway led into a maze of galleries with corridors and tunnels branching off in all directions. Most of them looked the same to Pyrgus, but the demons never hesitated. The colour of the light began to change, sliding from the bilious fungus-green into a softer, rosy hue, but he couldn't understand where it was coming from. At the same time the temperature seemed to be rising, a little at a time, until he found himself sweating. There was an increasing smell of sulphur in the air that was vaguely familiar, although he couldn't remember why.

They emerged from the maze after more than an hour. An odd thought occurred to Pyrgus. An invading army could wander for months in that labyrinth. Had it been built for just that purpose – as a protection for the place where the demons lived? Pyrgus didn't know and didn't really care.

They were standing in a cavern so vast Pyrgus couldn't see the other side. Before them, stretched out across the cavern floor, was an underground city, laid out in a mirror image of the ruined city he'd seen above. But this city was made from gleaming metals, not stone, and in far better repair. The polished surfaces reflected the dim red light, yet the whole city was somehow in shadow. Pyrgus didn't care, any more than he cared about the heat. Pyrgus didn't care about anything much.

The demons marched him through the gloomy streets towards the central plaza. In his drifting thoughts he mused about the demon world. Demons kidnapped people all the time and flew them off in metal ships. Somebody had told him that, although he couldn't quite remember who. Six million people called Americans were missing. He wondered why the demons wanted so many. Perhaps they were food. He wondered if an American would taste as good as a potato crisp.

There were demons on the streets, but none stopped to look at him.

In the centre of the plaza was an enormous dome-shaped building that extruded a metal ramp as they approached. It looked so friendly and inviting that Pyrgus almost broke into a run, but the slime-mould at the edges of his mind reached out and quickly pulled him back. His thoughts clicked into gear. They were all going to see somebody important. He stepped on to the ramp and forgot what he was thinking.

As they entered the building he saw there was machinery in the walls. How weird was *that*?

In the gently wafting thistledown that had replaced his mind, a new thought appeared. Nobody who was kidnapped by demons ever got back to their own world. The slime-mould seized the thought at once and threw it out. What a totally stupid thought that was! Demons only wanted to be *friends*.

The demons led him through into a large, high-ceilinged chamber (*throne room? Situation Room?*) where a red-robed demon studied a large map spread across a metal table.

The creature looked up as they entered. 'Crown Prince Pyrgus,' it said smoothly. 'How good of you to visit us.'

* * *

The world snapped into sharp focus as Pyrgus's mind cleared. He was in Hael, the demon world. He had no idea how he'd got there, but it was the only thing that made sense. Somehow Mr Fogarty's portal must have sent him here. He remembered the smell of sulphur and the barren desolation, the sullen, stark, unmoving sun, the rosy light, the metal city – he *had* to be in Hael.

Without the slightest hesitation, Pyrgus hurled himself at the demon in the scarlet robe ... and found his body wouldn't move.

'Don't upset yourself, Pyrgus,' the demon said. 'It will be easier on you if you avoid aggressive actions. And more convenient for me.'

If he couldn't move, could he talk? There were things he needed to know if he was to have any chance of getting out of here. 'How do you know my name?' he asked. It came out slightly slurred, but otherwise just fine.

The scarlet demon stared at him with huge dark eyes, but made no attempt to control his mind again. 'We've met before.'

Pyrgus blinked. He had no memory of ever seeing this creature.

'Don't you remember?' the demon asked, picking up his thoughts. 'Well, perhaps that's understandable. I looked a little different then.'

To Pyrgus's astonishment the creature began to expand in all directions. It grew upwards to a height of six feet ... seven feet ... eight feet and more. Its body burst out of the scarlet robe and took on slabs of rippling muscle. Its skull distorted and its face changed. Ram's horns erupted from its forehead and curled powerfully to frame the side of its head. 'Does this refresh your memory?' Even the voice had changed. The smooth, well-modulated tones now rumbled like a thunderstorm.

Pyrgus's mouth opened and closed like a fish. It was the creature Brimstone had called up, the creature that had tried to kill him just before his father's guards arrived. 'You're – you're – '

'Prince Beleth at your service!' laughed the demon.

The transformation was astonishing. 'Is that the way you really look?' asked Pyrgus.

Beleth shook his head. 'Of course not. All this is just part of the show we put on for old fools like Brimstone. He believes he's a Master of Illusion, but he never thinks to question what he sees himself.' The huge form began to shrink until Pyrgus was again faced with the creature in the scarlet robe. Somehow it looked no less scary than the thing with horns. This Beleth was a formidable opponent however he looked.

'Why, thank you,' Beleth said, again demonstrating how easily he picked up Pyrgus's thoughts. He glanced down at the map, then back at Pyrgus. 'I expect you'll soon be wondering how you got into this mess.'

Pyrgus, who'd started to wonder how he'd got into this mess, felt a nasty little chill crawl up his spine. How could you get away from something that read the plans in your mind as you were making them?

'Not very easily,' Beleth told him. 'So why don't you stop worrying about getting away and in return I'll satisfy your curiosity about one or two things that have been troubling you. How about that, Prince Pyrgus? Do we have a bargain?'

Pyrgus found his headache was getting worse. He didn't like the thought of making bargains with a demon, but just at that moment he couldn't figure out what else he was supposed to do. Clearly he *couldn't* get away just now, whether he worried about it or not. Besides, he *was* curious about how he'd managed to end up here and a few other things besides. Starting with why Brimstone had been so anxious to sacrifice him to this creature.

'Well,' said Beleth, 'let's deal with how you got here first and I'll tell you about Brimstone in a moment – save the best for last, so to speak. You're here because we interfered with your portal – that's why you're here. Not many people know we can do that.'

Pyrgus certainly hadn't known. He'd never heard a hint of demons interfering with portals before. He wondered if –

Beleth said, 'We're the ones who sent you off course when you tried to translate to the Analogue World. We had help, naturally. We needed to know House Iris portal coordinate settings. Catching you this time was a lot easier – we already knew the coordinates for your return so it was only a question of watching for the signal and diverting you as you stepped through.'

'But why?' Pyrgus asked.

'Because Brimstone didn't manage to fulfil his contract,' Beleth explained patiently. He smiled, showing little demon teeth. 'So now I have to do the job myself.'

'Just seven groats a week,' the old woman cackled. 'Won't find anything this good for the money anywhere in the realm, young man.' She grinned toothlessly and a knowing look crossed her features. 'Or as private.'

Brimstone stared at his new lodgings with distaste.

They consisted of one filthy room with a shuttered window. The bed was a heap of vermin-ridden straw in a corner. The only furniture was a rickety table and a single wooden chair. From now on he would sleep here and eat here –

'Meals is extra,' the old woman added, as if reading his mind.

– and venture out only after dark. 'I'll take it,' he told the harridan. He tossed her a few coins. 'Here's a month in advance – now piss off.'

She tested two of the coins between her gums and presumably found them satisfactory. 'Thank you, sir,' she said. The knowing look returned. 'Rest assured no one will know you're here, sir. Not while there's breath left in my body. Guarantee my tenants privacy, I do. *Guarantee* it.' She hesitated at the door. 'Bone gruel for supper,' she said. 'Very nourishing.'

Brimstone turned away as she closed the door and opened the shutter a crack. His room looked out on to an open sewer. He closed the shutter again. At least no one was likely to break in through the window. He went to the table, sat on the chair – which was hideously uncomfortable – and carefully counted the gold coins he had left. He could stay here for quite a while at seven groats a week if the bone gruel didn't kill him off, but he'd have to come out of hiding eventually.

He just hoped Beleth wouldn't still be looking for him when he did.

Pyrgus felt like a balloon tethered to Beleth by an invisible cord. Demons prostrated themselves as their Prince strode through the city streets. Pyrgus followed no more than a pace or two behind, but seemed to be floating rather than walking. His mind was racing now, even though he knew Beleth could pick up every thought.

'Patience,' Beleth cautioned over his shoulder. 'All will soon be clear. And rest assured I shall tell you everything. It's such a *delicious* plan, I've been dying to tell somebody. Of course I couldn't until now in case word got out. But since you're captive here now, I can tell you all. It's quite, quite marvellous!'

They crossed the perimeter of the city and stepped on to a gloomy metal plain. Stretched across it for as far as the eye could see were rank upon rank of heavily armed and armoured demons. They carried fire lances, stun wands, rocket launchers. They wore bandoleers of laser grenades and biological spell cones. Servo-assisted boots meant they could leap for fifty yards or more. Helicopter backpacks would enable them to fly. They were the most fearsome fighting force Pyrgus had ever seen.

'Salute the troops,' said Beleth.

Pyrgus felt his arm move of its own accord until it snapped off an awkward salute. As it fell back to his side, Beleth said, 'This is what it's all about.'

Pyrgus stared out across the vast army and tried to make sense of it all. 'You're expecting trouble?' he ventured. He wondered if Hael might be threatened with invasion.

'You could say that,' Beleth told him. 'Although expecting isn't quite the right word. It's trouble we shall be *starting* soon. With a little help from our friends. That's what your song says, isn't it?' He caught the confusion in Pyrgus's mind. 'Well, perhaps it's an Analogue World song. I know I heard it somewhere.

No matter. The point is any day now decades of careful planning will bear fruit. There are going to be ... changes ... in the Realm of Faerie.'

Pyrgus definitely *was* floating. When he looked down he could see his feet were nearly six inches off the ground. Beleth towed him like a child's toy through the ranks of stone-faced demons. The smell of brimstone was exceptionally strong here, intermingled with the heavy scent of cordite, as if wars and armies were particularly demonic things. Which they probably were, Pyrgus supposed.

'How do you get on with your father?' Beleth asked.

'Very well,' Pyrgus answered loyally, although it was far from the truth.

'I ate mine,' Beleth told him. 'He got old and feeble and useless, but he wanted to hold on to power. So I took steps. Tasted disgusting – stringy, tough, smelly ... you know how fathers are – but it's the custom here. You're supposed to absorb the essence that way. Rank superstition, of course, but, well ... tradition.' He shrugged.

'So you became King of Hael?' Pyrgus said. He had an idea that if he could keep Beleth talking, the demon might not take time to read his thoughts.

'Prince of Darkness,' Beleth told him. 'The title is Prince of Darkness. We've never had a king here, or an emperor – prince is the highest rank. I was a duke when I ate him. Anyway, the point is when I became Prince, there were a few changes round here, I can tell you. This place had stagnated for centuries. But I made *plans*, Crown Prince Pyrgus. Would you like to hear about the plans I made?'

'Yes, please,' Pyrgus said eagerly. Maybe it was his

imagination, but the more Beleth talked the more his control over Pyrgus seemed to be easing. Pyrgus still couldn't *do* anything and he had to be hideously careful about everything he thought, but in time ...

'I made plans to expand my sphere of influence. That's the way they put it, isn't it? Nobody talks about conquest, loot and pillage any more, although it's much the same thing and such *fun*. Perhaps since we're friends now, I should speak plainly. I made plans to conquer, loot and pillage the entire Realm of Faerie. And after that to march my legions into the Analogue World, although that's not really your concern. In short, Pyrgus, I made plans to become the greatest Prince of Darkness the universe has ever known.' He stopped, black eyes shining.

After a moment, Pyrgus said encouragingly, 'Wow, how were you going to do that?'

'We demons have had a long relationship with the Faeries of the Night – a little help here, a sacrifice there, the occasional blood contract. You know that, of course. What you may not know is that only months ago I personally negotiated a secret treaty with one of the more powerful Nightside leaders – '

'Lord Hairstreak!' Pyrgus exclaimed.

'Precisely!' Beleth nodded. 'What an intelligent young man you are – you would make an excellent demon. As you say, Lord Hairstreak. He has ambitions to conquer, loot and pillage the entire Realm of Faerie himself and I agreed to help him. Specifically, Pyrgus, I agreed to add my forces to his when he launched an attack on the ancient Administration of the Light. In short, your father's Government. That attack is now imminent.'

'Hairstreak is going to declare war on my father?'

'Perhaps not declare. One would prefer an element of surprise. But he is certainly going to wage war and these stout fellows all around you will help him win it.'

This was no longer a game to keep Beleth talking. Pyrgus was chill as an icicle. He knew there had been some trouble with the Faeries of the Night, but it had never occurred to him the situation was so serious that it threatened war. And with Beleth's legions allied to the Nightside, it was a war his father could not win. Furiously he fought the panic rising through his thoughts. 'Hairstreak plans to overthrow my father?'

'Yes.'

'And declare himself Purple Emperor?'

'Something like that.' Beleth smiled benignly.

After a stunned moment, Pyrgus said, 'Our people will never stand for it!'

'They may have to when they lose the war. But you are quite right to suggest they will not like it. Hairstreak knows that, of course, which is why he asked me to murder you.'

'Hairstreak asked you to murder me?' Pyrgus echoed.

'Nothing personal,' said Beleth. 'It's only politics.'

Beleth's control was definitely slipping. Pyrgus had both feet on the ground now and the sensation of floating had all but gone. None the less he followed the Demon Prince willingly as they left the military field and re-entered the great, gloomy, metal city. Escape was useless to him now, even if he managed it. Before he took any action at all, he had to find out everything that was going on.

Luckily Beleth seemed happy to talk. 'The point, of course, is that you are Crown Prince, the legitimate heir to the throne should anything ... unfortunate befall your father.'

Frowning, Pyrgus asked, 'You mean like getting killed in the war?'

Beleth glanced back at him in surprise. 'Oh, no – your father won't be killed in battle. That would make him a martyr. He must be killed before hostilities break out. And so, I fear, must you.'

twenty-seven

Blue felt like killing her father.

'I've been worried sick, young lady!'

'Honestly, Father, there was no need.'

'No need? Do you know what time it is?'

He had a point of sorts there. It was almost dawn.
But even so, there was no need for him to speak to her
like this in front of the servants. 'I'm sorry it's so late,
Father, but I was on an important mission.'

'I don't care if you were visiting the High Priest of
Coridon!' snapped the Purple Emperor. 'You don't
think I have enough to worry me with your brother
missing without you taking yourself off as well?'

'It was actually about Pyrgus that I – '

'I don't care. I don't care what you thought you were
doing. I'm sick of all this Secret Service business. I'm
sick of you sneaking around pretending to be some sort
of spy. You're a Princess of the Realm, not a grubby
field operative in Imperial Espionage.'

'Father,' Holly Blue said patiently, 'I really don't
want to go into this in front of other people, but the
books I brought back contain important information.
They may give us some clue to where Pyrgus has got
to.'

She watched her father carefully. He had confiscated

the books she'd brought back from Brimstone's lodgings almost as soon as she returned to the palace – the moment she'd admitted to stealing them, in fact. But she'd at least had time to glance at Brimstone's magical diary. It left no doubt that Brimstone had tried to kill Pyrgus as part of some ghastly demonic operation. It also showed that Brimstone's partner Chalkhill had captured Pyrgus in the first place. What had Chalkhill and Brimstone been up to? Were they behind the sabotage of the portal? Did they know where he was now? Since Brimstone seemed to be missing at the moment, Blue fully intended to pay a little call on Chalkhill and get the truth from him one way or another.

Her father's brow turned thunderous. 'Those books were stolen, young lady. Stolen by you. I never thought I would see the day when a daughter of mine turned into a common thief. Gatekeeper Tithonus will return them in the morning. In the interim, I suggest you go to your room, take off those ridiculous clothes and get straight to bed.'

How could your own father be so stupid? So maddening. So ... so ... so ... 'Father, you *can't* give them back. They could help us find Pyrgus – '

'I think you may safely leave the search for Pyrgus to those who know what they're doing,' her father told her coldly. His tone softened a little as he added, 'I know you're worried about your brother, Blue, but while you've been on your ridiculous escapade, Tithonus and I have ascertained that he is safely back in the realm. It will be only a matter of time before we find him.'

So they hadn't found him yet. She knew it! She knew it! 'Father, I – '

'Not another word,' her father said. 'Not one more word. I've had a long day and a long night and a great deal more worry than I needed – much of it, I might say, caused entirely by you. Go to your room.'

'But, Father, I – '

'No "buts",' her father snapped. He half turned so that his back was towards her as if firmly ending the conversation, then, because he could never resist, he turned back and said, 'What is that ludicrous fashion you're wearing? You realise it makes you look exactly like a boy?'

'Father – '

'Not another word!' her father said. This time he turned away without turning back. Had he done so, he might have noticed the mutinous set of Blue's lower lip as she headed for her room.

Chalkhill had to be very rich indeed – there was a fair-weather spell laid across his entire estate. You could see the break in the clouds for miles across the Wildmoor Broads and when Blue approached the main gates she noticed the temperature had risen so much it felt almost sub-tropical. To her surprise, the gates themselves were open.

Kitterick seemed surprised as well. 'Come into my parlour ...' he murmured.

It was late morning on the day after the row with her father. She'd borrowed Kitterick again from Madame Cardui and they were riding side by side in an unmarked palace ouklo, perfect for the Broads since it carried them above the spreading prickleweed. Now it floated serenely along Chalkhill's pristine driveway, allowing them time to admire the manicured lawns and jasmine-scented borders. As the mansion came into view, Blue's attention was drawn to a massive flower bed tightly planted with pink and white roses to spell out the word *Jasper* in flamboyant, flowing script.

'Must be his first name,' Blue muttered. Her expression showed distaste at the vulgarity.

'I believe it is, Serenity,' Kitterick confirmed.

'You must stop calling me "Serenity", Kitterick,' Blue told him. 'It's important Chalkhill doesn't realise my identity.'

'Of course, Serenity,' Kitterick nodded. 'What shall I call you?'

She was dressed in the clothes her father believed made her look exactly like a boy. After a moment's thought she said, 'Sluce. You should call me Sluce.'

'Sluce, Serenity?' Kitterick's nose wrinkled in distaste. 'A little ... merchant class, surely?'

'We're *supposed* to be merchant class,' Blue said firmly. The cover story was they were here to offer Chalkhill a new wrinkle cream that actually reversed the ageing process to leave the skin soft as a child's. Madame Cardui claimed it was exactly the sort of nonsense to guarantee Chalkhill would see them. 'Are all the arrangements in place?' Blue asked Kitterick.

'Of course ... Mr Sluce,' the orange dwarf confirmed with an audible sniff. 'We can move on a whistle.' He patted his briefcase and stared, mysteriously, up at the sky.

The ouklo reached the courtyard in front of the house and descended like thistledown to the gravelled surface. Blue and Kitterick both stepped off delicately. There were several gardeners at work within sight of the windows, but they ignored the visitors completely.

The mansion was a mixture of styles. The central portion had the look of a minor manor and would have been perfectly acceptable had it been left alone. But someone had extended it with two enormous baroque wings and added gothic towers inlaid with something crystalline that sparkled in the sun. An extra storey – clearly only built within the last few years – squatted on top like some monstrous cosy. All the external surfaces that did not sparkle had been painted a uniform pink. The windows were outlined in a delicate sky blue and their glass sprayed with a liquid spell that created the illusion of cherubs dancing.

'A little … sudden for my taste,' Kitterick remarked.
Blue shushed him. 'It's probably better inside.'
Kitterick shuddered.

Two enormous rock-crystal manticores guarded the front steps. Like the windows, they had been enchanted for they turned to watch as Blue and Kitterick approached. Blue gave them a wide, nervous berth, but they made no move to block the way. She jerked the bell-pull on the pulsing pink front door and was rewarded with the brief swelling of a phantom orchestra somewhere deep inside. The amount of money Chalkhill had spent on spells and nonsense was quite extraordinary.

They waited. Behind them, the crystal manticores settled back laboriously into their original positions.

The door swung open and Blue almost gasped. She had an impression of luxurious brown ringlets and deep, dark, soulful eyes. The boy was tall. He was dark. He was handsome. In fact he was the most handsome young man Blue had ever seen. He was wearing formal butler's uniform, but the trousers had been cut off into shorts, worn with ankle socks and soft, green, pointed shoes.

'Yes?' He didn't seem too pleased to see them.

Blue dragged her eyes away from his legs. 'I am Sluce Ragetus,' she told him boldly. 'This is Mr Kitterick. We're here to see Mr Chalkhill.'

She expected him to ask the nature of their business and had her story about the wrinkle cream all ready. But he only said, 'You can't come in.' He looked Kitterick up and down. 'He would clash with the furniture.'

Blue's jaw dropped as the door closed.

'Sluce *Ragetus*?' Kitterick exclaimed. 'No wonder he wouldn't let us in.'

Completely at a loss, Blue said, 'What are we going to do now?'

'May I suggest, Ser – Mr Sluce, that we walk around to the back? I understand from Madame Cardui that Mr Chalkhill owns some sort of swimming pool. He may be taking the waters or enjoying his enchanted sun.'

'You think they'll let us just ... go round to the back?'

'I see no one to stop us,' Kitterick said.

Which was surprisingly true. After her experience in Brimstone's rooms, Blue had expected tight security around Chalkhill's mansion, but so far there was really none at all. The butler who had refused them entry hardly constituted an armed guard.

A flower bed of foxgloves and bluebells sang softly to them as they walked around the side of the mansion. The path meandered through a heart-shaped grove and past a croquet green with luminous pink hoops. The swimming pool, when they reached it, was nothing short of breathtaking.

At first Blue thought it must be some sort of illusion spell, but as she looked closer, she realised this was actually exactly how the pool was built. Although she was no stranger to wealth, the extravagance astonished her. The pool had been cut from a single piece of amethyst, the largest she had ever seen, then rimmed in gold and filled with sparkling water driven by machinery that maintained its fizz.

Blue's eyes slid reluctantly away from the pool to take in the painted apparition reclining on a heavily cushioned lounger beside it. Although the creature was severely under-dressed, she could not decide for a moment whether it was a man or a woman. It was certainly plump and it was painted more extravagantly than Madame Cardui. The skimpy bathing costume was a mix of gold lamé and ostrich feathers.

'What on earth is that?' asked Blue underneath her breath.

'That,' said Kitterick, 'is Mr Chalkhill.'

They stepped back together, out of sight of the pool. 'What now?' Blue whispered.

'I believe,' said Kitterick, who never seemed at a loss in any circumstances, 'we might simply approach him openly. We appear, after all, to be honest merchants – travelling salespeople, if you will – with something to purvey. A certain … aggression is expected of us.'

'You don't think he'll find it suspicious that we've sneaked around the back?'

'That is precisely the point, Mr Sluce. We are not sneaking anywhere – we are approaching quite openly.'

'And then what?' Blue asked, irritated with herself at

how vulnerable she felt. She'd been more together tackling Brimstone's traps which were a thousand times more dangerous than this.

'Then,' said Kitterick patiently, 'we lay out our sales pitch, engage Mr Chalkhill in conversation and hope he – ' He stopped as a heavy hand fell on his shoulder.

The man was no giant, but he still towered over Kitterick. Blue had an impression of well-balanced features and a pockmarked skin. He was wearing the bottle-green uniform of a Security Guard Captain. There was a vicious-looking stun wand hanging from his belt. He glowered at them. 'What are you two doing sneaking round back here?' he asked.

Blue swallowed. 'Sluce Ragetus,' she said automatically. 'Here to see M-Mr Chalkhill. On business,' she added lamely.

Captain Pratellus's dark eyes bored through her, turned to Kitterick, then back again. 'Do you have an authorisation from Mr Chalkhill for your visit?'

'Well, no,' Blue said, 'but – '

'Do you have identification papers?'

'Well, actually – ' Blue began.

Kitterick turned and bit the hand on his shoulder.

'Is he dead?' Blue asked, staring down at the prostrate body.

Kitterick shook his head. 'No, but he will remain in a coma for several hours. And there will be a substantial headache when he wakes up. And tremors. Something of a limp. Blurred vision. Impaired hearing. A few facial tics. Some nausea, loss of appetite, occasional hallucinations, flatulence, a weakness in the back. The nerve damage will repair itself in a few years. Providing he rests, of course.'

'What are we going to do with him?'

'Perhaps you would be so kind as to help me drag him underneath those bushes. I doubt he will be missed for an hour or so. By which time we shall have finished our business with Mr Chalkhill. One way or another.'

Blue's heart was pounding as they stepped out on to the patio surrounding the pool. Chalkhill spotted them at once.

'Why, visitors!' he exclaimed. 'How unexpected. How intriguing.' He removed his sun-glasses and stared at Blue. 'A young man – how delightful.' His glance moved to Kitterick. 'And a small orange person.' He struggled from his lounger. 'I was just about to go inside. Will you join me? I find too much sun so *destructive* to the skin.' He hesitated, looking at Blue. 'Unless you'd *prefer* to stay out here?'

'No thank you,' Blue said quickly.

'Quite right,' said Chalkhill. He belted on a towelling dressing-gown. 'We shall go inside and Raul shall bring us iced tea with lots of sugar.' He smiled and his teeth sparkled and glinted. 'Then you can tell me who you are and why I have the pleasure of your company today.'

Blue glanced at Kitterick and found he was examining his fingernails. It looked as if she was on her own. They followed Chalkhill into a room dominated by a pink piano and several off-white singing chairs. 'Mr Chalkhill,' she said. 'I am Sluce Ragetus and this is Mr Kitterick. We represent Panjandrum Products, the well-known cosmetic manufacturers. The reason we are here is that our wizards have developed an astonishing new skin cream based on natural tachyons that generate a field capable of permanently reversing time.' She drew a deep breath and launched into her fake sales pitch.

Chalkhill sat entranced, twittering with delight and giving trills of pure excitement as she outlined the benefits of her imaginary cream. She had two sample jars, made mainly from suet, in case he asked to see the miracle, but he did not. 'This cream,' he said. 'It's not just for my face?'

'Oh, no,' Blue nodded brightly as Raul returned with a tray of iced tea. He set it down on a little table in front of Chalkhill and a strange look passed between them.

'Well,' said Chalkhill as Raul left again, 'aren't you the practised little liar.'

Blue blinked. 'I'm sorry?' But Chalkhill was changing before her eyes. He still looked the same man in his ludicrous bathing costume and fluffy white robe, but he seemed straighter somehow, taller, and his eyes had taken on a steely glint.

'You're not – what was it? Sluce Ragetus? You're not even a boy, however prettily you dress. Unless I'm very much mistaken, you are Her Serene Highness Holly Blue Iris, the Princess Royal, out on one of her famous slumming jaunts. Oh, don't look so surprised. I may not have recognised your reclusive brother, but it's well known that you like mixing with hoi polloi in various ridiculous disguises. Don't tell me you believed your subjects were too stupid to recognise you?' He rolled his eyes towards the ceiling and smiled broadly. 'My dear, in certain quarters you are positively a laughing stock.' The smile died abruptly as a Halek knife emerged from the folds of his robe. 'Tell your dwarf to sit still, Serenity. I'm perfectly well aware what it means to be bitten by a toxic trinian. Oh, and in case you feel I would hesitate to use this, let me tell you this is a *reinforced* blade. It cost me a king's ransom, but the Halek guarantee it *never* shatters. The ultimate weapon, you might say.'

Kitterick looked as if he might be prepared to risk it, but sat back warily at Blue's warning glance. 'Mr Chalkhill – ' she began.

'What now?' Chalkhill asked. 'Try to persuade me I'm mistaken? Oh, no, Serenity, this game is well and truly over. You know, it will be something of a relief to finish with this pose.'

'Pose?' Blue echoed.

'The fool with more money than sense. Here is a riddle for you, Princess Holly Blue: if a fool and his money are soon parted, how did he get it in the first place? You've seen my home. You'd have to be blind to believe it didn't cost. Where do you think I found it?' He stared at her, his eyes a piercing blue.

Blue decided to drop her pretence. 'I was told you poisoned your aunt,' she said coldly.

Chalkhill smiled and now his teeth no longer fizzed and sparkled. 'Ah, poor Matilda – she was like a mother to me. But then you should have seen my mother. Indeed I did poison my aunt – how word gets around – but that was not the source of my income. She only left me a small property. Everything else was provided by Lord Hairstreak.'

'Hairstreak!' Blue breathed. She felt a sudden chill crawl up her spine. 'Why would Black Hairstreak give you money?'

'Because,' Chalkhill said proudly, 'I'm something you could never be, despite your amateurish bunglings. I am Lord Hairstreak's most valued secret agent.'

It was Kitterick who broke the silence that followed. 'Past tense, surely, now you've told us.'

'I think not, trinian,' said Chalkhill. 'And I plan to tell you more.' He turned his attention back to Blue. 'You see, Serenity, I've always claimed a deep and lasting friendship with Lord Hairstreak. Of course nobody believed me. It was the perfect cover. People were always so busy laughing they never thought to suspect the truth.'

'A cover for what?' Blue asked contemptuously. 'Your interest in a glue factory?'

Chalkhill looked genuinely surprised. 'You of all people ask me that? I assume you're here because of your poor, dear, missing brother?'

After a long moment, Blue said, 'What do you know about Pyrgus?'

'What do I know? What do I know? Let's see ...' He glanced upwards as if lost in cheerful thought. 'I know he's next in line for the throne. I know that if anyone planned to overthrow the Purple Emperor and, let's say, replace him, it would make things tidier if the immediate heir was eliminated as well. I know – '

'You're planning to overthrow my father?'

'Not me, Your Serene Highness – Lord Hairstreak.'

She stared at him, unable to speak. It was all beginning to make a horrid sort of sense – the negotiations that had turned sour, the threat of war, Pyrgus's disappearance ...

But Chalkhill was talking again. 'You look surprised. I'm glad. You would not believe the care we took to hide what was really going on. Do you know, our first plan was to have my fool of a partner kill your brother? Dear old Brimstone, always playing with his demons. He thinks he controls them, but they've been leading him a merry dance for years – especially the ones in Lord Hairstreak's pay. Anyway, I arranged for some thugs to chase Prince Pyrgus down Seething Lane. Do you know the area by any chance?'

'Yes,' Blue said stonily, without bothering to explain.

'Then you'll know that when you reach the bottom, the only place to go is into the factory. Cunning, eh? I forced Pyrgus to trespass on our premises. He stole some glue kittens as well, but that was a bonus. Once he was in the factory, it was only a matter of time before our security people caught him and delivered him to me.'

'Is there a point to any of this?' Kitterick asked.

Chalkhill ignored him. 'I, in turn, delivered him to Brimstone. Lord Hairstreak had already primed one of his demon friends to ask for a human sacrifice. The idea was Brimstone would murder Pyrgus in one of his revolting rituals, then we – well, I really – would denounce Brimstone. What a show trial that would have been. It would have taken everybody's attention off what we were really up to.' He spread his hands sadly and sighed in a parody of his former self. 'But Brimstone messed it up. I'm afraid the old boy's well past his sell-by date. Some of your father's guards arrived on the scene and he panicked.'

Blue kept her face expressionless, but she was chill inside. She'd been the one who'd insisted the guards start looking for Pyrgus, but until now she'd had no idea how close a call it had been when he was rescued.

Typical of Pyrgus not to mention how much trouble he'd been in. She fought down her own surge of panic and said, 'So you sabotaged the portal and poisoned him?'

Chalkhill shrugged. 'I don't know about poison, but we certainly sabotaged the portal. What else could we do? And now he's out of the way, we can get on with the really important business of assassinating your father.'

'And you don't think we'll warn him?' Blue asked.

Chalkhill pushed himself to his feet and smiled. 'You disappoint me, my dear. I would have thought you'd have worked out by now that you're in no position to warn anybody. I shall kill your trinian at once, of course.' He shuddered. 'I loathe dwarves – they're so small. But I plan to keep you safe, Princess, at least for a while ...'

Blue flushed, but before she could reply, Kitterick said quietly, 'You won't get near me, even with a Halek knife.'

'You're probably right,' Chalkhill nodded. 'But as it happens, I don't plan to try.' He raised his voice. 'Now, Raul!' Five burly guards marched into the room, armed with flexible obsidian swords and stun wands. 'You may poison one of them, trinian, but the others will have your bowels on the floor before you have time to release your teeth.'

Blue glanced at Kitterick, then looked at Chalkhill. 'Have you ever heard Mr Kitterick whistle, Mr Chalkhill?' she asked casually.

Chalkhill blinked. 'Whistle?' He looked confused.

'Whistle for the nice men, Mr Kitterick,' Blue said.

Without bothering to purse his lips, Kitterick

emitted a piercing whistle. It seemed to emerge from the slot in his head. At once a stream of burly palace commandos smashed through the window while more descended on ropes in a shower of broken glass from the skylight. They were armed with stun grenades and lightweight rocket launchers.

'You didn't really think I'd come alone?' said Blue mildly.

Chalkhill dropped his knife. Despite the Halek guarantee, it smashed into a thousand pieces on the floor.

Twenty-eight

Henry gawped. Stupidly, he stood trying to figure out whether he'd heard a ripping noise or just imagined it because the fabric of reality had torn apart. Then he realised it didn't matter and tried to make sense of what he was seeing instead.

What he was seeing was an enormous hole in Mr Fogarty's shed. But it wasn't like a steam engine had driven through it or anything. Actually it was the edges that were peculiar. Around the edges of the enormous hole he could still see bits of the shed – pots, tools, shelves, the big lawnmower – but stretched and twisted as if they were melting. Everything had a shimmery quality, and never mind about the ripping noise, there was a high-pitched whining noise that somehow made you think everything was about to blow apart.

Henry hit the green button.

The hole closed instantly. No tearing noise, no noise of any sort for half a second. Then there was the clash and clatter of earthen plant pots smashing on the floor, shelves cascading their contents, tools toppling over. The whole shed creaked as if it were about to cave in. Henry ran for the door.

Once he was clear, he stood outside and watched the shed guiltily. How was he going to explain to Mr

Fogarty if the whole thing collapsed? For a moment it shimmered and shivered as if it would indeed collapse, but then things settled down again. He watched a little while longer, just to be sure, then decided everything was going to be all right. He wouldn't have to explain anything to Mr Fogarty. Except the breakages inside.

Henry pressed the red button again.

There was no ripping sound. That had just been his imagination. And what opened up outside caused far less damage than the enormous hole that appeared inside the shed. In fact it didn't cause any damage at all that he could see. He seemed to be looking down some sort of corridor, but the edges simply blended into the rest of the world without all that peculiar melting business. It was as if somebody had just built a corridor in Mr Fogarty's back garden. Sort of.

There was carpet on the floor of the corridor and expensive-looking crystal chandeliers at intervals along the ceiling. There were doors in the walls and other corridors branching off. There was another world in there! It had to be a portal! Even if this looked like nothing Pyrgus had described, it *had* to be a portal! He was looking at the world where Pyrgus lived!

Henry stepped into the corridor.

He swung round at once and was relieved to find he was looking into Mr Fogarty's back garden. The quality of the light seemed a little different now, but otherwise it was just as he'd left it. Nothing changed. Nothing broken. A single step and he'd be back again. So that was all right.

Except he couldn't very well leave the portal open. Mr Fogarty had gone to a lot of trouble with his codes and secret messages to hide this opening into Pyrgus's world.

And even though Mr Fogarty was a bit peculiar at the best of times, Henry could see the sense of keeping the portal thing quiet. If you left one open and somebody found it, the next thing you knew there'd be *tourist coaches* driving through and package holidays and things. Pyrgus would never forgive him. He had to close the portal.

Henry pressed the green button firmly. Mr Fogarty's back garden vanished and he was looking along a continuation of the corridor. He drew a deep breath and pressed the red button. To his immense relief, the portal opened up again. He closed it down and dropped the cube into his trouser pocket. Then, with a mounting sense of excitement, he set out to explore a whole new world.

He was inside some large, luxurious building. There were carpeted floors, well-finished walls, decorative mouldings, tapestries and paintings, ornamental statuary at junctions. Could this be Pyrgus's palace? It had all the trappings, but there was one thing that was really weird – it was empty.

At first Henry was quite relieved not to be bumping into people, but after a while he began to feel spooked. He wandered through empty corridors, opened doors to look into empty rooms. There was no sign of Pyrgus or Mr Fogarty, which mightn't be all that surprising since he'd no idea how long it was since they'd gone on ahead. But apart from them, there was no sign of anybody you'd expect to find in a palace. No servants, no footmen, no butlers, no courtiers, no sign of life at all.

It was as if everybody had been ... wiped out.

Henry opened yet another door and found himself staring into a linen cupboard. He closed the door, turned round and called, 'Hello...?' He waited.

Nothing. 'Hello ...? Hello ...? Is anybody there?' His voice didn't echo – there were too many carpets and curtains for that – but it managed to sound lonely all the same. Where *was* everybody? A palace this size should be teeming with people.

He wandered for another ten minutes before beginning to suspect he was going round in circles – there was a painting of a unicorn that looked terribly familiar. He still hadn't seen a living soul. He kept moving doggedly, but his unease continued to increase.

At the junction of two corridors, he thought he heard a distant voice. Henry stopped to listen. Nothing. He waited. Still nothing. Then he heard it again: not just one voice but several. And laughter.

Relief flooded over him like a wave. Until that moment he'd not realised how frightened he'd been in this huge empty palace. But now he knew there were people here, it was somehow all right. Was it Pyrgus? It was difficult to tell, but he thought the laughter sounded a little high-pitched for Pyrgus, certainly too high-pitched for Mr Fogarty. But whoever it was would help him. Especially when he told them he was a friend of Prince Pyrgus.

He started off in the direction of the sound.

Henry had never seen a naked girl before. She was standing near the edge of an enormous sunken bath at the junction of four corridors and surrounded by nothing more than pillars. She had auburn hair and large brown eyes and open features. Several other girls – mercifully clothed – were preparing her bath and tying back her hair. She was chatting to them with an easy familiarity.

Henry couldn't take his eyes off her body. He knew

he shouldn't look, but didn't know how to stop. Her body was so different from the way a boy's body was formed. He looked at her shoulders and her arms and her feet and could not breathe properly because of what he was looking at. His face was on fire with embarrassment and still he couldn't look away. His heart was pounding and his hands were shaking. He felt his legs begin to tremble.

The girl stepped down into the steaming waters of the sunken bath. She was much the same age as Henry himself, maybe a year younger. She was not particularly tall, but he thought she moved with grace. He thought she moved with *wonderful* grace. The water came up to her calves, then her knees, then her thighs, then she plunged and actually swam a stroke or two. She returned to the edge and lay back so that only her head was above the water.

Henry had no idea what to do. He wasn't a Peeping Tom. He knew it was unfair to the girl to look at her like this, knew he should turn and walk away (quietly, so she wouldn't know some ghastly pervy boy had seen her with her clothes off). That's what he knew he should do, but somehow his legs wouldn't work.

He had to do something. He couldn't stay standing here, looking and looking. It wasn't fair on her, whoever she was. He had to stop looking and go away.

Henry groaned.

One of the girls looked up and saw him.

'What do you make of it?' asked Apatura Iris, the Purple Emperor.

'Strictly speaking, Majesty,' Tithonus said, 'Her Serene Highness was within her rights to commandeer a contingent of palace commandos. As Princess Royal she is their Commander-in-Chief. Purely an honorary title, of course, but – '

The Purple Emperor waved a dismissive hand. 'I'm not talking about the commandos,' he said. 'To be honest, if she must make these ridiculous jaunts, I'd rather she had protection. I was wondering what you thought about the story she brought back.'

'The alleged assassination attempt?'

'Alleged? You don't think it's true then?'

Tithonus sighed. 'I don't think Jasper Chalkhill is the most reliable of sources.'

'He made the claims of his own accord,' Apatura said. 'Unless you disbelieve my daughter.'

'Oh, I believe Princess Blue, sire,' Tithonus said. 'She may be a little fanciful, but she was never a liar. Besides, we have corroboration from the trinian. It's Chalkhill I'm less sure about.'

'You don't think he's one of Hairstreak's agents?'

'Actually I do,' Tithonus said. 'Our espionage people have had their suspicions about him for some time now. Nothing they could prove, but – ' He shrugged, then went on, 'It's just that this whole idea of replacing you as Emperor …' He spread his hands helplessly and shook his head.

'But we know there was an attempt on Pyrgus's life. And it may yet be successful – we still haven't found him.'

'That's true, Majesty, but that's also a weakness in the story Chalkhill told Blue. As I understand it, he claimed the reason Lord Hairstreak wanted Pyrgus killed was so there would be no legal claimant to the throne after your supposed assassination. But there are two further claimants to the throne should you and

Pyrgus both be killed.'

The Purple Emperor looked at him thoughtfully. 'Comma and Blue.'

'Exactly, sire – Prince Comma, then Princess Blue. The moment Pyrgus should die, Comma becomes Crown Prince. The moment you should die, the Crown Prince becomes Emperor. If Lord Hairstreak really wished to clear a road to the throne, he would have had to assassinate Comma and Blue along with Pyrgus and yourself. There has been no indication of that happening and nothing in Chalkhill's story to suggest it was planned. I'm frankly suspicious the whole thing may be a fabrication.'

'For what purpose?'

Tithonus shrugged again. 'Possibly to sow confusion – these are troubled times. Or possibly the whole thing is a fantasy of Chalkhill's to make himself appear important. He may be one of Hairstreak's agents, but he is still a very unstable character.'

'So you don't believe any additional security measures are required?'

'Not at this time,' Tithonus said. 'At least not until Chalkhill has been properly interrogated. Which is something that has already begun, of course. We will find out the truth quickly enough.'

They were together in the Emperor's quarters, protected as always by the silence spell. Apatura walked to the window and looked out thoughtfully. After a while he turned back and said, 'I think you may be right, Gatekeeper. Additional security precautions at this time might be interpreted as a sign of weakness. You were correct not to put them in place when my daughter urged it and I agree it may be better to take no further action in this area unless something else emerges from Chalkhill's interrogation.'

'Thank you, Your Majesty,' Tithonus said. 'Now, perhaps if you'll excuse – '

He was interrupted by a loud knock on the door.

'I gave orders we were not to be disturbed.' The Emperor's voice betrayed his irritation.

'It may be news of Pyrgus,' Tithonus said. He unlocked the door and opened it.

Mr Fogarty pushed past him rudely. His eyes were glazed and he was carrying his pump-action shotgun.

The guards were rough, but not brutal. They marched Henry down flights of stairs and locked him in a room that seemed to be used as a temporary store. After a moment he righted a wooden chair and sat down, staring miserably at the door. He felt deeply ashamed; and not just for getting caught. He'd done a dreadful thing and he didn't know how to undo it.

He didn't feel guilty about coming across her. That had been completely innocent – he'd just gone in the direction of the laughter. He wasn't to know it was a girl having a bath. And what was she doing having a bath right there in the open anyway? When you had a bath, you went into the bathroom and closed the door.

All the same, when he *did* see her, he should have turned away. He should have turned away at once, not just stood there and stared. The thing was, it wasn't fair. Charlie once said, *How would you like it if some of the girls were looking at you and giggling when you were in the showers?* Henry wasn't sure, but he didn't think he would like it; certainly he wouldn't like the giggling and he wouldn't like it at all if he had spots.

He hadn't noticed any spots on the auburn-haired girl he'd stared at.

The trouble was he could still see her in his mind's eye. And that made it worse somehow. It was as if he'd taken photographs and was sneakily looking at them now. The girl would have hated it if he'd really taken photographs, but what was the difference?

To distract himself, he got up and wandered around the room. It wasn't very large and there was a lot of stuff in it, bric-à-brac and packing cases pushed against one wall. There was a small window high up. He wondered what was outside, through the window.

It wasn't that he wanted to escape or anything, but he did want to see what was outside. He pulled a case over to the wall and found a stool which he put on top. He shook the stool and it seemed stable, so he climbed on to the case and on to the stool to look out through the window. He couldn't see much except a sweep of well-kept lawn so he clung to the windowsill and pushed himself up on tiptoes.

'What do you think you're doing?' asked a voice behind him.

Henry stopped himself from falling, but only just. He turned awkwardly, fighting to keep his balance. A girl had entered the room. For a fraction of a second, Henry didn't recognise her, then he realised it was the girl he'd seen in the bath. She was dressed now, which was a huge relief. All the same Henry felt himself flush crimson.

'Come down!' she told him sharply. 'Come down at once!'

Henry climbed down slowly from the stool, wishing he were dead.

twenty-nine

Pyrgus felt the last remnants of the demon's influence fall from his mind and a fierce, dark anger flared inside him. How dare this creature talk so calmly about killing an emperor? How dare he threaten the Realm of Faerie? Pyrgus wanted to hurl himself upon Beleth and strangle the demon with his bare hands. Instead, he examined his cage for some possibility of escape.

The thing was designed like the cage that held the cat and her kittens in the glue factory, except larger. But not so large that Pyrgus could stand upright. He crouched behind the bars, glaring down on a frightening, hellish scene.

His cage was suspended from a chain attached to a mechanism in the roof of a cavern underneath Beleth's metal mansion. Directly below a pool of molten brimstone cast a red glow. Some thirty or more of Beleth's followers were working in the cavern, their skins scaled and armoured against the heat, their bodies muscular and bloated to allow them to handle the hot metal they were crafting into a monstrous missile beside the pool. Beleth himself had reverted to the fearsome form he had used to appear in Brimstone's Triangle of Art. A lantern hung from one huge curling horn.

Beyond the toiling demons was a levelled platform

on which contingents of miniature troops were drawing up in battle order. The technology here was very different from that of the Emperor's Situation Room. Triangulated projectors replaced the crystal globes so that the armoured demons Pyrgus had seen outside the city were re-created little more than eighteen inches tall across the platform surface. At first glance they looked like a toy army, but once you watched for more than a moment you lost the scale and found yourself drawn into the midst of the action even more effectively than any globe.

'Aggression!' Beleth growled admiringly.

The troops were grouping for manoeuvres. They had separated out into two broadly equal factions and as Pyrgus watched they hurled themselves upon each other. Light wands sparked and hissed. Balls of flame rolled viciously across the battlefield. Missiles exploded everywhere. But Beleth's troops seemed indestructible. They walked unscathed through gouts of flame, explosions, shimmering razor fields, somehow surviving to press their attack with mind-numbing savagery. These were the creatures who would soon be joining Hairstreak to oppose the forces of the Purple Emperor. Pyrgus's father didn't stand a chance.

'The reality will be entertaining,' Beleth said. 'But enough of this small amusement – I want to tell you now how you will die.' The ground shook as he walked towards a metal lever set beside the brimstone pool. He looked up at Pyrgus, now almost directly overhead, and smiled. 'Isn't real machinery fascinating? I mean, all these magical trapped-lightning devices are impressive, but you can't really beat the good old-fashioned cogs and gears and levers stuff. That's machinery you

can *understand*. I love it, Crown Prince. So satisfying.'
He reached out and fondled the end of the lever.

It was uncomfortable in Pyrgus's cage. Crouched as
he was, the muscles of his legs were beginning to
protest and would probably soon spasm painfully. His
headache was back, more vicious than before. Just two
more little problems in what had been a really lousy
day. He wished he could think of something cool to say
to Beleth, but nothing came to mind. Not that it mattered, since Beleth was still talking.

'You will die very slowly,' Beleth said. 'Very slowly
and very, very painfully. This lever operates the
machinery above your head. Once I pull it, the machinery feeds out the chain and your cage will begin to
lower. It's set to work extremely slowly. I doubt you'll
even notice the movement, but take my word for it,
you will be moving. Downwards.'

Pyrgus looked down. Below him the brimstone pool
seethed and bubbled.

'In time,' said Beleth, 'in such a long, long time, life
will grow uncomfortable for you. In time you will find
yourself coughing from the brimstone fumes. In time
you will find yourself sweating from the heat. In time
the stench of sulphur will fill your nostrils and your
eyes will begin to stream.'

'Now look here, Beleth – ' Pyrgus said.

But Beleth was not to be interrupted. He giggled.
'And it can only get worse. The temperature will rise as
you approach the brimstone pool. You will become
thirsty as your body fluids evaporate. Your skin will
prickle, then begin to blister. All so slowly, so very, very
slowly, allowing you to appreciate every second of the
exquisite, steadily increasing pain. No, please don't

interrupt – we're getting to the best bit. Eventually, after many, many hours of drawn-out torture, you will reach the brimstone pool itself. Slowly, oh so slowly, your cage will descend into the molten sulphur. It will begin to burn away your feet, starting with the soles. Then, as the cage sinks deeper, it will burn away your ankles and your legs up to your knees. Brimstone cauterises blood flow, so you will remain alive and conscious as your body is gradually burned away a fraction of an inch at a time. Your head and brain will be the last to go so you may even enjoy the supreme horror of watching the molten brimstone creeping up towards your neck before you lose consciousness for ever.' He gave a deep, throaty chuckle and stroked the metal casing of the enormous missile his demons were constructing beside the pool. 'The last thing you will ever see will be my Doomsday Bomb.'

'Doomsday Bomb?' Pyrgus echoed despite himself.

'The weapon that will allow me to take over your father's kingdom,' Beleth grinned. 'The destructive power of a small sun is contained within this metal canister. I will launch it from one of my vimanas – what your human friends quaintly call flying saucers. It will kill a million of your father's soldiers, give or take a dozen. Such a saving in manpower. It will destroy your palaces and raze your entire capital in a single burst of deadly light. You will die looking at it, knowing it will soon wipe out your family and your friends.'

'Why are you doing this?' demanded Pyrgus. 'I can understand why you might want to kill me, but why the long, slow torture?'

Beleth smiled delightedly. 'It is my nature.' His fingers curled around the lever. 'Oh, I do like this bit!' he exclaimed. 'It gives me such a thrill!' He pulled the lever.

The sweating demons stopped their work momentarily and turned to look up at Pyrgus's cage. There was a grinding of machinery and Pyrgus felt the cage jerk slightly before it settled, swinging slightly.

'Doesn't feel as if it's moving, does it?' Beleth called. 'But it is, take my word for it. You are on your final journey and it will take a long, long time. I shall leave you soon to enjoy your trip, but before I go I want to give you a little mental anguish to accompany your physical pain. I want to tell you how your father was betrayed and how he will be killed. I want to tell you what will happen to the Peacock Throne and the fate of your dear little sister. I want to tell you about the treachery and treason and the utter, total, absolute destruction of House Iris. I want to tell you about our plans to pillage the Realm of Faerie. I want – '

In his cage, Pyrgus experienced another stab of his peculiar headache. It felt as if there was pressure building up inside his skull. It made him nauseous and for one glorious moment he thought he might be able to throw up all over Beleth. But then the nausea died down and he was just left with the headache and the pressure in his skull. He put it down to nerves and tried hard to ignore it.

Below him, Beleth droned on happily.

'But Serenity – ' the guard protested.

'Just go,' said Holly Blue imperiously. 'I shall be perfectly all right.'

The guard looked at her uncertainly, then turned and marched from the chamber. His companions followed in smart order. Blue swung her gaze to the boy who'd sneaked behind a pillar to get a glimpse of her in the bath. He was a pleasant-looking creature in most peculiar clothes, but he certainly didn't look as if he had the courage to risk the sort of punishment meted out for that type of behaviour. 'Well,' she said coldly, 'are you going to explain yourself?'

'I'm sorry,' Henry told her miserably. They were no longer in the storeroom. The guards had marched him to opulent living quarters where the girl seemed entirely at home. And in charge.

'Sorry you did it or sorry you were caught?'

'Sorry I did it,' Henry said. 'I didn't mean to.' The guards had called her 'Highness' and 'Serenity'. That probably meant she was some sort of royal, maybe even a princess. He almost shuddered at the thought before another, even more awful thought caught up with it: she might be related to Pyrgus. Hadn't Pyrgus said he had a sister? Henry couldn't remember, but the idea was terrifying. If this was Pyrgus's sister, how could Henry ever look his friend in the eye again? Bad enough to peep at a strange girl, but to peep at your friend's *sister* … He made a massive effort to pull himself together. 'I was just looking for somebody and I sort of came on you by accident.'

'Who were you looking for?'

'Well, anybody really,' Henry said uncomfortably. 'The whole place was so *empty*.' He rallied and added, 'It's not as if you were, you know, in a private *bathroom*. I mean, you were right out in the open with – without – right out in the open,' he tailed off lamely. '*Anybody* could have seen you. I was just unlucky.' He realised what he'd said and added hurriedly, 'I mean not unlucky to have *seen* you that way. I mean you're very pretty, beautiful and all that, no spots or anything, but unlucky to have *come across* you when you didn't want to be come across. Although if you didn't want to be come across, I don't think you should take your bath out in the open like that.'

'Oh, so it was really *my* fault?' Blue asked icily. 'I'm the one to blame?'

'No, you're not the one to blame. I didn't say you were to blame. I just meant that if you'd taken your bath in a proper bathroom, I wouldn't have accidentally come across you. Anybody could have seen you.'

'Hardly. I ordered this wing of the palace cleared. I always do when I take a bath.'

Henry groaned inwardly. *That* was why the place had been deserted. The princess was taking a bath. Everyone had orders to keep well away. And he'd casually strolled in on her. He closed his eyes to shut out the embarrassment of it all. When he opened them again, he said, 'Are you Pyrgus's sister?'

Blue froze. Silent moments ticked by, then she said, 'What do you know about Pyrgus? Where have you come from? Who are you?'

'Henry Atherton,' said Henry. And told her everything.

Frowning, Blue walked to the window. 'Pyrgus is probably still all right. I've been trying not to think about it. I've carried an antidote to his poison ever since I heard about it, but there's nothing we can do until we find him.'

'I'm sorry,' Henry said. 'I don't know what's happened to Pyrgus – nobody's told me. I mean you're the first person I've talked to. Don't you know where he is? Didn't he come back to the palace?'

'He's disappeared,' said Blue shortly. 'And if we don't find him soon, the poison will kill him. It's all a bit complicated – '

He thought she might be about to say something else, but the door slammed open and an hysterical servant girl burst in. 'Mistress Blue – you must come at once! Something dreadful's happened!'

'What is it, Anna? What's happened?'

But the girl was beyond rational speech. She began to wail and rock and moan, hugging herself and weeping just inside the doorway. 'It's His Majesty, His Majesty!'

'Come on!' Blue grabbed Henry's hand and headed for the door.

They ran.

There were guards everywhere, shouting orders and getting in each other's way. One tried to stop them as they entered a corridor.

'Stand aside!' hissed Blue furiously. The guard did what he was told.

It was chaos in the corridor. 'Where are we going?' Henry asked breathlessly.

'My father's private quarters.'

There were people milling everywhere as they approached the open door. A tall man in a green cloak swept towards them. 'Serenity, you must not go in.'

'What's happened, Tithonus?' Blue demanded.

'There has been an incident involving your father.'

'What sort of accident?'

Tithonus didn't say *accident*, Henry thought.

Tithonus swallowed. 'Your father has been gravely

injured, Princess. *Very* gravely injured.'

Her father was dead. It was clear as day to Henry. The adults always tried to break it to you gently, which just made things worse.

'What happened?' Holly Blue demanded.

'An intruder. He had a weapon – '

'What has happened to my father?' Blue screamed. She tried to push past, but Tithonus blocked the way.

Tithonus seemed distressed. 'Serenity, there was nothing I could do. It all happened so quickly.' He caught sight of Henry. 'Who is this boy?'

Holly Blue stared up at Tithonus, a dawning look of horror on her face. 'Is he …? Is he going to die?'

Tithonus shut his eyes briefly. 'Serenity,' he said formally, 'it is my tragic duty to tell you that your father, the Purple Emperor, is dead.'

For a moment Blue said nothing. Then she said, 'I don't believe you. I want to see him. Is he inside?'

'Serenity, it is best you don't see him. The weapon – ' Blue tried to push past again. Again Tithonus moved to stop her. 'Child,' he said, 'the weapon is not like our weapons and it was discharged at close range. Your father's face – '

A boy in purple garments emerged from the room behind Tithonus. He was pale and looked as if he might be sick at any moment.

'Comma!' Blue shouted. 'What is it? What – ?'

The boy looked at her blankly, then shook his head. He seemed in a daze. 'I'm sorry, Blue,' he said.

'Tithonus,' Blue said. 'I will see my father!'

Something in her tone persuaded him to step aside. 'As you wish, Serenity. But it would be better – '

She was already pushing past him. Without a

moment's hesitation, Henry followed.

He had an impression of a large, well-furnished chamber before his attention was locked on the body. Much of the face had been blown away, as if by a close shotgun blast. The smell of blood was overwhelming. A red pool had formed on the carpet.

'Daddy, no!' Blue wailed. She took a step forward. 'Daddy, Daddy, nooooo!'

Henry caught her as she fainted.

Thirty

A plump, middle-aged woman in servant's uniform ushered Henry away. 'She'll be all right, poor thing – there's doctors to look after her. But such a shock ...' She pursed her lips briefly, eyes glazing with grief, then turned her attention back to Henry. 'Now, young sir, I haven't seen you before so I don't know your name.'

'It's Henry,' Henry said dully. He was shocked himself by what had happened. It was the first time he'd seen a dead body and the damage to the face was like something out of a horror movie. Except in a horror movie you didn't get the smell.

'Oh, like the Duke of Burgundy,' the woman said. She managed a small, conspiratorial smile. 'Only I don't suppose you're with the Nightside, are you?'

'No,' Henry said quickly, although he hadn't the least idea what she was talking about.

'I'm Goodwife Umber,' the woman said. 'You'll be staying at the palace, Master Henry?'

Things had suddenly got a lot more complicated than he'd bargained for. He took a deep breath and said, 'I suppose so.'

'I'll show you to a guest room. I'm glad you're staying. She'll need her friends around her at a time like this.'

The guest room was sumptuous, miles better than his room at home, although there didn't seem to be a bed.

'Sorry if it isn't what you're used to,' Goodwife Umber said anxiously. She looked Henry up and down. 'You'll be from country parts then?'

Henry nodded. He thought it best not to get into where he was really from.

'Well, you'll find fresh clothes in the wardrobe a bit more suited to the palace – just scrabble round until you get your size and if you have any problems call me. Underwear in the drawers.' She gave him a motherly grin and closed the door behind her as she left.

Henry quickly discovered the reason there was no bed in his room was that it wasn't a room but a suite. There was a bedroom off the main room and a bathroom off that with a sunken bath in the middle of the floor that was a miniature (but a large miniature) of the one where he'd seen Blue. There were earthenware jars around the edge and on investigation he found them full of scented oils. He went back to the bedroom and discovered the wardrobe Goodwife Umber had mentioned. It was, as promised, packed with clothing in a range of sizes. He picked out a green jerkin and some breeches that fitted well enough and found some soft green shoes to go with them. When he examined himself in the wardrobe mirror he had the creepy feeling he looked a bit like Pyrgus, even though the outfit was nothing like the clothes Pyrgus wore. Maybe it just meant he would fit in here, which was no bad thing.

He pushed open another door in the bedroom, vaguely imagining it might be a second built-in wardrobe, and discovered it was a little windowless study, which lighted itself mysteriously when the door opened. There was a desk and a chair and walls lined with books. It occurred to him he might learn a lot about Pyrgus's world from those books if he took the time. But he would probably learn a lot more if he explored the palace.

Henry went back to the main living room, opened the door into the corridor and looked out.

'Ah, there you are,' said Goodwife Umber, making Henry jump out of his skin. She seemed to have been standing in the corridor waiting for him. 'You'll be wanting something to eat now, I'll be bound. If you follow me, I'll get you something in the kitchens.' She looked at him approvingly as he emerged. 'Green suits you.'

'Thank you,' Henry said. The palace kitchens would be as good a place to start as any. Besides, against all odds, he was feeling peckish.

The heat of the kitchens, generated by two huge cooking ranges, met him like a wall. As he stepped inside, he had the feeling of walking into a period movie, something from Dickens or even earlier. Everything had an old-fashioned look, from the scrubbed pine tables to the haunches of meat hanging from hooks in the ceiling. He imagined the place would be a hive of activity at mealtimes. Even now there were twenty or thirty people lounging about chatting and drinking cups of something while they waited for the rush to start.

Goodwife Umber led him over to a fat woman in a cook's uniform cutting vegetables into an enormous pot. 'This is Head Cook Lattice Brown,' she whispered.

'You be nice to her or else she'll poison you.' She grinned to show she was joking, then said loudly, 'Any chance of something to eat for a starving boy, Lattice? Friend of Princess Blue.'

Lattice set down the knife and wiped her hands on a cloth. Every move was made with great deliberation. She looked at Henry from underneath her eyebrows. 'Friend of Princess Blue, is it? And does this friend have a name?'

Henry opened his mouth to answer, but Goodwife Umber beat him to it. 'He's called Henry, Lattice. Named for the Duke of Burgundy, but loyal Lighter not a Nighter, eh?'

'Duke of Burgundy's not called Henry,' Lattice said.

Goodwife Umber frowned. 'Yes he is. Henry Lucina.'

'No he isn't. It's Hamearis. You're not called Hamearis, are you?' The question was directed at Henry.

Henry shook his head. 'No, Ma'am – Henry.'

Lattice Brown grinned delightedly. 'Hear that, Goodie Lanta? Ma'am! What a nice polite young man. You just leave him here with me and I'll see he's well fed. Expect there might be a couple of kitchen maids'll want to keep him company as well, handsome lad like that.' She winked at Henry, who blushed.

Minutes later he was sitting at one of the pine tables spooning stew from a bowl, with a thick wedge of crusty bread on a plate beside it – 'for dipping,' Cook Lattice said. To his relief, no kitchen maids had joined him and, after a few curious stares, the rest of the staff quickly settled back to what they had been doing, which was mainly gossiping. Henry kept his head down and listened. Predictably, the main topic was the Emperor's murder.

'Head completely gone – '

'What, all of it?'

'So Bert told me and he's a guard. Just the stump of a neck left, but no blood. Gatekeeper reckons it was a slicer beam – only thing that cauterises as it cuts.'

'Not what I heard at all. Head wasn't cut off, just sort of bashed in. Some sort of new Nighter weapon.'

'Aye, it'll be the Nighters all right, ruddy trouble the whole bunch of them.'

'Wasn't Nighters. You know it wasn't Nighters.'

'Who's running the realm, that's what I want to know. Emperor gone, Crown Prince missing ...'

'Could be the end of House Iris.' This was from a gloomy old boy staring into a pottery goblet. Two women and Cook Lattice rounded on him.

'Want to watch your mouth, Luigi.'

'It's House Iris pays your wages. Ours too.'

'There's Prince Comma – '

'Little weasel!'

'Mind your manners, girl.' This from Lattice. 'Even if he is a little weasel, he's still the Emperor's son.'

'Aye, and if you had a mother like that – '

'Shhh!' Cook Lattice looked around as if worried about being overheard.

'Why should I shush? Everybody knows the truth. No wonder poor little Comma is the way he is – blood will out, I always say.'

A woman Henry gathered was called Nell said, 'They can't make him Emperor anyway – he's too young.'

'Prince Pyrgus will turn up,' said Lattice confidently.

'But if he don't, it'll be Comma. The Gatekeeper will be his regent until he's of age. That's the way they do it. But Pyrgus will turn up, mark my words.'

'What's happened to Prince Pyrgus?' Henry asked. He'd been a bit worried about attracting any more attention to himself, but if he was to find anything out he had to ask questions.

'Nobody knows,' Lattice said. 'Sent him off through one of those silly portals and he never came back. Or if he did come back, they don't know where he's got to. Never held with them myself. Wouldn't find me trotting off to some weird world full of idiots and giants and dandruff. People there have six fingers and bright blue skin, did you know that?'

'No,' Henry said.

'Larry told me,' Cook Lattice said, without explaining who Larry was.

Nell said, 'The one who killed the Emperor didn't have blue skin.' Her face took on a smug expression. 'My Tom told me that and he was there.'

'He was there, why didn't he stop him doing it?' Luigi asked sourly.

'Well, he wasn't there when it *happened*,' Nell said. 'No guards at all there when it happened. But Tom was the first in afterwards. One of the first anyway. Said the old man looked just like you or me. Five fingers, ordinary skin, no dandruff. Bald, though.'

Henry felt a sudden tightness in his chest. 'You mean it was somebody from – ' what on earth had Pyrgus called it? ' – from the Analogue World who killed the Emperor?'

'Didn't you know? Old boy called Mist, Misty something like that. Emperor went to the other world to find Prince Pyrgus and brought back this old boy with him for some reason. Cook Lattice's right – nothing good ever came out of the other world. Be safer with demons, you ask me.'

'It wasn't Mist, it was Fog; well, Fogary actually,' Luigi said. 'Had some wicked weapon with him. You wonder what they were thinking of, letting him bring it through.'

'Far too trusting, the Emperor. Far too soft-hearted.'

'Won't be trusting anybody now, God rest him.'

'God rest him!' everybody chorused, then fell silent.

After a moment, Henry said tightly, 'Fogary or Fogarty?'

'That's right,' said Luigi. 'Fogarty. The one who killed the Emperor. His name was Fogarty. They're holding him in the palace dungeons.'

'Where are these dungeons exactly?' Henry asked innocently.

The last time Henry had felt this scared was when Mr Fogarty had sent him off to rob his school. Except now was even worse. His heart was pounding so badly it sounded like a military drum. His legs felt weak and he couldn't seem to take deep enough breaths. He forced himself to walk down the steep steps to the palace dungeons.

It was a surprise when he reached the bottom. He'd been expecting something old-fashioned, like the kitchens – dark, stone-lined cells with fettered prisoners and moisture running down the walls. But the reality was something else. The stairs ended in a bright reception area that even had a pale blue carpet. He could see some cell doors off the corridor beyond, one of which lay open. The empty cell had bunk beds, a desk and chairs, much like the modern prisons he'd seen in police series on TV.

A burly guard got up from a desk and moved over to the counter to greet him. 'Something I can do for you?' he asked.

Henry uttered a silent prayer and drew a breath that still wasn't deep enough. 'Do you have a prisoner here called Fogarty?'

'What if we have?'

I will not be intimidated, Henry thought. The man wasn't really suspicious – it was just his manner. You had to be a bit peculiar if you were a prison guard. For Henry, the trick was to appear confident. 'A prisoner from the Analogue World? The man accu – the man who killed His Majesty the Emperor?'

The guard looked him up and down, but the confident tone seemed to be working. 'Matter of fact we do. You a relative or something?' Henry's heart skipped a beat before the guard suddenly guffawed. 'Relative, eh? Come to see your dear old grandad, what?'

Henry smiled back weakly. 'No, but I *have* come to speak to the prisoner.' This was the tricky bit. 'Orders of Princess Holly Blue.'

'Got a chitty?' asked the guard.

Henry stared at him. 'No,' he said eventually. A woolly brown rug thrown carelessly to one end of the counter moved suddenly, making him jump.

'Can't let you near a prisoner without a chitty,' the guard said. 'Not if you come from the Emperor himself, God rest him.'

Henry decided to try for sympathy. 'Look, I'm new round here. Nobody told me I'd need a chitty.

Can't you make an exception?'

'More than my job's worth,' the guard said reasonably. 'Why don't you just go back and get one from the Princess?'

Good question. He could see the woolly rug out of the corner of his eye and it seemed to be creeping along the counter towards him. 'Thing is,' he said to the guard, 'Princess Blue is indisposed at the moment – the shock. She saw her father and ... well, you can understand. So she can't really be disturbed. You can check that if you like.' He swung his head suddenly to look directly at the rug and it stopped moving. Two beady brown eyes peered up at him out of the shaggy surface.

The guard looked at him, chewing his lower lip. 'Not supposed to let you in without a chitty,' he said uncertainly.

'Yes, I understand that,' Henry said. 'But perhaps there's a form I could sign taking responsibility, then later I could bring you the chitty when Princess Blue is feeling a little better. It really is rather urgent.' The rug thing with the brown eyes slid off the counter and on to the floor. Henry found himself glancing towards it uneasily as it edged towards him. The guard paid it no attention at all.

'Maybe if you could tell me what it's all about ...?' the guard said thoughtfully. 'I mean, I'd like to help the Princess, but at the same time – ' He pursed his lips and shrugged.

At least he'd been expecting this. 'The Princess wishes to find the reason why this man murdered her father. In case there are further plots.'

'Bit young to be questioning a prisoner about stuff like that, aren't you?'

He'd been expecting that one too. 'The Princess thought he might be less on his guard with somebody my age.' He waited, having learned it was always a bad thing to say too much when you were chancing your arm. The woolly-rug creature – it had to be some sort of animal – had reached his feet now and was sniffing round his ankles.

The guard leaned over the counter and looked down at the rug. 'What do you think?' he asked.

'Pack of lies,' the endolg said. 'Kid wouldn't know the truth if it bit him in the backside.'

Henry struggled furiously, but the guards were well used to dealing with difficult prisoners and kept clear of his flailing feet. They half dragged, half carried him along the corridor, then held him firm while one unlocked a cell door at the end.

'Don't know why you're making such a fuss,' one said. 'You wanted to see the old coot who murdered our Emperor. Now you're getting the chance.'

They threw him bodily into the cell and slammed the door. Henry picked himself up and hurled himself forward, but the key turned before he could reach it. 'Save your strength,' a familiar voice advised.

Henry swung round. Mr Fogarty was sitting on the top bunk, feet dangling. 'Scrotes know how to make a lock. I've been trying to pick that one since they threw me in here.' He slid down off the bed. 'Didn't expect to see you, Henry.' He sniffed and looked him up and down. 'Specially dressed up like a leprechaun.'

'Mr Fogarty, what happened? What's – '

Fogarty placed his finger to his lips. 'Nice weather for the time of year,' he said. He went over to the bunks and pulled a pad and pencil from underneath the mattress. He wrote something and passed the pad to Henry.

This place may be bugged, it said. *Best write down anything important. We can eat the paper afterwards. Meanwhile make small talk.*

Henry groaned inwardly, but took the pencil. He thought for a moment, then wrote: *What happened to Pyrgus?*

'What have they locked you up for?' Fogarty asked loudly. He took the pencil and wrote, *Little scrat used my portal before I tested it.*

'Some sort of rug testified against me,' Henry said. He took the pad back and got to the heart of the matter: *Why did you kill the Emperor?*

Not sure I did really.

'Not sure?' Henry exploded. 'You're in here for murder and you're not sure you did it – ?'

'Quiet!' Fogarty hissed. He looked around in alarm and thrust the pad back at Henry.

'I'm not writing it down,' said Henry furiously. 'This is too important. I need to know what's going on. You can't do it with notes.' By the sound of things it would be touch and go whether you could do it with a full-length novel.

'All right,' said Fogarty. 'But keep your voice down. If we sit side by side on the bed, we can whisper.' He sat and motioned Henry to the space beside him.

Henry groaned aloud this time, but sat down obediently. Anything was better than passing notes. 'Did you kill the Emperor?' he asked bluntly but quietly.

'No,' said Fogarty in a whisper.

'You didn't shoot him with your shotgun?'

'No.'

'Who did then?'

'A demon,' Fogarty said.

Henry felt like strangling him. The last thing he needed right now was to have to listen to the old boy's batty beliefs. 'Mr Fogarty,' he said patiently, 'there are no such things as – '

But Fogarty cut in with an urgent whisper. 'Listen, Henry, I know you think I'm off the wall, but you'd better get it into that thick head of yours that there are more things in the big wide world than they tell you at school. Didn't believe in fairies, did you, until you caught one in a jamjar? Didn't believe you could open up a hole in space and step into a whole different universe, did you? So where do you think you are now – Blackpool? Know what I was before I took to robbing banks?'

Henry looked at him blankly. After a moment he shook his head. 'No.'

'Particle physicist,' said Fogarty. 'And a damn good one. Think that makes me stupid?'

Henry shook his head again, more urgently this time. 'No, but – '

'Know why I stopped being a particle physicist?'

'No, but – '

'Because they paid me seven grand a year. Seven *grand*! Even in those days that was peanuts. Could make more selling soapflakes and you don't need a degree for that, let alone a doctorate.'

Henry stared at him in astonishment. 'You're a doctor of physics?' he asked incredulously.

But Fogarty was in full swing. 'So I did what any sensible man would do and took up bank robbery. But

I never forgot my physics. There are lots of alternative realities – even that old fool Einstein knew it. And one of them's the reality people used to call Hell. Place is full of demons and their UFOs. Pyrgus is stuck there now, poor little sprog.'

Henry had been about to say something else, but now he said, 'Pyrgus is in Hell?'

'Keep your voice down,' Fogarty hissed. 'Yes, Pyrgus is in Hell.'

'How do you know? How could you know that?'

'Got it from the demon,' Fogarty said.

This was crazier and crazier. Yet there was something about Mr Fogarty's absolute certainty that was getting to Henry. All he could do was echo, 'Demon?'

'Listen,' said Fogarty in a whisper. 'Just button your lip, open your mind and *listen*! Demons, UFO aliens, all the same thing. Old days they called them demons, now they're aliens, but they're still up to their old tricks. Don't know how he got there, but I do know Pyrgus is in the alien world. Right now. You want to be old-fashioned about it, he's in Hell. I know because there's a demon in the palace. Didn't know that, did you? Neither does anybody else.'

'How do *you* know?' Henry asked suspiciously.

'Because it took me over. Demons are good at taking over people,' Fogarty said. 'They've been doing it for years. Read the UFO reports. You're diddling about minding your own business when your car stops, the flying saucer lands and a little scrat with a big head has grabbed you by the ear. Next thing you know you're so confused you don't know where you are. That's the way demons do it. Look them in the eye and you're finished. They shove your brain to one side and take control of your body. A good one can tell you what to think.'

'What happened?' Henry asked, drawn in despite his better judgment.

Fogarty said sourly, 'I wasn't expecting it, you see. Came through the wall and next thing was I was looking it straight in the eye. Battle of wills after that. It walked me all the way to the Emperor's quarters. There was no security at all for some reason. All the time it was inside my head, telling me I had to kill the Emperor. No problem there – I had my shotgun. But I was fighting back, of course. Only by the time I walked in on Tithonus and the Emperor, he was winning. I tried to throw him out of my head but I just couldn't do it.'

'You mean he's still in there?' Henry asked, aghast.

'Don't be stupid,' Fogarty told him shortly. 'After that I sort of blanked out for a bit. That's when I discovered Pyrgus was in Hell.'

'I don't understand this,' Henry said.

'It's two-way traffic when a demon takes you over. He gets into your mind, but if you make the effort you can get into his. Up to a point. I got hold of some of his memories. Pyrgus was taken to the head demon, character called Beleth. Don't know what happened after that.'

'OK,' Henry said cautiously. 'So what happened to *you* after that?' He still wasn't sure he believed the demon story, but he found he didn't *not* believe it either. Fogarty had hit home with the remark about the fairy in the jamjar. Maybe there *were* such things as demons. Maybe they *did* drive flying saucers.

'When I came to, I found I'd shot the Emperor. Close

range. Took half his head off. Demon disappeared then. His job was done – he'd made me do it, made my *body* do it anyway. Then left me to carry the can. That's why I'm in here now.'

'Don't worry,' Henry said. 'When I tell Princess Blue what happened she'll get you out of here.' He hoped to heaven it was true.

'Better make it quick,' said Fogarty. 'They're due to hang me in the morning.'

Thirty-one

Blue pushed the doctor's hands away and sat up. 'I'm perfectly all right now,' she said calmly. She looked around. Somebody had undressed her and put her to bed in her own quarters. There were three court physicians in the room and several servants. All of them looked concerned.

'Serenity,' the nearest physician said, the one who'd tried to keep her supine, 'we must advise that it is best for you to stay in bed. The manifestations of shock – and you have had a severe shock – are such that …'

A severe shock. That's what they will always call it, she thought as the physician droned on. A severe shock. Daddy was dead and the world was changed. A severe shock. She felt sick in her stomach and every muscle in her body ached from tension. But the strangest thing was that her head seemed detached, as if it was floating somewhere a foot or two higher than it ought to be. The result, no doubt, of a severe shock. But while her head stayed detached, she could cope.

'I would like you gentlemen to leave now,' she said firmly. 'I wish to get dressed.'

'Serenity – ' The physician caught the look on her face and decided not to argue. He and his colleagues took a fussy leave with much backing and bowing. The

last to go said, 'Serenity, there is a sleeping draught by
the bedside should you need it. And a relaxant in the
blue vial – just two drops on the tongue when necessary, but no more than twelve drops in any twenty-four
hours. And a stimulant in the red vial should you need
to counteract the effects of the relaxant – one drop on
the tongue will be sufficient. And the spell candle is a
lethe. Once lit, it will enable you to forget until it is
extinguished or burns out. There are further lethe
candles in the drawer. And – '

'Thank you, Argus,' Blue said politely. 'You have
performed your duties admirably.'

'Thank you, Serenity,' the physician Argus said, and
finally withdrew.

'Please lay out something suitable for me to wear.'
Blue pushed back the bedclothes and swung her feet on
to the floor. Her body felt light, like her head, but that
didn't matter. She had to find out why her father had
died, why this creature from the Analogue World had
decided to kill him. She had to ensure, absolutely, that
the murderer was punished – although she suspected
Tithonus would already have taken care of that. And
Pyrgus was still missing.

She turned her head at the soft knock on the door.
'Yes?'

Anna entered hesitantly with something in her hand.
'Are you all right, Mistress Blue? They told me you
were awake.'

'I'm all right,' Blue said. Anna was the one who'd
brought her the news. Somehow she knew she would
always remember that. 'What is it?'

'I don't know if I should be bothering you,' said
Anna uncertainly, 'but it's supposed to be urgent and I

know how you like to keep on top of – ' She tailed off and proffered a piece of paper. 'That young boy spying on you in the bath. Got himself into even more trouble by the sound of it. Anyway, he sent you this with one of the guards.'

Blue took the paper and unfolded it.

Beleth was gone, but his demons remained in the hot, sulphureous cavern, bolting the outer plating on the Doomsday Bomb. They glanced up from time to time, as if curious to see what Pyrgus might be doing.

Pyrgus was doing nothing, since there was nothing he could do. His back ached and his legs ached even more from his crouched position in the cage, but the pain, which had built steadily for a time, was now levelling out, with an increasing numbness, so he was able to ignore the discomfort. He was less able to ignore the pressure in his head, which had been steadily worsening. He put it down to the stress of his situation.

Despite the headache, his mind was racing. He wondered if his father was dead yet, if Beleth's demon army had invaded. He wondered if his sister had survived. He needed to take action, to break free, to escape from Hael and join the fight against the forces of evil. But his cage was strong, the locks secure, so that he was as helpless as the kittens he'd rescued from the glue factory. That rescue seemed so long ago.

Beleth was right when he said you would never notice the downward movement of the cage. The machinery – the proper machinery the Demon Prince had called it – made no sound beyond the occasional random creak. But when he compared his distance from the cavern roof to what it had been when Beleth left, he could see a difference. The cage was definitely dropping. It was dropping slowly, a fraction at a time, but it was dropping surely. Below him, brimstone seethed and bubbled. The stress of his situation made him feel as if his head were about to explode.

'What's this?' Henry asked.

'Your share of the papers,' Fogarty told him. 'There's somebody coming.'

Henry looked at him blankly, then down at the crumpled ball in his hand. He looked back up at Fogarty.

'We have to eat them,' Fogarty said.

Henry unfolded the paper to discover he was holding two small torn sheets. On one was written in his handwriting, '*What happened to Pyrgus?*' On the other were the words, also in his handwriting, '*Why did you murder the Emperor?*' Hardly the most incriminating documents in the world. 'I'm not eating these,' he said.

Fogarty looked as if he'd like to argue, but his mouth was full and there was already the sound of footsteps immediately outside. A key grated in the lock and the cell door swung open. Two burly guards marched in to take their places on either side. Then a smaller figure entered, dressed in black.

'Blue!' Henry exclaimed, relief flooding over him.

She looked at him coolly. 'Come with me,' she said.

'Come on, Mr Fogarty,' Henry said delightedly. 'This is Princess Holly Blue. I told you she'd get us out of here.'

But Blue's face was unsmiling. 'Just you,' she said to Henry. 'The monster who killed my father stays here until he hangs.'

'Is this true?' Blue asked, her eyes boring through his fiercely. She was holding a piece of paper in her hand. He assumed it was the note he'd sent her. 'You know where Pyrgus is?'

Henry took a deep breath. 'It's sort of complicated,' he said.

'Then you'd better simplify it for me,' Blue told him coldly. She waited, her eyes never leaving him.

Henry repeated the story Fogarty had told him about the demon.

He could sense her growing disbelief the more he talked. Not that he blamed her – he was still far from sure about Fogarty's story himself. Then suddenly her expression changed. 'Did you say *Beleth*?' she asked urgently.

'That's right,' Henry said. 'He's some sort of demon king, I think.' He regretted the choice of words at once: they sounded like something out of a Christmas panto. 'Look, I know this sounds pretty batty, but I've known Mr Fogarty for ages and he would never – '

But she cut him off. 'Beleth was the demon Brimstone called up – the one who nearly killed Pyrgus. How could Fogarty know that name? How could *anybody* know that name? Pyrgus didn't tell anybody. I only know because I saw it in Brimstone's magical diary. And there was another book with something to do with Beleth ...' She stopped, frowning.

'You mean you believe me?' Henry asked with relief.

'I'm not sure,' Blue said. 'If you've just killed someone, then pretending you were controlled by a demon is a very convenient excuse. All the same ...'

Henry knew what she meant. If demons really existed – and Blue herself seemed to accept that they did –

then why shouldn't they take over people? It occurred to him it was a point he might clarify. 'You believe in demons, don't you?'

Blue blinked in surprise. 'Nobody *believes* in demons,' she said shortly. 'They're just *there*.' She caught Henry's expression and added, 'In their own world, of course. Usually trying to get into this one. Nighters work with them a lot.'

'Can they take over people?' Henry asked. 'Like, control their minds?'

'Yes, of course,' Blue said. 'Everybody knows you must never look a demon in the eye.' She suddenly realised where this was going and said quickly, 'That doesn't mean I believe there's a demon loose in the palace or that it made Mr Fogarty kill my father.'

'No, but it's *possible*, isn't it?'

She stood lost in thought for a long time before she said, 'Yes, it's possible.'

'We need more information,' Blue was saying. 'I have to get another look at those two books.' She caught Henry's blank look. 'I don't know if he told you, but Pyrgus got involved with a Nightside sorcerer called Brimstone who tried to sacrifice him to this demon. I found that out when I stole Brimstone's magical diary and another book about Beleth. Only my father – ' she blinked, but went on without hesitation ' – didn't approve and sent the books back. I was only able to glance at them.'

'Where are the books now?'

'I think Tithonus may have them,' Holly said.

'Can you ask Tithonus for them back? I mean, if you explain they might be important ...'

Blue nodded uncertainly. 'I expect so. I'll send a servant.'

Minutes later, Tithonus's manservant, a taciturn individual named Atolmis, was presenting his compliments. He wore footman's uniform with a canvas sack slung over one shoulder. 'Grave news, Your Serene Highness,' he said formally.

'What is it, Atolmis?' Blue asked sharply.

'The Gatekeeper has asked me to suggest you remain in your rooms for the moment, Serenity. He's in the Situation Room. We have received information the Nightside has launched a full-scale military attack.'

Blue's face was already pale, but Henry noticed she blanched even further. 'I should go to the Situation Room,' she said. 'There may be something I can do.'

'The Gatekeeper would prefer you to remain in your rooms, Serenity. He fears for your safety,' Atolmis said woodenly.

'My safety? Why should there be a threat to my safety?'

Atolmis had large dark eyes that never seemed to blink. He turned them on Blue now. 'Since the death of your illustrious father, my master has assumed the powers of Regent pending the return of the Crown Prince. As Regent he is now in charge of the defence of the Realm. I was at his side until a short time ago. We are – ' He hesitated, as if selecting his words carefully. 'We are experiencing some difficulties in containing the Nightside attack.'

'But they are under-manned!' Blue protested. 'My – ' She stopped. Her contacts in the Espionage Service had alerted her to the state of the Nightside armies, but she didn't want to admit that.

Atolmis said dully, 'The Nightside has been joined by demon forces.'

Blue blinked. 'How? How are the demons getting through?' There were always one or two demons in the Realm of Faerie, invited in by sorcerers, necromancers and the like, but a breakthrough by a full-scale demon army was impossible.

'I'm afraid we don't know, Serenity. But they have already crossed the Teetion Valley and there is fierce fighting on the Plains of Lilk. Demon reinforcements are marching to join the advance party.' He took a deep, noticeable breath. 'Serenity, it may be only a matter of hours before they threaten the city. The safety of the Royal Family is my master's prime concern. May I assure him you will remain in your rooms?'

Blue nodded soberly. 'Yes, Atolmis. Yes, you may.'

'Thank you, Serenity,' Atolmis said. He half turned to take his leave, then turned back and drew a cloth-wrapped package from his canvas sack. He held it out to Blue. 'The books you requested, Serenity.'

'It sounds serious,' Henry said when Atolmis had gone.

Blue glanced at him. 'That's stating the obvious,' she sniffed. She caught Henry's hurt expression and added quickly, 'But there's nothing we can do directly and it only means it's more important than ever to find Pyrgus.' She untied the ribbon enclosing the package. 'Come on – you can help me study these books.'

Thirty-two

The book felt unpleasant the moment he took it in his hand. It was bound with boards, covered in some sort of animal skin that was smooth and pink and hairless, a bit like ... a bit like ...

It couldn't be a baby's skin, could it? Henry almost dropped the book in panic. Only the thought of Blue's contempt stopped him. But the closer he looked at it, the more he felt it, the more he thought it must be a baby's skin. It had the right texture, the right feel and if you peered really closely you could even see the little pores. It was stamped in old gold leaf with the words, *The Book of Beleth*. Henry shuddered.

All the same, he opened the book.

It was like nothing he'd seen before. For a start, the paper was strange. It was thicker than ordinary paper and had a funny smell. The surface was rough to the touch, slightly porous. And it wasn't a printed book. Somebody had handwritten every word, hand-drawn every picture. Different inks had been used, including one that looked suspiciously like dried blood. On the page he had opened, there were crude drawings of an eye, a hand, a foot, a crown, a crest and a set of long, curling horns. To one side of them were peculiar sigils. One that looked like the Roman letter *I* falling forward on its face was captioned 'Oblique'. Another, which consisted of six lines cross-hatched, had the word 'Manifold' beside it. None of it made any sense to Henry.

He closed the book and opened it again at the beginning. There was a sigil on the first page, inked in black and composed of curls and loops so that it looked for all the world like somebody doodling. Except there was a deliberate feel about it that made him certain it was no doodle. Below the sigil were six words that made the hair crawl on the back of his neck: *Beleth holds the keys to Hell*.

Henry found himself in the peculiar position of holding a book that actually scared him. He couldn't shake the feeling it was like something out of a horror movie. In his mind's eye, he could see the innocent young hero stumble on a tome like this in some vampire's crypt. Open it, or even touch it, and the minute you turned your back it would start to glow. Shortly after that, smoke would billow out to form something with large teeth and long claws.

He glanced across at Blue. She had the other book Atolmis had brought open on her lap. It was a lot smaller than the one Henry was holding and a lot less scary. He wondered how she'd feel about a swap, then dismissed the thought as unworthy. And stupid. He looked back at the thing in his hands. At least it wasn't glowing yet.

Henry turned another leaf and came upon a contents page. His nervousness increased. Listed in an ornate hand were:

It all seemed very spooky to Henry, most of it the sort of thing you shouldn't be reading at all. And none of it seemed to have much to do with Pyrgus. Henry decided to start at the beginning and work through, skipping anything that wasn't relevant. He turned to page five, *Concerning Works of Hatred and Destruction*.

It was a nasty chapter and, despite a resolve to read carefully, he found himself skimming it. But by the time he reached the end he was fairly sure there was nothing in it about Beleth and certainly nothing about Pyrgus.

The Hand of Glory described in the next chapter proved to have a ghoulish fascination. To make one, you waited until they hanged a murderer at a crossroads, then cut off the right hand of the corpse, wrapped it in a piece of winding sheet and squeezed it firmly to get rid of any remaining drops of blood. You then put it in an earthenware jar along with nitre, salt, long peppers and zimort.

'What's *zimort*?' Henry asked Blue, frowning.

'Shhh!' Blue said.

After two weeks you took the hand out and exposed it to the sun during the dog days, or dried it in a wood-burning oven fuelled by fern and vervain.

'When are the dog days?' Henry muttered.

'Oh do be quiet!' Blue snapped impatiently.

While the hand was drying out, you made a candle from the fat of a hanged man, mixed with virgin wax, horse dung and sisamie.

'What's sis – ?' Henry stopped himself and went back to the book. You jammed the candle between the fingers of the dried hand and the Hand was ready. Now all you had to do was light the candle and any-body sleeping in the house would be unable to wake up until you blew it out again.

Was that all there was to it? A cure for insomnia? It seemed a lot of trouble for very little, even though the book assured him that after it had been used a few times, the Hand of Glory took on a life of its own and would crawl about the place looking for somebody to strangle. You had to keep it in a locked drawer at night for your own protection.

He skimmed the next two chapters then started to read about the Rite of Conjuration. At once he realised this was in a completely different league to the super-stitious nonsense that had gone before. It was like a step-by-step technical manual, telling you how to call things up out of Hell. It described machinery you could set up, precautions you had to take, all the –

Henry stopped dead. He'd just had a brilliant idea. The most brilliant idea of his whole life. 'Blue – ' he said excitedly.

Blue closed her book with a snap. 'This is useless!' she said angrily. 'He mentions Pyrgus. I knew that already. There's stuff in here about some stupid pact with Beleth and how they tried to kill Pyrgus and how Pyrgus got away. But there's absolutely nothing about what's happening to Pyrgus now or how to rescue him or anything. Useless! Useless! Useless!' She pounded the book with small fists in frustration.

'I know how to rescue Pyrgus,' Henry said.

With Blue's eyes on him, Henry's confidence suddenly ran out and he hesitated.

'Well?' Blue asked impatiently.

He had to say something. But he couldn't say what he'd been about to say – it was just too loony. The trouble was he couldn't think of anything else.

'Well?' Blue asked again.

He was committed now. Henry said, 'The thing is, the Rite of Conjuration is sort of general instructions for calling something out of Hell. At least I think that's what it is. It talks about Beleth because this is *The Book of Beleth*, but you could use it to, you know, to call *anything*. I thought if Mr Fogarty was right and Pyrgus really is in Hell, we should be able to, like, conjure up *him*.' He hesitated, then added weakly, 'It would get him out.'

Blue was staring at him, her face an absolute blank. Then she said briskly, 'Worth a try.'

Blue led Henry up a flight of narrow steps to an empty

tower chamber with a lockable door. 'If we try this in my quarters we might be interrupted,' she explained. 'But nobody ever comes up here – and if they're looking for me, they won't know where I've gone. Now tell me what stuff we need and I'll go and get it.'

Henry consulted *The Book of Beleth*. 'There's trapped-lightning machinery, but that's only if you're calling Beleth himself. And there's … oh – ' He stopped.

'What's wrong?'

'You have to kill an animal and skin it to make the circle. I'm not sure I could do – oh, wait a minute: that's optional.'

'So what is it we *actually* need?' Blue asked him patiently.

Henry looked at the floor, which was bare wood boards without carpet or any other covering. 'We need something to draw a circle on this floor. And a triangle. I suppose chalk would do, something like that. And we need charcoal and incense – '

'What sort of incense?'

'Doesn't say. Oh, wait a minute, I think it must mean you use camphor as incense. Camphor. Yes, camphor.'

'OK.'

'And something to burn it in. Incense burner or a brazier, something like that?'

'OK.'

'And we need verbena wreaths – '

'How many?'

Henry consulted the book. 'Two.'

'OK.'

'And two large candles in their holders. It says black here, but I think white since we're trying to get hold of

Pyrgus – black's all witchy and demonic, isn't it? Sort of thing they used in the old Hammer movies on TV.' He caught her expression. 'You wouldn't know about that, would you? Anyway, two large candles. In holders.' He frowned. 'Do you know what Rutanian brandy is?'

Blue nodded. 'Yes.'

'We need a small bottle. And something called haematite – have you ever heard of haematite?'

'Bloodstone,' Blue said. 'I can get a piece. Is that all?'

Henry consulted the book again. 'It says you need a blasting wand, but if you read ahead that's just so you can control the demon. I don't expect Pyrgus will cause us much trouble.'

'If it works properly.'

Henry looked at her. 'What's that mean?'

'If it works properly,' Blue repeated. 'If your idea works. If we call up Pyrgus. If we don't end up calling up Beleth or some other demon by mistake.'

Henry felt a sudden tightness in his lower abdomen. 'You think we might?'

'It's possible.'

'So we do actually need a blasting wand, just to be on the safe side?'

Blue licked her lips. 'Well, to be on the safe side.'

'Do you know where to get one?' Henry asked.

'No.' She stared at him. 'I mean, if we had more time I could probably send one of the servants … but not if we're going to do this now; soon, I mean. No.'

After a moment Henry said, 'We'll just have to do without the blasting wand then. I'm sure it will be OK.' He glanced back at the book. 'The only other thing is something called …' he stumbled over the pronunciation. '... asafoetida? Asafoetida grass? Do you know what that is?'

'Yes, of course,' Blue said. 'You use it in cooking. I can get some from the kitchens.'

'Oh, no, wait,' Henry said. 'You burn that to dismiss the demon you call up. We don't want to dismiss Pyrgus – that's the whole point.'

'Maybe we should get some anyway,' Blue said. 'Since we don't have a blasting wand.'

'Great idea. Yes, get asafoetida. Get *lots* of asafoetida.'

She was only gone fifteen minutes collecting the things they needed, but it was the longest fifteen minutes of Henry's life.

Henry held the book and called out instructions while Blue painstakingly drew the circle and the triangle. 'Like that?' she asked as she placed the candles.

'Bit closer, I think,' Henry said.

'Like that?'

Henry said, 'They need to be nearer to the triangle.'

'If they were any nearer they'd be *in* the triangle,' Blue snapped. She looked ready to throw them at him.

'OK,' Henry said.

They finished eventually and stood back to inspect their work. 'Oh,' Henry said.

'Oh? Why are you saying *Oh*? Is something wrong? Have I somehow managed to get it *wrong* despite your detailed instructions?' She glared at him.

Henry licked his lips. 'It's just that you've drawn the full circle.'

'Yes, Henry,' Blue said. 'I have drawn a full circle. You told me to draw a circle, so I drew a circle. Odd thing for me to do, but there it is.'

'It's just that you're not supposed to complete the circle until you're inside it. Otherwise it isn't proper.'

For a moment he thought she was going to hit him, but she only said, 'Tell you what: I'll rub out a bit of the circle with my kerchief – it's only chalk. Then we get inside the circle and I'll draw it back again. Will that do?'

'Yes,' said Henry quickly, although he had no idea whether it would or not.

In a moment they were both standing inside the circle, carefully redrawn where Blue had rubbed it out to make them an entrance. Henry licked his lips. 'Which of us is going to do this?'

'The ceremony? You are.'

'Why me?'

'You're the one holding the book,' Blue said.

He couldn't believe he was actually doing it. He was actually going to attempt some sort of black-magic rite to rescue his friend from Hell. It was ridiculous. What was even more ridiculous was that it might go wrong and leave them facing something nasty. Something very nasty indeed. He didn't want to do it. But he didn't want to chicken out either, not in front of Blue. The thing to do was overcome the sheer terror and get on with it. He took a deep breath. 'OK, you – oh ...'

'If you say *oh* to me just one more time ...' Blue began. She closed her eyes briefly, then opened them again. 'What is it? What's gone wrong now?'

'We're supposed to light the charcoal and burn some camphor, but I forgot to tell you to get matches. Or a lighter.' Or a tinderbox or whatever they used to start fires in this world: he realised he didn't have the least idea.

'Fortunately I sometimes find it possible to think for myself,' Blue said. She touched the charcoal with a slim rod about the size of a pencil and a blue flame sprang up briefly before the charcoal began to glow red. She added camphor without a word.

Henry opened *The Book of Beleth*, turned to face the direction of the triangle, rolled his fear into a tiny ball so it couldn't interfere with what he had to do, and started to read aloud the opening prayers.

When he came to the name *Beleth*, he carefully substituted *Pyrgus*. He hoped to heaven it would work.

It couldn't work. It was absolutely ridiculous. Standing in a circle calling something out of Hell? How weird could you get? Nobody believed in this sort of thing any more. Nobody had believed this sort of thing since the Middle Ages.

Same as nobody believes in fairies or portals to another world, a voice whispered in his head.

Henry closed his eyes. 'I call upon thee, Be – Pyrgus – I call upon thee Pyrgus to come forth within the Triangle of Art, fair of form in such shape as will be pleasing to me, so that we may – ' And so on, following the heavily repetitive instructions laid out on the page before him.

After a while, he found the camphor fumes were getting to him. Blue had fed a lot on to the burner and he was beginning to feel a little dizzy. At least he thought it must be the camphor fumes because when he opened his eyes, the whole room looked funny. All its edges were softened and everything he looked at writhed and shifted, as if they'd fallen underwater.

It had to be the camphor fumes because he was

getting nauseous now and there was a ringing in his ears. He thought he might be leaning at an angle, but when he checked he still seemed to be standing upright. Was there a thunderstorm brewing up outside? Something was rumbling in the distance and it sounded just like thunder.

There was a huge amount of smoke in the room. He tried to signal to Blue not to burn any more camphor, but for some reason his arm wouldn't move. He was still chanting the ritual words from the book. Or at least his throat and mouth were still chanting the ritual words from the book because the rest of him didn't feel he had anything to do with it. The rest of him felt as if it was about to pass out or fall over or possibly go blind from camphor in his eyes.

The incense smoke was swirling in a cone above the triangle. It formed itself into a human shape.

Thirty-three

Pyrgus was choking so violently he could hardly breathe. His head felt close to bursting. Sweat was pouring from his face and body. The molten brimstone was less than an inch away from his feet now and the heat was so intense the soles of his boots had begun to smoke. It was a toss-up whether they would catch fire before the cage lurched and sent him into the brimstone itself. Pyrgus was certain it *would* lurch. Despite Beleth's boast about the slow, gradual death, the cage had twice dropped more than eighteen inches in the last fifteen minutes. Another drop like that and he would begin to burn. He would begin to die.

Through the fumes and the smoke he could see Beleth had come back. Presumably to watch the show. The Prince of Darkness liked to watch people in pain, liked to hear their screams and listen to their pleas. Except Pyrgus was determined to give him as little satisfaction as possible. No screams. No pleas. No show of pain. If possible he would swallow molten brimstone to give himself a fast death. Well, faster. Better than some inch-by-inch burn from the feet up.

'Are you hoping it will lurch again?' called Beleth. He had assumed his horned form once more so that his voice rumbled like distant thunder. 'Are you hoping for a faster death?' He smiled broadly. 'I'm afraid, Crown Prince, you will be disappointed. I had your cage lowered faster just so I could witness your demise before I – '

Beleth stopped. Inside the metal cage, the form of Pyrgus was flickering like a candle in a gale. One moment he looked solid, the next he was a wraith. Beleth's jaw fell open. Pyrgus was no longer there. Yes he was. No he wasn't. Yes he – Pyrgus had disappeared completely. He'd been crouched there, surrounded by the fumes and smoke, but now the cage was empty. Definitely empty.

Beleth growled. There was no mistake. Pyrgus was no longer there. The Demon Prince swung round to glare at his subjects, as if they were somehow responsible. But the demons working in the brimstone cavern looked as bewildered as he was.

'Where is he?' Beleth grabbed the nearest demon and shook him till his neck snapped. He threw the body aside. 'Where is Prince Pyrgus?' he demanded.

A thought occurred. Invisibility! That was it! The boy had concealed a cone of invisibility about his person. He hadn't escaped. Of course he hadn't escaped. Escape was quite impossible. Pyrgus was still inside the cage! He could still be felt, could still be *burned,* could still be *crushed* ...

Beleth stepped into the brimstone pool. The molten lava lapped over his feet like lukewarm water. As he moved towards the cage his foot caught on something just beneath the surface and he stumbled. His huge flailing arm struck the Doomsday Bomb which toppled from its stand and started to roll. 'Noooooo!' Beleth howled in sudden alarm.

Everything seemed to slow. The Doomsday Bomb rolled inch by inch towards the pool. One of the demon workmen tried to grab it, but missed. Beleth hurled himself forward, but missed the bomb as well. Gently, so very gently, it slid into the molten pool.

Beleth's scream reverberated through the cavern. A bubble erupted on the surface of the pool like some giant belch. Huge bolts of elemental energy snaked across the molten brimstone. From somewhere deep below there was a rumbling that rose to a roar. Beleth ran, but not fast enough or far enough. The brimstone pool erupted in a vast explosion that tore him limb from limb. A fraction of a second later the entire cavern collapsed, burying every living being in it.

Far above, the great metal city rang like a bell before its buildings began to topple and sink.

All of a sudden Henry wasn't doubting any more. All of a sudden, the self-conscious feeling left him and a wave of confidence swept in. He felt himself stand a little straighter, felt his voice grow stronger, felt – yes, definitely felt – a surge of energy flow through him that carried the words he spoke through space and time and alien dimensions. *The Book of Beleth* trembled in his hands. 'Come to us, Pyrgus, come!' There was power in the room. 'Come, Pyrgus, come!'

But the creature wasn't Pyrgus. And it wasn't trapped in the triangle either. Through the swirling incense smoke he could see something approaching out of a nightmare. It was human in form – two arms, two legs, a trunk, a head – but nothing ever born to human mother. It was small and thin and pale and grey with huge black eyes and skinny insect limbs.

'Don't look into its eyes!' screamed Holly Blue. Her voice seemed to reach him from far away.

It was a fuzzy photo in the tabloid press. It was an illustration from a cover of a flying-saucer book. It was like that thing they cut up after Roswell, the one everybody said was just a rubber dummy. It was one of the aliens that came in UFOs. But Blue thought it was a demon. And he'd called it with a magic rite that was supposed to conjure demons. Mr Fogarty was right. He'd been right all along. UFO aliens and demons were the same thing under different names!

'Don't look into its eyes!'

The creature seemed confused. It walked in a zigzag across the room, sometimes stopping, sometimes turning, sometimes actually backtracking a pace or two. Its small mouth moved. 'Kill the Emperor!' it said in commanding tones, then added in a thin, faltering voice, 'They're out to get me! They're *all* out to get me!'

Henry thought it might be blind.

The creature held its hands out like a child begging for food. 'You must kill the Emperor,' it whined. 'Or Beleth will punish me.' It blinked its blind, black eyes. 'But keep out of my mind, old man! I can't stand you in my mind!' It jerked its head to one side to look over its shoulder. 'It's the Government, you know. Them and the CIA. They've all got mind-control machines.'

It sounded hauntingly familiar. Especially the bit about the CIA. What would a demon in the Realm of Faerie know about the CIA? Henry did a mental flip and *knew*! 'Blue,' he shouted, 'this is the demon that took over Mr Fogarty!'

The creature turned towards Henry at the sound of the name. 'I'm sorry, Beleth,' it said plaintively. 'He wouldn't do what he was told. His mind was so slippery I couldn't hold him. Wouldn't do it. I was fighting the whole CIA.' It staggered towards Henry, arms outstretched. Blue screamed. It reached the edge of the protective circle and winked out of existence as if someone had turned off a light.

There was a loud groan from the triangle. Henry swung round, knowing he'd find Beleth there. His insides turned to water. There was something crouching on the floor.

'Pyrgus!' Blue shrieked.

'Don't leave the circ – ' Henry shouted. But it was already too late. Blue was running across the room.

Pyrgus was hunched up in the triangle, his head cradled in both arms. For some reason there was smoke coming from the soles of his boots. He groaned again.

Blue reached him and threw her arms around his neck. 'Pyrgus! Oh, Pyrgus!' Still clinging to him, she half turned. 'It worked, Henry! It worked!'

Henry thought what the hell and stepped out of the magic circle. The demon creature did not reappear. He moved towards the figure in the triangle.

'My head!' Pyrgus moaned.

Blue released him and fumbled in a pocket. 'I can do something about that, you poor thing!' She drew a syringe from her pocket, uncapped it and plunged the needle into Pyrgus's thigh. 'There,' she said. 'I've carried that around ever since I heard you'd been poisoned. It's the antidote – you'll soon be right.' She cradled him in her arms again.

She was right too. As Henry watched, Pyrgus gradually ceased rocking to and fro and in a moment took his arms away from his head. Blue released him and stood back, grinning. Pyrgus straightened up and looked around. 'Hello, Henry. What are you doing here?' Suddenly he was hopping on one leg as he tore off his boots. 'Ruddy brimstone!' he hissed.

Blue said all of a rush, 'Pyrgus, Father's dead – he was murdered. You're the Purple Emperor now. The Nightside are attacking and they have demon reinforcements. We're being over-run!'

Pyrgus said, 'Destroy the book!'

He had no reaction to his father's death, Henry thought. Almost as if he knew already.

'Destroy the book!' Pyrgus said again.

Henry realised suddenly Pyrgus was talking to him. 'What?'

'That's *The Book of Beleth* you're holding, isn't it?'

Henry looked down at the book in his hands. 'Yes … ' he said uncertainly. Then, more definitely, 'Yes, it is.'

'Destroy it!' Pyrgus snapped. He grabbed the tome out of Henry's hands. 'Look!' He ripped the hideous skin backing off the cover. Underneath, thin worms of blue light writhed across what looked like some weird type of printed circuit. Pyrgus threw the book violently on the floor. 'Stamp on it!' he commanded. 'Break it up!'

Henry blinked at him.

'For God's sake, Henry!' Pyrgus shouted. 'I haven't any boots on!'

Henry's paralysis broke and he slammed his foot down on the book. The printed circuit jagged easily, sending a mild electric shock across his toes. He picked up the jagged pieces of the book and dropped them in the brazier. They flared at once, filling the room with strange, green light. He turned to look at Pyrgus. His friend seemed taller somehow, more commanding.

'I need to see Tithonus now,' Pyrgus said.

Blue was looking a shade in awe of her brother as well. 'He'll be in the Situation Room,' she said. 'He's Regent for Comma now that Daddy's dead. Nobody knew where you ... well, you know – ' She shrugged. 'Comma was the next in line. So Tithonus has been running things – the war and so on – while you've been away.'

'I'm back now,' Pyrgus said a little grimly. His face softened briefly and he gave a tiny smile. 'Thanks to you two.' The smile vanished. 'Come on – we still have work to do.'

The guards looked stunned as Pyrgus, Henry and Blue stepped out of the suspensor shaft, but snapped to attention at once. 'Crown Prince Pyrgus!' one exclaimed.

'You address your Emperor,' said Pyrgus quietly.

'Majesty,' the guard acknowledged.

With Pyrgus in the lead, they were escorted down the corridor towards the Situation Room. The door guards came to attention at their approach. Pyrgus seemed extraordinarily confident to Henry, every inch an emperor. The doors swung open and they marched through.

Henry had a brief confused impression of crystal globes with moving pictures flickering in their depths and an enormous table that seemed to have a landscape modelled on its surface.

'They've definitely stopped,' a voice said. It came

from a broad-shouldered man in uniform who Henry didn't recognise. 'The demons are no longer coming.'

'They can't have stopped!' another voice exclaimed.

'They've stopped all right, Tithonus,' Pyrgus said.

Tithonus spun around, a stunned expression on his face. 'Pyrgus!' He caught himself and added more formally, 'Crown Prince. How good to – '

'No longer Crown Prince,' Pyrgus told him coldly. 'Do you acknowledge your new Emperor?'

'I – , Pyrgus, of course I – Majesty, I – '

Pyrgus cut across him by turning to one of the men in military uniform. 'General Ovard, do you acknowledge your new Emperor?'

'Of course, Purple Emperor,' Ovard said promptly.

Pyrgus said, 'General Ovard, please place Gatekeeper Tithonus under arrest.'

'Pyrgus!' Blue exclaimed.

'As you command, Purple Emperor,' Ovard nodded, his face wooden. He motioned to the guards who moved to surround Tithonus.

'Pyrgus!' Tithonus spluttered. 'Majesty, what is the meaning of this?'

Pyrgus strode forward until he was no more than eighteen inches from Tithonus. 'You are a traitor, Gatekeeper,' he said quietly.

Blue said, 'Pyrgus, this is *Tithe*!'

Tithonus said, 'It was necessary I took the title Regent, Majesty. You were missing. Comma is too young. The realm was under attack. It was important there was someone in command.'

A chill half-smile played across Pyrgus's lips. 'Beleth told me everything when he had me hanging in his cage,' he said. 'Including your treachery.'

'Treachery?' Tithonus echoed. He turned towards General Ovard. 'You can't believe this!' His eyes flickered to the other military men. 'Creerful, Vanelke – you must know this is nonsense.' They stared back at him without a word.

'Take him away,' Pyrgus ordered.

The guards dragged Tithonus struggling from the room. They almost knocked over Comma who was coming in as they did so.

Comma looked from Pyrgus to Blue, then briefly to Henry and back to Pyrgus. 'What's going on? What are they doing to Tithonus?'

'He was a traitor,' Pyrgus said simply. 'He was the one who tried to kill me. He was the one who arranged our father's death.'

Comma's eyes flickered towards the doorway. He managed to look guilty and frightened at the same time. 'How do you know?'

Pyrgus said soberly, 'Beleth told me. When he thought I couldn't escape and was going to die, he told me everything to make me suffer.'

'What did he say about me?' Comma asked quickly.

Pyrgus stared at him severely. 'Nothing, brother. Should he have said something?'

Comma shook his head violently. 'No. No, of course not. I – I was just …'

'Wondering?' Pyrgus finished for him.

Comma had the look of a trapped rabbit, but said nothing. The silence in the room stretched to breaking point.

'Why?' Blue asked to cut the tension. 'Why did Tithonus betray us? He's known us since we were babies. He's known our father for ever.'

'His sympathies were with the Nightside,' Pyrgus told her simply. 'He believed they could win.' He sighed. 'Beleth promised him he would be Emperor.'

'Tithonus? Emperor?'

'Don't get too excited,' Pyrgus said. 'Beleth promised Hairstreak he would be Emperor as well. And Silas Brimstone. And probably a hundred others we don't know about. Beleth lied to everybody – it's his nature. What he really wanted was the Realm of Faerie for himself. But Tithonus was the key. He was Gatekeeper, the one we trusted.'

Blue shook her head. 'I can hardly believe this.'

'Tithonus kept a demon hidden in the palace,' Pyrgus said. 'He used it as a sort of courier to carry messages to Beleth. That's how they planned the demon invasion.'

Henry asked curiously, 'How come the demons stopped invading?'

'You stopped them, Henry,' Pyrgus said.

Henry looked at Pyrgus, then at Blue, then back at Pyrgus again. 'I did?'

'You stopped them when you stamped on *The Book of Beleth*,' Pyrgus said. 'The book was the main control portal between Hell and the Realm of Faerie. Once you destroyed it, all the other portals ceased to operate.'

'What, between this world and mine?' Henry asked in alarm.

Pyrgus shook his head. 'No, just between this world and the demon world. Beleth set up the control device centuries ago and disguised it as a book so nobody would think to close it down. The rituals were psychotronic triggers so it could be used for conjuration, but its real purpose was to keep the portals open so demons could have easy access to the realm.'

'Good grief,' Henry said.

'It must have been Tithonus's demon who made Henry's friend kill Daddy,' Blue remarked.

'Yipes!!' Henry shouted, jumping to his feet.

They swung round in alarm. 'What's wrong? What's the matter?'

'Mr Fogarty!' Henry exclaimed. 'There was so much going on I forgot about him completely. We left him in the cell – getting ready to be hanged!'

'Then we must get him out,' Pyrgus said. He turned to one of several aides who hovered on the edges of the conversation. 'See to it.'

'Yes, Majesty.'

Yes, Majesty, Henry thought. His friend was an emperor. The new Purple Emperor.

Blue groaned. 'That was my fault,' she said to Henry. 'You wanted me to let him out, but I thought he was a murderer.'

'That was what you were meant to think,' Pyrgus told her. 'Mr Fogarty may have been a murderer *technically*, but it was the demon driving him to do it.'

Henry said, 'I don't think Mr Fogarty did murder your father, even technically – I think he fought off the demon.'

They both turned to him. 'Why do you say that, Henry?' Pyrgus asked him soberly.

'Just before you … you know, appeared in the triangle, there was this demon thing turned up – '

'I forgot to tell you,' Blue put in.

'I was scared when I saw it,' Henry said, 'but it was confused and I don't think it could see properly. It thought it was talking to Beleth some of the time and it kept saying it couldn't make somebody do what they were told. And it also said *Kill the Emperor* a couple of times. I think that must have been the demon Tithonus was hiding in the palace, the one that was supposed to make Mr Fogarty kill your father. Only I think when it tried to take over his mind, he drove it mental. He's a bit odd – Mr Fogarty,' he ended weakly.

'He is a wise and powerful man,' Pyrgus said seriously. 'I plan to ask him if he will serve as my new Gatekeeper.'

Blue said, 'If your friend didn't kill Daddy, who did? The demon wouldn't actually have been there, would it?'

'My guess is Tithonus,' Henry said. 'Mr Fogarty was locked up fighting the demon in his head. I think when he saw Mr Fogarty wasn't going to do it, he took the gun and shot your father himself, then blamed Mr Fogarty. Mr Fogarty was too confused even to contradict him.'

'I'm sure that's right,' Comma put in suddenly. He almost managed to smile. 'I'm sure everything was down to Tithonus. Just Tithonus. On his own.'

Pyrgus looked unbelievable in the full formal regalia of the Purple Emperor. The heavy robes and towering mitre-crown made him appear far taller than he was, while the ornate, multi-coloured Peacock Throne lent him a surprising dignity. Holly Blue was seated on a smaller throne beside him, dressed entirely in white and looking absolutely – Henry swallowed and dragged his eyes away. He was already in enough trouble for ogling the Princess Royal. All the same, she gave him a small, encouraging smile.

The throne room was hung with golden banners and thronged with courtiers in bright costumes. A stone-faced military guard in full dress uniform formed a colonnade along the centre of the chamber. Henry had to walk between them and the prospect scared him witless.

'Get on with it!' Fogarty hissed, poking him in the back. He was dressed in something that seemed suspiciously like wizard's gear – a robe with embroidered stars and a pointed hat – but somehow managed to look quite comfortable. There was a sash across his chest emblazoned with the insignia of Gatekeeper.

Henry stumbled forward, caught his balance and began the long walk to the throne. To his profound embarrassment, each guard saluted him as he walked past and the courtiers began to applaud. He felt his face turn to flame, but there was nothing he could do about it. He fixed his eyes on a point on the floor six feet ahead and kept on walking.

It felt like several years, but eventually he found himself at the steps below the throne. Remembering an earlier instruction from Mr Fogarty, he bowed. As he straightened up again, he saw Pyrgus and Blue walking at a stately pace down the steps towards him. Henry closed his eyes, wondering how on earth he'd got himself into this. When he opened them again, Blue was smiling at him broadly. But it was Pyrgus who spoke.

'Kneel!' he commanded in a voice that carried through the hall.

Henry went down on one knee. 'Like King Arthur's knights,' Mr Fogarty had told him, but he didn't feel much like a knight. In fact he felt a twit. To hide his embarrassment, he bowed his head again.

The chamber fell to a deathly silence.

'Take notice all persons present,' Pyrgus intoned in that remarkable new official voice of his, 'that in token of his courageous and unstinting service to Faerie Realm and Purple Emperor, this citizen of the Analogue World, Henry Atherton, is hereby awarded the most noble and meritorious title of Knight Commander of the Grey Dagger, our realm's most ancient Order of Chivalry, and shall henceforth be known throughout the land by his Faerie name, *Iron Prominent*!' A flunkey handed him a grey dagger on a purple cushion and he held it out to Henry. 'Of course we'll still just call you Henry in private,' Pyrgus whispered.

'Thanks,' Henry muttered.

'Arise, Iron Prominent!' Pyrgus commanded.

There was a trumpet fanfare and a swell of cheering as Henry struggled to his feet. 'Now,' Pyrgus whispered, 'there's somewhere you and I have to go.'

They were in a narrow street called Seething Lane and this time, thank heavens, Henry was not the centre of attention. Pyrgus was at his shoulder, dressed the way he was when Henry had first met him. Ranged around them was a company of the toughest soldiers Henry had encountered.

'That's it,' Pyrgus said, nodding. 'My father wouldn't close it down because of politics, but the Nighters are on the run now, so I reckon I can do what

I damn well please.'

The glue works at the bottom of the lane looked miserable to Henry. They were covered in grime and belching smoke, as gloomy a set of buildings as he'd ever seen in his life. Pyrgus gave a signal and the soldiers wheeled up an enormous wood-and-twisted-rope machine that reminded Henry of Roman catapults. The captain of the guard began personally to wind back the throwing arm.

'Have all animals been evacuated?' Pyrgus asked.

'Yes, sire,' said the captain.

'And the people?'

'Yes, sire.'

Pyrgus turned to Henry. 'We have one of the owners – Chalkhill – in jail. He'll be there for a very long time. The other one, Brimstone, has gone into hiding, but we'll find him eventually, I promise you that,' he said grimly.

Henry licked his lips. He was fascinated by the enormous catapult. Four soldiers were rolling a gigantic rock on to the throwing cradle.

'Have the coatings been applied?' asked Pyrgus.

'Liberally, sire,' the captain assured him.

The rock was on the cradle now and the soldiers stood back, panting and sweating. The captain finished winding back the ropes and wedged the wheel to hold them. 'Ready, Emperor!' he snapped.

Pyrgus stared down Seething Lane towards the gloomy factory. 'Fire,' he ordered quietly.

The captain knocked out the wedge and stepped back in a single movement. Henry actually felt wind on his face as the catapult jerked violently. The huge arm whipped forward with unimaginable ferocity. He watched as the enormous rock arced higher than the rooftops, then fell like a meteor towards the factory.

It struck dead centre on the roof of the main building, to one side of a smoking chimney, and crashed through as if the structure was matchwood. For a heartbeat there was total silence, then the spell coatings triggered.

A sheet of flame erupted sideways through the factory buildings, shattering windows and walls, collapsing roofs, hurtling stonework and fiery beams high into the air. The noise was deafening and the explosive spells went on and on. Henry watched chimneys tumble, metal gates twist into slag, melting machinery suddenly exposed as their gloomy housing disappeared. In moments it was over. In place of the Chalkhill and Brimstone Miracle Glue factory, there was nothing but a smoking wasteland leading out to Wildmoor Broads.

'That's for the kittens,' Pyrgus whispered.

Mr Fogarty said it didn't matter where he used the cube – it would still open a portal – but it was usually better to trigger it outside. So they decided to say their farewells in the palace gardens.

'You might keep an eye on the house,' Fogarty said. He was dressed in an amazing ermine-trimmed robe, which he claimed was the official uniform of his new position. 'I'll be popping back from time to time, but I expect to be spending most of my time here.' He glanced briefly at the sky and added seriously, 'None of the surveillance agencies know how to get to this world yet, so I should be left in peace for a time.'

'Yes, I will,' Henry said about the house. There would be trouble with his parents, but he didn't care.

'You can rely on me.'

Pyrgus placed a hand on his shoulder. 'And so can I.' He looked Henry deep in the eyes. 'Henry,' he said, 'I want to thank you. I owe you my life.'

Henry flushed. 'Oh, it wasn't like that,' he said, embarrassed. 'I mean, I …' He trailed off, not knowing what to say. After a moment, what he did say was, 'Well, I suppose I'd better be going.'

'Henry?' Blue said.

Henry pulled the cube from his pocket as he turned towards her. It was the first time she'd spoken to him since he'd changed back into his old clothes and he'd been wondering if she thought he looked stupid. 'Yes?'

'You remember you said you were just unlucky to see me without my clothes on?'

Henry flushed a deeper crimson than he had when Pyrgus thanked him. He swallowed and nodded. 'Yes. Wh – wh-why?'

'Did you really mean it when you said I was beautiful?' Blue asked him, smiling shyly.

Thirty-four

Even though he'd only been away a single night, Henry was expecting major hassles about where he'd been and had a cover story prepared. He'd gone to see Charlie and her parents invited him to stay the night. He'd tried to phone home, but there was a fault on the line. It sounded convincing enough – he'd stayed at the Severs's often enough before – unless they'd phoned Charlie's house last night. Which they might well have done. If they had, he was cooked. Cooked twice because they'd know he was lying to cover his tracks. Except what could he do? He couldn't think of a better story.

But though he got home in a state of nerves, he found them too wrapped up in their own thing to care.

'Hi,' Henry shouted as he opened the front door. He was desperately anxious to get it all over. 'Sorry about staying out. Phone wasn't working. Slept over at Charlie's.' He waited. If they'd rung the Severs's, this was where he'd find out.

His mother popped her head out of the kitchen, frowning vaguely. 'Oh, Henry.' She blinked. 'We assumed that's where you were. Could you come in here a minute?'

Henry groaned inwardly. He was hugely relieved she'd bought his story, but this was going to be another of those hideous kitchen conferences. He prayed it would be short. What he really wanted was to go to bed.

His heart sank when he found his father was in the kitchen too, although it was long past the time when he should have been off to work. Another biggie. The only good thing was Aisling wasn't there. He stood just inside the door and waited.

'Henry,' his mother said – it was always his mother who spoke first at these happy little family get-togethers, 'your father is leaving.'

Henry nodded numbly. 'I know. You told me.'

But his mother shook her head. 'No, I don't mean in a few weeks or a month or two. He's found a flat.' She glanced at Henry's father, who smiled weakly. 'We've talked it over and we've decided there's no sense in pro-longing the agony, so he's moving out this weekend. I just wanted to tell you again, to reassure you that this will make no difference at all to your, ah, situation. You'll still be here, you'll still have your room and your models. And your school. You and I and Aisling will still be together as a family unit and as we said before your father will visit frequently, so there's absolutely no question – '

'Fifty-fifty,' Henry said.

His mother blinked. 'What?'

Henry said firmly, 'I don't think it's right I stay with you all the time. I want to spend six months of the year with my dad.' He turned to his father. 'That's all right, isn't it? You've got room?'

'Ah – I – well, yes. Yes, of course it's all right,' his father said, his features a mask of surprise. 'Yes, if that's – I mean, if that's what you want.'

'That's what I want,' Henry said. 'I think Aisling

should do it too, but that's up to her.'

'Just a minute, Henry,' his mother said quickly. 'This could be very awkward. There's your school and the whole question of …' She tailed off under Henry's silent stare.

'I'm sure you'll work something out,' Henry said as he turned to leave the kitchen. 'You're good at that.'

The flying pig was on the dresser in his room. For a moment it looked more alien than anything he'd seen in the Faerie Realm. He turned the cardboard handle and the pig took off along its pillar, wings flapping strongly.

Pigs might fly.

Henry shook his head, smiling slightly. It was astonishing what had happened. Amazing. Incredible. He pulled the ornamental dagger from his pocket and stared at it, remembering. Then he looked around. There was a shelf at the top of his wardrobe where he kept his modelling tools in a shoebox. Nobody ever looked in there. He opened the wardrobe and stepped back as junk fell out, then reached up for the shoebox. There was a smell of glue as he flipped back the top. It reminded him of Seething Lane.

Henry took the cube from his pocket. He'd a feeling he'd be using it again soon, but for now the thing to do was hide it away safely. He dropped the cube and his dagger into the box, then stowed it away on the wardrobe shelf. Despite everything, life seemed to be looking up.

Iron Prominent, he thought. Knight Commander of the Grey Dagger.

And Holly Blue had smiled at him.